Also by Jennifer Antill:

*Small Acts of Kindness,
a tale of the first Russian revolution*

FORTUNE'S PRICE

JENNIFER ANTILL

The Book Guild Ltd

First published in Great Britain in 2024 by
The Book Guild Ltd
Unit E2 Airfield Business Park,
Harrison Road, Market Harborough,
Leicestershire. LE16 7UL
Tel: 0116 2792299
www.bookguild.co.uk
Email: info@bookguild.co.uk
X: @bookguild

Copyright © 2024 Jennifer Antill

The right of Jennifer Antill to be identified as the author of this
work has been asserted by them in accordance with the
Copyright, Design and Patents Act 1988.

All rights reserved. No part of this publication may be
reproduced, transmitted, or stored in a retrieval system, in any form or by any means,
without permission in writing from the publisher, nor be otherwise circulated in
any form of binding or cover other than that in which it is published and without
a similar condition being imposed on the subsequent purchaser.

This work is entirely fictitious and bears no resemblance to any persons living or dead.

Typeset in 11pt Minion Pro

Printed on FSC accredited paper
Printed and bound in Great Britain by 4edge Limited

ISBN 978 1835740 774

British Library Cataloguing in Publication Data.
A catalogue record for this book is available from the British Library.

For my friends Alison Carse, Mary Evans
and Michael Winwood

Lux perpetua luceat eis.

CONTENTS

	Who's Who in *Fortune's Price*	ix
Part One	Challenges	1
Part Two	Trials By Fire And Water	189
Part Three	Resolutions	289
	Historical Note	455
	Acknowledgements	459
	About The Author	461

WHO'S WHO IN *FORTUNE'S PRICE*

The most commonly used names of principal characters in the text are marked in bold.
*historical figures

The Belkin family
Vasily Nikolayevich, Count Belkin (Vasya).

Alexander Petrovich, Count Belkin (Sasha). Vasily and Katya's uncle, Nikolay's older brother. A senior officer in the Ministry of the Interior.

Ekaterina Nikolayevna (**Katya**), Princess Polunina. Vasily's sister.

Maria Vasiliyevna, Countess Belkin. Vasily's mother, cousin of Countess Antonina Stepanova Laptev.

Sophia Vasilyevna (**Sonya**). Irina and Vasily's natural daughter.

Yevgenia Alexandrovna, Countess Belkin. Vasily and Katya's grandmother, Nikolay and Alexander's mother.

Nikolay Petrovich, Count Belkin. Vasily and Katya's father, died escaping Moscow in 1812.

Prince **Polunin**. Katya's husband.

Matvey (Motya) (Matthew). Vasily's ward, formerly a serf.

The Bogolyubov family

Dmitry Vladimirovich, Prince Bogolyubov (Dima). Alexander Petrovich's former superior officer, mentor and landlord, friend and partner.

Stepan Dmitryevich, Count Bogolyubov. A cousin of Dmitry Vladimirovich. Killed in 1805 at the Battle of Austerlitz.

Belkin/Bogolyubov family serfs, retainers etc

Yakov. Vasily's manservant.

Pashka. The blacksmith on the Belkin estate.

The von Klein Sternberg family

Andrey Andreyevich, Baron von Klein Sternberg. Stepan Bogolyubov's son. Illegitimate under Russian canon law. Second lieutenant in The King of Prussia's Grenadier Regiment.

Astrella Andreyevna von Klein Sternberg. Mother of Andrey Andreyevich, daughter of Andrey Andreyevich senior (deceased).

Andrey Andreyevich (senior), Baron von Klein Sternberg. Andrey Andreyevich's grandfather. Deceased.

Friedrich Andreyevich, Baron von Klein Sternberg. An impoverished Estonian landowner. Andrey Andreyevich's uncle, son of Andrey Andreyevich (senior), brother of Astrella.

The Laptev family

Nadezhda Gavrilovna, Countess Laptev (Nadya) (Nadushka). An heiress. Younger daughter of Antonina and Gavril.

Antonina Stepanova, Countess Laptev. Countess Maria Belkin's first cousin, Nadezhda's mother.

Gavril Ivanovich, Count Laptev. Nadezhda's father.

Elizabeta Gavrilovna, Madame Stenovsky (**Lisa**). Nadezhda's older sister, married to Mikhail.

Mikhail Alexandrovich Stenovsky, Ivan's brother, now in prison in Siberia for his political activities.

Piotr Borisovich. An art student from Oryol.

Yevgraf. The Laptev family steward.

Other characters

Irina Pavlovna, the Baroness von Steiner (Irène). Vasily's former mistress and mother of his daughter.

Colonel Pavel Pavlovich **Kalinin**. Irina Pavlovna's brother. A diplomat.

Captain **Ivan** Alexandrovich Stenovsky (Vanya). A Chevalier Guardsman, younger brother of the Decembrist rebels Mikhail and Nikita Stenovsky. Old schoolfriend of Vasily's.

Madame Hélène. A seller of hats on Nevsky Prospekt.
Luka Ilyich **Kuprin**. A nobleman, formerly of the merchant class.

Prince **Yevgeny** Uspensky. A second lieutenant in the Pavlogradsky Hussars. Old friend of Vasily and Nadezhda.

Thomas Maltby. An English tutor.

Lieutenant-General **Zadachin**. A member of Grand Duke Constantine's staff in Warsaw.

Anna Grigoryevna Zadachina. Lieutenant-General Zadachin's wife.

Count **Angelov**. Friend of the late Stepan Dmitryevich Bogolyubov, who formerly served with him in the Napoleonic wars.

Rodionov. A notary. St Petersburg representative for the von Klein Sternberg family.

Praskovya. The wife of the wheelwright on Stepan Bogolyubov's country estate, Kluchovo.

Smirnov. A clerk at the Ministry of the Interior, Vasily's assistant.

Doctor Richard Webster. An English physician.

Konstantin Maksimovich. Son of Count Kukarin, a neighbour of the Laptev family in Oryol.

Bagrov. An officer from the Third Section of the Imperial Chancellery.

*Nicholas I. Emperor of all the Russias.

*General Zakrevsky. The Minister of the Interior.

*Count Benkendorf. The Head of the Third Section (in charge of public morals and security).

*Alexander Nikolayevich Mordvinov. Benkendorf's assistant from 1831.

At the theatre

Minnie Voronova. A dancer.

Lyubov Lebedeva. A dancer.

Count Malyshev. Minnie's protector.

*Rafael Mikhailovich Zotov. Assistant Director of the Bolshoy Kammeny Theatre.

Count Bolotin. Lyuba Lebedeva's suitor.

Soldiers

Denis Ivanovich **Borisov**. An ensign in the King of Prussia's Grenadiers.

Kirill Mikhailovich **Rosovsky**. A captain in the King of Prussia's Grenadiers.

Morozov. Andrey Andreyevich's orderly.

*Grand Duke Constantine Pavlovich. Older brother of the Emperor Nicholas. Commander of the Polish army at the time of the uprising.

*Field Marshall Diebitsch. First commander-in-chief of the Russian forces during the Polish campaign.

*Grand Duke Mikhail Pavlovich. The Emperor's younger brother. Commander-in-chief of the Russian Guards Regiment.

*General, Count Ivan Shakhovsky. Commander of Infantry during the Polish campaign.

*General Pavel Ugrumov. Commander of First Grenadier Division during the Polish campaign.

*Field Marshal Ivan Feodorovich Paskevich. Second commander-in-chief of the Russian army during the Polish campaign.

*Colonel Chevakinsky. Commanding officer of the King of Prussia's Grenadiers.

*Grigory Feodorovich **Filipson**. A first Lieutenant in the Duke of Wurttemberg's Grenadiers.

Vengerov. A captain in the King of Prussia's Grenadiers.

Steklov. A short-lived first lieutenant in the King of Prussia's Grenadiers.

Sidorov. A sergeant in the King of Prussia's Grenadiers.

*Ensign Ivan Romanovich van der Khoven. A Life Guard Grenadier, serving in St Petersburg during the cholera epidemic.

*Generals Lubensky and Skrzynesky. Polish generals.

PART ONE

CHALLENGES

*'The young shoemaker took pity on the veteran,
and gave the old man a fistful of golden ducats. At
once there was a great rumble of thunder.
"You did not keep your word," the princess said,
and disappeared. The boy found he had lost
everything that he had bought. He was dressed in
rags once again and his pockets were empty.
"It is not wealth, not ducats, that make you happy.
Only honest work, health, and a good heart.
Remember that, boy," said the old soldier.'*

From *The Golden Duck*, a Polish legend

CHAPTER ONE

June 1830 – St Petersburg

Perhaps, at last, his luck was changing. The lieutenant gripped the edge of the gaming table. Betting had commenced; he must raise his stake and hold his nerve. If he could win just once more, he would eat well this week, replace his worn-out boots, even repay some of his debts.

He wiped his kerchief across his brow. It was warm in the club. He leant forward, hand trembling, and shifted his token to the eight of spades. He added a second, and placed two more on the high card bar. Silence fell. The banker drew from the shoe and exposed the two critical cards. Both his bets had won!

Fighting to hide his relief, he drained his glass. 'I'm out, gentlemen.' He rose and smoothed down his uniform, but as he stretched to scoop up his winnings he heard a harsh voice reverberate through the haze of cigar smoke.

'Ah! I've found you, Klein, and a little bird tells me you're now in funds.'

His elation evaporated. Captain Ivan Stenovsky, swinging a riding whip, was walking towards him. The sturdy cavalryman was flanked by two junior officers. As the array of silver-gilt-edged white tunics advanced on him, the manager of the club stepped out. 'Excuse me, sirs. You cannot collect a debt in here. You know that.' Stenovsky thrust the man aside and, on reaching the lieutenant's table, swept his pile of chips onto the frayed carpet. One of the captain's companions stooped to retrieve them, then turned and hastened to the cash desk in the hall.

The lieutenant lunged forward in pursuit, but Stenovsky seized his arm and the remaining officer clasped his shoulder. As they marched him out across the crowded clubroom, gamblers grouped around the tables ceased their play and stared as if bewitched. A waiter put down his tray to turn to look; the glasses clinked; the samovar in the corner groaned and hissed.

The manager tried once more to deflect Stenovsky. 'It is against house rules to put pressure on a gentleman in here, sir. Kindly let the lieutenant go. You must pursue this at some other time. Our customers…'

The captain silenced the man with a shake of his whip. 'This isn't an establishment frequented by gentlemen, as I am sure you're aware.'

The manager eyed the whip and stepped back. They pushed the lieutenant on, out through the echoing hallway and into the street. A roar of chatter erupted behind them. It was light outside. He struggled to break free but, outnumbered, found himself swiftly propelled into the stinking alleyway behind the club. Stenovsky thrust his round head into his face and spat: 'Listen, you German bastard, you owe me money and I'm taking some of it back. I don't need an excuse, Klein. You're a dirty thief.'

'How dare you! This is a matter of honour...'

'I don't think so. We've already established that you're no gentleman, and you can't deny you owe me money. Indeed, I'd say you owe me more than money.' Stenovsky stepped back, flexing his whip. 'Turn him round.'

Stenovsky's companions glanced at one another. 'Captain, sir... are you sure?'

'Turn him round.'

They swivelled the lieutenant to face the filthy wall, striking his head on the rough bricks. Dazed, he hardly noticed the first blow, but as more followed he crumpled to the ground. He tried to roll away, but they held him down until a final sharp kick took away what remained of his breath.

'That'll do. Leave him there.'

As his tormentor and his acolytes departed, he lay gasping in the slime and wished he were dead. It was not the pain. That would pass. It was the shame, the ignominy, the hopelessness of his situation. He could hear footsteps. Had someone witnessed his humiliation? This was unbearable. He tried to get up, to make an escape, but his feet slipped beneath him.

'Come on, Andrey Andreyevich... I think you need some help.' It was the voice of his fellow officer, Denis Borisov. The ensign must have followed him from the club. He tried to push the man away but, determined to remain, Borisov tried to lift him from the ground. Unable to hold back tears of mortification, Andrey's knees buckled. Finally, he was swaying unsteadily on his feet.

Borisov, with some difficulty, shepherded him past the row of columns that fronted the nearby barracks. At the gates, he heard the ensign say, 'He's drunk.' There was a chink as the sentry pocketed a coin and signed them in without comment. Reaching his rooms at last, Andrey sank to the floor, aware that his orderly was surveying him with contempt.

Monday morning brought the inevitable summons. Two troopers escorted Andrey to the rooms of Kirill Rosovsky, captain of the company of the King of Prussia's Grenadiers, currently stationed in the capital. He stood to rigid attention while blinding sunlight shone into his eyes from a window high in the wall. Pain sat like a gridiron from his shoulders to his thighs.

The captain finally looked up from his papers and waved the escort away. 'At ease, lieutenant.'

Andrey shifted away from the light. Sweat broke out on his brow and his head throbbed. What did the captain know of the incident two nights before? Would he be arrested, end up in the guardhouse and be sent back to the main force in Novgorod? Might he be demoted? Or even dismissed?

Rosovsky ran his fingers through his thick brown hair and cleared his throat. 'I've arrived this morning to find a report about a disturbance at a common gaming establishment on Saturday night in which you were involved, von Klein Sternberg. Can you enlighten me as to what it was all about?'

'Not really, sir. It was just a private matter.' Andrey stared at the floor. Must he tell the whole story?

'Come now, lieutenant. It's reported that you were taken from the place by force by three cavalry officers. By the look of you, they didn't treat you kindly. There must have been a reason.'

'Yes, sir.'

'Are you in some sort of trouble? You have to admit that the circumstances seem rather strange.'

'Yes, sir.'

'If all you are able to say to me is "yes, sir", I'll have no option but to put you on a charge. Look, I know you were not the aggressor, and I also know you well enough to know this is quite out of character. What was going on? Do you owe Stenovsky money?'

'Less than I did, sir.'

'I'm told that he cashed in your chips and pocketed the cash.'

'Yes, sir.'

'Do you have other debts?'

'Yes, sir.'

'Then why were you wasting your money playing faro?'

'I was actually winning, sir.'

The captain frowned and his eyes narrowed. 'You're an intelligent man – at least, I thought you were. I seem to remember you passed out with distinction from cadet school and have, up to now at least, shown some signs of sense. Surely you know that trying to gamble your way out of trouble is a hopeless exercise? How much do you owe?'

'About a year's stipend, sir.'

'I see.' The captain fell silent for a moment. 'And do you have any savings? Do you get an allowance from your... err... grandfather, the baron?'

Andrey glanced down at the desk. The captain had been reading his record. 'No, sir. My grandfather died two years ago. Things didn't go well for him after the war. Part of our estate has been sold, but that has barely covered the debts. I have an uncle, my mother's brother, but life is no easier for him. I can't look to him for help.' He shifted on the spot. Thank God his grandfather *was* dead, he reflected. Had he known of his current situation, his disappointment – and, of course, his wrath – would have been unendurable.

'But you have always seemed to manage in the past.'

Andrey flushed. 'Yes, sir.'

The captain was waiting for further explanation, but, when none came, he slapped his palm down hard on his desk. Andrey flinched. 'I have to ask you to be open with me. Otherwise, I can't begin to help you. If you've accumulated significant debts, as it seems you have, and have no way of repaying them, as looks probable, I'm bound to question whether you can remain as an officer with the regiment. You may have to transfer to the line, or re-register as a private soldier. I don't want to see that happen, Andrey Andreyevich.'

Andrey's face burned. There was no help for it. He must confess his guilt, and hope that Rosovsky lived up to his reputation for humanity. 'It was a woman, sir. She turned out to be rather expensive.'

The captain sighed. 'Your stipend won't support a life of self-indulgence, lieutenant, and you say you have no other resources. I was unaware of that.'

Andrey nodded. People often assumed he must have something to fall back on – the receipts from an estate or family wealth – and for the sake of appearances he had allowed them to think it. But in fact, he now had nothing and, in a month or so of madness, he had spent a good deal of what he hadn't got.

But Rosovsky was continuing, 'I assume that you've managed to upset Captain Stenovsky? His behaviour seems extreme for a man simply pursuing a debt, particularly a man with his resources. Following his older brothers' disgrace five years ago, he must be the heir to a fortune.'

Andrey swayed a little.

'Take a chair, if you like, lieutenant.'

'I'd rather stand, sir, but thank you. Yes, the woman was formerly... err... Stenovsky's mistress.'

'And he lent money to you?'

'Before she left him, before she and I...'

The captain looked up sharply. 'I hope you're not still supporting her?'

'No sir, we parted a week or so ago.'

'I suppose she realised your funds had run out.'

'Yes, sir. It was all a terrible mistake. I see that now.'

'And who was this woman?'

Andrey shrugged and, unable to meet Rosovsky's gaze, named Minnie, a young but increasingly celebrated dancer from the Bolshoy Kamenny Theatre.

Rosovsky's eyebrows rose. 'Really! You should have had more sense... you couldn't possibly...'

'Afford her... no, of course not.' The confession made him feel better.

'Has she gone back to Stenovsky?'

'No. She's now under the protection of Count Malyshev.'

The captain snorted. 'He should be able to keep her in

trinkets well enough. Well, lieutenant, you've got yourself into a fine mess. You're not thinking of calling Stenovsky out?'

'I don't think so, sir. I am happy to fight him, indeed I probably should, but…'

'Well, you shouldn't be happy to fight him, and I am obliged to order you not to!' The captain paused, then said more quietly, 'You've been very foolish, but I think you know that.'

'Yes, I'm deeply sorry, sir.'

'I expect you are, and there's no easy way to help you. Perhaps you might like to see active service in the Caucasus? Life is pretty cheap there in every sense, but promotion prospects are excellent and there may be opportunities for bounty.'

The Caucasus! Although probably no more than he deserved, such a fate was unthinkable, promotion prospects or not.

But Rosovsky continued, 'An alternative that I am prepared to contemplate, since I don't want to lose you, is for the regiment to advance a loan against your future income. It will only cover some of your debts; you'll need to juggle the rest as best you can. Life won't be easy. There'll be no wine, women or song for some time. Otherwise, I could transfer you or discharge you from service altogether, although that would be a pity and, of course, wouldn't resolve your financial problems. Go away for a couple of days and think about it.'

'Yes, thank you.' Andrey breathed more easily. It seemed that Rosovsky still had some faith in him, had not written him off.

'Alright, von Klein Sternberg, you're excused duty for the next three days. If you are to remain with us, you need to get fit. The company is duty guard at the palace next week, as you know, and within the month we're off to summer camp. I'll recommend that the major has a word with Stenovsky's senior officer. Whatever the man thinks you've done to him, there's no justification for assaulting one of our grenadiers. I'll see you back here on Thursday, same time.'

The captain turned to his papers. As Andrey saluted and started to leave, the captain looked up. 'Do you have any resources at all?'

'Very few, sir.'

Rosovsky took some money from the drawer of his desk. 'Take this, and give a kopek or two to your orderly and tell him to look after you. I have it in mind to change your man – you need someone less money-grubbing. That's all.'

Rosovsky picked up his pen. The interview was over.

Andrey did not stir from his rooms for the next three days. His surly orderly had been replaced by Morozov, a young trooper of a kinder disposition. On Wednesday he was visited by Denis Borisov, who had rescued him from the alleyway, and who, it seemed, had later gone back to the club to retrieve his sword and shako. Borisov spared his feelings by pretending that his fortitude in the face of adversity had been admirable, and he began to feel better. He didn't hurry to discuss the circumstances surrounding the incident; although the ensign was aware of his liaison with the actress, he was unwilling to reveal the extent of his financial difficulties.

When Borisov had left, Andrey pondered the choices he must make. He was twenty-four years old. Were he to leave the army, he had no idea what he could do. He had never thought to be anything other than a soldier. There was no place for him back in Estonia; the estate there could barely support his uncle's family. He might get a job in government service, but he had little inclination for desk work, and had no-one to recommend him for a post. Since he could never stoop to accepting bribes, it would also take years to pay off his debts. Perhaps he should transfer to a line regiment – life would certainly be cheaper – but despite everything he still had a spark of ambition, a desire to succeed. There was of course the Caucasus, where his rival, Stenovsky, had served with distinction in recent years. But, although he was not afraid of action, he had no appetite for leading anxious soldiers through lonely mountain passes awaiting the tribesmen's attack. No, he must take Rosovksy's offer and face a dull and frugal future. At least he had not been sent back to Novgorod.

On Thursday morning, as he was hauling on his uniform to keep his appointment with the captain, his orderly, Morozov, brought him two letters. Andrey frowned at them; people rarely wrote to him. The first letter had a familiar scent. He eyed it with misgiving. He didn't recognise the hand, but that was not surprising; although she was a fine dancer, Minnie rarely wrote anything. There seemed to be more than a letter; it was probably another bill for fripperies long-since consumed and forgotten. To his surprise, however, a small wad of paper roubles fell onto the desk: a useful sum, if not a substantial one.

I'm sorry for your trouble over me,' Minnie had written. *'I hope this will help you. I have plenty now and won't miss this. M.*

He must send the money back, of course, even though she now had everything she might desire – everything apart from a young lover. The count was certainly well over forty, and she was seventeen.

He set the letter aside. He knew from the seal that the other was from Rodionov, the agent that his family used, or had once used, for business in St Petersburg. Since his grandfather's death, he had heard nothing from the agent, apart from a communication a year or so ago seeking to know if he was in a position to defray some of the family's obligations. It was then he had realised that he would receive no inheritance of any sort.

To Baron von Klein Sternberg,

Sir, would you be so good as to call into my offices on Nevsky Prospekt at your convenience. I have information that may well be to your advantage.

I remain etc,
A.F. Rodionov

Despite the encouraging tone of the brief note, Andrey wasn't optimistic. It would probably mean another appeal for funds from one of his grandfather's creditors, or an attempt to get him to pay the agent's outstanding account.

He would go after drill; there was, after all, nothing to lose. And he must return the assignats to Minnie. He should not take money from her.

❈

Later, having met the captain, Andrey walked along Nevsky Prospekt. It was well before the dinner hour, and the shopping street was crowded. As he dodged the carriages and pushed his way past servants loaded with parcels, his mood was sober. Rosovsky had left him in no doubt that his future would be difficult. The conditions under which the loan was to be advanced were onerous, and any further trouble or scandal could mean demotion at best.

He gazed at the now-unattainable luxury goods in the shop windows and wondered, yet again, how he could have been so stupid. He had lived for a few weeks in a bubble of profligacy, and had behaved like the owner of a vast estate with a thousand serfs, when in fact he had nothing, or less than nothing. It had, of course, been intensely thrilling when he had gained exclusive entry to Minnie's dressing room, when he had tasted the prestige of recognition as her lover. He had relished the intimate late suppers, the nights between satin sheets. But when one of his creditors had finally drawn a line and the truth had dawned on Minnie, the shock had been like an inoculation. As he came to himself, he found he felt nothing for the woman, nothing at all. The entire encounter seemed as empty as the tawdry spectacles in which she sometimes performed.

He felt a curdle of shame, and his steps faltered. The years fell away. He could hear the voice of his grandfather, berating him for some misdemeanour, extolling the virtues of honour and self-control. Would he be sent to languish in his room, be forbidden to school his horse, or worse, be taken by the collar and thrashed?

When a dog ran across his path, almost tripping him up, he shook himself and walked briskly on. He must put uncomfortable childhood memories behind him. What was done was done and, despite all, he could not entirely regret his adventure with Minnie. It had broadened his view of the world and had changed him. He had learned something of real passion and had discovered within himself a capacity for tolerance and humour, virtues that had not been encouraged by his narrow, and sometimes harsh, upbringing.

Rodionov's office was above a tailor's shop. Andrey walked up the steep stairway into the vestibule, where dim light filtered through clouded glass doors. A clerk in the outer office leapt up to greet him. 'Oh, Baron! How very good to see you. Mr Rodionov asked me to send you straight in. Can I interest you in some refreshment?'

'No, thank you.'

The agent opened his door. The plump little man smiled as he welcomed him with a flourish. 'Baron von Klein Sternberg! I trust you are well. Sit down, sit down, sir.'

Andrey watched Rodionov's pudgy hands shuffle piles of paper around his desk. The room smelt faintly of cats. Finally the agent found what he was looking for. Holding what seemed to be an official document, he said, 'I think I have some good news for you, sir. It may very well prove to be very good news!'

Andrey shifted in his chair. He supposed this should cheer him, but his body still ached and two hours on the parade ground this morning had not improved matters.

'Recently, as agent for your family, I took delivery of a box that appears to contain some items belonging to your late mother,' said Rodionov. 'Apparently the estate house near Torzhok that belonged to your late father's family was demolished a few months back – it was quite ruinous – and the papers were found in the attic.'

Andrey's stomach tightened. The very mention of his father filled him with guilty discomfort. But now the agent was in full flow. 'You are of course aware that there was a problem surrounding the marriage of your parents in that the ceremony, although valid, of course, was held under the Lutheran rites.'

Andrey was indeed aware of this. Some months prior to his birth, his father, a Russian count, had died, his head taken off by a cannon ball at the Battle of Austerlitz. For whatever reason, possibly lack of time, his parents had failed to go through a second, Orthodox, ceremony. This had had a calamitous effect on the status of their only child, Andrey. The original grant of nobility that pertained to his father's family stipulated that to inherit any title or heritable property in Russia, it was necessary to be of the Orthodox faith and the legitimate heir of parents married under the auspices of the Russian church. As it happened, due to his father's profligacy, there had been no wealth to inherit, but he resented the loss of his title and the sense that his background was tainted.

Rodionov was rehearsing these facts at some length, but now he said, 'The thing is this, Baron. It seems we may have been wrong with regard to your position. In the aforementioned box, the one from the attic, there was little of interest, just some old papers – bills, mainly – and rags. Apart from, that is, this document, which is a record of a marriage. It seems to show that your mother and father did, after all, go through an Orthodox ceremony.'

Rodionov proffered the paper. Andrey scanned it. It was discoloured but legible and yes, it did seem to be the written record of a marriage between his long-dead mother, Astrella von Klein Sternberg, and Count Stepan Dmitryevich Bogolyubov in September 1805. The ceremony had taken place at the church of St Andrew the First Named on Vasilevsky Island, here in St Petersburg, two months before Austerlitz, and six months before his own birth in 1806.

The agent, now pink with excitement, seemed hardly able to contain himself. 'This is of course remarkable in itself, Baron… or perhaps I should say Count! But what is even more interesting is that it appears that your father, although impoverished, did, after all, have some expectations, although at the time of his death these must have seemed very remote. He was a distant relative of Prince Dmitry Vladimirovich Bogolyubov, an elderly man of considerable substance. The prince was a senator and a senior figure at the Ministry of the Interior, but has now retired. As things have turned out, following the death of the son of another cousin some years ago, your father would have been Bogolyubov's sole heir.'

'But doesn't my adoption by my grandfather preclude me from inheriting?' Andrey's mother had died within a month of his birth and old Baron von Klein Sternberg had formally adopted his orphaned grandchild and ensured that he inherited his name and title. The old man had suffered from inordinate pride and, although in the end he also had nothing to leave Andrey, at least face had been saved.

'No, I don't think so. If the marriage was valid, it should not prevent you from claiming your rights. You would probably have to convert to the Orthodox faith, however.'

Andrey leant back. He knew that this news, coming at such a fortuitous moment, should cheer him, but his first reaction was one of uncertainty and doubt. To make what must be a very public claim on the prince's legacy would mean that his family history, up to now concealed from the world, would become common knowledge. But surely his present situation was equally unsatisfactory. If he truly was the heir to the Bogolyubov princedom, he should seek to claim it, even if he exposed himself to scrutiny and possible ridicule.

Rodionov was continuing to speak.

'I'm sorry, what were you saying?' said Andrey.

'I was asking, Andrey Andreyevich, if you want me to inform the prince. My clerk has already unearthed the record of the marriage at the church, and is seeking confirmation of its validity at the Consistory Court. I suspect that the prince wrongly believes that he has no living heirs. He is close to the Belkin family, particularly the head of the family, Alexander, Count Belkin. I'm told that at present he intends that they inherit his moveable assets and acquired property. His holdings in patrimonial land and any associated serfs may well revert to the

Crown, however, in the absence of a legitimate successor or a dispensation from the Emperor.' Rodionov had clearly already done a good deal of research.

'Very well, Rodionov. If you are happy that all is in order, you must contact the prince.'

'And I'll look after the box, shall I, sir? For safekeeping?'

Andrey hesitated for a moment. Very likely it contained nothing but a catalogue of old debts and defunct mortgage deeds. He had more pressing concerns at present. 'Yes, you look after it, Rodionov,' he said. 'I'll come and pick it up in due course.'

CHAPTER TWO

July 1830 – Dubovnoye Estate, Province of Moscow

Vasily Nikolayevich rode along the sandy track that led to the village. The morning was still and warm. Lime trees edging the wayside glowed, a bright green lattice masking the grey and silver upstrokes of the birches in the woods beyond. The crooning of woodpigeons drowned out other birdsong. A woodcock flew up and Vasily's mare danced sideways. He calmed her, rubbing his hand along her smooth neck, then urged her into a trot.

It was early, but a few peasants were already making for the fields, hoping to complete their work before the heat of midday. His spirit lightened. It would soon be harvest time, when he could go out to join them. As he rode past, they took off their caps. Some knelt on the ground, and he greeted most of them by name.

He passed the wooden church. The village was quiet; many of the izbas were deserted. Chickens scratched in the dust. A cat stalked some creature among the scrubby rushes by the pond. Women were weeding the kitchen gardens, or sitting on low wooden stools before their doors, working with yarn. Again, they stopped what they were doing and bowed. He wished that they would ignore him but, however uncomfortable their deference made him feel, he knew it was pointless to expect them to ignore the custom of years.

As usual he pulled up at the smithy, throwing the mare's reins to the boy who came out to greet him. The thick, acrid smell of burnt hoof drifted from within. The smith was working. He walked into the smoky gloom.

'Good morning, Pashka.'

'I'll be finished in just a minute, master. Sit you down outside, sir.'

Ten minutes later the smith emerged, wiping his hands. They sat together in silence for several minutes.

'Well, what's new?' Vasily asked at last. Pashka was his best source of information in the village, more alert to the current mood than the village headsman.

'All's well enough, sir. Weather looks set fair for harvest.' Vasily stretched his legs out into the sunshine as Pashka gave voice to the village's concerns. The controversial German cows, which Vasily had encouraged the estate manager to acquire to try to improve the poor quality of the soil, were still regarded by some in the village as an alien and unnecessary nuisance. There were also worries about the levies. Would Dubovskoye be subject to them this year? The army's hunger for men seemed insatiable, and the sudden disappearance for twenty-five years of a son could be a disaster for a peasant family. It would be best to be prepared. Vasily promised to make enquiries when he next went to town.

When Pashka seemed to have come to the end of

his catalogue, Vasily took his leave. He rode out to look at the offending cattle and then, satisfied that they were where they should be, returned to the estate office. Then he collected Annika, his deerhound, who was unreliable with chickens, and rode out towards the woods.

On his way he passed the cemetery. He pulled up for a moment at his father's grave. Count Nikolay Belkin had died eighteen years before, when Vasily had been just seven years old. Now contemplating the headstone, his heart twisted with sadness. He still remembered his father's carefree nature, his generosity and love. But the imagined dry tones of his Uncle Alexander overlaid his thoughts: *Your father was running the estate into the ground.* Well, that might have been so, but his own life would have been so different had he still been here.

1812 had been a terrible year. In addition to his father's death, their family home in Moscow was destroyed by fire when Napoleon occupied the city. Only government loans and the sale of the site had saved the family from bankruptcy. Leaving their country estate in the hands of a steward, Vasily, with his mother and sister, had moved to St Petersburg to live with his father's brother, Alexander, in the home of his close friend and patron, Dmitry Vladimirovich, Prince Bogolyubov.

Aware of an unopened letter from his uncle in his pocket, he rode on through the woods. He reached a clearing where he often came to escape the crowds that seemed to throng the estate house these days. Dismounting, he sat under a tree and opened the seal.

Bogolyubov Palace, St Petersburg
4th July 1830

My dear Vasily,

I hope that all is well with you at Dubovnoye.

As you know, I was not expecting to visit the estate this summer. Dmitry remains rather feeble after his bout of the gripe in the spring. I continue to try to step back from the Ministry, but the need to respect the Emperor's call for all men to fulfil their duty ties me to my desk for at least some of the time.

Nonetheless, I find I must visit you after all. An awkward situation, which I would prefer not to describe here, has arisen that we need to discuss. Accordingly, you should expect me to arrive towards the middle of the month.

When we meet we must consider your future, Vasily. You are almost twenty-six. I think we can safely put the troubles of the past behind us, and decide what you will do now. You know that Count Benkendorf received good reports of you when you served with the Ministry in Oryol, and would happily recruit you to the Third Section. The work is well paid, and considered important. You could expect to enter at the 10th rank, given your record. Please give the matter some thought.

Your mother and sister Katya send greetings to you all. They are, as usual, with the Court at Tsarskoye Selo, with Prince Polunin and the children.

Your uncle,
Alexander

Vasily set the letter aside. Could he and his uncle really put the past behind them? It was almost five years since the rebellion had been quashed, and more than two since anyone had suspected his part in it. The one man he had feared would betray him was dead, and only a handful of others, all trustworthy, knew anything at all. Yes, sadly, he probably could now safely return to the capital.

He unconsciously flexed his crop. He was happy here at Dubovnoye. It was satisfying to live voluntarily where he had previously been confined in disgrace. Thanks to the hard work of the steward, assisted by his grandmother, the estate had gradually recovered from its desperate financial position and had a future worth building. His greatest wish now was to secure his patrimony, and improve the lives of those who depended on him. He had plenty of new ideas and, with some help from Dmitry Vladimirovich, the means to adopt them. But clearly Alexander thought he should return to Petersburg and would be deeply disappointed if he failed to complete some further years in the service of the state.

Annika licked Vasily's hand and he scratched her ears. He knew he had been lucky. He had in the past travelled in Europe and had spent a year here in the country after his spell as a low-ranked government official in Oryol. He'd been hoping that his uncle might forget about the continuation of his career. Well, Alexander would shortly be here. They could battle the matter out then.

He looked for his horse. There was work to do in the estate office. Later he would ride over to the mill to visit the widow. She would find him some dinner and soothe his fears about the future.

Ten days later

'But how astonishing that it hasn't come to light before now!' Yevgenia, Vasily's grandmother, rose from her chair and started to refresh the teacups. His uncle, Alexander, had arrived an hour or so ago, and within minutes had told them the disquieting news that a man had emerged claiming to be the legitimate heir of their benefactor, Dmitry Vladimirovich, Prince Bogolyubov.

Beyond the veranda the sky was overcast; after many days of settled weather a storm threatened. The garden was devoid of shadow, all seemed faded, and small flies had emerged, some of which had penetrated the netting pinned to the wooden balustrade. Vasily looked at his uncle's tall, sparse form. He was obviously tired after the journey, and also troubled.

'I'm not so worried for myself,' Alexander was saying, rubbing his bony knees. 'I can always go to live with your sister, Vasily, or come here. I'm well enough provided for, but Dmitry is distressed. In the absence of a successor, he had been thinking of petitioning the Tsar to allow him to pass on some of his patrimony to you, even formally name you his heir.'

Vasily was surprised. He knew the prince to be attached to him, and he had been generous over the years, but such an idea was something new, and would mean an entirely different future. 'Well, I won't miss what I've never had, Uncle.'

'Don't joke about this, Vasya. Dmitry is really very

disturbed, and if von Klein Sternberg is successful, there's no doubt we'll all be worse off financially.' Alexander swatted away a fly. 'The affair will doubtless bring the family into the public eye, which is never desirable.'

'Who is this character anyway?' asked Vasily.

'He's a German.'

'A German? How can that be?'

'He's a Russian citizen of German descent from an ancient Estonian family. His name is Andrey Andreyevich von Klein Sternberg. He's about twenty-four years old.' Alexander briefly outlined the basis of von Klein's claim.

'Dmitry didn't seek to try to do something for him after the death of his father?'

'No. Initially there were several other heirs, and there was no love lost between the different branches of the family. Von Klein's father, Count Stepan Bogolyubov, was a cousin, a military man who showed open contempt for a career civil servant like Dmitry. The two men rarely met. Stepan received a fair proportion of the Bogolyubov wealth of course, through his own father, but, although a gallant officer by all accounts, he lived a wild and unstable life. When he died during the war, all his lands were mortgaged, and later reverted to his creditors.'

'So what has changed now?'

'Interestingly, it was when one of those creditors recently decided to pull down the estate house that the evidence concerning the marriage came to light.'

'And is he going to pursue his claim?'

'It seems he is. Of course, if he has a case and Dmitry won't accept it then he will have to fight it through the courts on Dmitry's death. Dmitry is in reasonable health, but he's not getting any younger.'

'Does von Klein Sternberg have any estate? What does he do? Has he made a secret of his birth up to now? I have to say, I've never heard of him.'

'He's a soldier. A second lieutenant in one of the grenadier regiments, the one that used to be the St Petersburg, but is now named for the King of Prussia. After the death of his father, and in the light of his dubious legitimacy, I suppose, he managed to acquire his maternal grandfather's name and the title of baron, I assume through adoption. Your friend, Ivan Stenovsky, knows the man and was very scathing about him when I made enquiries. It seems he hasn't a bean to his name, and is a gambler and a libertine.'

Vasily frowned and started to reply but his uncle continued, 'I know you won't want to hear this, but I think the time has come for you to return to Petersburg. You need to resume your career. Aside from that, the prince wants someone he trusts to look into all this, and I don't have time. Since General Zakrevsky has been in post I have been constantly occupied. He has been a real new broom. If you don't want to take up Benkendorf's generous offer of work in the Third Section, a slot can be found for you at the Interior Ministry, where you won't be overburdened.'

'If I come back, I don't want to have anything to do with police work.' Vasily had had enough of opening innocent people's mail and looking for conspiracy where there was none. When he had worked with the gendarmes in Oryol, their efforts in this respect had been half-hearted, but it had been part of their job.

'I thought that might be the case. I had in mind something like internal passports,' Alexander said. 'Or, of course, there is always roads maintenance.'

Permits or potholes! Vasily gazed out over the garden and sighed. Was he fated to remain a pen-pushing bureaucrat forever? When he had returned from Europe in 1825, he had been destined for a prestigious post in the Foreign Service, but fate – and perhaps what some might see as his own folly – had intervened.

'And Vasily, when you return to town, you can have the run of the apartment. Since I've been abandoned by all of you…'

'Oh Uncle, really!'

'Since I've been abandoned by all of you,' Alexander repeated, 'I've been bivouacking down with Dmitry most of the time anyway.'

Vasily reflected that living in the prince's spacious and opulent rooms on the ground floor of the Bogolyubov Palace hardly constituted 'bivouacking', but he let it pass.

Alexander leant forward. 'Look Vasily, I do need your help with this. It may not take too long to sort out, and I promise you that we'll discuss your permanent return here in time.'

His grandmother, who had been listening in silence, rose and put her hand on Vasily's shoulder. 'Do what your uncle asks, Vasya. Dubovnoye will still be here waiting for you. I shall be delighted when you return, but I think you should think about finding a wife to bring home with you. One with money, preferably. It will be like the old days, and I shall do what I can to keep myself alive until then.'

Vasily glanced at his grandmother, and then at his uncle. If he agreed to go to St Petersburg, it might not be easy to return here to the Moscow region, particularly if the prince achieved his goal of naming him his heir. Such generosity would almost certainly require the agreement of the Emperor. He could be expected to appear at court, become part of the autocratic system that he deplored and in the past had vainly sought to destroy. But he had resolved to put ideas of violent revolution behind him, and knew that he really had no excuse. He threw up his hands in consent. Alexander rubbed his long nose and then grimaced. Vasily recognised this as a smile.

'Can we postpone my departure for a couple of weeks, sir?' he said. 'I would like to see some of the harvest in, and enjoy a little more of the summer.'

'Oh yes, no need to come back to the city ahead of the crowds. I'll tell the minister that you'll start at the beginning of September.'

※

That night the weather broke. At the first crash of thunder, Vasily awoke from sleep that was already disturbed. The rain clattered on the roof like fistfuls of pebbles; the old wooden house shook and groaned in the wind. The thunder rolled again and his uncle's words revolved in his mind. He knew that he must help the prince, who had been more than a father to him since he had welcomed Alexander and his family into his home. Perhaps he was too pessimistic. Perhaps, after all, wealth and high rank might mean freedom rather than drudgery, might provide a route back to Irina, his mistress, and to Sophia, their child.

As the thunder rumbled again, he recalled a similarly foul night over a year ago. He had travelled all day from Oryol, to visit Irina and Sophia on Irina's family estate near Bryansk. He had been wet and irritable, and on his arrival he and Irina had embarked on a bitter argument.

When he had been reunited with his mistress after a forced separation of many months, they had enjoyed a brief period of ecstatic contentment. But the obstacle that had spoiled their joy in the past now threatened to destroy their relationship. Irina was not free. She was already married to an Austrian nobleman, from whom she was separated. Vasily had no doubt that she loved him. When Vasily's freedom, and perhaps his life, had been threatened, she had sacrificed her happiness to save him. But from the very start she had insisted that their affair must remain discreet; she would do nothing to threaten his reputation, his honour, or the advancement of his career. He had believed that when they were reunited her attitude would change, but he had been mistaken. Despite his entreaties, she would not contemplate coming to live in Oryol, and now his service in the city was coming to an end, she was evasive about committing to any plans for the future.

Thus, the following morning, as they sat together on the steps of the estate house presiding over the May Day celebrations, he had been in despair. With their little dark-haired daughter on his knee, he barely listened while the serf women and girls sang the old songs and danced their stately dances. From time to time he looked at Irina, lovely in her light gown, her shoulders covered with a bright shawl. He could smell the spring flowers that the women had draped around her neck and tangled in her red gold hair. Tears had filled his eyes. To argue like this was torture. He knew he must make peace with her, reassure her that he loved her and that, after all, he was content to continue with this half-life, even if that was untrue.

They had made up their quarrel on that occasion. He had postponed his departure from Oryol twice and continued to visit her. They had spent two uninterrupted weeks together during the late summer, two weeks of pain and pleasure that now he could hardly bear to recall. When he had ridden away that last time, nothing had been resolved – and, despairing that it ever would be, he had never returned. A few weeks later he had settled, alone, on his estate near Moscow.

Now they exchanged polite notes. He wrote to her of the estate and sent her his sketches. She replied with news of Sophia. He sent money and gifts for the child when he could. In time he was almost able to put both mother and child from his mind. He made the best of his life at Dubovnoye, went out in local society, rekindled a relationship with the miller's widow. But at times like this, when his life was about to change, he yearned for Irina, her love, her support.

※

August 1830

Taking his uncle at his word, Vasily did not hurry to leave for St Petersburg, but his plans were accelerated when disturbing news came from the south.

He had been in his study, shaking his head over a book written in English. He could hardly understand a word! It was the novel *Ivanhoe*, a fine volume that the journalist and teacher, Golovkin, had given him on his last day in Oryol. His lack of comprehension would certainly disappoint his friend, Thomas Maltby, his former English tutor, to whom he had written to warn of his return to the capital. Would it be worthwhile restarting his English lessons? He would have to go back to the beginning.

The door opened, hitting the wall with a crack. The lanky form of Yakov, his manservant, stood on the threshold. 'Vasily Nikolayevich, sir, the smith's boy is here. He says you're to go down to see his father now!' Vasily was relieved to set Sir Walter aside. 'Send for the cart, Yakov, and do try to open the door more gently.'

'Yes sir, sorry sir.'

As they were waiting for the dog cart to be brought round, Vasily's young ward Matvey appeared and insisted on being included in the trip. Yakov drove them down to the village, and Pashka emerged from the smithy. 'Thank you for coming down, sir. An ofenya is trading his wares in the village today. He says he needs to speak to the lord.'

Vasily nodded; what could the merchant want of him? An ofenya was no ordinary pedlar but a traveller, revered by the serfs, who sold books, church calendars and holy images. He was a tall, handsome man with a neat short beard. His shirt shone white, and his brown homespun coat was belted with red plaited strips of scarlet leather. A number of villagers had gathered round his stall, picking up the goods on offer. He was showing an icon to an old man, who stroked his beard as he contemplated the image.

A waft of incense sweetened the air. Vasily picked up several books and put them down again. Here was one containing woodcuts of bible characters. Sophia might like that. He reached into his pocket.

'Are you the master here, sir?' the ofenya asked him, taking some coins in payment. He led him a few steps away from the stall and continued in a low voice, 'You need to know, lord, that there's a pestilence approaching from the south.'

'What sort of pestilence?'

'It's not entirely clear, sir, but men say it is the cholera. The affliction has been raging in the east for some time, but it has now found its way into Russia. There was word of cases in Astrakhan and then at the Great Fair at Nizhny. It will have spread along the trade routes, up the rivers.'

Vasily stepped back. He knew that the disease was deadly. 'Have you come from Nizhny?'

'No sir, and even if I had, it's not clear that a man can pass it on to another through speech.'

Vasily fell silent for a moment. He had clearly failed to hide his fear. 'What should I do to help my people here?' he asked.

'Pray to God, sir, and tell every soul to do the same. All lies in His hands. But that aside, some say that drinking clean water and eating wholesome food prevents infection. Folk in the country seem to have a better chance of staying safe. They should stock up for the winter and stay at home. I am making my way home myself. I don't wish to spread disease.'

Vasily thanked the man for his warning and went to discuss the news with Pashka. 'Before I go to Petersburg,

I want to know that stores for the winter are adequate,' he said. 'Try to encourage folk to preserve what they can from their plots this autumn, so they don't have to make unnecessary trips to town.'

'Must you go to the capital, sir? You'd be better to stay here. Disease spreads like a plague in the city.'

'I should much prefer to stay, but I have duties to fulfil in St Petersburg.'

'Go sooner rather than later then, sir,' the blacksmith urged. 'The capital's a distance from Nizhny. It may well be spared entirely.'

As they drove back to the estate house, Vasily told Yakov and Matvey why he must return to St Petersburg earlier than planned. 'You both have a choice,' he said. 'Yakov, you can stay here with your family if you wish, and Matvey, you can go down to the south, to Golovkin's school in Oryol, as we had discussed. I can't really tell what would be the safest thing for you.'

'I'll be coming with you, sir,' Yakov said immediately. Vasily knew that he would not willingly leave the comfortable position he had occupied since their childhood.

Matvey remained silent for some minutes, and then said, 'You do realise, sir, that I never had any intention of going to Oryol. I was planning to find a way to avoid it, but hadn't quite worked it out. I am aware that it could mean sleeping with Yakov in the servants' rooms, but all the same…'

Vasily smiled. Clearly Matvey had not lost his gift for spontaneous, often unconvincing, invention. Once the property of the prince but now free, his hazel almond-shaped eyes were striking and his chaotic black curls, which a maid's scissors failed to tame for long, gave him the aura of a gypsy. The boy had grown rapidly in recent months, and was now almost as tall as he. His age was uncertain, but the flash of pimples on his forehead, his changing voice and a new self-awareness suggested that he was fourteen or perhaps fifteen years old.

Vasily was relieved that both Yakov and Matvey wanted to accompany him. Perhaps selfishly, he preferred that they stay together. As they drew up in the yard, he leapt down and hurried to find his grandmother. When news of the cholera spread, the roads would become crowded and possibly dangerous. Travelling restrictions might soon be imposed. They must leave Dubovnoye as soon as they could.

CHAPTER THREE

September 1830 – St Petersburg

Andrey Andreyevich stood by the turrets on the Anichkov Bridge and looked around for a droshky. He had been visiting Rodionov and the news was, on the whole, promising. While he was away at summer camp, the notary had rechecked the records at the church in St Petersburg at which his parents' marriage had taken place. The register, Rodionov said, had been 'indistinct' in places, but it seemed that it corresponded sufficiently closely with the copy at the Consistory Court to satisfy the requirements of evidence.

Prince Bogolyubov's agent had, however, made it clear that the prince refused to recognise Andrey as his legal heir and would fight the case. This seemed to represent a setback, but Rodionov was confident that, in time, the position would change. He would, he said, lodge a suit aimed at seeking a declaration of Andrey's status, and take the matter from there. Legal process always took time, and sometimes a certain 'greasing of the wheels' was necessary, but generally parties were more willing to compromise once a court declaration had been made.

On the back of his new expectations, Rodionov had secured a loan for him on reasonable terms. Andrey was unwilling to flaunt his change in fortune, but he could now clear his outstanding debts, set a little by for contingencies, and fulfil his long-overlooked duty to send funds home to his uncle. His career was moving in the right direction too. At summer camp the colonel had seemed satisfied with the performance of his men and had even praised the sharpness of their drill. This was encouraging; he was keen to erase the blot on his record that had resulted from his encounter with Stenovsky.

There were no droshkies to be had; he must walk back to the barracks. It being a clear September day, he decided to first take a stroll along Nevsky Prospekt. He set off down the broad street towards Palace Square and the Neva, crossing the narrow, not altogether fragrant, Catherine Canal. He turned along the Moika River. The blank eyes of ranked windows stared down from the facades of palaces and mansions ranged along the embankment; the ripples on the water shimmered in the sunlight. He soon reached the building site where the new St Isaac's Church was slowly rising from the ground.

The Bogolyubov Palace stood in a side street nearby. It would do no harm to take a look at it. As he stood before the expanse of russet stone, taking in the grey portico, intricate plasterwork, and rows of square glass between high mounted columns, he thought how extraordinary it would be to own such a place, to call it home. He didn't really dare to entertain the hope. Were he truly the prince's heir, the rewards might be enormous, but at present he felt he would settle happily for a little success, for some small relief – enough to secure his future and restore his sense of self-respect.

A doorman emerged from behind the varnished doors. 'If you come back on Thursday afternoon, you can take a look inside, sir,' he said. 'The prince opens the state rooms up to respectable folk on the first Thursday of the month.'

Andrey turned away. No, he wouldn't visit the palace. Why torment himself with dreams that might never be fulfilled?

But when after drill on Thursday the empty afternoon stretched before him, he found himself once again standing in the street outside. Ignoring the instruction from the doorman to leave his calling card, he climbed the stone stairway that led up to the square upper hallway. Enfilades stretched to right and left, and in front of him a glass door led outside into an inner court.

A liveried flunkey approached and took his sword. 'That's the way down to the garden, sir,' he said. 'It's not open today, but you can take a look from here.'

The well-tended garden lay between the wings of the building. Grey stone paths intersected a tender green lawn, and in the centre a fountain was playing. A man of medium height, of about his own age, was sitting on a bench reading a book, a deerhound at his feet. His soft dark hair flopped over his brow, and in his neat frock coat and loosely tied cravat, he recalled an illustration from a sentimental novel. As Andrey observed him, someone in a first-floor window caught the man's attention, and he smiled and nodded his head in response. He then returned to his book. This man was far too young to be the prince. Perhaps it was the younger of the two Count Belkins.

Andrey turned to the right through a vestibule into the expanse of ballroom, and then on into the saloon. The rooms had once been magnificent, and in their way still were, but clearly had not been altered in the fifty years or more of the palace's life. The mirrors were spotted and a little cloudy, the giant Chinese jars crazed, and the gilding of the picture frames damaged in places. The wooden floors under his feet were uneven, but they were extravagantly patterned, the sinuous designs snaking away into the gloom. He paused to look around him. How stunning it would all be when the smoke-rimed chandeliers were lit and the rooms filled with people! He retraced his steps, crossed the hallway and entered the opposite suite of rooms. Here were anterooms and drawing rooms, and a state bedroom, probably never used, the great bed hung with thinning silk scattered with tattered roses. He looked up at the pictures, classical and biblical scenes, uninteresting to his eyes and almost impossible to see. Everything was faded, melancholy, lifeless.

He paused in the dining room. Laid out on the long polished table were some drawings: sketches of a country estate – the house, the park, some peasants, a cemetery high above a river. As he examined the pictures, he heard voices in the adjacent room. Three women were walking there. Two of them paused at a window and started to converse. The third walked on and was now entering the dining room. He looked down again at the drawings. Footsteps were approaching; he turned round.

A slim girl stood before him. On seeing him she hesitated and glanced behind her. Finding herself alone, she ventured a tentative smile. She wore a dark dress under a light pelisse; such hair as he could see under her bonnet was black and her eyes were very dark. Her face gleamed, ghostlike in the ill-lit room. She could only have been about sixteen or seventeen years old. As he met her gaze, he felt a sensation that was close to pain; her face was the loveliest that he had ever seen.

'Oh, I'm sorry, sir,' she was saying. 'I thought you were my cousin, Vasily. Those are his sketches, you see. But of course, I can see now I was mistaken.'

What should he reply? They were not acquainted. Should he introduce himself? He returned her smile, still trying to find appropriate words, but then his dilemma was resolved. One of the older women called out, 'Come along Nadezhda, our cousins are waiting.' The girl contemplated him for a moment and then she turned away. She walked on through the dining room with her companions into the rooms beyond. She did not look back.

Andrey watched her leave with a wry smile. A cousin of the Belkins! Not much hope of success there. But in any event, his future was too uncertain to entertain the idea of any woman in his life. He looked at the drawings again. They must be images of the Belkin estate. The rambling old house and the soft landscapes populated by amiable serfs were quite unlike what remained of his family's lands in the forests and marshlands of the north.

He walked on and then, reaching the sunny divan room, turned back. The women seemed to have disappeared. He noticed a door concealed in the wall. It must lead to further rooms, perhaps to a private apartment. What a strange labyrinth this was! Returning to the top of the stairway, he could hear muffled voices and the chime of laughter. He looked down into the garden. The three women stood on the grass, talking to the young man he had noticed earlier. Andrey involuntarily stepped forward. He gripped the handle of the glass door and watched as the younger woman tossed back her head and started to remove her bonnet. She revealed her dark hair, which fell in soft ringlets down her slim neck. Her sweet face was bright and alive. Sinking down onto the stone edge of the fountain, she swung the hat by its ribbons as she stretched her legs and smoothed her skirts. The unsettling pain in his heart returned; he felt a dangerous pang of desire. She was indeed very lovely. What if… perhaps…

He heard a cough behind him. The lackey was holding out his sword.

Andrey's voice was thick as he buckled it on. 'Who's that in the garden?'

'That is Vasily Nikolayevich, Count Belkin, with his sister, the Princess Polunina, and their cousins, the Countess Laptev and her daughter, Nadezhda Gavrilovna.' The man intoned the names with an air of haughty self-importance. 'The count has just returned from his estate near Moscow. Was the palace to your liking, sir?'

Andrey hesitated. How should he reply? 'I think it's all rather beyond my reach,' he said. As he stepped out into the street he wondered if that would prove true.

※

After the freedom he had enjoyed in the country, Vasily found the daily routine at the Ministry of the Interior irksome. He rose every morning and shrugged on his stiff new uniform. Having taken breakfast with Matvey, he drove the short distance to the office with his uncle. The autumnal air was fast dissolving the city's summer stink. The streets and broad squares were quiet; only a few tardy government clerks scuttled to work under the shadows of still-slumbering palaces, past the iron railings and granite walls that confined the canals.

He arrived at about ten o'clock and, after some hours of doing very little, returned home in good time for dinner. No doubt through Alexander's influence, he had been promoted to Titular Councillor, with responsibility for the administration of the issuance of internal passports. This role was not onerous. Controversial decisions were made by servants of the Crown in positions more elevated than his own and clerks completed the paperwork. Cholera continued to spread in the south, and it was feared it would soon reach Moscow. The minister and most of the senior bureaucrats were fully occupied enacting preventative measures. Accordingly, no-one seemed to care how he spent his time. Indeed, as in Oryol, his immediate superior seemed surprised to see him at his desk.

He had therefore felt free yesterday afternoon to visit the Church of St Andrew the First Named on Vasilevsky Island, where Stepan Bogolyubov's Orthodox marriage service to von Klein Sternberg's mother, Astrella, had taken place. He had already examined a copy of the records lodged at the central registry of the Church Consistory Court, which seemed to confirm that the wedding had indeed been celebrated there. Accompanied by Matvey, who had carefully made a copy of the Court entry for the file, he had crossed the pontoon bridge across the Neva to the island.

They had stood for a while to admire the ships in the inner basin. Once beyond the monumental buildings on the embankment, the island took on the relaxed atmosphere of a provincial town. The Lines, rows of houses, were built in a neat grid system. Many of the dwellings were quite small, and were popular with middle-ranking army officers and merchants. The church fronted a broad tree-lined roadway. Built in a fluid baroque style, it sat behind low classical gateways, topped by a large tower and flanked by four smaller ones like minarets.

The priest in charge had been accommodating. As he searched through the wooden shelves in the registry, the bearded cleric remarked that recently there seemed to have been considerable interest in this particular entry. Vasily did not satisfy his obvious curiosity.

Today he had taken a droshky to make enquiries at the administrative office at the barracks of the Preobrazhensky Guards Regiment, where Count Bogolyubov had been serving as a major at the time of the wedding. And now, before dinner, he was descending the great stone staircase to the prince's rooms to divulge the fruits of his investigations.

He found the portly form of Dmitry Vladimirovich, his thinning grey curls in disarray, walking in circles around his drawing room. Alexander, erect in an armchair, watched his friend in exasperation, complaining that he had already sent a man to make enquiries at the church. The prince, however, dissatisfied with what he had heard, had insisted that Vasily go and check the facts once again.

'Well, Vasya,' the prince said, 'what have you discovered? Before you start, I must tell you that a case has been lodged by von Klein at the Consistory Court to seek a declaration that his parents' marriage is valid. I'll do what I can to hold that up. Your uncle's man confirmed that the register at the church was consistent with the record at the court. But he didn't add much. I'd like a few more details.'

'I'm not sure I uncovered more than you already know, sir,' Vasily said. 'We took another look at the register of marriages in the church. I assume Alexander's man told you that the record has been damaged. Vasilevsky Island was submerged in the flood of '24, as you know, and although the documents were not destroyed, they're not in good condition. The date on the record is correct, but the signatures are blurred. That of Stepan Bogolyubov is clear enough, but Astrella von Klein's mark is barely legible. One can see that her initial A is distinct – it's quite a flourish, in fact – and it's possible to make out the word "von".' Matvey had made a careful copy and he handed it to the prince, who looked at it and frowned. 'The names of the witnesses are just blurs of ink,' Vasily continued. 'But they are, of course, recorded at the court. One of the witnesses died some time ago, but the other, a Count Angelov, may still be alive, although initial enquiries have not found him here in St Petersburg.'

'His family home is near Moscow I think,' said the prince. 'Have you any idea, Sasha? I've rather lost touch.'

'No,' replied Alexander. 'But it won't be difficult to find out. He was close to the last Emperor, Alexander, a prominent member of his court. Polunin will know if he is still alive, and if so, where he can be found. I'll send a note to him. I'm afraid if there is a witness to testify that the marriage took place, the claimant's case will be improved. Mind you, it was almost exactly twenty-five years ago now. He may not remember.'

'Well, we can only hope.' The prince continued his peregrination. Alexander shook his head, called for a lackey and started to pen a brief note to his niece Katya's husband.

'The witness must be questioned if he is still alive,' said Vasily. 'Did no-one think of this before?'

'I think we assumed that all the witnesses would be dead,' the prince said.

'Yes, I certainly did,' said Alexander.

The prince sighed. 'Have you discovered anything else?'

'This afternoon, having applied through the military police, I visited the barracks of the guards regiment, with whom Stepan was serving in 1805. Major Bogolyubov had, it seemed, been granted two months leave of absence in order to marry. When he re-joined the regiment, his battalion had already left St Petersburg to march west to meet Napoleon. Stepan himself didn't actually join them until mid-October, a few weeks after the ceremony in St Petersburg. The Major must have enjoyed a privileged status to receive leave of absence at such a crucial moment. However, it was noted in his attestation that when he finally caught up with the army, he was reprimanded for overstaying his leave by three days, but there was no mention of any sanction beyond a warning. Anyway, what is important is that he was not with his regiment on the date that the marriage took place, and could well have been in St Petersburg.'

The prince looked miserable. Vasily realised that Dmitry had hoped that he would quickly produce some evidence that no marriage had taken place, and put his mind at rest. Well, there was nothing so far, but it was early days and there were other avenues to pursue.

'I know none of this looks very promising, sir, but further enquiries will have to be made. Angelov may be alive, and I do think it's strange that von Klein's grandfather, the bride's father, appeared to be completely unaware of any second marriage, and felt it necessary to adopt the boy. We have to ask, why did he do that if he was already the legitimate son of a Russian count? Perhaps Astrella never told him of the Orthodox ceremony. Or perhaps the old baron decided not to acknowledge it. As a Lutheran he would have recognised the legitimacy of the first one, after all. And then any hope of inheriting the princedom from your branch of the family, sir, would have seemed remote, even had he thought about it. You might well have had a son in due course, and there were others with a prior claim.'

'At least two others, in fact,' said Dmitry. 'Stepan's father, my uncle Dmitry, was of course dead, but there was my own brother, who later died childless, and the surviving son of another cousin, who subsequently managed to get himself shot in a duel. There might have been more if my sister hadn't married, finally, with a substantial dowry. In return she formally renounced any further rights to family wealth. She was about thirty – it was the only way my father could offload her. Of course, if we give in to this claim now, her family might well consider queuing up at the Land Court wanting their share. It will be open season…' The prince blew out his cheeks in disgust, and then, remembering himself, said, 'So what do you intend to do now, Vasily?'

'Seek to discover if Count Angelov is still with us. It might also be worth taking a trip up to Wesenburgh, to visit this uncle of von Klein's. He may be able to tell me something. I wonder if he knows about the case? If so he might not be willing to meet, but I feel I should try. I hope I can get the time off.'

'Oh, don't worry about that,' said Alexander. 'Your department know that you're simply a… that in addition to your duties, you've special work to do for me.'

Vasily turned once again to the prince. 'Are you sure you really want to fight this, sir? It may be possible to reach a compromise. As things stand, it looks as though there may well have been a wedding…'

'I don't think I can do that, Vasily. By all accounts the man is a rogue and a thief; definitely not worthy of the Bogolyubov name. The title goes back a long way, you know. And then there's his religion.'

Vasily said nothing. The aspirant heir might well not be scrupulous about religion, and the prince's title was not as ancient as he liked to pretend. The first Prince Bogolyubov's family had perished at the time of the Mongols and the princedom had been later revived. It was old, but not that old. No, the dignity of the title had little to do with the matter. Vasily knew that in addition to having a low opinion of the junior branch of his family, the prince was deeply concerned about his uncle's future, and also about himself. He thought of the Belkins as his family.

There seemed little more to say, and it was almost time for dinner. Guests had arrived; Dmitry Vladimirovich kept open house at the Palace. Matvey came down in a fine new suit. The prince greeted the lad cordially and thanked him for his clerking activity in support of his case. It was remarkable how quickly the elderly man had forgotten that Matvey had once been his slave, a kitchen boy, sleeping on a filthy scullery floor and swallowing dregs from discarded flasks of vodka. The prince had come to accept this particular rags-to-riches story. Vasily wondered if he would be able to accept another.

※

The following morning Vasily was in his study. He was penning a note to his friend, the Englishman Thomas Maltby, whom he hoped would take on Matvey's lessons once again. Five years had passed since Thomas had started the boy on his educational journey, and he would find his pupil had made good progress. As he put down his pen and blotted the ink, Yakov came to tell him that his old schoolfriend, Ivan Stenovsky, had sent up his card.

A few minutes later the clink of spurs chimed in the corridor. *My first friend, friend without price...* The words of Pushkin's poem floated unbidden into his mind. His heart twisted with sadness. Five years ago on a cold December day, here in this room, he had parted, seemingly forever, from Ivan's older brother, Mikhail. Then too the distinctive sound of spurs had rung out on the wooden floor, fading away and finally disappearing into an uncertain future.

He rose to his feet, seeking to collect himself, disturbing Annika, who muttered and sighed before settling back to sleep under his desk.

Mikhail had been a well-mannered, lithe, fine-featured man, who had hidden unshakable liberal convictions behind a reserved exterior. Ivan was nothing like his brother. He bounced into the room, knocking aside Yakov, and took Vasily's arms in a crushing grip. Then he slumped down into a chair. He was only a few months older than Vasily, but the hair on his egg-shaped head was already showing signs of thinning, and his fleshy cheeks were permanently flushed. His uniform strained uncomfortably across his chest and wrinkled up his well-muscled arms. Having failed to leave his sword in the hallway, it clanked alarmingly as he settled, disturbing the dog once again. She slid from the room with her tail between her legs.

'It's good to see you back, Vasya,' he was saying. 'I thought you might have called on us.'

'I was obliged to start work as soon as I arrived. I would have called this week.' In truth, Vasily hadn't rushed to call. Their relationship was awkward. They had been close at school; Ivan had been a staunch ally in a fight and, if he was honest, at times Vasily had relied on his protection. But their view of the world had diverged and now much between them must be left unsaid. While Ivan had been away fighting in the Caucasus, Vasily's warm friendship with Mikhail had developed. Now, of course, Mikhail and a third brother Nikita were state convicts in Siberia, condemned to permanent exile for their part in the revolt of 1825. Ivan, a supporter of the status quo, rarely acknowledged the existence of his exiled brothers, despite the fact that as a child he had been devoted to them.

'One of the reasons I'm here, Vasya, is because I've heard about the problem that's cropped up with regard to Dmitry Vladimirovich's estate,' Ivan was saying.

'He's not dead yet, Ivan!'

'No, well, you know what I mean. I understand that this man Klein has crawled out of a hole, and is pretending that he's the prince's rightful heir.'

'You mean Baron von Klein Sternberg? Yes, I know that you're acquainted.'

'I have come across him, and what I know of him isn't good. I hope you'll see him off.'

'My uncle, as I expect you know, asked me to return to Petersburg to investigate,' Vasily responded. 'But I have to say that thus far the case looks unpromising. On the face of it, the man seems to be what he says he is. There's evidence that a valid marriage took place.'

'You seem very calm about it! Surely there's a lot at stake for you, and for Alexander Petrovich too?'

Vasily shrugged. 'The prince has been a more than generous patron, and has supported my family for many years, but he never led me to believe that I had any long-term expectations. In any event, he's still free to dispose of a proportion of his wealth as he wishes. Some will certainly go to my uncle, and I expect some will find its way to me, heir or no heir. It's principally the land and the title to which von Klein has a claim.'

'You wouldn't be so sanguine about Klein if you knew more about him.'

'Well, enlighten me, Vanya. It's why you're here, I think.'

Ivan looked pained. 'No, of course I wanted to see you, always do, but you need to tread with care. Klein's a confidence trickster and a thief. When he came to St Petersburg – he'd been serving in Novgorod, spending his time kicking his heels in the garrison, not doing anything useful – when he came here on a temporary detachment, he pretended to be what he wasn't, kept an expensive mistress, who of course he abandoned when the money ran out. He borrowed a good deal…'

'From you, I suppose?'

'From me, among others. Of course, we've all been repaid now. He's managed to settle most of his old debts by borrowing on the back of his so-called expectations. It's all a sham; he needs to be stopped.'

'You surely don't see this claim as some sort of elaborate game? No-one in their right mind would embark on such an enterprise without some evidence, and in this case, to date anyway, right seems to be on his side. How well do you actually know him?'

Ivan shifted in his seat and looked at the wall. 'He hung around the theatre for a while, and you know I sometimes move in those circles.' Ivan seemed to have real antipathy towards the baron. This impression was confirmed when he continued, 'Of course, I could arrange his disappearance. We came close to a fight over the money he owed me…'

'Absolutely not, Ivan. What are you thinking of? That would be murder!'

'Not at all… a duel's perfectly fair.'

'Really? From what you've told me, von Klein's only experience of soldiering has been a spell drilling men in the provinces, interspersed by guard duty at the palace in St Petersburg. I suspect he can load a pistol, but not fire one with purpose. Whereas you…'

Ivan looked churlish. 'Put it this way, Vasya. If he crosses me, I may not be able to resist the temptation.'

Vasily frowned. Could von Klein really be as depraved as he was being painted? Ivan's opinion had certainly been believed by the prince, but without meeting the man or seeking information elsewhere, it was impossible to know. Well, time would no doubt tell. He should change the subject.

'Have you seen my sister Katya recently? Our mother's relations, young Nadezhda Gavrilovna, your sister-in-law, and her mother, are staying with her at present.' This too was a risky topic. Before his arrest, Mikhail Stenovsky had been betrothed to Nadezhda's sister, Lisa, and after his conviction for treason, Lisa had travelled to Siberia to marry him. She, like Mikhail, was likely to remain there indefinitely.

'Yes, I have actually. They always make me welcome. Nadezhda seems a nice enough girl but, being honest, I can't understand her family bringing her to the capital under the circumstances. She's tainted by her sister's connections.'

Vasily frowned. Didn't Ivan recognise that his own connections were equally "tainted"? 'I think the Laptevs want to show that, although their elder daughter was determined to flout convention, the family remains loyal to the Emperor. They're hardly the only family associated with the uprising that has subsequently paraded its patriotism and devotion to the Crown with some success. Otherwise, half of the elite nobility would be out of favour. Besides, Nadezhda is a good catch; just like you, she's now the heir to a sizeable fortune.' The jibe seemed to pass Ivan by.

Vasily sent for tea and they sat companionably enough until Ivan finally rose to leave. 'Will you be at the palace this evening?' he asked.

'No, thank God,' said Vasily. 'I've managed to avoid being placed on any court rotas. I'll be enjoying a quiet evening at home. The prince may well be going, although I suspect my uncle will try to dissuade him. I suppose Katya will be there though, with her new protégé.' They hovered, uncomfortable in the hallway. 'Ivan, look, please don't think of doing anything stupid,' Vasily said. 'This business with von Klein is awkward enough. The prince hates being the subject of tittle-tattle…'

Ivan slapped him hard on the back, propelling him into a rack laden with coats. 'Don't worry, old man, you can rely on me.'

Vasily extricated himself from the coats as the sound of Ivan's boots clattered away. Weary, he sat down in the drawing room. Annika, seeing that the coast was clear, joined him and leapt up, thrusting her wet nose into his face. Then she settled at his feet while he, pulling at a tassel on a cushion, considered Ivan's threats. Like most soldiers these days, he had too much time on his hands, and he probably missed the excitement of military action. But surely he couldn't seriously think that to dispose of the German would be in any way helpful to the prince's cause.

CHAPTER FOUR

Three days later – St Petersburg

Nadezhda Gavrilovna was sitting by the window of Katya's small drawing room in the Polunin Palace. She often sought out this spot in the morning. The north-facing room caught the reflected sunlight from the river. From here, she could watch ships in the waters in front of the fortress offloading their passengers and cargoes into cutters and lighters.

Her book was open, but she was not reading. She was preoccupied by events that had taken place at the reception and ball two nights before. Having been presented formally to the Empress a few days earlier, this had been her first outing into St Petersburg society. Accompanied by her mother, Countess Antonina Laptev, Countess Maria Belkin – and her daughter, Katya, with her husband, Prince Polunin – she had entered the three marble halls that ran along the riverside facade of the Winter Palace. Her stomach had quivered, tight with nerves; her eyes were confused by the crush of people crowded between the arches and columns. It was as if they were on a small raft, tossed in a shifting sea of fine clothes and unknown faces. How anyone could find anyone else here was beyond her.

And yet clearly there had been some underlying logic. At the opening of the ball, the assembly had lined up in proper order to greet the Tsar and his family. Then, engulfed by a tangle of bright medals and braids, evening coats and dress uniforms, her *carnet de bal* seemed to fill spontaneously and, before the dancing began, she found that what had been an embarrassingly empty card was satisfyingly complete. She only recognised one name: that of her old friend from Oryol, Prince Yevgeny Uspensky, who, much to her pleasure, had engaged her for the mazurka.

She had been surprised when she realised that the grenadier guards officer who claimed her for the waltz was the man whom she had recently mistaken for Vasily in the gloom of the dining room at Prince Bogolyubov's palace.

'Oh!' she had exclaimed, rather foolishly; but, having bowed, he had simply smiled, and led her onto the floor. The lieutenant was tall, and his eyes very blue. His skin, burnished by the summer sun, set off his remarkable fair hair. At first she had found him rather overwhelming, but he had danced tolerably well, and had kept up a steady flow of conversation, so that when the music stopped, she was content. He had asked her if, despite the absence of a formal introduction, he might take her into supper. She looked around for her mother, but failing to see her, she took the risk of agreeing. Surely only respectable people attended these events?

She had looked forward to meeting him later, but things had not turned out as she had hoped. When the mazurka was finally over, and Yevgeny had rushed off to his next assignation, the tall grenadier came to find her and took her arm. They had almost reached the entrance to the supper rooms when, like a balding pugnacious bear, her sister's brother-in-law, Ivan Stenovsky, blocked their way. His face scarlet, and his neck bulging over his stiff collar, he had snatched her elbow without a word and pulled her, quite roughly, from the side of her companion. The grenadier started to protest, but before she knew what was happening, another soldier, on Stenovsky's instruction, had walked her rapidly away and delivered her, confused and close to tears, to her mother and Katya, who had been standing nearby.

Her mother gave no sign that anything was amiss. Katya had smoothly steered her aside and found an acquaintance in the crowd with whom to converse. Both women must have noticed the incident, but nothing was said, and later, when she looked for the lieutenant, he was nowhere to be seen. After supper, dancing had resumed, but the evening had been spoilt, and she was pleased when the imperial family departed and it was time to go home.

Now, she sat by the window, her brow furrowed, fingering her book. The steam shuttle was making its way downriver but she barely noticed it. Of course, she knew nothing about the young officer; nonetheless, she found it difficult to dismiss him from her thoughts.

In the adjacent reception room, she could hear low voices in urgent conversation. She rose and, following the sound, encountered Vasily Nikolayevich and his sister deep in discussion, their heads close together. Hearing her, they looked up.

'Well, here she is,' Katya said. 'You can ask her yourself.'

Vasily greeted her with a short bow. Nadezhda smiled. She liked her cousin. Despite the fact he was rather short, he was not unattractive, and even when she had been an awkward fourteen-year-old in the country, he had always treated her kindly.

'Oh Vasya! I wish you had been at the ball!' she said.

'You didn't need me, Nadya.' His brown eyes were warm as he returned her smile. 'I gather you had no shortage of partners. But let's sit down. We need to talk to you about Ivan's extraordinary behaviour. We're not sure what he thought he was doing. Do you happen to have your *carnet*?'

She sent her maid for it and handed it to Vasily, who scanned the names before showing it to Katya. 'There, look – you're right, it was definitely him. Here's his name… it's a bit of a scrawl… "von Klein S"…'

'I have to say,' said Katya, 'if he knew who she was, he's got a nerve asking Nadya to dance.'

'What on earth are you talking about? Did I do something wrong?' Nadezhda's voice rose in alarm.

'No, no, my dear,' said Katya. 'But I think you've become an object of attention for an adventurer who is trying to take advantage of the family…'

'We don't know that,' said Vasily.

'I think we do,' his sister responded. 'He's a man with no money and a bad reputation, and now it seems he sees fit to taunt us by toying with an innocent young girl. Ivan was right to put a stop to it.'

Vasily turned to her. 'Can you tell me what happened?'

'It was over very quickly; there's not much to tell. The lieutenant was walking me towards the door, when Ivan Alexandrovich dragged me away. He was rough – my arm is quite bruised! But there was nothing at all improper in the baron's attention, nothing at all. He seemed very respectable. Why are you so concerned?'

'Von Klein Sternberg claims to be Prince Bogolyubov's heir,' said Vasily. 'I think you have heard the story? But he's never made himself known to us, and of course we haven't given him any encouragement. You couldn't be expected to recognise him.'

'Oh!' She had indeed heard about the man who Prince Polunin simply called "the pretender", and who in family mythology had already become a monster, determined to drive Dmitry Vladimirovich into an early grave and ruin the Belkin family. Could this really be the same man?

'I suppose his interest in you could have been innocent; he may not have been aware of the family connection. But if he did know your identity, he should have realised that dancing with you, and engaging you again later, would be tactless at best, and at worst might be seen as audacious provocation. I fear he may have started more trouble than he bargained for. I'll guarantee that Ivan was looking for a fight. I hope that von Klein didn't rise to it.'

'Fight him? You mean there could be a duel?'

'It's possible and I don't rate his chances. Ivan's a good shot.'

'Well,' said Katya, 'that would solve the problem nicely.'

Nadezhda felt an ache of disappointment. Had the

young man simply danced with her to upset her family, to make a cheap point? She had thought that he had genuinely liked her. 'But I had met him before, you know, at the prince's palace!' she said. 'I mistook him for you, Vasily. It was a Thursday afternoon, and he was taking a look around.'

'There you are!' said Katya. 'The man's been snooping, probably valuing the artwork in anticipation of throwing you out. He must have known he wouldn't be welcome there, and it's clear he's been stalking Nadya.'

'I doubt that. Why would he do that? I suspect von Klein danced with her because he recognised her and found her attractive, nothing more. But Ivan mustn't fight him, he knows that. News of von Klein's claim, his lawsuit, is already getting around. Were a duel to prove fatal, it would seem that we had plotted to be rid of him. If we're to defeat him, it must be through the courts. I'll go round to the lieutenant's barracks later and warn his commanding officer that there could be trouble.'

Vasily scanned Nadya's *carnet* again. 'Oh! You danced with Yevgeny Uspensky,' he said. 'Is he in town? I must look him up. It would be good to see him again.'

As they planned to invite Yevgeny to dinner, Nadya's mood improved. However, when Vasily had left and she had resumed her chair by the window, her eyes filled with tears. In addition to being handsome, Andrey Andreyevich had seemed charming, uncomplicated and gentle. Could it really be true that he was some kind of fraudster? And even if he was, she certainly did not want to see him destroyed. She must send to him, urge him not to fight on her account. To write wasn't at all appropriate, of course, but surely the danger justified a breach of propriety.

※

At the barracks, a mile or so distant, Andrey Andreyevich was putting his affairs in order. He wasn't surprised at the turn of events. He had known that given any encouragement, Stenovsky's quarrel with him would flare up again. He was no coward and in truth, had Rosovsky not expressly forbidden it, he would have issued a challenge after the painful incident at the club. The matter must be arranged quickly before anyone tried to intervene. He had already engaged a second.

When he had recognised Nadezhda at the start of the evening, perhaps foolishly he had pushed aside the knowledge of her connection to the Belkin family. Slender in white, a pink rose in her dark hair, the temptation to engage her to dance had been overwhelming and she had proved an unaffected and easy partner. He had been looking forward to further conversation at supper.

But Stenovsky had made his inexcusable intervention and Nadezhda had been snatched away. Andrey had found himself alone in the middle of the Great Hall. A crowd of dancers, fresh from the thrilling whirl of the mazurka, hurried past him, eagerly seeking refreshment. He looked for Stenovsky, who he now found engaged in conversation with an elderly man. The captain ignored him as he approached, but when his companion took his leave, he turned towards him and smirked.

'So you're after my brother's sister-in-law now, are you, Klein? We can't have that. I'm surprised they allow predatory scum like you out at night.'

The captain's words had startled him. Was Nadezhda in some way related to Stenovsky? That was unfortunate, but he would not apologise. Indeed, he had nothing for which to be sorry. She had readily agreed that he should take her in to supper. Stenovsky's behaviour was quite insupportable. A crowd of people had seen the captain force the young woman from his side, and now others could hear his continuing insults. 'This *is* a matter of honour,' he had said. 'Our differences clearly cannot be resolved. You will hear from my second.'

The challenge had been made and Stenovsky hadn't sought to interrupt or deflect him. It was clear that he was prepared to fight, that a duel must be arranged. As he turned on his heel, Andrey had heard Stenovsky behind him, emitting short barks of mirthless laughter that faded away as he left the ballroom and passed through the emptying halls into the night.

Now, in his shadowed rooms, Andrey's heart was heavy. His future was even more uncertain, and he might never see Nadezhda Gavrilovna again. In that event, he hoped she would remember him kindly, but there was nothing to be done. No man of honour could avoid this outcome and, despite a persistent tug of sadness, he was resolved to face whatever fate had in store.

CHAPTER FIVE

Early morning, two days later – St Petersburg

It was the middle of the night, so why was someone shaking him?

'There's a soldier here, Vasily Nikolayevich, sir,' Yakov was whispering. 'He needs you to go out with him now. There's some sort of trouble, but he won't tell me what. He says you're to take your pistols, if you have any... Well, I told him that of course you have some, and he said...'

'Alright, thank you, Yakov.' Vasily slipped from his bed and pulled on his clothes as Yakov passed them to him. 'What time is it?' Vasily asked.

'A little after five.'

The ensign from von Klein's company, Denis Borisov, was pacing the narrow hall. 'It's Andrey Andreyevich, sir. I'm afraid we've missed a trick. He's gone off to fight much sooner than expected. I was supposed to tip off Captain Rosovsky when the fight was due, and he was going to arrest the lieutenant and lock him up. But he's been sly. He asked me to be his second, as we expected, and he told me that the fight would be later this week. Then last night he went missing with a second picked from the Guards next door... a notorious *bretteur*.'

Vasily had wanted to prevent a duel at all costs. Whether the family liked it or not, von Klein may well be the prince's legitimate heir. Whatever his shortcomings, he could not be prematurely extinguished. When he had called on von Klein's company commander, Captain Rosovsky had been certain that, were a duel to take place, von Klein would ask his friend Borisov to support him. But he had been wrong, and their plans to pre-empt a fight had failed.

'Do you know where they've gone?'

'I think so, sir. The arrangement was to fight on Vasilevsky Island, at first light. That'll be in an hour or so.' Vasily threw on his cloak and Yakov handed him his pistols. With luck they would get there in time.

Two troopers stood in the stable yard, waiting to accompany them. The streets were empty and dark in the hour before dawn. Only the occasional spluttering street lamp or watchman's brazier lit the way. The bridge had undergone its nightly reconstruction and when Vasily flicked his government pass at the sentry, he waved them across.

Captain Rosovsky, whose family lived on the island, was waiting for them. 'We must try to persuade them to give up the fight,' he said. 'I can – probably should – arrest von Klein Sternberg, but I would prefer to give him the chance to back down voluntarily. If there's an inquiry it will make things easier.'

When they reached the end of the street, their way was blocked by a merchant's cart loading up for the day. It cost them several minutes. They emerged from the paved streets into a confusion of marshland and salt-blighted fields; there was no sign of activity on the island's distant edge. Moving westwards, they skirted the shoreline until at last they saw some figures on the remote strand.

'That's them,' said the captain. He turned to his men. 'You three stay here and keep an eye out. Come when I give a signal.'

It was dangerously close to sunrise. Vasily and Rosovsky walked out towards the embankment built to resist the surges of the tide. Their breath swirled around them. The damp earth beneath Vasily's feet felt soft as a sponge and gave up a smell of brine and mud; a rim of frost whitened the rough grass. He stared out to the empty horizon and shivered. It was said that out there, where the land comingled with the grey waters of the Gulf of Finland, the bodies of criminals lay and ghosts walked the shore.

They were now in clear sight but had not been noticed. The ritual had already begun. The two men were walking away from the markers with steady steps. When the call came, each would turn and approach his rival, aiming to fire as soon as he judged the distance to be right. As he and the captain broke into a run, Vasily heard the first shot. A flock of gulls flew up and wheeled away over the gulf. Andrey Andreyevich had fired much too soon and the bullet had passed harmlessly through the air. The lieutenant stood frozen, his head bowed, his pistol hanging at his side. Stenovsky had come to a halt. He seemed to be waiting, his hand on his hip.

'Stenovsky, von Klein Sternberg, stop this at once!' Rosovsky yelled as if on the parade ground. Ivan

Alexandrovich paid no attention and was now advancing again with deliberate steps. The distance to his target was enough to make a shot challenging, but there was little doubt that he had the skill to kill von Klein. Vasily drew his own pistol and cocked it.

'Ivan! Ivan, stop!' he shouted. 'My uncle and the prince would deplore what you're doing. I beg you…'

Ivan turned and regarded him with a sneer. 'This is nothing to do with your damn family problems, Vasya. Go back to bed, and let me finish it. It's not only bad manners to interrupt a fight, it's the action of a coward.'

'You're the coward, Ivan. If you kill this man now in cold blood, I swear you'll have to fight me next.'

'Don't be ridiculous!' Stenovsky was raising his arm.

Vasily was desperate. How could he stop him? He fired his own pistol in the air. 'I mean it Ivan, I'll damn well fight you with this, your own brother's gun, and you know what? Mikhail would forgive me the deed. What's happened to you? Where's your sense of honour? This man isn't a worthy opponent; he isn't worth killing. You know that, we both know that, and he certainly isn't worth being cashiered for.'

Stenovsky stared up at the sky, his face unreadable. The pistol remained half raised. Was he hesitating? Vasily must try once more.

'Ivan, I beg you, stop and consider. You're clearly the victor here… you don't need to kill him to prove it.'

Stenovsky shook his head slightly. He raised his arm further. His aim was steady. He was going to fire.

'For God's sake, Vanya…'

The shot cracked through the morning air.

Vasily spun towards von Klein. He feared the worst, but the tall man remained on his feet. His head was still bowed. His pale hair had fallen over his face but his lips were moving, perhaps in prayer. Had Ivan intended to kill him? If so, he had clearly failed.

Rosovsky shouted for his men. 'Take the lieutenant in charge,' he ordered. 'Put him in the guardhouse.'

Vasily watched Borisov approach von Klein. 'Will you come with me, sir?' Von Klein raised his head and looked at the ensign, his face expressionless, his shoulders slumped. He was breathing heavily and blue circles of weariness stained the skin beneath his eyes. He seemed about to speak, but then, pulling himself erect with some difficulty, he looked into the distance and, with a faint smile, handed over his pistols. He stumbled a little as the three grenadiers marched him away.

Vasily looked back. Ivan hadn't moved from the marker post. He seemed to be in a daze, swaying a little back and forth. Then he turned, gave his guns to his second and walked with slow steps across the rough ground towards the sea. He was probably best left alone. Vasily could hear Rosovsky taking von Klein's second to task. The officer from the Semenovsky Guards was shrugging his shoulders and waving his hand dismissively. Duelling, it seemed, was all in a day's work.

In silence, Vasily and Rosovsky followed the soldiers and their charge from the field. Vasily looked up at the captain. Like most grenadiers, he was tall. His face was long and angular beneath thick brown hair. Vasily thought that he seemed familiar, but he had been unable to remember where or when they had previously met.

'Well, I suppose that's a result of sorts,' the captain said at last. 'Once he has cooled off in the guardhouse for a few days, I'm afraid I'll have to pack him off back to the main force in Novgorod. I don't think the colonel will insist on demoting him, but it's possible. This is a second blot on his record. It's a pity; in many ways he's a promising soldier.'

Vasily wondered what other crimes the German had committed. He didn't look like a rogue, although his deception with regard to the timing of the duel had certainly shown some propensity for guile.

'Will you inform Stenovsky's superiors?'

'Yes, I shall. They know that it's not the first time the men have quarrelled. The captain's something of a bully, isn't he?'

'Sadly, yes. But you say it's not the first time they've fallen out?'

'No, a couple of months ago there was a dispute over debts and a woman– a dancer… significant debts, and the woman was well out of von Klein's league.'

A propensity for deceit and a history of indebtedness, gambling and expensive women. There seemed to be some justification for Stenovsky's poor opinion of von Klein. He must accelerate his investigations into the man's past.

They had reached the door of Rosovsky's house. 'Do you want to come in, have some tea, Vasily Nikolayevich?' The captain paused. 'You don't remember me, do you?'

'Well, you seem familiar, but I'm sorry, I can't place you.' As he spoke, Vasily's memory cleared. He had first met Kirill Rosovsky five years ago. They had been at a meeting of the Northern Society a few weeks before the failed attempt to seize power that had ended in death for some and exile for many. Like himself, the captain had, it seemed, managed to evade the full force of imperial vengeance.

'Of course, you were at that meeting at Obolensky's…'

The captain instinctively glanced back along the street. They were not observed. 'Yes, in the early days after the event more of us escaped serious punishment than you might think, Count. When I was released, fortunately without charge, but tainted by association, I was transferred from the Guards to a grenadier regiment. An effective demotion of course… It's as well Kondraty burnt all the records before he was taken…'

'It seems we're both lucky men.'

'Indeed. Lucky, older too certainly, and probably wiser.' They regarded one another for a moment. The captain shivered slightly in the morning air. A clock somewhere struck the half hour.

'I must leave you,' Vasily said. 'Perhaps we should take a drink together soon for old time's sake.'

'Yes, I should enjoy that, Count Belkin. Thank you for your help today.' Rosovsky shook Vasily by the hand and, turning towards his door, paused and asked, 'Did your pistols really belong to Mikhail Alexandrovich?'

'Yes, he sent them to me as a gift, through his wife's family, when he was imprisoned in Reval.'

'Ah… I see.' The captain shrugged, sighed and looked down at his boots. 'A sad business altogether, Belkin.' He clasped Vasily's shoulder for a moment, before disappearing into his house.

As Vasily walked back towards St Isaac's Bridge, the streets were becoming crowded. The name of the hanged revolutionary leader, Kondraty Ryleev, brought back the exhilaration, the terror, and ultimately the frustration, of the uprising five years ago. His own small part in the affair had changed the course of his life, and although he had turned his back on radical politics, his views were unaltered. Did Rosovsky feel the same? Did he still long for a different, better, form of government, aspire to free the peasants from slavery? Perhaps. But with a family to support, it seemed that the captain had reconciled himself to accepting life in Russia as it was.

What should he himself do? His immediate goal, of course, must be to try to refute von Klein's suit, but then perhaps, since any prospect of changing the current regime was remote, he too should compromise and resign himself to the yoke of imperial service. In Oryol he had made a promising start, and regardless of the prince's legacy, his prospects of advancement and reward were probably assured. It was not what he had imagined or dreamed, but perhaps it would, after all, be the right course.

CHAPTER SIX

A few days after the duel on Vasilevsky Island, Vasily escorted his mother to the shops. Following the death of her husband eighteen years earlier, Maria had never remarried, and when she looked to her son to accompany her on such excursions, he was generally happy to oblige. Nevsky Prospekt was busy. Shoppers hurried by. Wisps of hay whirled in the cooling autumn air as carts, interspersed with carriages and droshkies, rumbled past on their way to the cavalry barracks.

Having taken refreshment at Wolf and Beranger's, Vasily walked with Maria and her maid the short distance to her favourite milliners. It was one of the leading establishments of its type in the city. The signs above the door advertised the shop's wares in French, German and Russian, and its square-paned window was well stocked with goods.

The door swung open as they approached and the familiar figure of their neighbour, the wealthy merchant Luka Kuprin, emerged. He was followed by the proprietor of the shop, Madame Hélène. She inclined her head as

Kuprin bowed in farewell. She was an attractive, well-endowed woman of perhaps forty. The glossy black curls beneath her cap were untouched by grey. The merchant rose, his eyes gleaming, and briefly took her hand.

'Farewell Luka Ilyich,' they heard her say. 'Please convey my compliments to Madame Kuprina.' The squat grandee trudged away, fingering his beard. He climbed into his glossy carriage and his extravagantly-dressed lackey jumped up behind.

'Ah, Countess Belkin!' Madame Hélène had noticed them hovering at the window. 'How good to see you! Of course you have come for the hat... you need not have bothered; I could have had it delivered and dressed at the palace.'

'I wanted to see what stock you have in for the season,' Maria replied. She stepped inside and looked around. 'You have created a wonderful showroom here, Madame Hélène!' she exclaimed. 'The best in St Petersburg! But I don't think you know my son Vasily. He has been living on our estates after a period of outstanding service in the provinces. He's now been promoted and works with his uncle, the First State Councillor, at the Ministry...'

Wincing at his mother's effusive introduction, Vasily gave a short bow and expressed himself delighted.

'Oh, but I do know you, sir!' Madame Hélène's blue eyes regarded him steadily. 'I am sure you came in some years ago with the Baroness von Steiner.' Vasily felt himself flush. The milliner must have a prodigious memory! He had indeed come into the shop with Irina. They had been taking a drive during those magical few weeks in 1825 when they had been enjoying the first sweet delirium of fresh passion. He had wanted to buy silk flowers for her bonnet.

Now, muttering something incoherent, he ignored his mother's pained expression and sat down on a circular seat covered in buttoned red velvet. With some relief, he noticed the girls in their large black aprons being summoned from the workshop. The work of adjusting the new hat got underway.

'I see our neighbour, Kuprin, has been calling on you,' Maria remarked.

'Yes. He is the owner of this shop, you know. I am hoping that he will allow me to rent further space in the property next door. I have been here in Petersburg for almost twelve years, have been a good tenant, and would so like to expand. Business is good, but customers now want to see other merchandise on sale when they buy their bonnets: shawls and furbelows, ribbons and the like; even jewellery, perhaps.' Madame Hélène spoke excellent French with a slightly unusual intonation. Vasily wondered about her origins; she certainly was not Russian, but he did not think she was French.

'I hope he agrees to your plans,' said Maria. 'I am sure you will do well if he does.' As she spoke, one of the girls offered Vasily a candied plum steeped in honey from a box sourced from the nearby confectioners. 'I'm testing those sweetmeats,' Madame Hélène said. 'I may have some packed in miniature hat boxes as a gift for customers.'

Vasily wiped his brow. It was stuffy in the shop, and the sugary fruit had set his teeth on edge. Restless, he got to his feet and stepped outside for a few moments. When he returned, he stood in the doorway and looked around. Several bonnets were out on display, and in the corner close by stood a pile of large white boxes, each with 'Hélène' written on the side in sweeping black letters. A male employee was sorting through them.

As he watched, Madame Hélène bustled over and pointed to each box in turn. 'That is to go to Millionnaya, and those two to Princess Bezborodko, that one over there to the theatre… and oh! I almost forgot…' She turned and walked to the back of the shop and picked up a card from a fragile gilt table. 'I've ordered the usual flowers from the florist; they will be ready by now. Please attach this card and be sure to deliver them to the stage door.'

'Is that all, ma'am?'

It seemed that it was, for Madame Hélène turned briskly away and devoted her attention once again to his mother's bonnet.

※

Vasily took his mother back to the Polunin Palace, where she had now taken up permanent residence. They took tea with his sister Katya and her children in the large drawing room and he sat quietly in a corner while Maria, chattering among discarded boxes and bags, showed off her purchases. Katya had recently refurbished the room; bright, soft sofas had been introduced and the heavy shutters were concealed behind light silk drapes. A new painting from Italy had been installed over the fireplace. Vasily admired it; it would be a fine thing to buy things like that on a whim! Of course, if all turned out well and von Klein's claim were refuted, he too might… The prospect of wealth suddenly seemed very tempting. He shook his head. At present, that didn't seem likely.

Prince Polunin and his Uncle Alexander appeared on the threshold and stood for a moment surveying the scene. They indicated to Vasily that he should join them and together they made their way down to the winter garden. Under the high glazed roof, servants were watering the plants, and the scent of wet vegetation filled the air as they walked the marbled paths.

'I have enquired at the court with regard to your witness Angelov's whereabouts,' Polunin commented. 'And I'm afraid that, somewhat inconveniently, he is not here in Russia. Since the death of the former emperor he has been serving in Warsaw, in the suite of Grand Duke Constantine. The Duke delights in his role as commander of the Polish army, and he's unlikely to be returning to Petersburg in the foreseeable future.'

'That's a pity,' said Alexander. 'We can't ask questions and take evidence by letter; someone must go to see him in person, I think.' He glanced hopefully at Vasily.

'I'll go, of course, if it's necessary, but I would first like to visit the von Klein Sternberg estates,' Vasily said. 'I want to understand more about the man's background and learn more, if I can, about the circumstances surrounding the marriage.'

'Estonia's not so far distant. I think a trip could be arranged,' Alexander said.

Prince Polunin swept aside a trailing vine. 'Aren't you concerned about the cholera?' he asked.

'At present areas to the north-west are unaffected; a trip there will be safe enough,' replied Alexander. 'But, between ourselves, despite Zavretsky's assurances, the disease hasn't been contained in the Volga region. It's spreading rapidly in the south.'

Vasily nodded. Just yesterday he had heard alarming rumours of a case in Moscow. What's more, the disease seemed virulent: mortality rates had reached sixty percent in some regions. He looked at Alexander and felt a spasm of guilt. His uncle seemed even thinner than usual and his face was etched with weariness. He had been involved in arranging committees, quarantine measures and troop deployment in affected areas for some weeks. Could he really continue to sit idly wasting time in the internal passport department while many other officers were now fully engaged in fighting the disease?

'You know, Uncle, Mama won't like it and nor will Dmitry, but I do think I should seek a transfer to public health. My present work can hardly be seen as vital, and the von Klein matter could wait for a while. I understand from Rosovsky that the lieutenant is likely to be packed off to kick his heels in Novgorod, and is unlikely to return.'

Alexander's face brightened. 'You are right,' he said. 'Maria won't like it, but if you feel you should play your part, you must. In fact, we could combine some further private investigations with combatting this wretched plague. If you are serious, I'll see what I can do to speed matters along.'

'It's almost dinner time,' Polunin said. 'You're both intending to dine here, I hope?'

As they made their way back to join the family, Vasily sighed in weary resignation. Life was clearly about to become more challenging, and his hopes of a quick resolution to von Klein's claim, followed by a speedy return to his estates, were receding by the day.

※

Nadezhda was stitching at her embroidery frame, grateful for the clear light in Katya's small drawing room. The work demanded concentration and temporarily drove away thoughts that tried to creep, uninvited, into her head. She worked with precision and determination for at least ten minutes before setting her needle aside.

A launch was passing, filled with passengers from a steamship that must have docked this morning at Kronstadt. How diverting it must be to travel to distant places. Vasily had told her of his trip to France and Germany some years before. Perhaps one day she too might go. She briefly pictured herself strolling with Andrey Andreyevich through the Bois de Boulogne, or along the Champs-Élysées. He would smile at her as he had smiled at the ball. She sighed and shook her head. When she had discovered that the duel had not resulted in the death of either party, she had thanked God with all her heart. It seemed that Ivan had been deemed the victor of the fight; how shameful it had been to have secretly hoped for his destruction! Baron von Klein Sternberg had been taken back to barracks under arrest and would, it seemed, be punished, but at least he still lived, and while he lived perhaps there was hope that they might meet again.

It had probably been unwise to send him that note. It was reckless to write to an unattached man – it could lead to embarrassment, even to disaster. As it happened, her intervention had come too late; the duel had been fought more quickly than expected. Andrey Andreyevich may never have received the message at all. She would probably never know.

She thought about picking up her work again but she could hear voices in the drawing room next door. And now here was Yevgeny Filipovich with Katya and her mother. She heard Katya's voice. 'Go in to see her, Yevgeny. She will be delighted! We shall stay in here... not far away.' Nadezhda knew that her mother in particular had hopes that Prince Uspensky and she would form an attachment. They never would, of course; she had known Yevgeny too long, knew his weaknesses too well.

Yevgeny almost danced into the room. Nadezhda couldn't help laughing. Despite the fact that he had fought in the Turkish War and been promoted to second lieutenant, he remained an unconvincing soldier. His overlong curly hair flopped into his eyes. His new uniform did not suit his extravagant, almost foppish, manner.

She listened as he described, in elegant French, his latest exploits. The military life clearly continued to frustrate him. He had come to St Petersburg to try to transfer from the Pavlogradsky Hussars, with whom he had served for almost three years, into a more prestigious guards regiment based in the capital. The project was not going well.

His company had been engaged in summer manoeuvres outside the city, but he had found the temptations of the capital irresistible, and as a result of constantly travelling back and forth had been late on parade twice. His passion for horse dealing meant that he had concluded some sharp transactions that had upset his colonel and his staff. Worst of all, however, he had during a drinking bout removed the statue of a naked nymph from a palace garden and taken it to a restaurant. Having spent the evening toasting her with his comrades, he had deposited her outside the home of a senior officer, her intimate parts garlanded with weeds and ivy. For this latter misdemeanour he had spent three days in the guardhouse.

'You know it wasn't the owner of the palace who complained,' he said, frowning with disgust, 'or the officer, but the owner of the restaurant! Damn cheek, I call it… we spent a fortune there. Anyway, the upshot is that my probationary period has been terminated and I'm sent back to Oryol, back to the Hussars. It's a bit of a bugger really. I was given to understand that some fun was tolerated in the guards…'

'Are you sure that you're really suited to army life, Zhenya? That there's nothing else you'd rather do?'

Yevgeny looked downcast. 'That's just what Vasily Nikolayevich said last week.'

'His advice is generally sound.'

'I know, he's the very best of men, very sensible and all that… but I have to confess that I'm disappointed. I wanted to make a success of being a soldier, to show my family that I could do it, that I could stand on my own feet, be a real Russian. Anyway, I'll give it one more go, but it means that I'll be leaving Petersburg in a week or so.'

'Oh, that's a pity,' said Nadezhda. Yevgeny seemed genuinely disheartened. She changed the subject. 'Have you heard from Miss Roberts?'

Yevgeny brightened a little. 'Yes, she's back in England now. I have it in mind to visit her.' Nadezhda knew that he was very fond of her former governess. Miss Roberts was unlikely to entertain an approach from the feckless young prince, but perhaps when he finally settled down…

As she thought about marriage, she had an idea. 'Zhenya, there is something you might do for me. It's rather a lot to ask, but it would very much help me. I wouldn't ask you, but now you're leaving town it would be possible to accomplish without too much embarrassment. I do find the pressure to find a husband, not just from my mother but also the princess and Maria Vasilyevna, overwhelming. I'm just seventeen! I have plenty of time to marry. If you and I could appear to have reached an understanding, an attachment, then this procession of unwanted suitors would cease. There might be something of a reckoning when the truth is revealed, but you could be at home with your family in Italy by then…'

'I don't need to pretend, Nadya… I am attached to you.'

'Not in the way they wish.'

'Well, I'm not so sure about that…'

'But I am.' She felt herself flush with embarrassment.

Yevgeny looked at her. 'Nadya… you've found an admirer! You sly hussy…'

'Oh no… really!'

'I don't believe you, but don't worry, I won't give you away. I say! Is he married?'

'Yevgeny, really! No, he isn't.' She realised as soon as she spoke that he had trapped her into a confession. 'Please don't ask me more. In different circumstances he might be considered perfectly respectable…'

'No, I understand. You can rely on me to keep your secret, and also to pay you enough attention to keep your family off the scent.' Yevgeny seemed highly diverted by the plan. He stood up and bounced around the room, humming a tune. The trinkets in the display case quivered. He soon resumed his place by her side.

Nadya heard a slight rustle of silk. Katya and her mother, Maria, were peering round the door. That was excellent! The sight of them both, heads together in close tête-à-tête, should satisfy their curiosity and serve her purpose perfectly.

※

Andrey watched the spider progress across the stone-flagged floor of the cell. Could he count to ten before she reached the wall? Probably. But now she had started to scuttle more quickly, and he had only reached eight when the beast disappeared. He mentally docked himself fifty kopecks. What could he do to amuse himself now? He rose from the low pallet and paced up and down the confined space between the bed and the door.

He had been imprisoned for several days. The only human he had seen was the warder who brought food twice daily, and occasionally replaced the fetid bucket in the corner. In the daytime, some light filtered down through the curtain of cobwebs at a small high window. At night, the cell was completely dark, but the absence of a candle was no deprivation since his only reading material was the graffiti on the walls. They had removed his belt and anything sharp from his person, so in addition to being unable to hang himself, he could not make his own contribution to the graphic images, jokes and expletives.

He had expected to be summoned to explain his actions within hours of his incarceration, but several days had passed. Had they forgotten him? The day before yesterday – or was it the day before that? – he had heard Denis Borisov outside his cell, trying to persuade the warder to allow him to visit, or at least to bring a book or two, but the request had been firmly refused.

When he had first been locked up, he had felt light-headed, relieved to find himself alive. As he had waited for Stenovsky's shot he had been convinced that his life was over; he had felt a sense of profound sadness that he had to leave a world that at that moment seemed full of beauty and promise. When he was reprieved, the feeling of release made him grateful, almost joyful, and this sensation had lasted for some hours.

As the reality of his situation began to dawn on him, however, his elation turned to depression, and then to resentment and anger. How had he found himself in this impossible situation? He was not to blame; surely his actions had been dictated by honour. But if he was not guilty, who was? Stenovsky's hatred of him was understandable – he had indeed stolen his mistress, failed to repay the debts he owed him, and then appeared to take liberties with another woman with whom the captain was connected. But he had not deliberately set out to provoke him. As for the Bogolyubov legacy, he wished he had never heard about it. The tantalising possibility of a change in his fortunes, coming so fortuitously, seemed like a cruel chimera. Of course, if he managed to prove his case his life would be transformed, but if the prince continued to deny him his rights, it may be years before he could enjoy the benefits. He was unwilling to borrow more money against such an uncertain prospect, and so he faced continued penury. Even worse, he knew that his case was becoming the source of gossip and that in society some regarded him as an adventurer and a fraud. Belkin's words about him sidled into his mind, *'This man isn't a worthy opponent, he isn't worth killing. You know that, we both know that...'* It seemed that whenever he tried to expunge the past and regain his integrity, his sense of worth, of honour, something stood in his way.

As time passed his anger abated and, bored, he started to concentrate on ways to amuse himself. Fortunately, he was used to his own company. The rodents and arachnids provided sporadic entertainment. He tried to kill the first and laid bets on the progress of the second. He sang French, German and Russian songs to himself and then translated them, trying to make them scan. He tried to recreate the military calculations and equations taught to him at cadet school. He was just rehearsing the formations and distances between the ranks at his troop's last parade when the cell door opened. The captain wished to see him.

※

Andrey waited for the words of rebuke, but for a few moments Rosovsky simply contemplated him in silence. He knew that the captain was not given to the abuse and foul language deployed by some officers in such situations. But in a way, that made it worse. It would be painful to listen to Rosovsky expressing his profound disappointment that he had, once again, failed to meet the expected standard of behaviour. He felt his anger and frustration revive.

'Well, von Klein Sternberg, I've discussed your case with the colonel,' he was saying. 'You're lucky that he's more tolerant than I of your chosen method of resolving arguments. I remember ordering you expressly not to fight Stenovsky, I think?'

'Yes, sir.' Andrey feared the worst.

'You were also lucky that no-one was injured, because then we might have had to involve the military police,' Rosovsky continued. 'Anyway, it has been decided that you can keep your rank – for now, at least – but you can no longer stay here with the company in St Petersburg. That would send quite the wrong message to your fellows, I think you'll agree. The colonel has indicated that you should return to the regiment in Novgorod and serve in the military settlement.'

Andrey stared down at his feet. Although he had known this would be the likely outcome, it wasn't welcome. His duties would be difficult and frustrating: supervising farmers who didn't want to be soldiers, and soldiers who didn't want to be farmers. He would be forced to apply to the letter an extensive book of rules and conditions of service, enforced by a regime of harsh and often cruel discipline. He was unlikely to be able to bring much humanity to the task. It was no life for a competent officer with an ounce of self-respect. In fact, as far as his career in the army was concerned, it was likely to prove a dead end. He had no choice but to comply, but he really might have to review his plans for the future.

As if he read his thoughts, Rosovsky continued, 'It won't be forever, lieutenant, but I can't promise a quick return to the active units. A period spent in the settlement should give you time to reflect, and to get your finances back into shape. You still owe the regiment money, and this way you will have few opportunities to fritter away your pay.'

Andrey felt a twist of irritation. He had hardly been living a profligate life in recent weeks. The first repayment of his debt to the army had been made in full and on time. But arguing wouldn't get him anywhere.

'There's a detachment leaving for Novgorod next week,' Rosovsky said. 'I expect you to accompany it. In the meantime, you are confined to barracks.'

'And Morozov, sir?' Andrey liked his new orderly.

'If he wishes to come with you, he can. He may not, of course.'

Andrey nodded silently. Rosovsky's grave manner relaxed for a moment. He leant forward. 'Look, Andrey Andreyevich. I know this is difficult for you, but I hope you can see that antics that reflect badly on the regiment can't go unpunished. I'm aware that you feel you were deliberately provoked and had little choice but to fight Stenovsky. I'll do my best to bring you back to us. As you know, some troops have been mobilised and sent west due to the unrest in France and Belgium; it doesn't look as though that will come to anything, but something else may arise. If we are put on a war footing, I shall seek to recall you. I can't promise more than that. That's all.'

Dismissed, Andrey made his way back to his quarters, relieved not to have to return to prison. Morozov was waiting for him with a clean set of clothes and a towel to take to the bath house. He quickly assured Andrey that he would be happy to accompany him to Novgorod, and indeed would welcome a move to the country.

'Oh, this came for you, sir, while you were... err... away.' He handed Andrey a slim letter.

The Polunin Palace, English Embankment
Baron von Klein Sternberg,
It has come to my notice that you may be intending to challenge Captain Stenovsky following the incident at the recent ball.
I write to urge you not to take up arms on my account. I will think no worse of you if you show humility and resolve your differences amicably and I beg you to do so.
I remain etc,
N.L.

He frowned as he re-read the note. It was quite inappropriate, of course – the girl barely knew him – and what was she trying to say? Was this simply an admonition designed to distance herself from responsibility for his actions, or had she written out of genuine concern for him? He closed his eyes and recalled the moment she had been snatched from his arm, her sweet face etched with concern.

He rubbed the back of his neck. Her plea not to fight Stenovsky had come too late, of course. But what if he had received it earlier? That was pointless speculation. And now he should throw the note away. As he started to crumple it in his hand, something stopped him. He smoothed out the paper, folded it, and pressed on the seal. Then he placed it with care into the drawer of his desk.

CHAPTER SEVEN

October 1830 – Estonia

The carriage lurched sideways. The autumn rains had barely started, and although the road through the forest between Reval and Narva had yet to become a muddy quagmire, random craters and potholes caused the vehicle to roll and pitch. Vasily wished that he was on horseback, riding at the rear with the two officers from the Internal Guard. But he must sit inside, maintaining his dignity as a representative of the Ministry.

His work in the Estonian capital had concerned the cholera. Although the disease remained confined to the south and east of the empire, as a precaution envoys were already being sent out to communicate official advice from the General Medical Council in St Petersburg. Accustomed to similar work in Oryol, he had completed his business within a week.

There had been little time for sightseeing, but they had enjoyed Reval's narrow cobbled streets, crowded with merchants and sailors; the wide main square; the tall buildings with steep gabled roofs and church spires like black needles pointing to heaven. One evening they had taken a walk by the Baltic Sea and watched the waves churning, grey and rough, in the rich autumn light. The city fortress loomed, an implacable presence above the town ramparts, brooding over a tumble of rocks below. Vasily, his heart hollow with sorrow, recalled that his friend Mikhail had been confined here in the early months of 1826, and that there had been no news from Siberia for some months.

As he travelled home, he planned to take a short detour to visit the von Klein Sternberg estate. He was curious to know more about the lieutenant. There had been no further progress in his investigation of the prince's case, and many questions remained unanswered. Here in the land of Andrey Andreyevich's birth, he may find some clues regarding what actually happened before Stepan Bogolyubov left his new bride to meet his fate at Austerlitz in 1805.

'We'll soon be turning off!' shouted the coachman. Once off the main road the countryside changed. The dense woods became sparser, separated by expanses of marsh grasses, pools and greyish fields. Some were already ploughed, others were planted with limp, stunted root crops. They passed the mean huts of a couple of lonely villages, some derelict, their damp thatch lifting in the breeze. Seabirds from the north cried overhead and once, Vasily saw a golden eagle soaring high over distant trees.

The ancestral home of Andrey Andreyevich stood on a low bluff. A rutted driveway swept up the slope and around the back of the farmhouse. The place seemed to be deserted. Only a small part of what had once been a fine stone structure remained standing. The rest was ruinous, its stone walls scorched, its thatch removed, the timbers of its roof a stark skeleton. Grass grew in the gaping doorways. Vasily surveyed the scene. Would he learn anything of use here? It seemed doubtful. But someone was living here. In the yard behind the house, a tattered brichka was drawn up, and a plough, thick with fresh earth, stood by a well-built barn. A horse's head nodded over a stable door.

The carriage came to a halt, and for a moment they sat in silence. The veterans from the Internal Guard seemed unwilling to dismount. The horses stirred restlessly.

'Good God!' said Yakov finally. 'What a dump...'

'I think there must be someone around though,' said Vasily.

The coachman, remembering his role, descended slowly from the box and lowered the steps. Vasily stepped out and stood in the yard, wondering whether to approach the only part of the house that seemed habitable. Suddenly, from nowhere, a heavy brindled terrier hurtled towards him and, snarling, took a firm grip on his trouser leg. Vasily felt sharp teeth graze his skin. He lashed out at the dog with his cane. The coachman went for his whip and Yakov, leaping from the carriage, was about to deliver a hearty kick to the dog's flank when a heart-stopping yell was heard from the direction of the house. The dog released Vasily, retaining in his jaws a sizeable swatch of green uniform.

A man stood in the yard, his face purple below his thick yellow-grey hair. He was tall and broad-shouldered, Vasily guessed in his mid-forties. 'Leave my dog alone and get out of here!' he shouted. 'We've paid our taxes, you damned jackals, and I've got a quittance to prove it. Can't you leave a man alone?'

Vasily, resisting the temptation to examine his injured leg, waited for the tirade to cease. This must be some relative of von Klein's. He probably should have sent a message in advance. 'Get back in the carriage, Yakov,' he said. Then, turning to the coachman, he told him to return down the driveway and wait. He indicated that the guards should follow behind.

'I'm not leaving you here alone, sir,' said Yakov.

'I think it's the only way I'll get to speak to him. He thinks we're on some official business. I need to reassure him.'

'Well, let me stay with you.'

'No, I'll be safe. He isn't armed – and look, his wife has come out to investigate.'

'I'm coming back with the guard in half an hour, sir, whether you like it or not…'

At one end of the house the walls still seemed sound, and the roof had been repaired. A woman stood in the doorway. The man stared, saying nothing. Vasily stood alone as the sound of the wheels and horses' hooves faded, then he walked, limping slightly, towards the house. The dog, apparently regretting the savage attack, sloped along beside him. Vasily stopped and held his fist towards it in a gesture of friendship. The dog licked it, but then growled. He was clearly only on probation.

'Baron von Klein Sternberg?' Vasily ventured.

'Well, who else would I be?' the man retorted. 'More to the point, who are you, and what are you doing bringing armed guards onto my land?'

'Yes, I'm sorry, sir, I'm returning from official business in Reval. I should have sent ahead, it didn't occur to me... My name is Belkin, Vasily Nikolayevich, Titular Councillor at the Ministry of the Interior, but I am not here on Ministry business. I have come on behalf of my patron, Prince Bogolyubov, and was hoping to be able to speak with you about the case of your relative Andrey Andreyevich von Klein Sternberg.'

If he recognised Vasily's name, the prince's, or indeed Andrey's, the baron did not immediately show it. The woman broke the silence. 'Friedrich, let the officer come in. We need to hear news of Andrey.'

The baron was clearly still undecided, but then, muttering, he turned and led the way into the house. 'He's in some sort of trouble! I knew it!' he said immediately. 'He doesn't understand his duty to his family!'

'Can I offer you refreshment, sir?' the woman interrupted. 'You must forgive my husband. Our life is not easy at present. And is your leg hurt? I can arrange for your trousers to be mended...' She took the piece of cloth from his hand and turned to ring a bell. It seemed that despite their circumstances, the baron had at least one servant. A neatly dressed maid appeared and later returned with tea.

Vasily looked around. The room, which seemed to be the only living room, was moderately large, clean and filled with a mixture of good quality painted and light wooden furniture. A large desk covered with papers at the window must have served as the baron's office. 'I suppose you're surprised at the way we live?' the baron said.

'Well, yes, a little, sir.'

'Part of the house burned down just after my father, Andrey's grandfather, died three years ago. I was farming our land over near Johvi at that time. Times have been hard, the harvests the worst for years. We don't have the money to rebuild, but we've more or less restored what we can... Anyway, councillor, what can I do for you?'

'Firstly, I apologise again, sir, for catching you unawares. It was thoughtless of me. Before we start, could I send for my people and the carriage? I hope not to delay you too long, but I can't leave them out on the road.'

The baron called a man in from the yard and sent him to find the carriage. 'I'm afraid they'll have to rest in the barn,' he said. 'There's nowhere else, but there's plenty of hay at this time of year.'

As Vasily started to relate the history of his nephew's claim to the prince's title and wealth, von Klein Sternberg became agitated; whether from excitement, irritation or disbelief, it was hard to tell. It was clear that he knew nothing about the current legal proceedings, and it was also plain that his opinion of his nephew was not high. Did no-one have a good word to say about the lieutenant?

'I thought that Rodionov, the notary, was your agent in the capital, sir – I was certain that he or Andrey Andreyevich would have told you. After all, if your nephew's claim is valid, it must make a difference to your family.'

'Must it? I don't see why. We're not expecting much from Andrey Andreyevich. He sent some money home in the past, but then it dried up completely for a while. A small sum did arrive recently, but I'm not sure he thinks he really owes us anything. As for the notary, he stopped communicating with us when he realised that we were more or less bankrupt. I suspect he only got in touch with Andrey Andreyevich because he could smell money.'

'In fairness, sir, I don't think that the lieutenant had much money to send. Although he receives a higher salary in the grenadiers, his expenses are high… he has to keep up appearances.'

'I know. But my father would insist on Andrey entering a "good" regiment. The boy loved horses, is very skilled with them, in fact. The family hoped he might obtain a commission in the cavalry, but that proved too expensive. And of course, he's bright – did well at school and in the cadet corps. My father brought him up strictly, too harshly at times – concerned, I suppose, that he might turn out like his father. But he did what he could for him financially. He said it should pay off in the end, and from what you tell me he may have been right!' The baron gave a snort of what might have been laughter. 'So, why have you come all this way to see me? I assume that since you are acting for the prince, your interest lies in refuting Andrey's claim?' The baron seemed unperturbed by the thought.

'The prince, who does indeed deny the claim, has asked me to investigate the matter, that's true, sir. And you are right that I have a personal interest in seeing the lieutenant's case fail, but I must deal with the matter honestly. I confess also to being intrigued by the story of the relationship between Stepan Bogolyubov and your sister, Astrella. What particularly exercises me is why, if they did go through a service according to the Orthodox rite, no-one here appears to have been aware of it.

'I'll be honest with you, councillor,' said the baron. 'I was always led to believe that my sister's marriage, while legally valid, was never followed by an Orthodox ceremony. What's more, as far as I am aware, Astrella gave no necessary undertaking that her son should be brought up in the Orthodox faith. The impression that my father always gave was that time had run out, that no second marriage took place because the count had to return to his regiment, and then, of course, he was killed.'

'Where were you then, sir?'

'Fighting Bonaparte like everyone else. I graduated from the cadet corps in 1805 and only left the army in 1818. My sister Astrella died shortly after giving birth to Andrey. I came home irregularly, and when I did return it seemed she and the count had been written out of the family story. Stepan died heavily in debt, you know, and there was nothing to claim on Astrella's behalf, no dowry to retrieve. My father treated Andrey as his own son. He adopted him formally and passed on his title. Andrey went away to school in Reval when he was twelve or so; I barely knew him really. He came home from time to time, holidays and the like, but I was living over at our farm near Johvi.'

'And your father never spoke of your sister?'

'Hardly at all... He was quite a difficult man, of the old school. He never tired of reminding us that our line goes back to the thirteenth century, to the Knights of the Sword, far more ancient and distinguished than that of most Russian nobles – although a lot of good that does us now. His pride and dignity were hurt by what he saw as Astrella's disgrace. She was already with child when she married Stepan, and he wanted to expunge the past as far as possible.' The baron paused, and then continued, 'Even had he been aware of a second marriage, you know, he may well have chosen to deny it. Stepan's creditors turned up here in droves after his death, hoping to recoup their losses, threatening lawsuits and the like.'

'Is there anyone on the estate now who was here at the time of the marriage?'

'There are a few former serfs, but they live in the village some distance away, and would know little or nothing of Astrella's affairs. After the land reform here several years ago, many of the more enterprising left, seeking their fortunes elsewhere, and others are now dead. Conditions here are poor; one can hardly scratch a living, whether peasant or landowner, as I know to my cost. And then of course, after the war, the blockade meant the closure of the ports and there was nowhere to send the grain. Later, when that eased, prices collapsed.'

Vasily nodded. It was not surprising that many of the serfs had wanted to leave their former owners behind when they were able.

'Since then it's been difficult to get the peasants who remained here to fulfil their remaining obligations. We've had to make many economies. In the past we always used to employ a steward. At around the time the count married Astrella, the man here, Goossens, came with his wife and daughter from Flanders. He didn't last long. One or two others followed, but in time, my father took on most of the administrative work, and even some of the farm work, himself. It was the only way to make ends meet.'

'Do you know what happened to Goossens, where he went?'

'No, I'm afraid not.'

Uncertain how to pursue the matter further, Vasily rose to leave.

'Won't you stay and dine with us, councillor, and stay the night?' said Friedrich's wife. 'I think we can manage to feed you all, despite Friedrich's grumbling. I don't think you should try to make the journey to Narva tonight. We can heat the banya and the barn can be made comfortable.'

They spent a convivial evening at the ruined manor house. Friedrich proved, in the end, a genial host. As Vasily was bidding farewell the following morning, the baron handed him a small package. 'This is all I have of my sister,' he said. 'Be so good as to return the items when you've reached your conclusions, sir. I don't hold out much hope that Andrey will prevail, despite your opinion that his case seems good. Like you, I cannot help feeling that there is something not quite right, but we shall see… God moves in mysterious ways. If you see Andrey, tell him to contact us. If he has no money at present… well, so be it.'

Vasily nodded, unwilling to reveal that the last news he had of the baron's nephew was that he was incarcerated in the guardhouse in disgrace.

As the carriage swung off down the drive, he opened the package. There were a few recipes written in a neat hand and also a small picture. It showed a woman of about twenty, with a high forehead and narrow nose. Her hair was pale blonde, the same hue as that of her son, Andrey Andreyevich.

CHAPTER EIGHT

October 1830 – St Petersburg

'I would guess there'll be as much drama on this side of the curtain as on the other,' Katya observed to Nadezhda. The two women peered down from Prince Polunin's box on the *bel étage* into the depths of the theatre. Nadezhda tried to see through the gloom but the lighting was poor and the atmosphere, pungent with the scent of cologne and human sweat, was blue with cigar smoke.

'You'll see more when the curtain goes up,' said Vasily. 'There'll be more light then, and no-one will pay any attention to the stage for at least ten minutes. They'll be too busy trying to spot their acquaintance and see who's with whom. I suppose that's why there's an overture…'

The orchestra started to tune up. Nadezhda felt a tremor of anticipation. Tonight she could relax, be herself. She had created a breathing space. Yevgeny Filipovich, now safely on his way back to the hussars in Oryol, had skilfully persuaded her family that he admired her without making any commitment. This had been enough to raise her mother's hopes. Her only regret was the absence of Andrey Andreyevich.

The noise in the theatre was becoming almost unbearable: a clamour of voices, the clatter of feet on the wooden floor, the shriek of stringed instruments. It was particularly raucous down in the pit, where a crowd of men, young and old, some in uniform and others in frock coats, were shouting greetings to one another, clambering over seats, and striking poses.

'There's no-one of note in the Emperor's loggia,' observed Prince Polunin as he scanned the boxes with his collapsible telescope. 'We won't need permission to laugh or applaud.'

'Look, there's Madame Hélène, in Kuprin's box. How he's packed it with people!' said Maria.

'No doubt he wants to get his money's worth,' said Katya with a sly giggle. 'But Madame is certainly dressed for the occasion!'

Nadezhda didn't know Madame Hélène, although she had seen her distinctive hat boxes at the palace. The milliner was sitting in conspicuous splendour at the front of the merchant's crowded box. Her hair was piled high and graced with a large feather, combined with what looked like a piece of fruit. Her shoulders glowed white against the rich blue of her gown; a pale flower was carefully placed in the folds that stretched across her ample breasts. She held a pair of the new-fangled opera binoculars, which she raised to her eyes from time to time to look around, trying perhaps to spot a valued customer. As Nadezhda watched, Kuprin offered her a sweet, which she accepted with a gracious nod.

'Is she really the best milliner in St Petersburg?' Nadezhda asked Katya.

'Certainly among the best; she's been established on Nevsky for several years and dresses all the best people.'

But now the conductor's baton was tapping and the orchestra was falling silent. The first notes were heard and the curtain rose on a view of a fine country house standing in parkland. As Vasily had predicted, the audience immediately used the reflected light to look about them, greet acquaintance and comment to their neighbours. As a result the music was at times inaudible, but finally the din abated.

The popular comic opera was liberally interspersed with dance. When the dancers appeared, the young men in the pit responded with cheers and rowdy applause as their preferred artists took their turns on the stage. One young woman was particularly well received. She emerged from the wings in a full skirt that fell to her calves. Almost transparent, it afforded a fine view of slender legs clad in pink tights. A group of men standing in the parterre roared their appreciation.

'She hasn't even begun to dance yet!' Nadezhda objected. 'What's so special about her?'

'Oh that's Minnie, Minnie Voronova,' said Vasily, leaning forward to get a better view. 'She's a talented girl, apparently – but probably more to the point, she has the patronage of Count Malyshev. He'll make sure that she receives more than her fair share of adulation…'

She was a slender woman of below average height, almost boyish in appearance. She looked little more than seventeen. The music to which she danced suited her quick athletic style. Her legs worked so fast that they were hardly visible as she moved almost soundlessly across the stage. She spun and leapt, and the applause from her claque became more intense. At the end of the performance, she kissed her hands and threw them outwards. Her eyes sought her patron in the boxes and when they found him, she removed the lace fichu from her neck, put it to her lips and held it towards him. The cheers and ecstatic shouts of admiration were deafening. As she left the stage, her supporters were treated to a coy backwards glance and a twitch of her skirt.

Prince Polunin leaned forward. 'And now here's Lyuba Lebedeva. She's been a great favourite for some years now. She's a fine performer; she'll be well received.' An altogether more substantial dancer ran onto the stage, and seemed instinctively to pause for a moment to bask in the adulation from the pit. There was indeed a good deal of applause, but there was also a descant of whistling and some low hostile groans. Polunin turned to Vasily. 'That's a bit unfair!' he said. 'I'm afraid Malyshev's up to his tricks.'

'What tricks?' Nadezhda asked.

'He's hired some young bucks to rubbish the opposition.'

To Nadezhda's eyes, Lyuba appeared at least as accomplished as Voronova. Indeed, she preferred her more measured approach and her dignified fluidity of movement. But although she was beautiful, she didn't have the gamine appeal, the raw sexual attraction, of the younger dancer. Now she was joined by a partner, and the fine *pas des deux* that followed was met with animated applause. But it was certainly more muted than that received by Minnie. As she took her bow, Lyuba's smile seemed forced and her partner didn't try to hide his discomfort. Once the corps had danced their last turn, the audience settled down and the opera continued.

When the dancing commenced in the second half, Lyuba took the stage first and although most of the audience applauded her warmly, a low hissing arose from the right flank of the parterre. Apparently unfazed, she danced with grace and skill, but she remained on stage only briefly at the end of her performance. As she ran to the wings, a man in the pit shouted, 'Time to draw your pension, Lyuba!'

A scuffle ensued. One of Lyuba's supporters had taken offence. Fists flew, but the ushers in their imperial livery quickly intervened and both offenders were escorted out. Nadezhda felt sorry for the dancer; how hurtful the insults must have been, how mortifying.

Minnie's turn came a little later. As she danced with a slim but muscular partner, every lift and each swoop of their entwined bodies was met with groans of ecstasy from Malyshev's hired apostles. She was undoubtedly talented and alluring, but Nadezhda was irritated by her insouciant smiles and the faux innocence of her oversized eyes.

She heard Prince Polunin behind her, speaking in what he believed to be a low voice to Vasily. 'Of course, that little bundle was formerly Ivan Stenovsky's mistress, you know.'

'Really? I knew that he admired her, but...' Vasily seemed surprised.

'Yes, he took it badly when she left him. Well, better to have loved and lost...' the prince ventured. Vasily didn't reply.

Nadezhda was straining her ears to hear more, but as Minnie and her partner completed their dance, the pit erupted with wave after wave of adulatory cries, hoots and resonant applause. The little dancer had been Ivan Stenovsky's mistress! What a colourful life Ivan Alexandrovich seemed to have had. What a singular person he was! When he had called at the palace recently, there had of course been no mention of the duel, but he had been very subdued. His recent conduct had, it seemed, not gone unnoticed by his colonel. Perhaps as a result, his manners had improved. He now paid her the attention appropriate to the sister of his brother's wife. She had tried to be equally courteous, but continued to dislike him and was determined to keep her distance. Tonight, during the interval, she had spotted his broad frame standing behind the seating on the left flank of the parterre. Now as she looked down, he was in the same place, leaning against the wall, neither applauding nor looking at the stage but staring fixedly at the ground. Did he come here to torment himself?

But the finale had commenced. The young lovers' misunderstandings had been resolved; the elderly nobleman, who had aspired to the young woman's favours, was being married off to a widowed neighbour of appropriate antiquity. Having been lampooned earlier for his enthusiasm for foreign luxuries and innovations, the master of the house was resolving to allow his serfs to return to their traditional customs. In short, the order of life was restored.

※

The family did not stay for the vaudeville. Maria Vasilyevna claimed to be exhausted, and Katya said that she too found the atmosphere of the theatre fatiguing after a while. They waited in the vestibule while Matvey called for their carriage and Yakov retrieved the coats.

'I don't know why they always satirise landowners who try to improve their land,' Vasily complained. 'If people don't innovate, we'll never get anywhere…' He remembered his German cows.

Prince Polunin smiled. 'You mustn't forget this is the Imperial Theatre! Order, the status quo and the Fatherland must always prevail.'

The doors to the street opened and an autumn draught curled around the halls. Maria shivered. As Vasily moved his mother to a less chill spot, they heard footsteps on the stairs leading from the upper foyers. Madame Hélène was on her way down, taking each step at a time. Her shoulders were hunched and her expression was sombre. She dabbed at her eyes with her kerchief. Under her powder, she looked much older than her years. Vasily wondered whether she was ill, but as soon as she saw their family group, she quickened her step and straightened her back.

'Count Belkin! Countess!' she exclaimed, now apparently quite recovered. 'How good to see you; how lovely you look as always, Countess!' The usual pleasantries were exchanged and then she continued, 'I see that, like me, you do not like the vaudeville.'

'Oh, we sometimes stay,' said Vasily. 'But my mother is fatigued, and I have to make preparations for a journey.'

'Are you travelling for pleasure, Count? You've left it a little late in the year.'

'No, I have business in Warsaw.'

'I don't envy you the journey, and indeed is it safe to travel? I understand the disease…'

'At present the cholera is largely confined to the south and east, Madame. There are no quarantined areas elsewhere, apart from up in Archangelsk. I believe, however that there have been cases in Novgorod.' As he spoke, Vasily realised it would have been better not to mention this; Novgorod was not that far distant. But it was too late. He added that he hoped that the progress of the disease would be slowed when the winter came.

'Yes, the movement restrictions are causing my business some problems,' Madame Hélène said. 'At one point, everything sent from Moscow was being stopped for fumigation. I'm concerned. The government should consider the needs of commerce.'

'Can we offer you a ride home, Madame?' asked Katya.

'That's very kind, Princess, but Luka Ilyich has called his coach.'

They took their leave of her. On the way home, Katya remarked, 'I wonder what happened to Madame Hélène. She was clearly distressed when she came down the stairs.'

'Perhaps she really is concerned about her business,' said Vasily. 'There are problems with supplies, and if the disease did take hold here, many of her clients would probably leave town. I'd certainly expect your family to leave.'

'But she looked quite happy earlier in the evening.

Perhaps Kuprin said something to upset her!' said Katya.

They dropped Vasily off at his home, and he went up to the drawing room of the apartment. Yakov brought tea and sat down with Vasily to drink it. Despite the disapproval of his uncle, Vasily had always tried to treat his servant, if not as an equal, at least as a human being. They had been together since childhood and he usually enjoyed his company.

'I'm a bit concerned about Matvey,' Yakov said.

'Are you? He seems pretty content to me.'

'Sveta, the maid, says that he's taken to creeping out of the house in the evening. I don't know where he goes.'

'Really?'

'Yes, and he takes a stout stick with him. I don't know why he needs that.'

'I suppose if he wants to go out for a walk, there is no real reason to object. He knows how to look after himself. The stick is probably a good precaution… there are some rough types about, even in the Admiralty District, at night. I wish he had some friends of his own age. I do wonder about school.'

Vasily leant back. Should he be concerned? On one occasion he had spotted Matvey shadowing him when he had gone to Rosovsky's home for dinner. He hadn't thought too much about it, but it was clear that his ward had become his self-appointed bodyguard. Since he had rescued him from the cruelties of Prince Bogolyubov's kitchens, the boy's devotion had been unwavering. When he had been forced to escape from St Petersburg in the winter of 1825, Matvey had stowed away in order to be with him. After days on the road in freezing temperatures,

Vasily had been close to death, and the child – for he had only been a child at that time – had nursed him back to health. Matvey had been with him ever since, and having been freed, showed no sign of wanting to leave. He had wanted to go with him to Poland and had only been diverted from the idea with difficulty.

'I'll have another word with him before we go, Yakov,' Vasily promised.

'I suppose the trip is really necessary.' Yakov was not fond of travel, particularly in the autumn, and had already endured the trip to Estonia.

'Yes, von Klein's case is coming up again in court shortly. I must catch up with Count Angelov and find out how much, if anything, he remembers about Stepan Bogolyubov's wedding. The count must be getting on a bit. He's been in Constantine Pavlovich's suite for several years. My uncle has been urging me to go to see him ever since I returned from Reval, and of course he's made sure that the minister has now, conveniently, found me some work in Warsaw.'

Yakov stood up. 'It would be good if the weather changed.'

'Yes, the trip would be a lot easier if there were some snow. But there's no sign at present. I could take another man, Yakov.'

'No, I can't let you go without me, sir. You'll get into trouble. Well, I'm off to bed. Was there anything else?

'No, I'll see you in the morning. Nine o'clock will do. I don't have an early start tomorrow. I've been summoned to see Irina's brother, Colonel Kalinin. I'm not sure what he wants.'

The following day, as Vasily walked the short distance to Pavel Kalinin's home on the English Embankment, he prayed that all was well with Irina and his daughter. There had been cases of cholera to the south of the Kalinin estate in Bryansk, but they should be safe enough in the depths of the country.

He paused for a moment outside. It was painful to dwell on memories of the rambling apartment, its bright rooms and broad views, where for a few months he had achieved a level of joy and excitement that could probably never be repeated. He recalled Irina's bright hair, the sweet lemon scent of her fair skin. He would give a good deal to see her again. Today, when he was shown in, Margarethe, Irina's companion and Pavel's mistress, came out to greet him. For a moment his heart lifted. 'Is Irina Pavlovna here?' he asked. But Margarethe shook her head. 'No, Irina and Sophia are in the country. I'm spending some time with Pavel before he goes abroad once again. I hope to be able to return to Bryansk very shortly, provided the roads are free from quarantine restrictions.'

'Are they alone?' In the past Irina had felt solitary in the deep forests that surrounded the estate, particularly in winter.

'No, she has Pavel's cousin and his family with her – they've fled from the disease in Moscow – so she'll have company when the winter snow comes. Both she and Sonya are well, and seem content enough.'

Vasily would have liked to know more, but Pavel Pavlovich now emerged from his study. It had been two years since they had met and his appearance hadn't changed. His remarkable claret-coloured hair still glowed above the pale freckled skin and green-grey eyes that he shared with his sister. Vasily took a seat, not entirely at ease. The colonel had a sharp wit and a caustic tongue, and rarely revealed much of himself. He had certainly been involved in some way with the failed uprising in 1825, but if he was truly a liberal, his views did not seem to have affected his diplomatic career.

'Thank you for coming over to see me,' Pavel said. 'I hear you're off to Poland, and I wanted to have a brief word with you before you go.'

Vasily was taken aback. How did the colonel know his plans? He supposed he had discovered them through his work at the Foreign Ministry.

'Do you really need to make this journey?' Pavel continued.

Vasily frowned. Was there something he had missed? This was the second or third time this question had been put to him. 'Yes. I have official work to do there, and also there's the family matter…'

'So your uncle has arranged the trip?'

'Yes.'

Pavel grunted. Vasily knew that he didn't care much for Alexander Petrovich.

'And the family matter?'

Vasily told the colonel about the prince's legacy. The colonel pondered for a moment before asking, 'How much do you know about Poland?'

'I've read a briefing note from the Ministry.'

'That won't help you much. If you're determined to go, you need to be aware of a few facts, if only to make sure that you don't upset the sensibilities of the Poles you meet.'

Pavel settled in his chair. Vasily forced himself to concentrate; a lecture was clearly in prospect. 'Poland is a very singular place,' the colonel started. 'Its borders have been so changed by a series of forced partitions over the past sixty years that the idea of Poland is now hard to grasp, to define.' He leant back, looked at the ceiling and ran his slender fingers through his hair as he continued, 'One might have thought that this constant upheaval would gradually erode the Poles' sense of identity, which is, I suppose, what the great powers hoped. But it's never easy to entirely destroy a nation. It's often forgotten that Poland has a culture that stretches back hundreds of years, and indeed, for much of that time the country was regarded as among the most advanced societies in the world, both culturally and constitutionally.' Pavel picked up a pen and started to draw interconnected rectangles on the paper in front of him. 'The current situation stems from the settlement that followed the Congress of Vienna in 1815. What now remains of Poland, the "Congress Kingdom", exists as a semi-independent fiefdom of Russia. Russia is supposed to respect its constitutional rights. This isn't a particularly comfortable position. Some Poles, for economic reasons or due to concerns about security, are content to embrace their overlords. Many, however, increasingly hope for the restoration of independence, and see the current hybrid arrangement as the foundation for building a free Polish nation in the future.'

'But how autonomous is the Kingdom now?' Vasily asked.

'In theory at least, the Poles have responsibility for domestic administration through their own elected body, the Sejm. Foreign Policy and, of course, security are run from St Petersburg. The Tsar of Russia is the King of Poland. Nicholas's envoy, Novosiltsev, supervises the activities of the Sejm. And then of course there's the Grand Duke, Constantine Pavlovich, the Tsar's older brother. He's the commander-in-chief of the Polish Army. It's made up of both Russian and Polish Troops. He effectively acts as Viceroy and he's a great enthusiast for the Polish nation – is married to a Polish woman in fact.'

'But there are reasons for concern?'

'Yes, things have not gone entirely to plan. The late emperor, Alexander, promised the new Kingdom liberalism and freedom, but these promises were gradually abandoned. Towards the end of his reign the Polish Sejm lost its autonomy, censorship was imposed and prominent liberals in universities and the like were purged. The discovery of Polish connections to our own abortive liberal uprising in 1825… you remember that, of course, Vasily?'

Kalinin looked quizzically at Vasily, who felt himself flush. Was Kalinin laughing at him? If so, he didn't much appreciate it.

'The discovery of Polish links to our own uprising in 1825,' the colonel repeated, 'inevitably influenced the attitude of our new Tsar, Nicholas. With his customary light touch, he redoubled the efforts of Russian agents and police in Poland, and imposed Russian law in cases that touched his interests. The result was the inevitable arrest of intellectuals and revolutionaries, real and imagined. A procession of Polish dissidents made their way to prison or exile.'

'That can't have been popular.'

'No, but of course Nicholas's actions are understandable. Since the day that the Congress Kingdom was created, hardcore nationalists have been working towards full independence. Poets and intellectuals have started to pen patriotic odes and uplifting histories of the Polish nation. Many soldiers, particularly young officers, have been frustrated by a lack of promotion opportunities. Their lives are dull, and they chafe against the endless drills and parades; they resent the harsh discipline. Many Poles still look back to the perceived glories of the Napoleonic wars, even though they were badly let down by their hero. Secret societies meet regularly. The kind of organisation which I think you're familiar with, Vasily, where intellectuals, dilettantes and young officers meet to grumble, drink, sing songs, and plot revolution…'

'I know there has been turmoil in Paris and unrest in Belgium,' Vasily interrupted. 'But has there been any trouble in Warsaw?' He wasn't in the mood for the gentle mockery to which he was being subjected, particularly since it had in part been Pavel's influence that had first drawn him to radical ideas.

'Frankly, I think that the place is a powder keg, but a powder keg is only dangerous when someone lights a fuse.' Pavel paused, put down his pen, and considered for a moment before he continued. 'In Warsaw there has been some evidence that unrest elsewhere in Europe hasn't gone unnoticed: street demonstrations, anti-Russian graffiti, a "to let" sign hung on the gate of Constantine's palace. The authorities here in Russia seem unperturbed, however, and a trip to Poland now should be safe enough. But don't expect a warm welcome.'

'I appreciate your concern,' Vasily said. 'I was aware of some of this, but I've fallen out of the habit of thinking about politics. In the current climate there seems little point.'

Pavel gave a slight nod. 'Yes, I can understand that.' He paused for a moment, and then continued, 'Look, I'm not trying to frighten you. Just be alert, do your business, whatever it is, and come home. And Vasya, you mustn't mind me pulling your leg a little. I always felt you were rather an unlikely revolutionary... but for a while, you seemed to take quite well to it.' Pavel favoured Vasily with one of his rare smiles. He hummed a little to himself and changed the subject.

Vasily finally rose to leave.

'Have you heard from my sister, Irina?' the colonel asked.

'Not since I've been in Petersburg. I wrote to tell her that I was coming back to work here, but...' Vasily looked away towards the river.

'I'm sorry, truly sorry, Vasya, about your separation, but it's probably for the best. It wasn't really a tenable situation long-term...'

'Do you have word of her husband?'

Pavel shrugged. 'Fit as a flea, I'm afraid. I wish I had better news for you.'

Vasily didn't comment, but he was strangely affected. The colonel had rarely shown any interest in his feelings in the past. He left the apartment, if not cheerful, in better spirits than when he arrived – although later, when he considered their discussion, he was at a loss to understand why.

CHAPTER NINE

Sunday 16th November 1830 – Warsaw

Vasily stood on the eastern bank of the Vistula in the grey afternoon light. Across the river, the cupola on the tower of the Royal Castle rose above the city. He had arrived at the checkpoint at Praga that morning. Now it was past three o'clock, but the necessary checks and formalities were still not complete. The Polish officials were surly and taciturn, and their interpretation of his paperwork seemed deliberately obtuse. When they demanded a second inspection of his boxes, he left Smirnov and Yakov to unpack them and took a brisk walk along the deserted riverbank. A heavy flat-bottomed barge was drifting upstream. The first few snowflakes of winter floated down and an occasional early candle glowed in the windows of the scattered houses.

They had left St Petersburg before the end of October and had travelled for almost three weeks. They had enjoyed a smooth ride in a Ministry carriage as far as Narva. There they had been obliged to leave their escort behind and hire a more robust vehicle, together with two professional postilions, who were accustomed to navigating the sometimes-atrocious roads that passed through Estonia and beyond.

They had stopped for three nights at Riga and then, crossing the long wooden bridge over the river, they travelled on through Livonian forests, filled with pine, larch and birch. Bearskins hung on the walls of the post houses along the way, and their sleep at night was disturbed by the howling of wolves. The carriage was often in danger of becoming stuck in deep sand or tipping into gullies. At one remote spot, barely resisting the temptation to cover their eyes, they navigated an almost perpendicular descent onto a rickety pontoon bridge over a rushing river.

After Mitau the roads improved, and once over the Polish border they became quite good, having recently been repaired by order of Grand Duke Constantine. They crossed the Neiman River, not far from the point where Napoleon had marched into Russia eighteen years before. The better roads in Poland were not mirrored by the condition of its people. The poverty of many of the villages through which they travelled was dispiriting. The hovels were thronged with wretched-looking peasants. Many of these were Jews, who proved themselves adept at running repairs when, as happened regularly, a part of the carriage broke or failed.

At Pultusk they had enjoyed a night at a good post house, and as they drove along the bank of the Narew River, the road was paved. At first the countryside was flat and monotonous, but finally their route passed through an undulating wooded region, where the leaves of oak trees fell in brown drifts onto the green well-tended verges that edged the final versts to the Polish capital.

Now, itching and uncomfortable, their clothes crumpled and grimed with the dust of travel, they were tantalisingly close to their destination. As Vasily returned to the customs post, he gloomily contemplated the city on the far bank, which seemed so near but felt unattainable. To his relief, when he arrived, formalities seemed to be complete.

'Yes, all we've got to do now is fill in the residency forms before we cross the bridge,' Smirnov said doubtfully, his round, normally cheerful face strained and tired. The two postilions sat by the coach looking bored.

At last, the battered carriage made its way across the crowded pontoon bridge that spanned the Vistula. They passed in front of the Royal Castle and drove along the fine broad thoroughfare of Nowy Swiat, where an array of stylish shops reminded Vasily of Paris. Turning off into a side street, they soon came to a halt outside a plain stone house standing back from the road behind high railings. Two Russian soldiers, grenadiers in heavy greatcoats, stood on guard at the open gates. This must be the home of Lieutenant General Zadachin, where the Ministry had arranged lodgings. The drivers dropped Vasily and Smirnov at the front door, and then drove on with Yakov to stout wooden gates that led to the stable yard.

The door swung open as they approached. Vasily shrugged in discomfort as he pulled out his letter of introduction to the general.

'Oh yes, Count Belkin, we've been expecting you,' said the doorman. 'Since you need to rest after your journey,

Madame will not expect you to join her for dinner tonight. Food will be delivered to your rooms.'

Vasily's head was swimming with fatigue. In addition to supper, all he needed was a bath and then sleep. 'Thank you. I wonder if you could arrange for these to be delivered?' He pulled out some papers: a letter to Count Angelov, requesting a meeting; and his formal introduction to an official in the office of Novosiltsev, the Tsar's personal commissioner. Then he and Smirnov made their way to their rooms.

❧

Monday 17th November

The following morning, having slept deeply, Vasily descended a curved stone stairway into a spacious hallway. In one of the upper rooms, he could hear the voices of young children squawking brightly. They must be the general's grandchildren; he knew that the officer had retired from active service and was now attached to the Grand Duke's suite.

In the dining room, a young woman came forward to greet him. 'Count Belkin! Welcome to Warsaw. I hope that you slept well and that your rooms are comfortable?' This must be the mother of the children, probably the general's daughter. He glanced round the room. A small group had gathered. An older woman sat at the table, but she didn't stir. As if sensing his uncertainty, the young woman added, 'I am Anna Grigoryevna, General Zadachin's wife.'

He tried to hide his surprise. The older woman, it seemed, was the general's widowed sister. A plump elderly Frenchman was introduced as the former tutor to the general's sons, presumably from an earlier marriage. Having taken food from a sideboard, Vasily sat down. The meal continued in silence. Madame Zadachina had resumed her place at the head of the table. She was a tall, slender woman. Above the full sleeves of her plain day dress, the pale triangle of her neck and shoulders was covered with a wisp of gauze. She was no great beauty. Her fair hair, swept up into a ribboned roundel, flanked her slightly overlong face with two looped plaits. Her nose was also long, but her blue eyes were soft and expressive and her mouth generous. Vasily wondered how she had come to marry a man so much older than herself. But after all, it wasn't so unusual. His sister Katya had done much the same and seemed content enough.

As he sat enjoying his rye bread and sausage, a lackey appeared and handed him a message. It confirmed his meeting at the government offices later that day. As he tucked it away, the Frenchman turned to him with a peevish expression. 'I'm surprised that you decided to visit Warsaw now, Count. Although the atmosphere is less volatile since the tumult in France died down, the city remains tense. Just last night there was rumoured to be some sort of trouble, although I understand it came to nothing.'

'You mustn't upset yourself, monsieur,' said the general's sister. 'It was a false alarm. In any event, my brother has assured me that in the city at least, there are many more Russian troops than Polish, and the Polish officers like and respect the Grand Duke.'

'I don't intend to stay very long, sir,' said Vasily. 'But cholera is no respecter of politics and the minister is keen that…' He was going to say "all parts of the Empire" but wondered if that was appropriate here. 'And the minister is keen that the Kingdom of Poland should be as well prepared as possible. We have learned something from our experiences this year, I think. In addition, I have some urgent family business to attend to.'

'Do you have pistols, sir?' asked the Frenchman.

'Yes, I do.'

'When you go out, I suggest you take them. And don't fall into any disputes; it can happen quite easily if you're incautious.'

Vasily glanced at Madame Zadachina, who frowned but said nothing. But perhaps the Frenchman was right. Hadn't Kalinin described Poland as a powder keg? Yesterday the city had seemed calm enough, but the officers at the barrier had barely concealed their hostility. He should try to complete his business and leave as quickly as was reasonable, even if that meant a swift return to tedious days on the road.

※

Vasily's meeting with the Polish Interior Ministry did not delay him long. He was politely received at the Government Palace, but it was clear from the start that the Polish authorities were not interested in advice from St Petersburg. They assured him that were the cholera to arrive, which was by no means certain of course, their plans were well advanced. If direct decrees were issued by

King Nicholas, they would, as required, pay heed to them, but he should remember that the Congress Kingdom looked after its own internal affairs, and of course their doctors were known around Europe as being second to none.

'Surely they want to learn from our experience?' Smirnov said as they walked back to their lodgings.

'You would have thought so, but they are sensitive when they think we are meddling in their affairs. It's disappointing, but I can understand it,' said Vasily. 'Besides, I'm not sure that we have all the answers; some of our recommendations are contradictory, to say the least. Never mind, Smirnov, we can go home shortly.'

'But we've only just arrived, sir!'

'Well, we can't leave until I've caught up with Count Angelov, which might take a little while. I understand that the Grand Duke keeps his suite busy with reviews and parades. We should look around the city too. I'm told there are some fine paintings in the castle.' Vasily did not speak with much conviction. Warsaw's situation on the slopes above the broad river was certainly attractive, but the atmosphere did feel oppressive. Small detachments of Russian troops in grey greatcoats were on regular patrol, a sombre military display among the colourful markets and spacious public gardens. As he and Smirnov walked along Nowy Swiat, a gang of Polish cadets pushed past and almost sent the clerk flying into the gutter.

Outside the gates of Zadachin's house, the Russian grenadiers had today been replaced by Polish soldiers. The doorman handed Vasily a note with an elaborate seal.

Count Belkin,

I shall be happy to receive you on Wednesday morning after the Changing of the Guard, which takes place at the Place de Saxe. I suggest that you come to the parade, which will commence at 10.30 in the morning, and look for me among the Grand Duke's suite afterwards.

Angelov

At least here was some progress. Vasily felt disappointed at the outcome of this morning's meeting; perhaps he shouldn't give up too easily. The count had been in Poland for some time and may have suggestions as to how to take matters further.

Smirnov disappeared upstairs to write his report. Vasily could again hear children; this time the sound was coming from the drawing room. He found Madame Zadachina entertaining her daughters as their nanny looked on.

'Oh, Vasily Nikolayevich, do come in... that is, if you like children,' she said. 'I shall send for coffee.'

The prospect of coffee was enticing. He took one of the leather-covered chairs. Anna's two girls were playing contentedly. They were sweet, soft children of about three and five, with pale hair and their mother's grey-blue eyes. The younger of the two wobbled towards him, a painted wooden horse in her hand. He reached out and took it, asking its name. The child, overcome with shyness, snatched the toy back and ran to her mother. Remembering his own daughter, his throat tightened and tears came to his eyes.

Anna regarded him closely. 'You must forgive her. She's not used to strangers. Do you have children?'

'I have a daughter, Sophia,' Vasily replied without reflection. 'She is just four.'

'Ah! Much the same age then. So you know how valuable these moments of peace are.'

Vasily smiled, but found himself unable to reply. Seeming to sense his distress, Anna hurried on. 'Well, this, the older one, is Louisa, and the other is Masha. They're good girls, aren't they, Nanya?'

'Oh yes, ma'am.'

The children were soon taken away, and Vasily, clearing his throat, started to make enquiries about life in Warsaw, the nature of the Grand Duke's court, the scope for excursions in the summer. Anna was an easy companion and time passed quickly.

'Was today's meeting successful?' Anna asked.

'Not really. I'm not sure that the Kingdom's representatives are very interested in receiving advice from Russia, even when public health is threatened. The minister in Petersburg will be disappointed.'

'The situation is difficult,' said Anna after a moment of reflection. 'The Poles are a proud people, and, it must be said, have not been kindly dealt with in recent years. The rich and powerful set, the people that we Russians generally mix with, are reasonably content. They complain, of course, but in fact are happy enough to deal with Novosiltsev, to receive compliments from the King when he visits, to play the courtier, to collect their medals and awards. They know that their rights, their lands, are secure enough under an autocratic regime. It's the lesser nobility, and of course the young, who are resentful and dream of independence. The Grand Duke doesn't mix much with them. His Polish courtiers, and some Polish generals, give him the impression that he is much loved, that the army would do anything for him… and then of course, there is his wife.'

'Yes, he's married to a Polish woman, isn't he?'

'Joanna Grudzinska, the Princess Lovich. She's a fine woman actually – dignified, beautiful and good company. She puts up with Constantine's eccentricities, his temper tantrums. He's devoted to her and generally takes her advice.'

Vasily remembered how, after the death of the Emperor Alexander in 1825, Constantine's portrait had appeared in the shop windows along Nevsky Prospekt. At that time everyone thought that he would be the next Tsar. Had he been, the December rising might not have occurred, and the course of Vasily's own life might have been quite different.

The clock on the mantlepiece struck four. Anna rose. 'I must go upstairs and change. My husband dines here this evening and will be pleased to meet you.'

Vasily took her lead, bowed, and left the room. Although he still felt weary, his spirits had risen. Anna Grigoryevna was a pleasant woman. He wondered what he would make of her husband. Anna had barely mentioned him.

※

When Vasily entered the drawing room an hour or so later, wearing his best uniform and doused liberally with cologne, the general himself was seated by the fireplace.

He was a tall man, very thin, with a narrow, handsome face. He wore the dark uniform of a senior cavalry officer. It was hard to guess his age, but he must have been well over fifty. He was flicking through a journal, but noticing Vasily, he set it aside and rose.

'Delighted to meet you, Count Belkin. Welcome to Warsaw, and to my home. I'm glad we could help out the Commissioner by accommodating you and your men.' He waved forward a lackey with a glass of wine. 'Have your meetings gone well today?'

Vasily explained that they had not and was, in reply, treated to a lengthy ramble about the shortcomings of civil servants, particularly in Poland. From this, he concluded that the general might be well made and presentable, but that he was not very acute.

During dinner it became plain that Zadachin, in addition to being dull, was also an extreme conservative who was fond of the sound of his own voice. His sister and the Frenchman had remained largely silent, eating their food with resigned application, while the general regaled them with a blow-by-blow account of today's parade on the square. Only Anna sat looking at her husband as if hanging on his every word. Vasily felt painfully sorry for her; imagine this every evening!

The general droned on. Vasily's lids drooped as he toyed with his food, but then he was roused by a sharp knock on the door. A young captain stood on the threshold. His fresh face was flushed and he was breathing heavily. 'The general is needed at the palace at once! There's been a revolt at the Military Academy; an attempt seems to have been made on the life of the commander-in-chief!'

'Is the Grand Duke unhurt?' the general barked, rising from his seat.

'I believe so, sir, but it's not sure…'

The two soldiers made haste to leave. The captain turned at the doorway. 'When we have gone, lock all the doors and don't admit any strangers, Anna Grigoryevna. There's no cause for alarm. The army is prepared. Most of the Polish troops will remain loyal, I'm sure of it…'

The general was calling for his coat. He had not comforted or even taken leave of his wife. The sound of boots retreated and doors slammed shut. With a small gasp, the general's sister fell insensate to the floor. It was therefore several minutes before it was revealed that every Polish servant in the house had disappeared.

CHAPTER TEN

As soon as he was free to leave the drawing room, Vasily sought out Smirnov and Yakov. They were playing draughts in their small sitting room, with beakers of Polish beer and black bread and cheese at their elbows. They seemed largely indifferent to the news of trouble, until the sound of musket shot crackled in the street.

'Can we go out and take a look, sir?' asked Smirnov, his eyes bright with excitement.

'Certainly not!' Vasily spoke sharply. Hadn't he explained the danger? 'We must stay here until calm is restored. That seems to be the likely outcome. I should go down and check that the drivers are still with us, and then look to the ladies.' He went through the kitchens to the stable yard. The general's Russian coachman had been sent home from the Belvedere Palace and Vasily told him to secure the substantial wooden gates that led to the street. His own drivers, unfazed by the disturbance, were drinking and playing cards in their quarters above the stables.

When Vasily returned to the empty drawing room, he could smell the pungent aroma of hartshorn. The voice of

Anna Grigoryevna echoed somewhere close by, seeking to calm the children's nanny and her two Russian maids. One of her daughters was crying. Bells rang out. Sporadic gunfire and explosions, raucous shouts of '*Do broni!*' and the crash of breaking glass drifted up from Nowy Swiat. There seemed no option but to wait and hope for relief. Vasily put a log on the open fire and stared into the flames. Kalinin had been right. He shouldn't have come. Travelling all this way to question Count Angelov would probably not change anything. The prince and his uncle should have bowed to what seemed inevitable and accepted that the German, whatever his shortcomings, should have his damned legacy.

Anna finally returned. She poured a glass of vodka, which Vasily downed thankfully. Handing him another, she took one herself. She seemed calm, although a reddening of the skin around her neck betrayed her anxiety. They exchanged a few empty phrases. After some minutes, she rose and opened the pianoforte in the corner. She rippled the keys and then closed the lid again. It was almost midnight, but she did not seem to want to retire. To try to distract her, he started to relate the true reason for his journey here. The story about the prince's fortune seemed to engage her attention and they became absorbed in conversation until an insistent knocking on the front door startled them. The Polish doorman had departed, and so Vasily went into the hallway.

'Who's there?' he shouted. Hearing the captain's voice, he unbolted the door.

The officer, his face sheened with sweat, stepped into the drawing room. 'The situation isn't good,' he said. 'The

Belvedere Palace was briefly overrun by the rebels. The Grand Duke has escaped. He hid in the attic with his valet, but General Gendre and the Vice President Lubovidsky were murdered in the confusion, and no-one knows what has become of Frederick Fanshawe, the Grand Duke's secretary.'

'And the general?' Anna asked.

'Your husband is safe, but several Russian officers are missing, believed captured.'

'Do you know anything of Count Angelov?' Vasily asked. Had he been killed, his journey here would have been pointless.

'No, I'm afraid not, but I don't think he was at the palace this evening.' The captain sat down heavily, his sword scraping on the floor. Anna handed him a drink, which he downed in one. He continued, 'As was planned in the event of trouble, all Russian regiments have left their barracks. They engaged in a fighting retreat through the streets, without many casualties it seems, and most are now assembled in front of the palace. A number of Polish regiments, the Grodno Hussars and some uhlans, have remained loyal to the Crown and have joined them. The Grand Duke is refusing to allow Russian soldiers to return to the town to restore order. He seems to think that it is up to the Poles to sort out their own problems. He was encouraged by pledges of support from some of the Polish commanders, who I suspect downplayed the extent of the trouble. Meanwhile, as you can hear, disturbances continue.'

As if on cue, an explosion caused the lamps in the room to flicker. Fine porcelain in a display cabinet shivered and chinked.

'So we should remain here?'

'I don't think that there's much alternative. The streets are dangerous. Some townsmen – a good number of them – have stormed and taken the arsenal. There's a vast store of weapons there, including thirty thousand muskets, so it's a serious setback. It's thought the Grand Duke will withdraw his troops to an estate a little way out of the city, close to Mokotów. He intends to negotiate with the Poles tomorrow. I have to say I'm disappointed by his inaction. We certainly outnumber the rebel troops, and could have subdued them.'

'But presumably not if you include the armed civilians,' Vasily said.

'That's hard to tell, but if we'd acted quickly, had some leadership, the arsenal might have been secured. Indeed, it should never have been left unguarded. We were aware of rumours that an uprising could take place, but when it didn't happen yesterday, everyone relaxed…'

'Will you remain here with us, Captain?' Anna asked.

'No, I've been sent to find out what has happened to the Grand Duke's Fourth, the Polish Jaegers. They're his favourite regiment, you know. He refuses to believe that they've gone over to the rebels.'

'But it can't be safe, sir,' said Vasily. 'Why not wait until morning?'

The captain rose. 'No, I must go now. I'll be careful.' He bowed and left.

Anna Grigoryevna's equanimity had deserted her. She started to tremble. Vasily picked up a shawl that she had discarded and put it round her shoulders. He then drew her towards him and briefly enfolded her in his arms.

Tuesday 18th November

When Vasily woke the following morning, he found himself in the chill drawing room, lying on a leather-covered ottoman. Someone had covered him with a thick quilt, and both he and the quilt were in danger of slipping to the floor. The streets outside were silent. There was no sign of Anna.

They had talked into the early hours, rising from time to time to feed the fire. They had withheld little from one another. He had spoken of Sonya, and of course about Irina; how he was in theory a free man, but didn't really feel so. She had told him about her marriage to the general.

'I wasn't in love with him, although I hoped that I might eventually come to it,' she said. 'He was our neighbour, a widower, with lands adjacent to our own small estate in Penza. I married him with my eyes open. I wanted to help myself and my siblings to a better life. My poor father... we were not so poor that we didn't have some ambitions.'

'It's not an unusual story, Anna. My sister, who married a man much older than herself, would like me to court an heiress like my cousin Nadya.'

'But you won't do that?'

'No, I think not. If I can't marry for love, I would rather look for a local landowner's daughter near Dubovnoye... try to put the estate there on a firmer footing.'

'Ah, love...' Anna said. 'That would have been a great bonus!' She glanced down at her wedding ring. 'But you mustn't think me unhappy. The general is kind and he delights in his girls. But, oh dear, how dull he is! He runs the household like a military campaign, and a pretty tedious one at that. Try as I might, I can't truly respect him...'

She fell silent. A log toppled in the grate and sparks flew up. She rose and moved aside the fire screen. As she turned back, he thought he could discern a gleam in her eye. 'So we are both trapped and lonely, Vasily Nikolayevich, are we not? Perhaps we should try to make an escape together? Not a complete one, of course, but...'

Vasily held her gaze, feeling a pulse of arousal. He had supposed that they had clung together earlier for simple comfort, but she seemed less plain than he had at first thought her. In fact, when animated, she was not plain at all. A sudden splutter of gunfire in the street reminded him that this was not the time for precipitous passion, but in any event, he very much liked her.

She shivered at the interruption and sat down beside him. He put his arm around her shoulders. He remembered kissing her plaited hair as she settled against him, smelling her floral scent, and then after some minutes, shamefully, falling asleep. Now, alone and a little embarrassed in the cold morning light, he rose and made for his rooms.

※

A little later, shaved and dressed in civilian clothes, Vasily collected his small band. There was no sign of other members of the household and he could hear the sound of renewed shouts and explosions in the streets. He went upstairs to a window and looked down to the corner of Nowy Swiat. The shopping street was crowded with townsmen, many carrying weapons. Looting had started again and rioters were shattering any shop windows that had been overlooked the night before.

He walked briskly back to the stairwell. At the front of the house, there was no sign of a guard, Polish or Russian, but the gate between the railings was firmly locked and chained. As he watched, a small group of men, some armed and some laden with sacks, ran past the secured front door towards the stable yard. Had the coachman remembered to close the gates? He found his pistols and ran down the stairs.

As he had feared, the two heavy gates were standing wide open. Two men in workers' smocks were already inside, running up the yard, making for the stables and his own carriage. They were quaintly equipped with halberds, presumably stolen last night from the arsenal. The two postilions emerged from their quarters, one with a club, the other with a musket. The looters, surprised, wavered and stopped, the ornamental axes crowning their weapons glinting in the frosty morning sunlight.

Vasily knew that he must close the gates, even if this trapped the two looters inside the yard. Pulling out his pistol, he hurried to release the right-hand gate. Bolting it, he turned to the other, but it swung towards him. There were men hidden behind it! Before he could take aim, they were upon him. His gun spun from his hand as he fell to the floor. He felt a sharp kick in the back.

They dragged him out into the street. The wooden gates slammed shut behind them. They started to march him towards the swarming crowds in Nowy Swiat. Dazed and in pain, he could barely walk. One of his captors took him by the shoulders and, spitting in his face, said in a mix of Polish and Russian something about the Tsar, dogs, hanging and revenge. He then hit him in the stomach, and as he fell to the ground, kicked him again.

When he came to, his hands were bound behind his back and cobbles dug into his spine. He could smell horse dung. His eyes absorbed a blurred patchwork of different blues – the sky and other blues, darker, softer, shifting chaotically above him. Heavy boots clattered close to his head. Someone bawled out a command. As arms lifted him up from the road, he could taste blood and feel a crushing pain in his side. He started to fall away once again…

CHAPTER ELEVEN

Vasily opened his eyes and immediately closed them. His head seemed to be bound by a band of steel. He risked opening his eyes once more. Above his head, lines of white mortar wavered between red bricks. A shaft of light fell across his body from above. It was impossible to ignore the unmistakable prison stench. He tried to sit up and pain ran through his back and into his guts. Nauseous, he lay back with a groan, shivering with cold.

He closed his eyes once again and relived the scene in the stable yard. How could the coachman have been so careless with the gates? And how could he himself have been so rash? He wondered what had happened to Yakov, and indeed to Anna and the other occupants of the house. Had he saved them or put them at risk?

He heard a noise. A grille in the door was sliding open. He was being observed. Muffled voices – adults in conversation, children's cries – floated in from outside. They seemed to be speaking in Russian. He could make no sense of it.

Later he heard the jingle of keys and the scrape of

bolts. A man entered wearing a heavy black cloak and carrying a bag. 'So you're awake... good. I am a doctor. I need to take a look at your head,' he said in rapid French. He threw his cloak aside and swiftly peeled off the band of steel, which proved to be a bandage. He grunted and, setting it aside, briefly examined Vasily's bruises. Then, grunting again, he said, 'There's nothing much to do but wait. There may be internal damage. Who knows? Time might tell. I'll give you a sleeping draught.'

'Where am I?' Vasily asked him.

'In the castle prison,' the doctor replied. 'But I'm sorry, I am not at liberty to say more...'

'I'm very cold.'

Another grunt. The doctor walked to the door and called out for a blanket. He then turned to his bag and started to prepare a draught. Vasily thanked him.

'Don't thank me, Russian,' he said with a scowl. 'My job's just to make you fit to hang...'

Vasily started to struggle up, attempting to protest. The doctor caught his shoulder and pushed him back. 'Don't worry, you'll probably get a chance to explain yourself. Here, drink this, and then try to rest.' Clearly unwilling to linger, he thrust a vial into Vasily's hand, threw the musty blanket over him, and picked up his cloak as he left.

※

Wednesday 19th November

The following morning, Vasily woke to find food and water by his bed. He felt drowsy; the draught had been powerful. He soon fell asleep once more, and was woken by the sound of his cell being unlocked. Two Polish soldiers stood over him. 'You must come with us to see the major,' one said.

They hauled him to his feet. He swayed, trying to find some sort of balance. They supported him out of the cell and up shallow steps into an empty courtyard. His body ached but his legs seemed to work well enough. A gate led through to a smaller court, where they halted for a moment while he caught his breath. He looked up and staggered backwards. A roughly crafted gallows stood in their path. Four thick ropes hung from the cross beam, their ends freshly severed, swaying as if their dismal burden had just been cut down. Perhaps they were indeed going to hang him!

One of the soldiers laughed at his obvious fear and walked him on, past the gallows and through a door into a long corridor. At last he found himself in a small chamber, confronting a middle-aged Polish officer. This must be the major. The officer rose from his desk and, dismissing the guard, motioned Vasily towards a chair opposite him. Vasily, wincing, sat down.

The tall soldier, speaking excellent French, asked him a series of predictable questions. Who was he? What was his business in Poland? Why was he not wearing uniform? Where were his papers? What was this personal business he said he needed to complete? The major's manner was relaxed, almost friendly. Perhaps it was aimed at lowering his guard, but in any event, Vasily had no reason to lie. As he gave his replies, his inquisitor jotted down a few notes.

'You can easily verify my story,' Vasily said. 'My

arrival should have been noted at the customs post, and of course at the Ministry.'

The officer shrugged. 'Well, of course, if you are a spy, Russian, you would hardly come to Warsaw without some sort of cover,' he said. 'The city is in chaos and there's no way to check anything. My duty is simply to record your details. As to whether your story is believed... well, you will have to rely on your luck and honest face.'

'I've no way of proving who I am,' Vasily said. 'But I have no quarrel with the Polish people – far from it. I was sent here to offer help.' He wondered if he should say more, express some sympathy for the Polish cause, but although that sentiment would have been genuine, to express it here seemed inappropriate. Instead, when the major did not respond, he asked, 'But can you tell me if Madame Zadachina and her children are safe?'

'I've no idea. The situation is what one might call "fluid". Russian civilians who didn't manage to escape with the Grand Duke are being arrested and brought in. They won't be ill-treated.'

'And how did I get here?'

'You were extracted from your difficult position by a citizens' patrol in Nowy Swiat and brought in by my troops for your own safety. How safe you will turn out to be under the circumstances, I don't know. Much will depend on whether an agreement is reached between the Russian Grand Duke and the Polish Administrative Council. If that happens, you could well be released, unless someone decides that you *are* a spy, of course. If no truce is concluded, at best you could be here for a long time... at worst, who knows?'

Vasily looked down at the desk, frowned and rubbed his sore brow.

'If it's any comfort to you,' the Pole continued, 'most of those executed thus far have been Polish, officers and gentry who proved unwilling to join the rebels on the night of the revolt. The Grand Duke has every incentive to come to terms. The Council has recalled the Polish army stationed outside the capital. Whatever some senior officers might say, the majority of the troops will support the revolution, and when they get here, you Russians will be outnumbered by almost four to one.'

The major rose to his feet and shouted for the guard. He said, 'I'm afraid I'm now going to have to confine you in less comfortable accommodation. I'm likely to have more prisoners to house, uncooperative Poles as well as Russians. Because of your uncertain status I can't allow you to mix with the rest.'

They took Vasily to a small austere cell in an ancient tower, part of the original fortifications of the castle. The light outside was fading. Only the drip of water seeping down a wall onto the stone flags broke the silence. Vasily sat on the thin pallet and pulled his blanket closer about him. His whole body ached and he was uneasy. The major had tried to reassure him, but could an accord be reached between the Grand Duke and the Poles? He sighed. This morning, had fate not intervened, he should have met Count Angelov at the Belvedere Palace. The captain had said Angelov had not been at the palace on the night of the attack, but would he be able to find him again? Just now, he didn't much care; resolving a dispute about rights to wealth and privilege seemed meaningless.

A jailer brought food, a candle and another blanket, which he said came with the compliments of the major. Vasily stretched. He felt very weary. Despite his pain, he believed he might sleep again. Moisture continued to drip intermittently down the algae-streaked wall, the chill air smelt stale, but the tall flame of the tallow candle gave out a dim glow. In the shadows he conjured up the face of Irina. Five years ago, she had sacrificed her own happiness to keep him out of a prison like this. He felt guilty, and his heart ached for her. Then he recalled how his friend, Mikhail, had survived in a cell for over a year and, alone, had faced interrogation and possible death. The thought gave him courage. But it would be a strange irony if now, four years later, he came to share a similar fate, not as the liberal revolutionary he had been, but as a reluctant representative of autocracy.

※

Friday 21st November

He heard the city clocks strike four in the morning. After more than twenty-four hours in his cell, his drowsiness had become persistent wakefulness. He stared into the gloom, tracking the progress of a moonbeam that crept along the wall. Yesterday evening he had thought that he had heard the sound of distant voices, the clack of passing feet, but now only the occasional hollow drip of water disturbed the thick, almost tangible silence.

The clocks struck the half-hour, and then the hour. Dawn would not break until almost seven. Somewhere outside he heard a shout and the rumble of wheels. His body tensed. The sound of boots rang out in the corridor. The bolts of his door rasped open. When two guards entered, he struggled stiff-limbed from his bed and grabbed the blanket. He clung to it as they led him, shuffling and unbalanced, from the cell.

Out in the yard a huddle of prisoners was gathered in the moonlight, surrounded by soldiers. He was led in amongst them. An open cart stood close to the gates, the horses shifting their feet on the cobbles, the chink of their trappings jingling with incongruous cheer around the walls.

The major appeared as if from nowhere, accompanied by two junior officers. One carried a lantern. 'Good,' the major said, peering at a list in his hand. 'You all seem to be here. Shine the light, lieutenant!'

The lantern lit the face of each prisoner in turn. When identified, the first man selected was marched to a far corner. He had the bearing of a soldier but wore civilian clothes. The lieutenant next questioned two youths, gypsies with tangled hair. One started to argue, but the major shook his head and they, too, were quickly marched away. Next it was the turn of an elderly man who, trembling with fear or cold, seemed to be wearing formal court dress from the end of the last century. The major waved him towards the waiting wagon. He was soon followed by two further men, but then a character with a long moustache, who looked like a Cossack, was sent to join the gypsies. Vasily alone remained. He eyed the wagon. It seemed to promise some prospect of escape and was surely the option to be preferred.

'That one's for the road,' said the major. Vasily sighed with relief, but it seemed that the officer was not speaking of him and was indicating a rolled bundle that lay on the ground. Two troopers picked it up and, staggering, tipped it into the wagon. It fell onto the wooden planks with a crash. Vasily guessed it was a body. A knot of fear felt tight in his chest as the major finally approached him. He tried to maintain an impression of calm.

'Well, Count, it seems that you are destined to leave us,' the major said. 'The order only came in an hour ago… most of your compatriots have already joined the Grand Duke. I'm sorry to mix you up with all this riff-raff, but we can't afford any mistakes.'

Vasily, his tension melting away, felt slightly faint. He nodded towards the remaining prisoners. 'What will happen to them?'

The major shrugged. 'Playthings of fate… like the rest of us,' he said. 'You'd better get on board, sir.' He paused for a moment. 'I hope we may meet in better times. Good luck.' He spun away and disappeared into the shadows.

Vasily heaved himself painfully into the cart, clutching his blanket like a talisman. The vehicle rumbled out through the castle gates, accompanied by a small troop of horses. A breeze stirred the early morning air; he sensed the sweet breath of freedom.

※

In a little over an hour, the wagon was approaching the village of Mokotów, where the Grand Duke had been living for four days, surrounded by his troops. The dawn was breaking. Sometimes from afar, sometimes close at hand, Vasily could hear the silver call of a bugle. On each side of the track, hundreds, perhaps thousands, of soldiers were hunched on the open ground under blankets or bulky greatcoats, often with no packs on which to rest their heads. Some were huddled together for warmth, others were stretching and getting to their feet, stamping in the frosty morning air. Here and there fires had been lit, and steam was rising from round black cauldrons. A few officers who had risen early from their billets walked among their men, greeting them, talking to their sergeants.

The wagon drew up outside what appeared to be the village inn. Vasily looked around. There was nothing here – no guards, no checkpoint – but two figures were standing some distance away. They appeared to have been waiting, watching the Warsaw Road. Now they were stirring, and one was starting to run towards him. It was his servant, Yakov. He was grinning broadly, carrying a thick cloak over his arm. As Vasily sank into its folds, weak with relief, he breathed in the garment's familiar scent, a consoling mix of camphor and cologne that spoke of civilisation. They embraced; although Yakov was laughing, his cheeks were wet with tears.

Vasily heard a quiet cough behind them. He disentangled himself and turned. Colonel Pavel Kalinin stood contemplating them, arms crossed, his bicorne hat a dark wedge above his pale, impassive face.

'Pavel! My God! What are you doing here?'

'Until a few moments ago, I was waiting for you.'

'But why are you here at all?'

'I'm not here for the sake of my health, Vasya. I'll explain all as we go. There isn't a lot of time. We must all leave here today – this morning, in fact.'

Vasily's spirits fell. He had been hoping for some rest.

Kalinin took them to his quarters in the grounds of the large estate house, where Constantine and his Polish wife were lodged. As Pavel sat drinking tea, Vasily stood in a wooden tub while Yakov poured buckets of hot water over his battered body. To his surprise, he had been reunited with his possessions, and also with Smirnov. Even the tatty old carriage with its two long-suffering drivers appeared to have been allowed to leave the city. Anna and her household were also safe.

'The day after we met in Petersburg, I was asked by Count Nesselrode to travel here to try to assess the state of affairs,' the colonel was explaining. 'Constantine wrote detailed twice-weekly reports from Warsaw to his brother, the Emperor, but Nicholas had a bad habit of leaving his foreign minister completely in the dark when it came to the question of Poland. Both brothers like to promote the notion that all is well here. But Nesselrode was suspicious. He'd received alarming reports from his friend, the Prussian Ambassador, and they proved to be accurate. I'd only just arrived when rumours of an incipient uprising arose. Intelligence sources mistook the date, however…'

'Yes, that was the day we arrived in town,' said Vasily. 'I wish I'd known you were here.'

'I'm not sure I could have been of much help to you. The actual revolt took place so soon after the false alarm…'

Yakov was now handing Vasily a towel. Pavel studied his bruises. 'I say, Vasily, you're a bit beaten up.'

'I'm better than I was. Go on...'

'I've been staying with my old friend, Fanshawe – George Fanshawe. He's served in the Russian army for years. I'd introduce you to him but he's pretty cut up at present. His younger brother Frederick was killed during the attack on the palace... I fear you may have brought his body with you in the wagon. Better fellow you couldn't hope to meet... a great pity.'

'Yes, we did have a corpse on board, I think.'

'Apparently the insurgents were going to spare him, but he stupidly offered them snuff from a box with the head of Constantine painted on it. One of the villains took offence and ran him through.'

'My God! What bad luck!'

'Yes, I never fail to be surprised by the vagaries of fate.' Kalinin paused briefly and then continued, 'When we heard that the bunt had started, we did as instructed and drove straight to the Belvedere. Later we continued on here with the Duke's train and the loyal troops. Since then I've been party to the negotiations. I think we've done well under the circumstances. Having failed to act decisively when he could, Constantine's position isn't strong, but we've reached a reasonable agreement. He's got a safe conduct out of Poland for himself and his men, but he must leave at once. He's had to promise to intercede for the Poles with his brother, the Emperor, and has pledged not to re-enter the country with troops from Lithuania. The Polish regiments that remained loyal are obliged to return to Warsaw today. I'm not sure I'd want to be in their shoes when they get there.'

'A Polish officer at the castle told me that some Poles who were unwilling to join the revolt were executed.'

'Well, execution is possibly a polite way of putting it. Certainly, on the first night there were reports that Poles, both officers and civilians, who refused to take up arms were lynched or hacked down by the mob where they stood.'

'And the Russian civilians?'

'Some fled with the Duke; a few were killed by the mob. Others were confined to their homes, and those who the Poles believed harmless were given safe passage. Most were released yesterday afternoon, and were permitted to use their carriages and take what possessions they could with them. We've had to leave a couple of senior officers behind, effectively as hostages, and a handful of people who the Poles were convinced were spies.' Pavel drew out a snuff box and took a pinch.

Yakov, having taken back the towel, ran his finger over Vasily's bruised face and frowned. He then dropped a clean shirt over his head. The touch of fresh linen was cool on Vasily's skin. 'Thank you, Yakov. It's very good to see you.' Vasily gripped his servant's arm with affection.

'I'll fetch the razor, Vasily Nikolayevich, sir. You could certainly do with a shave.' As Yakov stepped from the room humming to himself, Pavel frowned. Vasily knew that the colonel thought him too familiar with his servant. Well, he would just have to tolerate it. Although lazy at times, Yakov had rarely let him down.

'I was concerned,' Pavel said. 'No-one seemed to know what had happened to you. Then yesterday your name appeared on the list of Russian detainees. I assumed you would be among those released. Yakov and Smirnov took it in turns to look out for you all afternoon, and into the evening, but when you didn't arrive, I had to call in one or two favours.'

'I had no way of proving who I was.'

'No, so I gather. Anyway, I managed to convince the Poles of your blameless republican convictions.' Pavel smiled and took more snuff. 'I really wish I'd tried harder to persuade you not to come. I'd like to give your uncle a good kicking…' He sneezed.

'Don't be too hard on him, Pavel. He wouldn't have put me through this deliberately. By the way, on that subject, did Count Angelov make it out of the city?'

Vasily waited anxiously for Pavel's reply. It would be a serious irritation if his recent trials had all been for nothing.

'Yes, he's here. You'll be able to catch up with him during our ignominious retreat to the border. No doubt it will be a slow and uncomfortable business.'

Kalinin rose and drained his tea. 'I'm very pleased to see you back safely,' he said. 'I'll have to spend time with the Grand Duke, but we'll meet on the road, no doubt. Don't forget to insist on a decent billet enroute. As a representative of the Ministry, you're entitled to proper treatment.'

'Thank you for getting me out of this mess, Pavel Pavlovich.' Once more he was in the colonel's debt.

'Ah, my life wouldn't have been worth living if I'd left you behind, Vasya. Margarethe, and of course Irina, would never have forgiven me.'

CHAPTER TWELVE

30th November 1830 – Lubartów, Poland

Count Angelov had sent his well-sprung carriage. As it swayed along the highway, Vasily's head drooped but he jerked himself awake. There was no time to sleep. It was not far from his billet to the fine palace where the Grand Duke's suite was staying overnight, and where he finally hoped to meet the count.

It was the ninth day of Grand Duke Constantine's retreat from Warsaw. As Kalinin had anticipated, progress had been slow and cruel. In rain and sleet, the column struggled to travel twenty versts a day. In addition to the Duke's entourage and seven thousand soldiers, the company included fifty wagons and carriages carrying refugees: men and women with their children, servants and dogs. While the Duke's party had gone on ahead, Vasily and Smirnov had worked with army and civilian officers to ensure that civilians were housed and fed every night. But they could not do much to help the common soldiers who, without proper clothing, were dying from disease and starvation along the way.

Now he entered another world. The brightly lit anteroom on the first floor was warm. A vivid Turkey carpet covered the floor and gold leaf glinted from the plaster mouldings. Two fine views of Warsaw graced the walls, and a clock ticked loudly on the mantlepiece. There was no sign of Angelov. Instead, here was General Zadachin, gleaming in his dark uniform as if at a state reception. Anna stood at his side, regarding Vasily closely as the general explained that Angelov would be along shortly. Vasily could not supress a surge of frustration. Would he never meet the man? He felt uncomfortably shabby. Yakov had done his best with his uniform, sponging it, trying to steam out the creases, but it still hung limply on his body. He had lost weight; his face was still bruised and his hair too long.

'Well done, Count Belkin! Very well done!' Zadachin slapped him on the back. Vasily flinched. Anna noticed his discomfort and frowned. 'You put up a good show! Stopped those ruffians doing any damage. We're very grateful, aren't we, my dear?'

Anna nodded. 'Yes, of course.'

'I suppose that the Poles arrested your family, sir?'

'Yes, but keeping the looters out of the house did mean that we have retained our personal effects, and most importantly, we didn't lose the coach and horses. Many people were left without vehicles, you know.'

Vasily, who had carried a collection of destitute Russians in his own carriage over the past nine days, was well aware of the shortage of transport. 'One thing I don't understand, sir…' he said. 'Why have we taken this cross-country route? It's made the journey much longer.'

'We must avoid Polish troops where possible. Most of their army are on the march to Warsaw. There's a detachment of uhlans not far away in Lublin, so we've had to skirt to the north. They shouldn't attack us – in theory a safe conduct has been granted – but one cannot be sure. And of course, when we do meet the Poles, Constantine Pavlovich finds it painful to receive offhand salutes and open contempt from officers and men whom he regarded as his own; whom he believed loved him, would remain loyal to him.' Zadachin paused, shook his head, and continued, 'But don't despair, Belkin, we are only a hundred versts of so from the border. Three or four more days should find us on the shores of the Bug.'

'What will the Grand Duke do when we reach Russia, General? Will he return to Petersburg?

'No, it's his intention to march up to Brest, and wait on his brother's orders. It's my duty to stay with him. I fear that there will soon be a declaration of war. News of the rising should have reached the capital by now.'

'I thought the Grand Duke had promised not to re-enter Poland with an army.'

The general shrugged. 'I'm not sure the Emperor will set much store by promises made under duress, and in any event, I don't think Constantine will be in command. He regards his career as over. All very sad, but there we are...' The general's lean face flushed, and he paused for a moment. 'My wife and the children will of course travel on to Petersburg,' he continued. 'In fact, Count, I should be obliged if you'd keep an eye out for them. I assume you are returning to the capital?'

'Yes, once we reach the border I shall be making

straight for home. I shall be pleased to be of service to your family, General.'

'Good, excellent. Well, I must go to the Duke. The princess is unwell and he is not, as you might imagine, in the best of spirits. Who's your commanding officer, Belkin? I will commend you to him.'

'I suppose you mean the minister, but sir, I think General Zakrevsky is rather preoccupied with the cholera…'

'Yes, well, I'll do what I can! Well done, Belkin!'

Zadachin looked for a salute, but then, remembering Vasily's occupation, made do with his brief bow. The general marched briskly from the room. As she turned to follow her husband, Anna raised her eyebrows and favoured Vasily with the fleeting hint of a smile.

※

'Ah, Count Belkin, we finally meet! I'm sorry to have been so elusive, but we have all, I think, been rather overtaken by events!'

'We have indeed, sir.'

Count Angelov proved to be an unremarkable man of about sixty. His head, which was completely bald, shone as pink as the polished rose quartz paperweight that sat on the desk between them. He wore civilian clothes, the star of the Order of Saint Ann firmly attached to his black frock coat. He seemed friendly enough, however, and listened to Vasily's story with interest.

'You were a witness at the marriage between Stepan Bogolyubov and Astrella von Stein, I think,' Vasily said.

'I wonder if you could tell me what you can remember about the events surrounding the ceremony?'

'Well, Vasily Nikolayevich, I don't need to tell you that it was many years ago – twenty-five or more. But I can remember something of it. It was the year that my father died. In fact, that was why I was in St Petersburg. The war was on. I should have been with my regiment, of course, but I had been granted leave of absence due to my father's illness. Stepan Bogolyubov had also taken leave, I suppose in order to marry.'

'Were you in the same regiment; is that how you met?'

'Oh no, we went back further than that. We knew one another as boys. Our family estates were near Torzhok, not that distant from one another. We went fishing and hunting together, held card parties and the like. It was quite by chance that I ran across him in Petersburg. I went down to the English Club one evening. I remember it particularly because I was feeling rather guilty. I shouldn't have been at the club at all, of course, but I was finding the atmosphere at home oppressive and needed to get out. I remember looking into the card room and seeing him there. I drew the line at gaming when my father was on his death bed, of course, and went to take a glass in the saloon. A little later he came looking for me. I remember him coming towards me, holding out his hand. He was a very fine, handsome man, and he seemed to glow with health and life... I can see him now!' Angelov drew out a kerchief and blew his nose, clearly affected by the memory. '"Angelov!" he said. "You're just the man I need! I'm getting married the day after tomorrow and I'm looking for a witness." They married at that church just over St Isaac's Bridge, on the island, you know…'

'Yes, I looked at the register there. All seemed to have been done correctly, although the record was indistinct.'

'I remember that it all went on for quite a long time. There was an excess of singing and the bride wept a good deal. Stepan Dmitryevich seemed embarrassed by it. He shifted about from foot to foot, but he was never a patient man. Afterwards we went to drink champagne at the Hotel de France and then he swept her off. It was the last I saw of either of them. But there's no doubt you know, Belkin – a marriage certainly took place.'

Vasily looked down at the shining desktop. So there was a living witness to the marriage. The prince's case seemed even more unpromising. 'I know that the other witnesses are dead, sir, but can you think of anyone else who was there?'

'I don't recall anyone. Despite all the ceremony, there were no people of note there. Just a few servants; she had a maid, I seem to remember, and he had a lackey, or possibly his orderly, with him. There were the usual gawpers I expect but I can't remember now.'

'Did you just meet Astrella once?'

'No, we dined together the evening before the wedding, at a restaurant, I seem to recall. She was a lovely girl, but very young, I do remember that. Stepan seemed devoted to her – well, as devoted as he was ever likely to be…'

'Did she go straight home to Estonia after Bogolyubov had gone back to join his regiment?'

'I think they intended that she leave town and go to live on his own estates near Torzhok when he returned to the army. She certainly didn't want to go home to Estonia. I got the impression that Stepan and her father hadn't rubbed along well. There seemed to have been some unpleasantness. But anyway, it would be natural that he wanted her to live at his own home. I couldn't see either of them enjoying life in the Estonian wilderness for long. I seem to recall my sister, who still lives nearby, speaking of her arrival.'

Vasily frowned. This didn't add up. He had assumed that Andrey Andreyevich had been born in Estonia and that Astrella had lived there permanently – apart from, presumably, the short period that she and Bogolyubov had spent in St Petersburg. Perhaps he was mistaken. Now was the time to show Angelov the picture of Astrella. He groped for his satchel.

'I have a portrait of Astrella, Andrey Andreyevich's mother. It was given to me by her brother, Friedrich, when I visited him in October. May I show it to you?'

'Oh yes, yes indeed! You have been very thorough, Count...' Angelov looked at the picture. He drew out a pince-nez and, moving the lamp on the desk towards him, examined it again. He shook his head. 'No... I don't think so.'

'You don't think what?'

'No, that's not her.'

'Not her?' The room seemed to shift.

'No, it's nothing like her. The Astrella he married was quite different; dark, well appointed...' Angelov cupped his hand over his breast. 'Very well appointed...'

'Are you sure?'

'I admit that it was a long time ago, but I assure you she was nothing like this scrap of a blonde... I doubt if Stepan would have been much attracted to this… Although I have to say she looks more German. I remember being surprised that the Astrella I met came from the frozen north.'

'That's very odd. Friedrich is unlikely to make a mistake about his own sister.'

Angelov paused for a moment. 'Well, yes, I suppose you're right. it seems that all indeed may not have been as it seemed. There may well have been two women in the case, which – given Stepan's rather reckless attitude to life in general, and the fair sex in particular – I wouldn't find entirely surprising.'

'And you'd be prepared to swear that this wasn't the woman whose marriage you witnessed?'

'With the normal caveats about it being a long time ago, of course. I was fond of Stepan Dmitryevich, but he's long dead, and has no reputation to spoil. But, you know, I hardly think my distant memories alone will be sufficient to see off Baron von Klein Sternberg. You will have to find out more, pursue things further. My sister may be able to help you.'

Vasily rubbed his head. Could it be true that another woman had married Bogolyubov within weeks of his marriage to Astrella von Klein Sternberg? And would it be possible to prove that after all this time? He had hoped that this meeting might conclude the matter, but it seemed it was not to be.

CHAPTER THIRTEEN

December 1830 – The Military Settlement of the King of Prussia's Regiment, near Novgorod

It was dusk when the message arrived. A cantonist, coming to rigid attention, held out the paper. 'A dispatch for you, sir.' The lad looked neat enough; his uniform was brushed, his shoes clean, but his hand was shaking and, as Andrey inspected him, his eyes flickered away, not meeting his gaze.

'Thank you, soldier,' he said. 'Very good. Dismissed.'

Visibly relieved, the cantonist clicked his heels and turned. Andrey watched him march swiftly back towards the settlement office. It seemed that even the simple task of delivering a message to an officer filled these child soldiers with terror. Had the boy expected a reprimand, or worse? The atmosphere of random brutality in which the children lived was unlikely to make good soldiers of them.

He walked away from the drill field towards his quarters, skirting the rows of grey huts that stretched almost a verst in both directions. It was bitterly cold and the paths and tracks were deserted. As he passed one of the communal wells, a bucket was rolling on its side, rattling in the wind. If it wasn't retrieved, the woman who had lost it would suffer tomorrow. He picked it up and stood it firmly against the low circular wall. A dank odour rose from the well. He resisted the temptation to pick up a stone and drop it into the depths.

He reached the square wooden house that he shared with three other junior officers. Lamplight glowed in the windows. As he walked up the steps, he heard a burst of laughter and the clink of glasses. His comrades must be entertaining. He pushed the door open.

'Oh! It's the German bogatyr! Have a drink, Sternberg,' one of the officers lurched from his chair and reached for a flask of vodka.

'Thank you, but I have a report to write, and…'

The men groaned in unison. 'Always so busy. Why work so hard?'

'It's because he's a German. They're always on the make…'

'Well! We all know about his prospects!'

'We must take him to town again. Find him his princess!'

The men laughed. They were clearly very drunk. A glass fell to the floor, and shattered. He must make his escape. They were not bad fellows, their ribbing wasn't really malicious, but he wouldn't spend the evening drinking. Apart from wishing to avoid a hangover, he had work to do and wanted to read his message in private. As soon as Morozov had taken his greatcoat and cap and pulled off his boots, he took hot water for tea from the samovar and retreated. Behind him he could hear hoots of derision and further explosions of glass.

He sat down at his desk and broke open the seal.

Semenyovsky Barracks, St Petersburg
28th November 1830

Andrey Andreyevich,

I did not think to be writing to you so soon, but I must ask you to prepare to return to St Petersburg. The King of Prussia's Regiment, excluding the troops attached to the military settlement, is to be put on a war footing imminently, and our company will march to meet it en route to the west. As I anticipated, the colonel has agreed that it would be appropriate for you to re-join us. I hope that this news will be welcome to you. A formal request to your commanding officer will follow tomorrow.

Rosovsky

Andrey breathed deeply. The vague ache of anxiety and dissatisfaction, which had troubled him since his arrival here, dissipated. In some ways, life in Novgorod had been better than expected. His accommodation and food were acceptable and the regiment had even created a reading room and library. But he had had little time to enjoy them. Perhaps because he had been marked out as a troublemaker, the major had seemed determined to keep him busy. In October, the harvest over, the farmer soldiers and the regular troops had worked on construction projects before the onset of winter. On most days Andrey had been ordered to go out to make sure that there was no slacking. At the end of the month, regular drills, inspections and parades had resumed and he had spent three days a week on the drill field with both the regular troops and the settlers. On other days he was occupied, either with the military education of the young cantonists, the children of the farmers, or with tedious paperwork.

Although he was happy to be busy, his hard work thus far had received little recognition. The atmosphere here was dispiriting. Discipline was strict, some might say brutal, both on and off the parade ground. Tyranny extended to the farmer-soldiers' wives, who were expected to work in the fields while producing as many children as possible. Beatings and punishment rituals, which seemed to him unnecessary, occurred so regularly that he feared that in time he might become indifferent, inured to cruelty. This depressed him deeply, and he knew that if he were forced to stay here for long with no hope of escape, for the sake of his own sanity, he must seek a discharge from the army and, despite the obstacles, try to find occupation elsewhere.

The issue of the Bogolyubov legacy was no nearer resolution. The appeal court had declared the validity of his parents' marriage, but Rodionov had written that the old prince still refused to meet him, or concede that he had any rights. There was little that could be done. Only when the prince died could he move to make his claim on the estate. He could try to force the prince's hand in the meantime by using his title, Count Bogolyubov, but that seemed presumptuous; he had neither the resources nor confidence to do the rank justice. But today's summons from Rosovsky meant he could set these problems aside. There might be a real campaign! It was what he had been trained for, and regardless of the legacy, it must be the way to get his career back on track.

He shouted for his orderly. 'I've news for you, Morozov. We're off to war!'

The young man took a step back. His face flushed and he swallowed. 'War, sir? Where? When?'

'I'm not sure. I just know that we're going back to Petersburg to rejoin Rosovsky's company. You'll need to get our things together; the order will come in the next few days.'

'Oh!' Morozov was clearly terrified by the prospect.

'Don't worry, lad, we'll all be in it together. We'll make our fortunes, you see if we don't!'

This, it seemed, didn't much encourage Morozov. A broad-shouldered, sweet-faced young man with hair like ripened wheat, he had been drafted from his village during one of the annual levies two or three years ago. His family had been unable to pay a bribe or quittance and so, despite the tears of his mother and pleas of his father, he had been marched away to the army for twenty-five years.

Andrey watched him slope away, his cheeks pink, his shoulders hunched, and felt for his misery. Morozov was a good orderly, cheerful, hard-working and discreet. But how would the young man cope with the rigours of a winter campaign? Indeed, how would he himself perform? He'd heard there was trouble in Belgium; perhaps that was where they were heading. He read Rosovsky's letter again, then set it aside and looked through the window across the silent parade ground. There was no light to be seen. Almost anywhere must be more enlivening than here.

CHAPTER FOURTEEN

12th December 1830 — St Petersburg

Nadezhda shivered. Despite her fur-lined cloak and thick stockings, it was cold on the edge of the Field of Mars. When she had stood here shortly after her arrival, the leaves on the trees that edged the vast parade ground had been just turning brown. Now their naked branches seemed to scrape the low December sky. Mist from the river smudged the outlines of palaces and townhouses on the perimeter and crept up the columns fronting the barracks of the Pavlovsky Guards. In the centre of the field, under an awning, churchmen had gathered ready to bless the troops. Ranks of infantrymen stood erect, unmoving on the field. The harsh echo of commands and the sounding of bugles vibrated in the chill air. Horses' hooves clattered as officers cantered backwards and forwards, seeming to vie with one another to produce the most stylish impression.

When the exhausted messenger, who had galloped all the way from the Prussian Embassy in Warsaw, had arrived in St Petersburg, the Emperor had met the news of the uprising with equanimity. His calm resolve was not shared by Count Nesselrode, the Foreign Minister, and his colleagues on the Council, who had been horrified, if not totally surprised, by the news. All was now on a war footing, and a series of parades aimed at raising the spirits of the people and the troops had been ordered.

None of the family had really wanted to come, but Prince Polunin had insisted. The rising in Poland was no small matter, and it was important to demonstrate loyalty at this difficult time. They stood together, surrounded by senators and members of the court. The Emperor had not yet arrived. 'I wonder how long we must wait,' Nadezhda's mother murmured to her. Her breath clouded the frigid air.

Mama looked pinched with cold, but was a picture of health compared with Katya, whose face was pale, her eyes under-smudged with shadows. She was worried about the fate of her brother, Vasily. Although most of the Russians had now managed to leave Poland safely, nothing had been heard of him for some weeks. Alexander Petrovich was also in the crowd, his face gaunt and strained, his nose even more prominent than usual. He wandered from group to group, engaging people in conversation. Perhaps he was seeking news of his nephew.

But now the Emperor was arriving with his suite. All finely mounted, they were followed by the carriage of the Empress and her ladies. The imperial coach was deeply padded within, its top edged with carved gilded oak leaves, the box swathed with pale blue hammer cloths, decorated with gold tassels and fringes. The crowd clapped and cheered; the women in the carriage waved graciously; the Tsar gave a signal. The parade got underway.

Marching, salutes and inspection followed. Troops of cavalry pivoted and span, their horses' tails flicking, their harnesses jingling. Nadezhda did not really understand what was happening, but the spectacle warmed her blood. The wheeling strict manoeuvres of the troops, carefully choreographed, in perfect harmony, seemed faultless to her untrained eyes.

'You won't see better drilled soldiers anywhere, although I'm not sure if any of it has much to do with fighting a war,' she heard Prince Polunin comment dryly to one of his fellow senators. 'Many of them will be off within the week. Then we'll see what they're really made of.'

It was then that she noticed Andrey Andreyevich. This was unexpected! He must have been recalled from Novgorod. He marched with another officer, behind Vasily Nikolayevich's friend, the captain. The King of Prussia's Grenadiers wore pristine green uniforms with dazzling white crossbands. The major on horseback, who rode with the column, doffed his hat as he passed the Emperor and then wheeled aside as his troops marched past. Andrey saluted, turned crisply and marched to the rear. Nadezhda's heart beat faster. She felt slightly sick. Supposing something went wrong, if he or his soldiers should make a mistake? Yevgeny had told her terrible tales about the retribution that followed mishaps on parade. Andrey might find himself in more trouble, in the guardhouse again. But all seemed well. Second Lieutenant von Klein Sternberg appeared entirely serene, in step and at one with his men. Her eyes refused to leave him. His tall frame was erect, the badge on his shako gleaming. A low moan escaped her lips. How arresting, how noble, how truly beautiful he looked. If only they could meet before he left for Poland.

Her mother turned to her. 'Are you alright, Nadya?'

'Oh yes, Mama. It is cold, isn't it?' Despite the chill, her cheeks were hot.

'It will be over soon and then we can go home, thank goodness. Oh look. Isn't that young Matvey?' Matvey was indeed pushing his way through the crowd. He was looking for someone. His unruly dark curls tumbled out from under his soft cap, touching the fur collar of his greatcoat.

'He needs a haircut,' said Antonina. 'He'll catch it when his master gets back.'

'He's not his master anymore, Mama.'

'No, well, you know what I mean…'

They watched as the youth bowed briefly to Alexander Petrovich, and gave him a letter. Alexander studied it carefully and frowned. Stepping aside, he ripped the letter open. He then grimaced in his odd way, which Nadezhda recognised as a smile; the contents had clearly pleased him. Alexander looked about him and spoke briefly to Matvey, then, on seeing Katya and Polunin, made his way to their enclosure.

'What is it, Uncle? Is it from Vasya?' asked Katya.

'It's a note from Pavel Kalinin, sent with the diplomatic mail from Brest. That man seems to get everywhere. Anyway, it's good news. He has seen Vasily and he is on his way home,'

'Oh, thank goodness!' Katya looked around for her mother to pass on the news, but then paused. The Emperor was leaving. They heard his astonishingly resonant voice echoing across the field. 'Farewell, my children!'

'Long life to you!' the ranks of troops on the field cried out in response.

The parade was at an end and the order to dismiss was given. Once their men had marched off, a number of the officers came to the edge of the parade ground, seeking acquaintance and family in the crowd. Ivan Stenovsky had thrown the reins of his mount to a colleague and was striding, as ever a little too large for his white uniform, towards them. He engaged Prince Polunin in conversation.

'Ah!' said Alexander. 'There's Rosovsky. I must tell him that Vasily's safe.' The captain received the news with obvious pleasure and then lingered, speaking to Katya and Antonina. It seemed that within the week his company would indeed be leaving the capital to rejoin the regiment on their way to Poland.

Nadezhda looked for Matvey. In recent weeks, in Vasily's absence, he had often come to visit her and Katya. Perhaps because they had first met some years before, she found him amusing and easy company. She knew he had been lonely and would be overjoyed at the news of Vasily's return. Now he was wandering at the edge of the field, straining to see the last departing soldiers. She was trying to catch his attention, when to her horror she overheard her mother speaking to Captain Rosovsky. 'Of course, Kirill Mikhailovich, nothing has been said, but we have every expectation that when this upset in Poland is over, Yevgeny Filipovich will come home and offer for Nadya. That means, of course, that she may spend some time in Italy…'

They were discussing her! How could her mother have been so indiscreet, so tactless? Why did she find it necessary to tell the world all her business? To boast and gossip was in her nature, of course, but to tell Rosovsky, Andrey's senior officer, the lie that she herself had fabricated about her relationship with Yevgeny… it would only be a matter of time before Andrey himself came to hear it, and then where would that leave her? Any hopes that he might harbour some small affection for her might as well be forgotten. There was really no choice. She must try to put the matter straight.

※

Andrey and Denis Borisov marched their troops the short distance back to the barracks. They parted at the gatehouse and Andrey returned to his rooms. He felt satisfied. The parade had passed without mishap, the men had performed well, and the spectacle and excitement of the event had buoyed his spirits.

He had been surprised and gratified by the warm welcome he had received on his return to St Petersburg. The duel, the spell in the guardhouse and the uneasy weeks spent in Novgorod, if not forgotten, now seemed insignificant. Overcoming an initial sense of diffidence, he had enjoyed taking advantage of the pleasures of the city before it was time to depart.

His fellow officers were in a state of excitement at the prospect of a fight, and preparations for the march to the west were well underway. Rosovsky had ordered him to waste no time in checking out his kit. It seemed that much needed to be renewed or replaced; he must exchange his rapier for a sabre, and acquire a new satchel, white woollen campaign trousers, shirts, foot cloths. If he didn't want to march the whole way to Warsaw with his men, he must also find himself a decent horse. Finance was an issue. He must see Rodionov and borrow more money; there was no choice. But his stipend should increase when they were on active campaign. Rosovsky hoped for a decent uplift. Moreover, if he fought well and received a bonus – and, with luck, promotion – that would defray the cost further.

※

Two days later, Morozov brought two envelopes to Andrey's room. The first was confirmation of a loan sufficient to pay for his new equipment and a solid mount that he hoped would carry him safely to Poland and, God willing, home again. The other was a personal letter. It was unsigned, but he recognised the hand. It seemed Nadezhda had noticed him at the parade and was pleased to see he had returned. But now she urgently needed to speak to him before he left for Poland. She asked him to meet her at the Cathedral of our Lady of Kazan at the time of Vespers tomorrow. She would, she said, be accompanied by her maid.

When she had written to him before the duel, he had been surprised and perplexed. Now he was filled with doubt; surely it wouldn't be wise to meet her. He didn't want to provoke another encounter with Stenovsky, particularly now, on the brink of war. Nor did he want to attract the attention of her cousin, that smug civil servant Belkin, whose aim must be to blacken his name and thwart his expectations. Nonetheless, his need for female company and affection had not left him, and in the bleak landscape of the military settlement, he had found himself cheered and comforted by the memory of the girl's elfin face, her sweet smile, the mixture of impulsiveness and innocence that he imagined in her.

He fingered the edge of the letter. He could be away for some time. If he turned his back on her now, she would likely forget him. But if they met, he might learn her mind and perhaps, as a result, ride away with hope and purpose in his heart. He hoped to return from Poland with his reputation restored, perhaps even enhanced, but if he didn't return, perhaps she might remember him with regret and on occasion pray for his soul. God knew nobody else would.

The Kazan cathedral would be busy at that time. Surely there could be no lasting harm in what might be explained away as a chance encounter. If she was prepared to risk her reputation, of course he should see her again!

※

Clouds of incense hung sweet in the humid air; the robes of priests swished on the marble floor while the choir sang. Those attending the service stood clustered beneath the great arch in the candlelit brightness before the royal gates. Andrey was relieved. The cathedral was a good choice. It would be possible to linger discreetly among the more distant shadows behind the pillars of the nave.

He recognised her at once. Insubstantial, ghostlike in the half-light, she wore a pale fur-lined cloak and bonnet and carried a muff. As he approached, his misgivings returned. Would an idle observer believe that this was really an accidental meeting? Her maid wandered away towards the porch and stood out of earshot but never out of sight. Could she be trusted? Nadezhda must have faith in her discretion.

As they faced one another, she looked down. Breaking the silence, he said, 'I've come as you asked, but I'm not sure how wise it was.' He knew he must sound distant, cold.

She looked up at him sharply. 'Well, you came, Andrey Andreyevich, so it seems that we are both equally unwise.'

He liked her directness, the way she returned his fire. She was right – they were certainly equal fools to be here. She said nothing more but continued to regard him. She was as delicate and lovely as he remembered; he couldn't sustain this chilly distance for long.

'There was something you wanted to say to me?'

She ignored the question. 'When did you return to Petersburg?'

'A week ago.'

'And when do you leave for Poland?'

'Within the week, but it's forbidden to speak of that. We can't stand here too long. Why did you want to meet me?'

'I'm sorry,' she said. 'It's true we don't have much time. The truth is that since the incident at the ball, I've been troubled. I felt so guilty about the danger my family – my sister's brother-in-law – led you into, for no good reason as far as I could tell. At the very least, before you went away, I wanted to express regret, ask your forgiveness and know that it hasn't ruined your future.'

Andrey hesitated. Of course she didn't know the whole story. Stenovsky had had other reasons to fight him, Rosovsky other reasons to deplore his behaviour, but this was neither the time nor place for that sort of honesty.

'I received your letter,' he said finally. 'But it came too late to make any difference.'

'I'm pleased that you received it at least, that you know I didn't want you to fight.'

'But I was obliged to make the challenge, to go through with it,' he said. 'Stenovsky provoked me beyond reason. There's nothing to forgive, and now we're off to war I hope that the incident will be forgotten.'

She looked away from him into the great church. The footsteps of passers-by and the sweet low tones of the choir crept into the silence that deepened between them. She frowned a little, lifting her hand as if to wave these intrusions away. She seemed to be struggling to say more. He knew he must help her. For better or worse, he had decided to come here today; they may never meet again; death may be waiting for him in Poland. He moved closer, feeling a strong impulse to reach out, to stroke the soft wool of her cloak, to wrap her in it closely, feel her warmth and shut out the world.

'I'm not going to lie to you, Nadezhda Gavrilovna.' His throat felt tight and his voice was hoarse. 'I've had plenty of time to think since we last met – too much, in fact.' He looked down. 'And you have been much in my thoughts.'

His words released her tongue. 'I hoped that may be so. I do need to tell you that you may hear rumours; indeed, I think it is possible that you will hear directly from Captain Rosovsky that I am as good as promised to someone...'

'Promised? In marriage?'

'Yes.' She paused. He felt a sour twist of disappointment. This was not what he had expected. She had salved her conscience with an apology, and now, having revealed his feelings, he was to be discarded, dismissed. He really should not have come.

'But the thing is... I'm not in any way committed. I didn't want you to think otherwise.' And now she was telling him of some agreement to feign an attachment, a pact that she had reached with some wealthy hussar. It seemed that this youthful princeling, of whom he had never heard, was himself riding to war, so the subterfuge, she said, could safely continue for now. He, Andrey, must be assured that this was all to the good: her family would not plague her with other suitors while the army was away.

There was a breathing space. Andrey frowned. What should he think of this? Surely her capacity for irresponsible deception should worry and repel him, but somehow it didn't. Despite her assured manner, she was little more than a child.

'I see,' he said.

His gravity seemed to alarm her. 'It's a stupid game and probably very wrong,' she hurried on. 'Yevgeny thinks it a great joke, but then that's his nature. But I could think of nothing else... no other way. I so wanted to give myself some time, in case...' She paused and shook her head. 'You can't understand how difficult it is to be a woman, Andrey Andreyevich, and particularly a woman with expectations. My family, my mother in particular, can't wait to find an eligible man, get a contract signed, have all safely settled. The pressure is absurd, the risk of consenting to a lifetime of unhappiness immense. But I can't be too hard on my parents. Since Lisa went to Chita to marry Mikhail, and gave up all her rights, I am their only heir.'

He had forgotten about the older sister, deep in Siberia, married to a convicted criminal. In truth, he had barely considered Nadezhda's actual circumstances at all. He had thought of her in the abstract: a source of comfort, and certainly an object of desire. Recently he had felt much the same about the prince's elusive legacy. Too much calculation and analysis seemed to destroy the power of possibility, of hope.

'You said you needed space,' he said.

'I had expected that we, you and I, would meet again. That…' She shrugged and looked into his face. Her eyes had filled with tears.

'And you think that I might make you happy? You can't really know that, Nadezhda Gavrilovna. We barely know one another and, as things stand, I have very little to offer you.'

She shook her head a little but said nothing more. It was warm in the church and she started to pull off her muff. Whether by accident or design, she dislodged the gloves that lay folded within it. Gloves and muff fell to the floor and lay in a soft heap on the cold marble slabs. She raised her hand to her mouth. 'Oh! Oh dear!'

He stooped to retrieve the gloves and, smiling into her eyes, toyed with them for a moment. 'One glove is generally considered sufficient encouragement on such occasions, Nadya.' She laughed, more at ease now. He examined the gloves and, on impulse, kissed each in turn. Resisting an overwhelming urge to kiss her too, he tucked one into his breast and returned the other. As he let his hand rest lightly on her arm, he felt her fingers brush his cheek.

Her maid was approaching. There was now much more to say, but clearly no time. Had they reached some kind of understanding? Perhaps. 'I would very much like you to write to me,' he ventured. 'Letters sent to the barracks will generally reach me in time… and if you can tell me where to send to you without embarrassment, I shall reply if I can.'

'I don't think that will be possible; my mother keeps a keen eye on the post.' Her voice was full of regret.

'No, of course not.' He squeezed her arm gently, and then reluctantly stepped back. 'So, until we meet again…'

As he bowed and turned to leave, he heard her say softly, 'God keep you safe, Andrey. I won't forget you.'

Outside the cathedral, he waited beneath the curved colonnade and saw her emerge. A barouche, its hood raised and displaying the Polunin coat of arms, stood waiting by the road. It was driven by a youth in a shaggy coat, his unruly hair flowing freely from beneath his overlarge hat. Nadezhda and her maid climbed in, the driver cracked the whip and the carriage jolted away. He watched it disappear at a scorching pace down Nevsky Prospekt, towards Palace Square.

CHAPTER FIFTEEN

January 1831 – St Petersburg

When, just after Christmas, Vasily finally returned to St Petersburg, he found himself plunged into a family crisis.

They had left Brest Litovsk on the Polish border with a large number of civilians, including Anna and her children. Their progress had been slowed by the terrible roads and also by the volume of soldiers and baggage travelling in the other direction. Every inn and post house had been packed with army officers who were initially unwilling to give up their beds, even to women and children. They had spent some days in Riga, where Kalinin had left them, claiming to have pressing business to pursue in the west. The last stage of the journey from Narva had been enjoyed in the relative comfort of an official carriage. When they had finally reached Saint Petersburg, Vasily gave Smirnov leave of absence until after new year, and then he and Yakov went home, where he slept for twenty-four hours.

Thus it was that he didn't immediately notice that Matvey was missing, and that there was also no sign of

Annika, his dog. When Yakov finally woke him, he went into the boy's room and found the bed stripped and his drawers empty. Concerned, he ran downstairs to find his uncle or the prince.

Alexander was at the Ministry, but he found Dmitry Vladimirovich sitting by his fire in the drawing room. The prince rose and embraced Vasily with his habitual warmth. 'I'm pleased and relieved to see you, Vasya. You must have had quite an adventure!'

'Yes, sir... I've much to tell you. But what has happened to Matvey?'

'Ah yes, Matvey.' The prince frowned at the Turkey carpet.

'Well, where is he? He seems to have vanished and taken all his things. My dog's gone too.'

'I think he is at Maltby's. In fact, I know he is. The thing is, there was some unpleasantness a week or so ago and he took off with the dog, but now you've returned I'm sure he'll come home.'

'Unpleasantness?'

'His part in the business was not so serious, but... Sit down, Vasya, and I'll try to explain. I'm afraid it's that man von Klein again.'

'Von Klein? I thought he'd been sent to Novgorod to drill peasants.'

'They called him back to fight. He's re-joined his company and has marched off west now. But it seems that before he left, the baron had some sort of assignation with young Nadya.'

'With Nadya? What sort of assignation? I thought she was committed to Yevgeny.'

'Oh, I don't know. It seems a bit of storm in a teacup to me, but Katya and Polunin, and of course the girl's mother, seem to think she's behaved very badly. They believe if Uspensky comes to hear of it he'll throw her over, and of course that would never do. Anyway, it seems they met, she and von Klein, at the Kazan Cathedral, before he went away. They were seen by a friend of Katya's, who of course went trotting off to tell your sister straight away. Nadezhda claimed that it was a chance meeting, but that seems rather improbable and no-one believes her. Even if she is telling the truth, she should never have spoken to him. Her maid isn't a proper chaperone.'

'But what did Matvey have to do with it?'

'Apparently he drove her there in Polunin's barouche, dressed up as a coachman. They took the carriage without permission. Nearly smashed it up on the way home too. Your uncle was most distressed.'

'But why has Matvey gone to Maltby's?'

'Prince Polunin was really angry. He can be very stuffy, you know. The maid's already been sent back to Oryol. Nadezhda is confined to her room while guidance is awaited from her father.'

Vasily snorted. He knew Nadya's father well. Not much sense would come from that direction. 'And Matvey?'

The prince hesitated. 'Polunin insisted that he be punished. He wanted to send him to the stables, to be dealt with by the coachman, but Sasha drew the line at that.'

Vasily frowned. The Polunins clearly couldn't forget that Matvey had once been a serf. At least his uncle had saved him from serious humiliation and possible injury. 'So?'

'Alexander brought him home and gave him a thrashing here... a few strokes of the cane, nothing dramatic, but enough to placate Polunin. The next morning, the boy and the dog had gone. We got a note from Maltby within the hour. He said that "Matthew", as he calls him, was very upset and that he'd look after him until you came home. Alexander did go round but Maltby sent him away, politely of course.'

'Oh, really!' Vasily failed to stifle his anger. Over the years, neither he nor the boy's tutor, the Englishman Maltby, had ever laid a finger on Matvey. They had congratulated themselves on turning an illiterate urchin into an educated young gentleman without once resorting to physical punishment, despite what had sometimes been extreme provocation. His uncle was well aware of that.

'I should go round to see Maltby if I were you, Vasya. Bring him home,' the prince said.

Vasily spent a few minutes telling Dmitry about his meeting with Angelov and his doubts about Stepan Bogolyubov's second marriage. Then he followed his advice.

He found Maltby and Matvey at home, happily eating some strange confection called pikelets. A bright fire was burning and a large atlas lay open on the table. When Vasily was announced, Annika yodelled in ecstasy, while Matvey almost smothered him in his embrace. The boy seemed to have grown even taller in the two months he had been away and his voice had become noticeably deeper. If he had been mortified by his treatment at the hands of Alexander, he didn't immediately show it.

Despite the early hour, champagne was opened. The story of Matvey's adventure trickled out. It seemed Nadezhda was Matvey's best friend; he would do anything for her and he was proud to have helped her when the coachman hadn't been available. He didn't want to talk about his treatment at the hands of Alexander and asked Vasily politely not to mention the matter further. He knew nothing, he said, of Nadya and Baron von Klein Sternberg. He had stayed outside the cathedral with the carriage and had not seen them together. As far as the close shave in Nevsky Prospekt was concerned – well, the other driver hadn't looked where he was going...

'But you'll be coming home now, Matvey?' Vasily asked, wondering how much of this story was true.

'Oh yes, of course, sir. But you mustn't leave me alone with Alexander Petrovich again. What he did wasn't right, you know, not now I'm free.'

'That's not entirely so. He's the head of the family, you're a part of his family, and sadly, he has every right...' As he spoke he caught Maltby's eye. The gaunt Englishman gave a slight shake of his head. It was clearly better to let the matter rest. 'Well, never mind,' he said. 'But Matvey, I can't really blame my uncle. Your actions were, to say the least, questionable.'

'I'll come home tomorrow, sir, if that's alright with you. We are looking at some maps later, and Mr Maltby has ordered fish and sweet pastries for dinner.'

In the end Vasily stayed for dinner too. He showed them where he had travelled on the map, and described his adventures. When they had heard the whole story, Maltby opened another bottle of champagne.

Snow had started to fall when Vasily, somewhat unsteadily, finally walked home. Annika cavorted behind him, snout in the air, teeth snapping, trying to catch the soft flakes. He stood for a moment, warming his hands at a watchman's brazier. As the logs sparked and flickered, he stared into the glow, wondering why and how von Klein had contrived to meet Nadya. What had he been up to? Perhaps he had indeed been stalking the girl, as Katya had suggested. Surely Nadya didn't actually like the German, hadn't encouraged him? No, she barely knew him, and she had been told he was a wastrel – although, if he were honest, he was probably no more a wastrel than Yevgeny. Perhaps von Klein had been deliberately seeking to provoke the family, to force them to notice him. They had, after all, resolutely refused to engage with him up to now. Anyway, there was little to be done, and if the lieutenant didn't survive the fighting in Poland, his claim would not matter in any event.

※

Alexander came to find Vasily the following morning as he was pulling on his heavy coat, intending to drive to the Ministry. They embraced warmly, and then, before Vasily could speak, Alexander stood back and raised his hand. 'I know, I know, you're going to tell me I shouldn't have done it – and indeed, had you been here, I would have expected you to deal with the boy. But he behaved very badly, you know, and both Polunin and I thought that he couldn't be allowed to get away with it. I've grown very fond of Matvey and I'm sorry that I was obliged to punish him. I doubt it did him much harm, but he seems to have taken it badly.'

Vasily remained silent for a moment. He didn't want to argue with his uncle, not today. Indeed, there was little point. His opinions and habits had been formed too long ago. 'I expect he'll survive, sir. I'll talk to him if he raises the matter, otherwise I think it's best forgotten. He's coming home later this morning.'

'That's good. Tell him he mustn't take it personally!'

Vasily frowned. In what other way could one take a beating? But Alexander was hurrying on.

'But why are you in uniform? You don't need to go to the Ministry. I suppose you've written a report on your meetings?'

'There isn't much to write. Smirnov sent the Riga reports back at once. In Warsaw there was only one meeting, which wasn't very fruitful. The revolt started that same day, and that of course was the end of discussions. If you've time, Uncle, we'll have some tea and I'll tell you the whole story.'

As he recounted his experiences, he watched Alexander's face change from an expression of lively interest to concern. He clearly realised that he should have thought twice before sending him to Poland. When he had finished, Alexander blew his nose ostentatiously and sent for tea.

'I understand from Dmitry that there's reason to hope that the Petersburg marriage might have not been what it seemed,' he said.

'It's hard to know what to think, but Angelov was adamant that the bride, who called herself Astrella, wasn't the Astrella in the portrait I'd been given by Friedrich von Klein Sternberg. But it was all a long time ago. Further enquiries need to be made. The count thinks his sister in Torzhok may be able to help. I'll go to see her shortly. I think that the cholera has abated in the Moscow area?'

'Yes, we removed the cordon sanitaire a month ago. But Vasily, I don't think you need hurry to pursue this. You look as though you need to rest and put on some weight. Even if, as predicted, the campaign is a short one, von Klein will be away for a while, I expect. By the way, did Kalinin come back with you to Petersburg?'

'No, he left us at the Polish border. When his work with the Grand Duke is finished, I think he may be bound for Austria.' Vasily shifted uneasily in his chair. On the journey, the astute colonel must have noticed his growing closeness to Anna, although he had made no comment. Of course, he and Irina had parted, but he hoped that her brother would not mention the matter to her.

'You brought Zadachin's family back?' Alexander seemed to have read his thoughts. 'The general has written a fulsome report about you to Zakrevsky, I understand. You'll certainly get some award from the Emperor for services rendered... even a promotion. Yes! You'll be catching me up soon, Vasya. And Benkendorf still wants you to join the Third Section.'

Vasily contemplated his teacup. He knew he must resign himself to remaining in the capital for a few months. But he didn't want to become a secret policeman, and flaunting some medal on his breast would provoke ribaldry from his military acquaintance. He yearned to escape, to return to the country and settle down in Dubovnoye as a private citizen, and in time perhaps find a wife. He hoped that someone had thought to bring the cows into the barn for the winter.

But now he could hear voices and laughter, and footsteps in the hall. Matvey must have come home.

CHAPTER SIXTEEN

January 1831 – St Petersburg

A week after New Year, Russia's declaration of war against Poland seemed inevitable. Envoys from Warsaw, hoping to engineer a peaceful compromise, had been sent back to Poland by the Russian Emperor with an uncompromising message to their leaders. It seemed certain that Nicholas would soon be deposed as King of Poland. The army was on a war footing, some were already in adjacent Lithuania and others continued to march west. General Diebitsch, fresh from his triumphs in Turkey, had been appointed commander-in-chief. Grand Duke Mikhail, the Emperor's younger brother, was to lead the elite guards regiments in what was anticipated would be a decisive and rapid campaign to restore order.

Ivan Stenovsky expected to receive his orders imminently. He suggested to Vasily that before his departure, he and the Polunins join him in his family's box to enjoy the first night of the latest operatic spectacular. Perhaps, he suggested, Vasily would like to bring Madame

Zadachina with him. She was now safely settled with her children in her husband's apartment nearby.

The party was also joined by Alexander and Dmitry Vladimirovich and Ivan's formidable mother. Matvey, quickly restored to general favour, had also decided to come, but Nadezhda and her mother were absent. Following the incident in the church, her father, in a rare demonstration of resolution, had decided that their daughter would be safer at home in the country, and they had returned to Bashkatovo, the Laptev seat in Oryol Province.

As the curtain rose, Vasily felt Anna's hand creep across his lap. He caught and squeezed it. On the long journey back from Brest Litovsk, he had come to admire Anna's humour and resilience and was truly grateful for her friendship. He realised how lonely he had been, and no doubt she had felt the same. But the few opportunities they had found for real intimacy, while satisfactory, had contained no hint that their affair was anything other than temporary. Her husband, the general, would after all return in time.

The first half of the performance passed by quite pleasurably. The plot was slight and the music tuneful but unmemorable. The spectators in the pit became restive. Some left the auditorium to stroll in the lobbies, waiting for the return of the dancers at the beginning of the second half.

Vasily was surprised that Ivan had abandoned his usual position close to the stage. The captain's attention seemed to be turning to the prospect of war, and his enthusiasm for ogling the dancers diminished. The same could not be said for other enthusiasts, who, as usual, cheered and whistled each turn with energy. The rivalry between Lyubov Lebedeva and Minnie Voronova seemed as intense as ever, although Lebedeva seemed less disturbed by her rival's supporters this evening, and to Vasily's eyes danced with great confidence and grace. Perhaps she had become inured to the catcalls and insults.

The curtain rose after the interval. The singing resumed for a time, followed by a general display from the corps de ballet. The front of the pit seemed to surge like the sea. Carnations and roses soared towards the stage like bright birds. One of the dancers had lost a floral wreath from her hair, and as it drifted behind the departing performers, a liveried steward ran across the stage and bent to retrieve it. A man in the balcony shouted, 'Clear off!' The orchestra struck up a gypsy dance. It was now Minnie's turn to shine and her lover's claque was out in full force. Violins playing at top speed excited the crowd to such a pitch that the hubbub became almost unbearable.

Minnie's small face appeared from behind the wings, full of life and mischief. It was followed by an enticing pink leg and the slow extension of a satin-clad shoe. The pit fell quiet. She burst onto the stage, pirouetting with rapid steps across the great wooden expanse, spinning along the edge, just avoiding the lights. Reaching the far side, she whisked round and, having executed a dramatic leap, repeated the performance, aiming to return to the spot where she had started.

Vasily noted her perfect timing and admired her speed, but then something changed. The dancer's feet seemed to falter, her momentum slow, her legs tangle, her feet slip. Unable to stop herself, she twisted sideways and, out of control, she teetered on the brink. She tried to throw her body away from the abyss, but with her arms flailing in the air, she fell with a screech into the darkness of the orchestra pit.

The audience groaned, the orchestra fell silent, and then the pit exploded with shouts and whistles. The curtain fell.

Ivan was on his feet. He turned to Vasily. 'I must go to her. Will you look after my mother?'

'Of course…'

Without another word, the captain pushed his way out of the box.

⁂

The curtain soon rose again and the performance continued. Stenovsky did not return. At the end of the show, Anna left discreetly, while Vasily and Matvey took Madame Stenovsky home in their carriage. There was no sign of Ivan at his mother's, and when he and Matvey got back to their apartment, Vasily was surprised to find the captain pacing up and down his drawing room, drinking his wine.

'I hope I'm not intruding, Vasya. I didn't want to come back to the box – I was too agitated – but when I got out of the theatre, I found I didn't want to go home either. Poor Minnie; it's a bad business!'

'Yes, indeed it is. Do you know how the accident happened?'

'I think she just tripped over her feet. She does take risks, dancing so close to the edge of the stage.'

Matvey fixed Ivan with his bright steady gaze. 'Are you sure she tripped?'

'I think so. What else could have happened?'

'Sabotage!'

'Oh really, Matvey. What sort of sabotage? You've been reading too many novels,' Vasily said.

'Well, it's clear that half the audience didn't like her. They prefer Lebedeva…'

Vasily frowned at Matvey and shook his head. The boy's imagination seemed to be as overactive as ever.

'Oh, it's not unknown,' said Ivan. 'A bit of grease in a strategic spot, shoe tampering, that sort of thing. But not in this case. Lebedeva is far too professional to stoop to such tricks. Her family is from a long line of performers. She's proud of it and, unusually for a dancer, has always managed to avoid any scandal. Her followers are, as a result, quite a respectable bunch, despite appearances, and I suspect that she will manage to marry one in the end. Lucky man!'

'Did you think to examine her shoes? The stage?' Matvey persisted.

'Matvey!' Vasily wondered how the guardsman would react to being interrogated.

'No, it's a fair question,' said Ivan. 'As it happens, I did try to go onto the stage out of curiosity, but the ushers closed ranks and said that the curtain would be up again shortly. There was such a crowd in Minnie's dressing room that there was no chance to examine anything, even if I had thought of it, which I didn't. It's a bad business though. Minnie seemed to be in pain, couldn't move her leg…'

'Well, let's hope that Count Malyshev looks after her until she's recovered.'

'Who knows? He's not known for his philanthropy.' Ivan frowned and fell silent. Vasily looked at his old schoolfriend's flushed countenance. Poor Ivan. He obviously still carried a flame for the little dancer.

'Have a drink, Vanya, and I'll send for some supper,' he said. 'I expect you're hungry.'

'Yes, yes indeed.' For once, Ivan didn't sound very keen. He frowned as he held out his glass for more wine, and muttered, 'At least now she's rid of that German…'

Vasily sent for the bottle. Was Ivan referring to von Klein? He recalled that after their duel Rosovsky had said that, in addition to debt, the two men had quarrelled over a woman. Had that woman been Minnie? If so, the captain's antipathy towards the lieutenant may well have principally been caused by jealousy, and his condemnation of the man's character exaggerated. He watched as Ivan, his face flushed and sullen, gulped down more wine, and wondered, not for the first time, if the German was truly as black as he had been painted.

⋈

The following morning, Vasily sat in his study reading a letter from Friedrich von Klein Sternberg. It was not helpful. Friedrich wished him well, and confirmed the date of Astrella and Stepan's Lutheran marriage, which was much as he had expected. The Estonian had not been able to think of anyone further who had lived at the estate when Stepan was in residence. He added that he had recently received a further contribution towards farm expenses from his nephew Andrey, which had been very welcome.

Vasily set the letter aside. It seemed he must look further afield if he were to get to the truth about Stepan Bogolyubov's marital status. If von Klein felt rich enough to send funds home, he must, rightly or wrongly, be feeling confident about his prospects.

His thoughts were interrupted by the arrival of Matvey, who had, it seemed, been to the theatre. He skidded into the room and shouted, 'There's news, sir! Minnie Voronova has broken her leg! She may never dance again!'

PART TWO

TRIALS BY FIRE AND WATER

⊗

'We redeemed our error with our blood… and the problem was resolved under the ramparts of Volya.'
**Nicholas 1 on the Polish uprising,
to Fredrick William lV of Prussia, 1845**

CHAPTER SEVENTEEN

Easter, April 1831 – Siedice, Poland

The Easter ceremony was coming to an end. Priests moved through the ranks bearing icons and banners crowned with crosses of gold. The regimental drummers followed with the colours. Laughter and greetings filled the soft spring air as companies dispersed. After weeks of marching through forested marshy terrain, only occasionally enlivened by flocks of birds fleeing from the sound of distant cannon, the King of Prussia's Grenadiers were now encamped close to the town of Siedice, ninety versts to the east of Warsaw.

Andrey turned away as his company was dismissed. His heart lifted. The tall figure of Kirill Rosovsky was approaching. He had barely seen the captain in recent weeks. Almost immediately after the grenadiers had crossed the Russian border in early February, the Commander of Infantry, General Shakhovsky, had appointed Rosovsky to the staff.

The captain waved aside Andrey's formal salute and gave the Easter greeting: 'Christ is risen!'

'He is risen indeed! Have you come with General Ugrumov, sir?'

'Yes, he's making a tour of the camps. He's engaged now. It would be good to catch up with your news.' Rosovsky relieved a trooper of a basket of provisions, purchased from the sutlers who now thronged the camp. They walked a little way from the crowded parade ground and settled at the edge of the woods, where a rivulet bubbled through lush green grass.

'Some decent food at last!' said Andrey. He sat down, bone-weary from weeks of constant marches.

Rosovsky squatted beside him. 'Yes, I know you've not been well fed…'

'It's been pretty bad, particularly for the men,' Andrey mumbled between bites. The flat pie was meaty and rich. 'We had to station sentries around the kitchens. You can imagine. Your replacement, Vengerov, ordered some unnecessarily harsh punishments.' He sighed as he wiped his mouth with the back of his hand and reached for a bottle of wine. Captain Vengerov was a remote and chilly officer. Worse, he clearly regarded Andrey as a troublemaker who should have been left behind in Novgorod.

'We left Russia in too much of a hurry,' said Rosovsky. 'But Diebitsch wanted to take advantage of the frost.' Rosovsky laughed. 'What frost?'

'Well, it got cold enough, eventually…'

Andrey brushed the crumbs away. Sparrows flew down to peck at them. He stretched out, eased his stiff shoulders, and lifted his face to the sun. He felt almost human. He had spent the last two nights in a comfortable bed. There had been adequate food and hot water. Morozov had patched up his fraying field uniform, cleaning off the mud, purging it of lice with a heated knife.

'How do you think it's all going?' Andrey asked. 'We have missed you, sir. No-one tells us much.' In Rosovsky's absence, he and the ensign, Denis Borisov, had not had much faith in their immediate superiors. First Lieutenant Steklov was a dull man, too fond of his drink, and Vengerov was Vengerov.

Rosovsky frowned and said nothing. 'It can't be good,' Andrey prompted. 'Diebitsch said it would all be over in a week, finished in one blow, but it clearly hasn't really begun. I suppose the plan for a swift march on Warsaw was frustrated by the weather.'

'Yes, the thaw meant that we couldn't move troops and equipment over frozen rivers as planned. The Polish mud, about which Napoleon regularly complained, if you remember, made the roads all but impassable.'

'I know all about that... the men have been exhausted by the marches. I thought my mare would break down and I'd be marching too, but she came through alright. When the ground finally did freeze it snowed heavily, and in the absence of stores we had to seize food and fodder from the peasants. They turned against us after that, of course.'

'The Poles rallied more quickly than expected,' said Rosovsky. 'They know we outnumber them, but they've fought intelligently, defensively. We've rarely been able to engage them in any size, although the fight at Grochow was, on balance, a victory for us.'

'Why didn't Diebitsch take the opportunity then to press on to Warsaw?'

'Our forces weren't up to full strength. The guards, under Grand Duke Mikhail, are still up in the north-east, pinned down by the Poles under Skrzynesci. I think Field Marshall Diebitsch is hoping that we'll soon join up, after which a determined assault must be made.' Rosovsky offered Andrey another pie. 'But Diebitsch's wavering concerns me. He seems to lack the will to bring the thing to a real fight. The Emperor seems to be losing faith in him and it's sapping his confidence.' He shook his head. 'At least you saw some action at the Liw bridgehead. I'm sorry I wasn't there with you.'

'We didn't do much. Spent most of the day in reserve watching the Prince of Prussia's Grenadiers repulsing Uminsky's cavalry, while hoping not to be mown down ourselves.'

'But you lost some men.'

'A few unlucky troopers were hit by a rogue long shot. No officers were harmed.'

Andrey fell silent, reliving the terror that had gripped him when the guns first roared out over the Liwiec River. He had expected the smoke, the thunder of the cannon, the agonised screams of the wounded but, nonetheless, he had briefly struggled to control his fear. An iron ball had cut a vicious swathe, bouncing through the regiment's ranks just yards from where he stood. He had involuntarily glanced at Borisov beside him. Sidorov, the company sergeant, was watching them, chewing a plug of tobacco. The seasoned soldier had sensed their alarm. 'Unlucky shot, sirs!' he had said, and then more quietly, 'Just stand nice and steady. That's all you have to do. I'll take care of the rest.' He spat into the trampled grass as the bodies were taken to the rear.

Then he bellowed down the line, 'Close up! Close up, boys.' Within seconds, strict order was restored; the carnage might never have happened. Finally, the Poles were repulsed, the bridgehead taken and the river crossing destroyed. It had been the only real action Andrey had seen.

Rosovsky's voice interrupted his thoughts. 'Have you lost many men from disease? Your numbers are down.'

'Some have died from fever; others fell by the wayside through lack of food and exhaustion. Why do you ask?'

'Cholera has reached Brest and Riga, and there have been cases reported among the townsfolk here in Siedice. Of course, the Poles are now blaming our army for bringing it with them, but that's not proven. Stay alert, Andrey. If the disease takes hold it could seriously weaken us. I wish to God we knew how it spreads.'

They finished their food, drank more wine and walked back through the camp. The men had erected small shelters of woven boughs, green with budding leaves, and now, the privations of the march forgotten, they sat beneath them, enjoying the plentiful supplies.

A number of officers, including the general's staff, were gathered outside a small farmhouse at the edge of the camp. All wore their parade uniforms in honour of the feast day. Medals and stars shone in abundance. Rosovsky presented Andrey to General Ugrumov, a man of around fifty with receding curly hair, unmarked by grey, his small mouth topped by a neat moustache. A cascade of imperial orders, won fighting Napoleon, tumbled below the bright oak leaves on his stiff collar. The general enquired if it was his first campaign and then, distracted by Captain Vengerov, turned away.

'It looks as though we're leaving,' Rosovsky said. Ugrumov's officers were calling for their horses, preparing to move on. 'Well, Andrey Andreyevich, look after yourself. Don't fall foul of Vengerov. When we get to Warsaw I'll be re-joining you for the final push, no doubt.'

'I look forward to that, sir.'

There was a distant rumble of cannon fire from the north. Even today it seemed the enemy continued to resist. The general climbed into his carriage and left the camp at speed, his escort riding behind him. Andrey watched the group disappear and then went to seek out Denis Borisov. The celebrations would continue for some days and he intended to enjoy them. As he crossed the parade ground he encountered his orderly, who met him with a careless salute.

'A letter for you, sir!' Morozov proffered a slim packet and then lingered, grinning slyly.

Andrey took it. Turning it over, he recognised the hand. She had kept her promise to write.

※

8th May 1831

The sun was setting over the Bug River. Andrey stood with Borisov on the edge of Granne, a settlement scattered along the sloping north bank. The river here was wide and shallow. Sappers had constructed a fine pontoon bridge that was now supporting a steady stream of traffic.

Field Marshal Diebitsch had at last decided to move north from Siedice in the hope of uniting his thirty-five thousand men with the Grand Duke's guards' regiments. Today the avant-garde under Ugrumov had moved up. The area around the bridge was thick with troops. Flat-capped field engineers, clad entirely in green, were checking the structure's timbers and ropes. Staff officers were directing the companies to their bivouac areas and lining up wagons and guns for transfer across the water. The cavalry were being diverted to a ford a little way downstream where the horses were able to swim across without difficulty.

Andrey and Borisov's quiet contemplation of the scene was disturbed by a summons from Captain Vengerov. With reluctant steps they returned to the house in the village that had been secured for officers' use. Under the low roof, the air was humid and thick with tobacco smoke. Vengerov himself, the major who commanded their battalion, and a first lieutenant sat at the wooden table. They had empty shot glasses before them and their faces were grim. The major waved Andrey and Borisov to a seat without ceremony and sent for more vodka.

'Bad news, I'm afraid,' he said, looking down at the table. 'We have more cases than ever today. I'm afraid Steklov has succumbed. He died an hour ago.'

Andrey caught his breath. Cholera was indeed a rapid killer. The lieutenant had seemed perfectly fit this morning. The disease had been present in the army for some weeks, but the King of Prussia's men had been spared until now.

Vengerov scowled. 'The disease is killing more men than the Poles.'

Andrey looked at him. That was true, but the regiment

had hardly seen any action thus far. Perhaps that might change.

'Yes, and it hasn't come at a good time,' the major added. 'We're moving to Nur tomorrow. Lubensky may still be occupying the town. The Field Marshall's concerned that the general will come at us from the rear while we're chasing his compatriot Skrzynesci back to Warsaw. We were already short of officers before Steklov's death, so you, von Klein Sternberg and Borisov, will both have to step up. Borisov will take your place, Sternberg, in an acting capacity, and you'll become acting first lieutenant.

Andrey's heart turned over. Promotion seemed barely credible; he had hardly distinguished himself thus far, but perhaps he shouldn't be surprised. Whether due to disease or battle casualties, progress through the ranks could be rapid in wartime. Denis Borisov flushed with pleasure. As he and Andrey expressed their thanks, Vengerov glowered out of the window as if smelling something unpleasant. 'We don't really have much option,' he muttered.

'You'd better go and sort yourselves out, lieutenants,' said the major. 'We haven't much time. We march out to Ciechanowiec tomorrow and then on to Nur.'

※

The following morning, Andrey and Denis Borisov, riding alongside their men, left Granne and took the road to the west. Their column, a mixed force of nine thousand, was led by several squadrons of Uhlan lancers, followed by sixteen guns. More guns and a troop of cuirassiers brought up the rear.

They overnighted at Ciechanowiec and the following day crossed the soft-banked curving reaches of the Nurzec River and turned south-west towards the town of Nur. On the way, the grenadiers were ordered to halt, but no instruction came to fall out. In the warmth of the quiet afternoon, bees were buzzing among the wild flowers in the lush verges; men could be heard murmuring in low voices to one another. They were in good spirits and keen to see some action. As they stood in the road, they could hear the lancers moving off ahead of them.

'I wish we knew what was happening,' said Andrey. 'We're never told anything.'

'Oh, it doesn't bother me,' said Borisov, grinning cheerfully. He was still delighted by his unexpected elevation. This morning he had taken obvious pleasure in inspecting the men's muskets, checking their action, and the sharpness of their bayonets.

'But we've no clue what we'll find in Nur, if anything.' Andrey pulled at his chinstrap. His shako felt hot, heavy. Wearing it on the march meant that action was at least possible.

'I don't think the powers that be know either,' said Borisov. 'That's why we've been going backwards and forwards ever since we got here.'

Andrey grunted. He remembered the paper exercises he had enjoyed puzzling over at cadet school, planning campaigns and manoeuvres. They had known the disposition and size of the enemy, the nature of the terrain and other useful facts. He wished he had such facts now. The tedium of campaigning would be much reduced if he had something constructive to think about.

As if in answer to his prayer, a few minutes later Rosovsky trotted on his horse towards them from the front of the column. He reined in. 'We'll be moving on soon,' he said. 'The scouts spotted a couple of squadrons of enemy Uhlans on the road. Our lancers gave chase, but when the enemy saw the size of our force they fled. Some prisoners were taken, who've confirmed that Lubensky is still in Nur with twelve thousand men.' As he collected his reins he added, 'Oh, by the way... congratulations on your promotions, gentlemen.'

He wheeled his horse and was gone.

The town of Nur was flanked to the south by the River Bug. A broad semi-circular strip of sparse woodland ran around the northern perimeter. As the troops came within sight of the trees, the column came to a halt and was called to battle order. The King of Prussia's men were placed at the rear, so could not see the two Polish infantry divisions drawn up against them by the trees.

In his new position at the front of his troop, Andrey heard the Poles open fire, followed by the order for Russian guns and carabiniers to respond. His heart beat faster. Now perhaps they would see some action! But it was the Emperor of Austria's Grenadiers who were ordered forward in support of two squadrons of cuirassiers on their heavy horses. It did not take them long to drive the Poles back. The horsemen pulled up at the edge of the trees and turned back, while the infantry pursued the enemy on through the woods into the town.

Andrey's regiment was moved forward, but then yet again was ordered to halt on the open field. Once more in reserve! Frustrated, Andrey kicked up a cloud of dust and looked back. A group of horsemen was approaching along the Ciechanowiec road. Among them he recognised the porcine features and flushed cheeks of the Field Marshal himself. 'He doesn't want to miss the fun!' said Borisov. As he spoke, six or seven squadrons of lancers, responding to an order from a member of Diebitsch's staff, galloped away across the field to the right, their irregular four-cornered shapkas gleaming in the afternoon sunlight; their swallow-tailed pennants furling out behind them. The horse artillery followed, dragging the dark cylinders of the guns behind them.

'They've gone to block the Czyzew Road. That's where Lubensky will likely try to break out, and that's where the action will be,' Captain Vengerov commented, pulling out his pipe.

They watched as Diebitsch and his staff followed the disappearing guns. The horses of the cavalry that remained snorted; their harnesses clinked. Soon they heard men's voices, the grate of wheels. The baggage train was still arriving.

Andrey turned to Sergeant Sidorov. The old soldier shrugged. 'We'll likely be here for a while,' he said. 'They'll only call on us if they need us.'

They stood for two hours or more, hearing the steady pulse of artillery, shouts and the clash of arms not far to the right. It was close to sunset. As the sky darkened, a staff officer arrived with news. As expected, Lubensky had left the town and had made a stand. When it was clear that his forces were outgunned, the Polish cavalry, having essayed a couple of heroic charges, had broken through the Russian lines and fled along the road to the north, towards Czyzew. Meanwhile, the Russian lancers had foiled an attempt by the Polish infantry to form squares, and had driven them into the woods to the west, where they were now fleeing to safety. The Russians had suffered few casualties, but had taken a hundred or so prisoners and inflicted some losses on the enemy. Nur was now thought to be enemy-free.

'Aren't we pursuing them?' Borisov asked.

'Apparently not.' Andrey shook his head. Why did Diebitsch never give chase? But it would soon be dark, and the Field Marshall had achieved his main objective. Lubensky could no longer threaten the Russian army as they marched on Warsaw.

Soon the troops still standing on the road to Ciechanowiec were ordered to move forward into the town. Muskets should not be loaded; the battle was over. Vengerov ordered Andrey's troop to march in the rear, just ahead of the baggage train. Andrey, recognising the deliberate slight, was soon joined by Sidorov. 'I'm looking forward to my dinner,' the sergeant said, untroubled.

The ancient trees on either side of the track rose tall and solid against the darkening sky. The men marched in threes, singing as they went. Andrey contemplated their blanket rolls, the flasks bouncing against their square packs, their cartridge pouches adorned with the three-flamed grenadier badge. All seemed in good order and his mind drifted. In recent months he had only dwelled on Nadezhda's soft attractions intermittently. Much of the time he had been too exhausted – and in any event, he had tried to empty his mind of everything to do with Petersburg and the prince's legacy. But the brief and affectionate note he had received from her in Siedice had cheered him. He would have liked to reply, but of course, that was impossible. Now he found it easy to conjure up her features. Perhaps it was his unexpected promotion that brought her so sharply to mind. Did it make him more worthy of her? Was she now more attainable?

His daydream was disturbed by the sight of a trooper, two ranks up the line, who seemed to be swaying, then crumpling slowly towards the ground. Andrey heard a sharp crack and Sidorov's voice. 'That's a sniper, sir. And he's aiming at you and me.' More cracks and another man was down, this time immediately in front of him.

His mind cleared. 'Take cover! Prepare to fire, and keep your heads down!'

The company scattered. Andrey drew his sabre as he flung himself behind a tree to the right of the path, with Sidorov beside him. The grenadiers crouched around him, loading their muskets. They bit the cartridges, spat, and having filled the pan and the barrel, rammed the ball down. He heard reassuring clicks as the guns were primed. Nothing stirred between the trees, but the air was filled with shouts and further shots. Much of the straggling column seemed to be under attack. In the gloom there was no sign of the enemy, but now shadows could be seen slipping towards them between the trees. A guardsman fired his musket prematurely.

'Hold fire!' snapped the sergeant.

The enemy was now thirty or forty yards distant. A scatter of musket shot passed harmlessly over their heads. Andrey ordered fire to be returned, but mainly for effect; few balls, if any, would hit their target. He felt the sting of smoke in his throat. His eyes were watering; he blinked. The Poles wavered. Then, urged on by their officers, they advanced again.

His grenadiers stood, bayonets raised, poised to withstand any onslaught with steel and rifle butts. Andrey frowned at his sabre, wishing he could exchange it for a musket's reach and weight. His heart was racing, but as the Poles approached, it slowed. Only a few were seasoned troops. Many were very young, conscripts probably, eccentrically dressed and variously armed. His men would be more than a match for them.

Not all of the enemy were novices, however. He heard Sidorov shout 'Watch it, sir!' as a large Polish sergeant-major made straight for them, a young trooper at his heels. The Pole lurched forward. Sidorov pushed Andrey to one side and swung his rifle butt at the man's head, sweeping him into the path of a guardsman, who thrust his bayonet forward and skewered him to the ground. Unbalanced, Andrey staggered back, avoiding the spurt of blood, and now finding himself face to face with the young soldier, he clumsily parried an uncertain blow from what appeared to be some sort of agricultural instrument. The youth wavered for a moment and Andrey, recovering his balance, leapt forward and with all his strength dealt his assailant a blow with the flat of his sabre, which caused him to lose his grip on his weapon and flee back into the trees.

Andrey looked about him. He could hear a more serious engagement continuing up the line, but here there was no imminent danger; few of the enemy seemed keen to fight and they were mainly intent on continuing their flight through the woods. In the gathering darkness, no orders came to pursue them and Andrey was content to let them go. A few enemy soldiers lay on the ground, dead or wounded, but apart from the two men hit by the sniper, his troop had avoided serious casualties. As Andrey went forward to examine the state of a corporal who was sitting, stunned, on a nearby tree root, he heard a shout behind him. Morozov was running towards them from the rear, closely followed by a motley collection of drivers, orderlies and cooks. 'It's the wagons, sir! They're stealing the wagons! We can't hold them off.'

Andrey cursed Vengerov. The captain should have mounted a rear guard behind the baggage train. They must turn back. He ordered Sidorov to gather as many men as possible. Forced to move in ones and twos along the forest track, they squeezed past the long line of heavy carts and the camp kitchen. The sound of shouts and gunfire grew louder. He called the soldiers to halt and gave the order to load. With Sidorov close behind him, he moved forwards to stand at the edge of the woods. A laden cart was disappearing into the dusk, escorted by Polish uhlans. Some twenty yards away, a group of Polish foot soldiers, grasping bright torches, were making off with some baggage.

'How many wagons have gone?' asked Andrey.

'That's the third or fourth, I think,' Morozov replied.

'And the horses?'

'We let them loose… they'll likely return.'

Andrey hoped he was right. He was fond of his mare and didn't want to lose her.

The line of grenadiers emerged from the trees and fired. The flash and smoke of musket shot saw off the raiders. A small band of horsemen wheeled by, clearly contemplating intervention, but on seeing the ranks of Russians and not knowing what lay behind them in the gloom, they thought better of it.

'Should we give chase?'

Sidorov shook his head. 'I wouldn't get in among them uhlans, sir. We'll be skewered like sheep. Better to save what we've got.'

Horses and stable doors came to Andrey's mind as he ordered the formation of a rear guard before the troop turned back towards Nur. They followed behind the rescued wagons. Progress was slow and it was pitch dark when they reached the town. Captain Rosovsky was standing at the town gates holding a flaming torch. He was clearly relieved to see them. 'That was a bloody mess,' he said. 'We had no idea that the enemy foot had fled east. We thought they'd gone north. Are all the wagons saved?'

'All but the last three, or perhaps four. Morozov thinks they were just carrying company records and some religious paraphernalia.'

'Well, that's something. Well done, Andrey. I'll make sure you get the credit.'

'Thank you, sir. Have we taken many losses?'

'It's not certain yet… not too many, I think. Although there are a few wounded, and they took some prisoners. Captain Vengerov's out of action. Took a blow to the head.'

'Oh! I'm sorry to hear that.' Andrey knew his words sounded unconvincing, but having shown his true worth in an emergency at last and achieved some recognition, he didn't want Vengerov's bile to blight his achievement.

Rosovsky raised an eyebrow and smiled. 'Yes, I'm sure you are. Some of the prisoners have already escaped. But I'm sorry to say that there's no sign of Denis Borisov. I fear he may be on his way to Warsaw.'

CHAPTER EIGHTEEN

May 1831 – Bashkatovo Estate, Oryol Province. Three hundred and fifty versts south of Moscow

Spring at Bashkatovo only lingers for a week and soon defers to the sultry lassitude of summer. During these precious few days, the tulips bloom, birds change their tune, and the uncurling leaves on the lime trees flush green. Enjoying the welcome warmth of the season, Nadezhda was sitting with her maid at the edge of the parterre that stretched before the great estate house. Her nose wrinkled against the sun, she watched as the gardeners removed the protective sacking from the statues, washed down the white marble, and scrubbed the paths and steps. The geometrical flower beds were empty, dug over, awaiting tender plants from the glasshouses. On such a radiant day, the recently arrived French novel recommended by Aunt Darya could not hold her attention for long.

When she had arrived home in the frozen weeks of early February, accompanied by her mother, she had expected to be bored and in disgrace. Indeed, her father had greeted her with a certain coolness, and the possible return of cholera had meant no trips to the nearby town of Oryol. Overall though, she was not distressed about her banishment from the capital. Unlike her mother, she did not regret society, and considered relative solitude a price well worth paying for her satisfactory tryst with Andrey. By bravely stifling her scruples and acting boldly, she believed she had not only avoided an awkward misunderstanding, but had also extracted some commitment from the intriguing lieutenant. Her only regret was that the discovery of their meeting at the church had resulted in trouble and pain for her friend, Matvey.

Before she had left St Petersburg, her cousin Vasily had called on her. He seemed less robust than usual, but appeared to have largely recovered from his ordeal in Poland. He was kind enough not to ask questions about her recent embarrassment, but knowing she was condemned to return to Oryol, he had given her some sound advice. Since, he said, her older sister Lisa had forfeited her rights by following Mikhail into exile, she was now the sole heir to much of the Laptev estate. She should take advantage of this forced exile to learn what that role meant. There was no reason why a woman could not undertake estate business very competently. His own grandmother, and also his friend Irina Pavlovna, were doing so with great success.

Accordingly, on her arrival she had embarked on a programme of self-improvement. She had tried to progress her reading beyond Aunt Darya's novels, although her father's library was rather lacking in books. She had spent time with the steward in the wood-clad estate office, absorbing facts about the farming year, crop yields and markets. She had learned to drive the gig and she had also, to her mother's amazement, interested herself in the economics of the household.

It must be admitted that on a day like today, she set such tasks aside and fell to daydreaming about Andrey Andreyevich. Before leaving the capital, she had bribed a servant to deliver a brief note to the barracks addressed to him, for forwarding. She told the lieutenant that she had returned to Oryol, but did not, of course, give the reason why. It would not do for him to know that his reputation within her family had sunk even further. She hoped that her message had reached him, but she knew she could not expect a reply.

She thought of him often, although her memories were few. Were her feelings for him genuine? A handsome face could, of course, hide ugly habits. But beneath his fine exterior and cool reserve, she had observed glimpses of sensitivity and humour that truly touched her heart. After dinner, when not required to play the pianoforte in company, she spent hours improvising on popular romances and old love songs. Gazing upwards at the music room ceiling, where brightly drawn cherubs and goddesses played, she rippled the keys and tried to remember him. Now, sitting in the garden, these thoughts returned. What exactly had he said when he danced with her? Did he still have her glove? What might a future with him hold? Had God kept him safe from the Poles?

Her maid was attracting her attention. A liveried footman was approaching. 'The countess would like you to attend her, miss,' he intoned.

Returning to the house, she passed beneath the row of pillars and through the great front door. Gathering her skirts, she climbed past the caryatids and monumental urns that flanked the grand stairway. Her mother and Aunt Darya were in the morning room. The blinds were drawn against the bright sunlight, and so she did not immediately notice that Aunt Darya's eyes were red with weeping, or that her mother's handsome face was marred by a pinched rigidity around the mouth. An unsealed letter lay discarded on the polished surface of the table. What could this mean? Had someone died? Her heart quivered as she remembered Andrey Andreyevich, fighting in Poland, but of course the news could not concern him. Little information about the progress of the war reached them here in the country, and with the exception of Ivan Alexandrovich, from whom nothing had been heard, none of the family was directly involved.

'Sit down, Nadezhda,' her mother said. 'We have had some disturbing news from Ekaterina Nikolayevna.' She glanced at Aunt Darya, who lowered her kerchief from her nose. 'I fear we have all been let down by Yevgeny Filipovich.'

'Let down? I thought he was occupied with his regiment in Poland.'

'Yes, so did we all. But there has been, it seems, an altercation with his superior officer about some horses and an issue with his servant's behaviour in camp. As a result he has resigned his commission. I don't know the details, but in any event, he is no longer with the army, and was last seen disappearing back to his parents' home in Italy. He was obliged to detour through St Petersburg, where Vasily dined with him. It seems he has decided to marry one of the sisters of an old friend, an officer whom he encountered in Brest Litovsk. He told Vasya that he and you were never more than just good friends. He can't understand how we came to think anything else.'

'Oh!' Nadezhda grimaced, hoping her face expressed sufficient distress. It wasn't difficult; the news was both surprising and vexing. She had hoped that the fiction of her attachment to the young prince might have lasted a little longer than this. After all, like Andrey, he should have been occupied for the duration of the fighting.

A deep sob sounded in the breast of Aunt Darya, and Nadezhda found herself embraced in a cloud of lavender water and camphor. 'Oh, my poor dear! What a terrible disappointment for you!'

She was not a good actress, and she shuddered and sniffled unconvincingly.

Her mother rose to her feet, and drew herself erect. Her voice resounded with savage resolution through the anteroom and along the enfilade. 'Never mind, my dear. Such matters generally turn out for the best. We never much liked the idea of you spending much of your time in Europe, and we do not know Yevgeny Filipovich's parents at all. Much better to find you a solid and respectable local landowner. When this wretched plague has passed, your father and I will redouble our efforts to secure an appropriate match.'

An appropriate match! A local landowner! In her mind's eye, Nadezhda could see a vista of eternal swamps, through which the tall figure of Andrey Andreyevich was fading into distant mist. The pain in her heart, like the tears on her cheeks, suddenly felt all too real.

CHAPTER NINETEEN

15th May 1831 – St Petersburg

Vasily sat on the edge of Anna's wide birchwood bed. It was very early, but daylight was already edging the shutters of her room. He should not have stayed so long, but Anna would be departing from Petersburg today or tomorrow, and they had wanted to enjoy one last night together.

The recent letter from her husband had not been a surprise. Cholera was rampant in Poland. Several officers had died. The general felt fortunate to have been spared. Anna was instructed to leave the city without delay and travel with the servants and her children to his sister's country estate, where he would join her. Zadachin was right to be worried. Petersburg had been free from infection up to now, but Vasily knew that the disease had already reached the city of Riga, had recurred in Moscow, and was now raging through cities to the south of the capital. It was only a matter of time before the first cases appeared here.

Anna was stirring, opening her eyes. 'Must you go so soon?' She sat up, attempting a smile. He pulled her to him, kissed her hair and then her lips. She trembled slightly. For a moment he thought that she might weep, but then she drew away from him, visibly collected herself and shook her head. 'No, you're right… you have to go. It's time.'

He knew their affair of a few months was over. They had found real comfort in one another's company since their return from Poland and, with some effort, they had managed to avoid excessive emotional commitment. He feared she might find their parting painful, but she was putting on a brave face.

'And thank you for your gift. I shall treasure it,' she said. Last night he had given her a necklace, a slim chain of gold from which hung a circle of diamonds. He had called it a token of friendship. He hoped she had accepted it as such.

'Will you write to me?' she said.

'Yes, of course. Why not?'

'Good. There mustn't be any bitterness or regret. And Vasily, look after yourself. Do you really have to stay in Petersburg? It's only a matter of time before the disease arrives here.'

'I'll be sure to follow my own advice, Anya. That should see me through.' He sounded more confident than he felt, but he couldn't leave. He was needed here for the duration of the emergency.

'Well, I shall pray for you, my dear.' She rose from the bed, put on her robe and opened the shutters. 'Now you really must go.' She remained with her back to him, staring at the window. He hesitated for a moment and then left the room without a word.

He walked home through the bright, empty streets. He felt grateful to Anna. She was blessed with a good deal of common sense, and had accepted the limitations of their relationship with good grace. She might well miss him, as he would miss her, but neither of them should grieve too deeply. The general, for all his shortcomings, would continue to protect and care for her; her children would continue to bring her joy. Nonetheless, as he walked on, Vasily could not resist a sharp tug of regret. He was alone once again, and was likely to remain so.

He turned to walk along the Moika, and stopped at the Blue Bridge. Shifting reflections shadowed the surface of the water. Reproachful dust swirled up from the pavement. On the left bank, a string of wagons had pulled up outside one of the larger palaces. Another family was leaving the city. It was almost summer, a time, of course, when many folk went to the country, but the exodus had certainly started earlier this year. All who could were wisely seeking places of safety away from the capital's teeming streets, dank canals, and the stink of its sewers. He thought of the fresh breezes at Dubovnoye and wished that he too could escape. But that wasn't possible. His duty lay here, and, once the threat of cholera had passed, the Polish war would probably be over. Had von Klein survived it, Vasily must restart his investigations into the facts surrounding the Bogolyubov marriage. He couldn't know where that quest would take him, or how long it would last.

❈

10th June 1831 – St Petersburg

'As I said to the minister, when it comes to the source of the disease, I am no wiser than you, Alexander Petrovich. Nor do I know why it spreads. What I do know however is that medical assistance, when given promptly, can certainly improve the patient's prospect of survival.'

The English doctor leant back in his chair, fingering his empty wine glass. As a servant hurried forward to refill it, Vasily scrutinised him. Doctor Webster's hair was streaked with grey and the skin on his square, pink-cheeked face had a leathery sheen that spoke of his years in the tropics. Vasily knew that he was in his early forties, but he seemed a good deal older. He had served with the British Army in India, and was now returning home by a circuitous route. This was the second time they had met. The first had been at the Ministry when, following the outbreak of cholera in Riga in May, the doctor had been called in as an advisor to the Medical Council. Now his uncle had invited him to the palace for dinner.

Alexander frowned. The answer hadn't satisfied him. 'Yes, I see… but that doesn't help much when it comes to introducing preventative measures. And as far as medical treatment is concerned – as you know, Webster, we're building temporary hospitals, but we don't have enough doctors to staff them.'

'There's been no revival of the disease in India on this occasion?' the prince asked.

'Not a general outbreak, not since '21, but it flares up here and there quite regularly. The country is never completely free of it.'

'You've clearly had a good deal of experience of the malady over the years,' said Alexander. 'You must have some opinion about why it occurs where it does, and how it spreads.'

'From what evidence we have it's not simple to deduce, but it's clear that, like most other diseases, it is generally most active where people are living in poor and overcrowded situations. That knowledge in itself is not of much use; once cholera takes a hold, it is no respecter of rank or place, as you know.'

Vasily nodded. In general, the wealthy suffered less than the poor, but news had come recently from Poland that Field Marshall Diebitsch himself had succumbed to the disease.

'Outbreaks generally prosper in periods of hot weather,' the doctor continued. 'But not always. The infection may occur in one district but can then, quite unexpectedly, appear somewhere new for no discernible reason. Despite that, I tend to the view that it spreads by contagion, person to person. I don't think that it travels in the air through some miasma, or that it can contaminate goods and so on…'

'No, I think we reached that conclusion last year when we stopped fumigating merchandise at each cordon sanitaire,' said Alexander. 'Unfortunately, I think the practice has been mandated once again this year. Isn't that right, Vasily? It seems nothing much has been learned.'

Vasily nodded. In recent weeks he had helped to introduce the new arrangements. He remembered the queues of wagons that had built up last year at the barrier on the highway to Moscow. The road had been clogged for several miles. When some enterprising peasants had found ways to evade the measures, police and troops had been sent out, fights and general disturbance had ensued and, in the end, the scheme had been abandoned.

Vasily looked round the table. The prince's dining room was unusually empty. The trickle of people leaving the city had recently turned into a flood and there were rarely new faces at the table. Matvey was out at his lessons with Maltby, and apart from the aged dependant who always dined here, Doctor Webster was the only guest.

'Some of the measures taken thus far are probably necessary,' said Webster. 'The disease is very likely to enter the city. I'm surprised that there are still no restrictions in place at Kronstadt.'

Alexander mopped his brow. 'That's now in hand. Between these four walls, I can tell you that one or two possible cases have been reported already. An official announcement is expected within the next few days.'

Vasily knew this was true. Most of the army was now in Poland, so the police, now on alert, would bear the brunt of enforcing any additional measures that might be introduced.

Dr Webster turned to the prince. 'You have decided not to leave town, sir?'

'Yes. I know that most of society has departed, but I think we're safe here in the palace. I don't visit my estates regularly.' Vasily knew that Dmitry Vladimirovich disliked the country, and in any event would not leave his uncle to face the epidemic alone. Alexander had already imposed a strict household regime, based on the Ministry's recommendations. The movements of the servants had been restricted, and water and other drinks, and all fresh produce, had been banned from the palace. Fortunately the wine cellar was full, the kitchens well stocked with preserves and dry goods, and such water as was drunk in the house was always boiled.

'I am sorry that I cannot do much to be of practical use,' Dr Webster was saying. 'You aren't encouraging visiting physicians to help in the hospitals, despite the shortage.'

Alexander shook his head. 'No. The minister, General Zavretsky, is worried that the ordinary folk won't like being treated by unknown foreigners, although many of our own doctors originally came from abroad.'

Webster shrugged. 'Well, I'm happy to do what I can, even if only in an advisory capacity. As I said, early treatment is vital. One must learn to recognise the first signs... low spirits, loss of appetite. If the disease is allowed to take hold, there is less than a fifty percent chance of survival. In some places, where medical assistance is sparse and the people deprived, over eighty percent of the afflicted die.'

Vasily caught his breath. He had known that the death rate from the disease was high, but these numbers were frightening. He wished once again that he had insisted that Matvey go to Tsarskoye Selo with Katya and Polunin, but the boy had been adamant that he wished to stay in Petersburg and continue his studies.

Webster seemed aware of the shock his words had caused. 'I know that you are taking precautions here, and that is good,' he said. 'But I suggest that you keep liquid opium in the house. A good dose of that, if taken in time and kept down, will in some cases do the trick. Bleeding is recommended too, and warm baths, although I am less convinced about their efficacy.'

The conversation moved on to the fighting in Poland. The consensus was that it was all going on too long. The doctor suggested that the appointment of General Paskevich, following Diebitsch's recent death, would make a difference.

'Yes, but the Poles are clearly losing in any event,' said the prince. 'They should have sought terms after their defeat at Ostrolenka, but they're stubborn and their aspirations to be free of Russian control are unrealistic.'

Vasily shifted in his seat. Although his experiences at the hands of the Poles in Warsaw had been uncomfortable, he couldn't agree. Surely a people deserved the rights that had been promised? But he said nothing, preferring not to provoke an argument.

'So an advance on Warsaw is likely?' asked the doctor.

'As soon as the new commander-in-chief takes up the reins,' said the prince.

It occurred to Vasily that there had been no word of Second Lieutenant von Klein Sternberg since his departure to the front. Had he survived the war thus far? In any event, this was no time to pursue his investigations into the pretender's claim. He looked at the prince. His kindly benefactor was ordering more wine. Dmitry seemed lively enough. God grant that he remain so.

CHAPTER TWENTY

Monday 22nd June – St Petersburg

> *In response to information received from Riga and other towns with regard to the appearance there of cholera, all measures have been taken to secure the city against the spread of the disease. Along all roads leading from these infected areas, the administration has erected barriers. All letters, goods and parcels received from there have been fumigated. In short, everything has been done to deal with the matter, but notwithstanding all these precautions, cholera, for a number of reasons, has penetrated the city.*
> **The Governor General of the City of St Petersburg**

Vasily snorted and set the document aside. Today's announcement merely confirmed what many already knew. There had been cases of cholera in the city for some days and the Ministry had already issued a stream of directives aimed at containing them. The police had been implementing these with enthusiasm, as if combatting a crime wave, despite the fact that many of the rules were contradictory and some plainly idiotic or impossibly repressive. A general fast, announced by the Church, had added to the growing sense of panic as crowds flocked to pray for deliverance. Unsurprisingly, therefore, Vasily's day of rest yesterday had been disturbed by trouble. The mob had been dispersed with difficulty, few policemen and even fewer troops being available.

He rose from his desk and looked out of the window. He was also concerned about Matvey. This morning, as he was leaving home, he had found the boy at the top of the great flight of stairs, busily consuming a large bag of fresh apricots.

'Where did you get those?' He had shouted as he gripped the boy's arm. 'You know you mustn't eat fresh fruit! You'll put us all in danger.'

Matvey looked alarmed but said nothing. 'Where did you get them?'

Matvey squirmed away and looked at the floor. 'I got them at Ekaterina Nikolayevna's,' he mumbled.

'But there's no-one at my sister's. They're all at Tsarskoye Selo...'

'The doorman's still there. He gave them to me. He said they were going to waste.'

Vasily realised that the fruit must have come from the palace's winter garden. There would be peaches soon, and grapes. There was probably no danger in eating fruit from there. 'Well, don't have too many. You don't want to make yourself ill, for any reason.'

Matvey threw him a resentful look. 'I was going to leave some here for Yako and take the rest to Mr Maltby.'

Vasily felt guilty. He was still inclined to suspect the boy of mischief, but more often than not his suspicions proved unfounded. Maltby was getting on in years now, and Matvey usually saved his tutor's legs by taking his lessons at his home. 'Well, alright, but please be cautious, Motya.' He spoke more gently.

'Don't worry, sir. I do know the rules...' Matvey grinned and slapped Vasily on the back, presumably aiming to reassure him. Before Vasily could protest, the boy had disappeared down the stairs. Vasily watched him go, feeling a customary twist of affection mixed with anxiety. Should he have insisted that Matvey leave town?

He moved away from the hot glass of the window and turned to the police reports that lay on his desk. He loosened his collar. It was before ten in the morning and his room was already suffocating. To open the window, however, would be to admit the noxious stink of lukewarm canal that pervaded the streets.

He rubbed the back of his neck as he turned the pages. A house close to the monastery in the Coachmen's District where disease had been found had been sealed off; an entire family living near the shopping arcade had been taken forcibly to the nearby lazarette; a Dutchman had been freed just in time from a mob of townsfolk convinced he was a spy aiming to spread disease. Clearly those who remained trapped here were deeply disturbed; the merchants and workmen saw the disease as a silent fiend from hell that was stalking the city. In the absence of facts about the source of this curse, or the purpose of the ever-changing "directives" emanating from the Cholera Council, they had dreamed up a plethora of explanations: divine retribution, poison, foreigners seeking revenge.

Helpless in the face of these problems, Vasily turned to his schedule of meetings for the day. As he read, he became aware of raised voices in the outer office. Smirnov's head appeared around his door. 'Young Matvey's here to see you. He seems very distressed.'

What could this be now? 'Show him in.'

Matvey slid into the room, his face gleaming with sweat and his hair even more unkempt than usual. 'Sir, sir, you've got to come, sir!'

'Calm down. What's the matter?'

'It's Mr Maltby, sir. I think he's sickening. We must find Doctor Webster.'

Vasily frowned. Surely Maltby couldn't have succumbed. He was so fastidious in his habits. But one couldn't say the same about his neighbours. The area in which he lived was very mixed.

Matvey was continuing, 'I got to Mr Maltby's as usual and we started work, but he wasn't himself. He was subdued and kept yawning. In the end he said he had a pain and took to his bed.'

'Did he ask you to fetch a doctor?'

'No, he gave me some reading and told me to go home, but I know that if he does have the cholera there's no time to waste.' Matvey's voice faltered and he fell silent, blinking away tears.

Vasily looked down at his desk. Matvey was right. A doctor must be found. Webster was much the best choice. He was probably "observing" at the main isolation hospital in Sennaya Square. Vasily put on his hat and they set off along the Fontanka River. The streets were quiet, and there were no droshkies to be found. As they walked, they covered their noses against the ripe smell that hung above the water. Vasily surveyed the green surface. *The poor drink and wash in that every day; no wonder they sicken and die,* he thought.

A procession of dark wagons loaded high with coffins was approaching. The small rough-coated horses strained to make progress as the heavy wheeled carts rumbled and scraped over the stone pavement. The drivers sat, shoulders hunched. There were no priests or mourners, but a scattered group of townsfolk ran ahead. Once the frightened people had flashed by, Vasily and Matvey stepped aside to let the dead pass. The sweet medicinal odour of pitch, which doused and sealed the coffins, briefly cleansed the air.

Further along the embankment, the streets became crowded. A gentleman passed them, walking at speed. 'I wouldn't go down that way, sir,' he said. 'There's trouble in the market.' He hurried on. Soon they heard cries and a series of crashes. But that was not surprising. The square, which surrounded one of the largest markets in the capital, was always filled with noise.

Obukhovsky Prospekt, the main thoroughfare, was jammed with people. Some were leaving the square, but the majority were swarming towards it. 'We'll have to get out of this,' said Vasily. 'Take a detour.' They turned off, cutting through narrow, foul-smelling courtyards between noisy tenements, where grimy washing hung from the windows and a filthy mix of mud and urine liaised underfoot. These were some of the worst slums in the city, a place where the destitute, dissolute and depraved lived and died side by side in uneasy partnership. Few policemen or officials ever showed their faces here. Vasily wondered if he should have brought his pistols, but guessed they would be of little use.

They emerged halfway along the side of the square. To their right stood the many-domed Church of the Saviour; to the left, the houses that had been converted into the isolation hospital. Things were far from normal. The place was alive with people, but no-one was occupied with business. All the traders had disappeared, and the low wooden pallets on which they usually displayed their wares were either bare or supporting onlookers.

Vasily climbed up onto the nearest pallet, and looked towards the hospital. Almost at once, as if orchestrated, the windows seemed to disintegrate and a waterfall of glass tumbled down the building's facade. Pillows, straw mattresses, medical equipment and chamber pots flew through the air onto the pavement. Crashes and cries came from within. Occasionally the surge of people at the entrance would separate to allow a stretcher carrying a patient to be borne away.

A cart carrying the sick came from Sadovaya Street, passed the church, and made its way slowly towards the hospital. It was followed by a group of women, their faces swathed in shawls. Within a few moments the cart was surrounded by a mob, the driver thrown to the ground and the patients carried off to God knew where.

Matvey had removed his cravat and was now carrying his jacket. 'You should take off your hat, sir,' he said. 'They'll think you're an official... or worse, a doctor.'

Vasily pulled off the hat and crushed it under his arm. To the left he could see that the gates of the church were firmly closed, but a couple of guardsmen stood, unmoving, under the columns of the market guardhouse nearby. More and more people were streaming into the square, many coming from Nevsky, others from the embankment of the Catherine Canal.

Vasily was filled with despair. There was little point in approaching the hospital; they would never be able to extract Webster. But unless they reached him or some other doctor soon, Maltby could die. He knew his service uniform would attract attention. For Matvey's safety and his own, they must seek refuge in the guardhouse.

Matvey stared around at the chaos, his face etched with grief. As Vasily pulled him in the direction of the military post, he thought that for a moment he was going to resist. But then he acquiesced, muttering with frustration. They hadn't progressed more than a few yards when a boy ran forward and snatched Vasily's hat from beneath his arm. He waved it in the air. 'A doctor! A doctor!'

A group of men encircled them. Vasily was seized by a wave of fear. This didn't feel good.

''E aren't a doctor!' Matvey yelled, his carefully acquired accent reverting to street argot. ''e's from the Ministry, an' 'e's 'ere about the roads! Look, 'e's in uniform, 'as a badge. Doctors don't have 'em!'

A red-bearded peasant in a tattered smock seemed to be the ringleader. 'Let's be seeing your jackets,' he said. The crowd surged forward. Men snatched Vasily's handkerchief, then his watch and chain and the silver medal he had received on his return from Warsaw. His

227

jacket was pulled from his back, and as he was jostled back and forth, fingers probed his pockets, his trousers. The stink of sweat and vodka made his head spin as he tried to master his fear.

'What's this here!' From Matvey's torn jacket, a small bag emerged. Vasily's heart sank. Had the boy brought some useless prophylactic with him? He had been told to carry nothing in his pockets. Now there *would* be more trouble…

'Poison! Poison!'

'The government's trying to murder us!'

'They're spies… The officer's not a road inspector, he's a Pole!'

'I'm not a damned Pole!' Vasily shouted, his stomach churning.

The crowd was not convinced. Someone pulled his arms behind his back. The red beard peered into the bag and shook it. A shower of sticky apricot kernels scattered over the cobbles. The man gave a humourless laugh, then turned his attention to Vasily's handkerchief and, sniffing it, remarked, 'That's sweet. Who does your washing for you… some fancy whore, I'd say.' He threw the cloth down onto the pavement and ground it to tatters with his heel.

'What shall we do with them?' said one of the men restraining Matvey.

'Let the servant go, and give the master a thrashing!' a woman cried.

This met with general approval, and Matvey was released. 'You shouldn't beat my master,' he cried, desperation in his voice. 'He's here to help a dying friend…'

'Poison him, more like! Or force him into the hospital!' A merchant's boy in a round narrow-brimmed hat waved a stout stick. 'The toffs want to do away with us all, that's clear enough. Besides, I thought you said he was here about the roads…' Mutters of agreement rumbled through the crowd. The men holding Vasily shoved him forward. He stumbled, dropped onto his knees on the cobblestones, shut his eyes and, with a sense of sick resignation, waited for the first blow to fall.

'Let that man go at once!' A voice that could only be that of a soldier blasted across the square. Vasily heard the slap of running boots and the rattle of muskets. He looked up.

'Thank God!' he breathed.

Four guardsmen were approaching, bayonets fixed. The mob surrounding them fled. Now Matvey was pulling him up and arms were supporting him. His legs trembled, sweat poured down his face, and he reached for his kerchief – but of course, it had gone.

※

A very young officer in a tall plumed helmet greeted them at the guardhouse. He introduced himself as Ensign Ivan Romanovich van der Khoven and claimed to be in command of the small band of lifeguard grenadiers manning the building.

Matvey reached out and snatched at his sleeve. 'Our friend is dying! We must get to the hospital to find the doctor.'

The soldier shook his head. 'I'm sorry, I can't help you.

I don't have enough men, as you can see – just twelve. I've sent to headquarters for support, but God knows if the message has got through. I should have been relieved by now in any event but there's no sign of anyone. All I can do is send out the occasional squad to people in obvious trouble. I've twenty or so prisoners downstairs in the cells and my first priority has to be keeping them there.'

As he spoke, Vasily heard insistent rattling coming from below, accompanied by shouts of, 'Help us, brothers! Let us out!'

'They're trying to loosen the grilles. I think they'll hold firm, but… Look, I'm sorry, sir, you'll have to excuse me. Make yourself as comfortable as you can. We all have to wait this out.' Some moments later they heard him shouting threats at his charges in the basement.

They made their way into the inner guardroom, where they found a number of high-back Voltaire chairs. Vasily, his heartbeat finally slowing, his legs barely working, slumped into one. Matvey stood staring at a large clock on the wall. It was a quarter to twelve. They had left the Ministry an hour ago. How long must they wait here while the minutes ticked away?

The room slowly filled with people of the better sort, most rescued from the mob by the guardsmen. They included an elderly regimental *kapellmeister* who had been ambushed in his droshky. His three-cornered hat had been taken for that of a doctor. The old man was trembling. Like Vasily, he had lost his jacket and belongings in the fray. He sat in the uncomfortable chair, unable to speak a word. Later, the distinguished courtier Bibikov staggered in. He immediately started to give orders to van der Khoven, instructing him to fire volleys over the head of the crowd. He received a polite but firm refusal.

All seemed like a dream. As time passed, Vasily's fear of the mob receded but his concern for Maltby grew sharper. Matvey, who had remained uncharacteristically silent, paced back and forth, glancing at the clock, looking out through the grimy windows or walking out onto the steps overlooking the square.

At four o'clock, a procession emerged from the hospital. A throng of people, led by priests bearing censors and icons, carried patients, stricken with disease, towards the church. The mob, shouting hysterically, surged behind them. They surrounded the guardhouse and started to respond to the cries for help from the prisoners. The bars of the cells in the basement rattled ominously.

'Right!' shouted van der Khoven. 'All civilians into the inner guardroom! Stay in there and keep calm!' He left, slamming the door behind him. Vasily's fear revived. He should have brought his pistols. The soldiers were heavily outnumbered. Stones clattered against the walls. As the crackle of musket fire overlaid the tumult outside, debris flew through a window, propelling glass across the floor. A woman screamed. Matvey grasped Vasily's arm, his face grey.

But soon they heard cries of, 'Hurrah!' The small squad of soldiers, despite the odds, had, it seemed, faced the mob down. Below, in the basement, the prisoners fell silent as birds at dusk.

For a while all was quiet, but when the church emptied disorder resumed. The guardhouse was apparently forgotten, as the crowd tossed and heaved outside the hospital. At last they heard the sound of a trumpet, and a roll of drums. Van der Khoven ran out to the steps, the plume on his helmet askew, closely followed by Vasily and Matvey. A detachment of very young soldiers was marching through the square in loose columns, clearing the crowds away with great efficiency.

'It's the trainee sapper battalion,' van der Khoven said.

The engineering students were soon followed by a detachment from the Ismailovsky Guards regiment, and finally the bright blue jackets of the Corps of Gendarmes appeared. Two heavy guns, their fuses smoking, were being dragged to the centre of the square. Soon the market was filled with uniforms, and there was not a civilian in sight. It occurred to Vasily that he had not spotted a regular policeman all day.

As soon as van der Khoven gave them leave, Vasily and Matvey crossed the square to the hospital. As they crunched through broken glass and kicked aside the wreckage, gendarmes were leading bewildered functionaries, doctors and orderlies down the steps of the building. They soon identified the tall figure of Webster, carrying his bag, seemingly as unruffled as if he had just been making a call.

'The idiots locked us up!' he commented, shaking his head. Vasily noticed a large bruise on his cheek. 'Said they were sending envoys to the Emperor, that we'd been poisoning the patients and when he heard about it he would hang us! A lot of nonsense, of course. But it's good to see you, Vasily Nikolayevich, and you, Matthew. How can I help you?'

He agreed to come with them to Maltby's at once.

※

The streets around the square were deserted. Eventually, they found a droshky to take them to the Englishman's small apartment off Nevsky Prospekt. Vasily searched in vain in his pockets for his stolen watch, but even without it he knew it had been at least nine hours since Matvey had left Maltby to come to find him. He prayed that Matvey's diagnosis was mistaken.

Maltby lived on the third floor. Matvey went ahead, taking the stairs two at a time. When Vasily and Webster reached the door, the boy had already crashed through the sitting room into the bedroom beyond. They were greeted by the stench of vomit and faeces. Vasily knew at once that his worst fears had been realised. Webster stretched his hand out. 'I'd stay out here for a moment, Count, and try not to touch anything…' He followed Matvey into the bedroom.

Vasily looked around the room where he had spent so many happy evenings. A vase of red roses stood on the dining table, still fresh. The decanter, as usual, stood half full on the dresser. A book lay open on the table by Maltby's armchair, another on the patterned rug by the fire screen. It seemed as though his friend had just walked out for a few moments and would shortly be back.

There was no sound from the bedroom. He could not bring himself to enter. Finally, Webster emerged. He pulled a towel from his bag and wiped his hands. 'He's been dead for some hours, Vasily Nikolayevich. He wasn't a young man. It's very likely I couldn't have saved him in any event. Young Matthew should come out of there now. It's better not to take any risks.'

Vasily stepped round an upturned water jug and walked into the bedroom. Maltby's body was lying on the bed. Webster had closed his eyes. His face was sunken and pale, his lips were blue, but he was recognisably himself. Vasily felt a savage stab of loss and could have given way to tears, but for Matvey's sake, he knew he shouldn't succumb. It would have been comforting to touch Maltby's hand for a last time, but he couldn't do that either. The youth was standing at the window, gazing sightlessly at the glass. Vasily walked over to him and took him by the shoulder. 'We must say goodbye to him, Motya,' he said. They'll need to take him away and seal the apartment.'

Matvey closed his eyes and rubbed his temples. 'I can't believe he's gone, sir. I…' He couldn't continue.

'He'll never completely leave you, leave either of us,' Vasily said. 'All the discussions we've had, all the things he's taught us… they'll stay with us.' He felt that was true, but wasn't sure it offered much comfort. He turned away, not knowing what else to say, and went back into the living room. Matvey moved to follow him. Webster held out a sealed package. 'This was addressed to you, Belkin. I'd leave it a day or so before you open it. I don't believe infection is transmitted by paper, but nothing is certain.'

'Thank you, sir. And thank you for trying to help us at the end of what must have been a difficult day.'

The doctor shrugged. 'I've known worse,' he said.

Two days passed. The Emperor sailed on his yacht from his refuge outside town to St Petersburg, despite the fact he was mourning the death of his brother, Constantine, who had succumbed to cholera while on the border of Poland. Nicholas toured several trouble spots, and his imposing presence subdued the crowds. The increasingly deserted streets of the city assumed an eerie calm as the people were driven indoors and the number of cholera cases climbed steadily.

Alexander and the prince insisted that Vasily and Matvey stay at home. Maltby's death and their experiences in Sennaya Square had clearly upset them. When Vasily recalled that it was said that low spirits made one susceptible to the disease, he was happy to comply with their wishes. Outwardly Matvey seemed calm, but he was unusually quiet and spent a good deal of time in his room. On the afternoon of the second day, Vasily roused the boy, and together they retrieved Maltby's package from one of the many unused rooms in the palace. A box inside was addressed to Vasily, and a letter to Matvey.

Matvey watched intently as Vasily opened the box. Inside lay Maltby's fine English gold watch, an object the tutor had treasured. A short affectionate note expressed the hope that Vasily would wear it and remember him. Vasily blinked away rising tears. Maltby had often been generous when he had most needed it, and now he had been so again.

Matvey picked up his letter and broke the seal. He perused it for several minutes and then dropped it on the table, his face scarlet. 'Please read it, sir,' he said as he rushed from the room.

Vasily's heart was full as he saw Maltby's familiar hand. The letter had obviously been written some time ago. Had the Englishman already been ailing? Or had he had some premonition of death? As Webster had said, he hadn't been a young man.

Dear Matthew,

You must take this letter to Mr Lewis, my agent, on Nevsky Prospekt. Vasily Nikolayevich knows where he can be found. Lewis keeps a copy of my will, within which you will discover my wishes for the disposition of my small estate in the event of my death; an event which I fear is not far away.

In short, what I have, Matthew, is yours. It is not a great fortune, but enough to give you some independence when you go on to the university and build on the work we have done together. There are also my books and my few effects. Please sell what is of no use to you.

How does a teacher without close family reward one's most promising student? If that student is dependent on the charity of others, however well-intentioned and honest, there is always the risk that for whatever reason their generosity might come to an end. I go to my grave happy, knowing that you will not be without resources.

I know you will work hard and remember me. You must be a good and respectful friend to Vasily Nikolayevich. He has made you what you are, and he loves you as I do. He will have charge of your legacy until you come of age.

Your friend,
Thomas Maltby

CHAPTER TWENTY-ONE

July 1831 – St Petersburg

Vasily returned to work three days after the Emperor's visit to the city. The rioting had ceased and the police. who had prudently retreated into their police houses, now re-emerged to charge and incarcerate suspected troublemakers. These arrests, often arbitrary, had repercussions. Those with influence bribed their way out of trouble, while the less well-connected were thrown into prison to await trial. Vasily was relieved to learn that some regulations had now been relaxed and concern about body-snatching had meant the banning of post-mortems. But a vigilant eye was still being maintained on the cordon sanitaire to ensure no-one entered or left the city without appropriate papers.

One evening Vasily came home to find his uncle in a state of agitation. 'A footman has fallen ill,' he said. 'Webster thinks it's just dysentery, but we've isolated him.'

'The number of cases is still going up,' said Vasily. 'I wonder if you shouldn't think of leaving. It probably isn't too late.'

Alexander shook his head. 'You know Dmitry won't go, and I still have to put in an appearance at the Ministry from time to time. Besides, given the number of barriers between here and Dubovnoye, the journey could take weeks.' Vasily knew that Alexander could evade the regulations if he needed to, but he valued his uncle's help and advice, and, despite his concern, was relieved that he was resolved to stay.

Matvey joined them and they descended to dinner. As they were starting on a depleted offering of dried meat and preserves, they heard noises from the direction of Kuprin's mansion next door. Vasily rose to look out of the window.

'His wife's ill,' the prince said.

'You didn't tell me,' said Alexander.

'I didn't want to concern you. Two or three of their servants have had the disease, I understand, but only one has died.'

Vasily could see some policemen approaching and, as he watched, a smartly dressed man who must have been a doctor climbed into a flashy gig and drove away. 'I think she may be worse than ill,' he commented. 'The police have arrived.'

The prince, ever inquisitive, sent a servant for news. He quickly returned. 'Madam Kuprin has fallen victim to cholera, sir,' he said. 'She succumbed early this morning, I understand. She is to be laid out at home, but it will not be possible to pay respects to the body. Mister Kuprin is, however, welcoming callers.'

'They're not going to seal the house?' Alexander asked.
'No, sir.'
'We've stopped doing that now, Uncle,' said Vasily.

'People took against being locked up with the dead. It was one of the causes of the riots.'

'Someone will have to go round out of courtesy, I suppose.' Alexander's thin shoulders drooped. Relations with the merchant next door had never been warm. He looked hopefully at Vasily.

'I'll call tomorrow morning, sir.'

※

As promised, the next day Vasily walked the short distance to the house next door. It was dark and stuffy in the cavernous drawing room. A sickly honeyed smell, mixed with lamp oil, pervaded the air. As Vasily waited, sweat ran down his spine. He crossed the room, his feet soundless on the rich woven carpet. The shutters were closed but the gilded furniture that cluttered the room gleamed with reflected light. A red glow flickered on the silver revetment that over-laced the icon in the corner. Waxy-leaved pot plants stood hunched in the corners. On one of the overstuffed sofas an embroidery frame lay discarded, and on a side table one of Madame Hélène's black and white hat boxes, with its flourish of a signature, stood accompanied by a miniature replica offering confectionary. Its lid was open.

'I'm sorry to have kept you, Count.' Kuprin greeted him with his customary brusqueness. His thick dark hair, peppered with grey, was tidy and his beard freshly trimmed. He showed no outward sign of grief; perhaps he had not yet fully grasped the reality of his wife's death. Vasily pronounced the usual words of condolence.

'She went very quickly, you know, Belkin,' the

merchant said. His eyes were wary and he kept his distance. He waved his square-fingered hand towards the discarded embroidery. His ruby ring flashed. 'Just two nights ago she was sitting there after dinner, stitching away, as lively as she ever was. Then she said she was retiring, had a pain. I was woken in the night by comings and goings, and called a doctor. He gave her the recommended treatment, camomile and opium; bled her too... but it did no good.'

'I'm sorry, sir. Cholera can be a rapid killer.'

'Yes, so it seems.' Kuprin walked towards the window and stared down into the street for a few moments. As he turned back, his face seemed more troubled. He nodded towards the hat box. 'And she'd just taken delivery of a new bonnet... I wanted to cheer her up. She found staying in the house, not going out, very wearing. I thought the hat would be a reminder of normality, you see.' He shrugged. 'I've sent to them to come and take it back.'

Kuprin noticed the box of sweets. He barked at the lackey, who had been hovering at the door. 'Those should have been taken away!'

'Yes sir. Sorry, sir.' The offending box was removed.

Having made an offer of practical help if needed, there seemed nothing further to say. Vasily bowed and withdrew. The sun still scalded the pavement outside but the air in the street felt fresh on his face. He paused for a moment and stood in the shade of the stable yard arch. As he did so a carriage drew up to the steps of Kuprin's house, and the familiar figure of Madame Hélène climbed out. She was dressed in silk of the deepest black. It was clear that having opted to remain in the city, she had decided to collect the unwanted hat herself.

CHAPTER TWENTY-TWO

August 1831 – Blonie, fifteen versts to the west of Warsaw.

'They say that it was the cholera that killed the Field Marshall, but I'm not so sure.'

Andrey blinked. 'What do you mean you're not sure, Filipson? What else could it have been?'

'It can't have been a coincidence that the day before Diebitsch died, Count Orlov came all the way from Petersburg to present him with what must have been a rather stiff rebuke from the Emperor,' insisted his companion, a first lieutenant from the Duke of Wurttemberg's Grenadiers.

Andrey shook his head. 'You think he killed himself?'

'That, or foul play…'

'Orlov killed Diebitsch? That's ridiculous!'

Filipson fell silent for a moment. He was a solid young man of Scottish ancestry with thick reddish-brown hair, a large nose and unexpectedly generous eyes. 'Well, perhaps,' he conceded. 'But my lads were on guard duty the day after the Field Marshall died. I saw the body – they embalmed it with indecent haste, you know – he looked pretty fit before he died! The barber who attended him was shocked that he expired within hours of his morning shave.'

They were walking along the village street towards staff headquarters. The sun was hot. Filipson started to whistle, abandoning his tune from time to time to greet men to right and left. The young grenadier had, like Andrey, just been seconded to the staff. He was an engaging comrade. Aged just twenty-one, he had been a first lieutenant for almost two years. His father, an impoverished landowner from Kazan, had somehow persuaded a senior officer to take him on at fourteen, well below the legal age. Grigory Ivanovich had been chaotically educated, but there was little he didn't know about the workings of the army, and his amiable character and store of anecdotes meant that his merits had been quickly recognised by his superiors.

Andrey considered. Could Filipson be right? It was common knowledge that the Emperor had been dissatisfied with Diebitsch's sluggish performance. There had been rumours for months that Nicholas had wanted to replace his Field Marshal with Ivan Paskevich, the new commander-in-chief.

On the other hand, prior to Diebitsch's death, the tide of war had seemed to be turning. The bloody fight at Ostrolenka in May had been a clear victory for Russia. Now, the Poles had largely retreated behind Warsaw's well fortified walls, where it was said they were becoming increasingly divided by political wrangling. Moreover, cholera had been rife within the army in May. Even the Tsar's brother, Grand Duke Constantine, hadn't been spared. It was difficult to know what to believe.

Andrey's mood was buoyant. A few days ago, the call had come to join the staff of the Infantry Division under Major General Gurko. The staff always seemed short of suitable men, and now that the Russian army was united and moving forward in force, there was a good deal of work to do to prepare the way for the final attack.

When the two men arrived at headquarters, they found Gurko himself giving out the orders of the day. Andrey was to leave camp immediately, his task to restore a bridge destroyed by the enemy on the main road to the capital. Bidding his new friend goodbye, and still wondering about the true fate of the late Field Marshal, he went to find his horse and escort.

As he rode out of the village, accompanied by a protective squad of Cossacks, the air became fresher. A light breeze cooled his face. It was good to have something useful to do. His mare, sensing his mood, sprang brightly along the sandy track. His mind wandered freely. The cholera had finally arrived in St Petersburg in June, which was troubling news. He knew that Nadezhda was safely in the countryside, but what about Minnie? To his surprise, he now found himself recalling their affair with little sense of guilt, and even some amusement. He remembered his Uncle Friedrich. He had spent little money while on campaign, and on his higher pay he would soon be able to send another contribution to his family. He hoped they had begun to forgive his previous neglect and would be proud when they learned of his promotion.

After five or so versts they reached an estate house in a small village. Its wealthy Polish owners, loyal to the Emperor, were unconcerned about admitting the enemy. Having dined there with the engineer who would supervise the restoration of the bridge, they rode on to the river. Repairs proceeded without disturbance, but the work continued until dawn. During the night, small detachments of troops arrived and, when the bridge was passable, they crossed and took up a position on the far side of the stream.

As Andrey returned to Blonie the next morning, he met the advance guard leaving the town. The army had begun its march towards Warsaw; the final struggle must surely be imminent.

※

25th August 1831 – Warsaw

The men of the King of Prussia's regiment stood watching the first light of dawn reveal the highway to the Polish capital. They were to the west of the city, close to the heavily defended suburb of Volya. Only the intermittent cheep of a courageous bird, the squeaking wheel of a gun carriage, the chink of metal on metal, broke the silence. Then, as the rising sun blazed over the roofs of the settlement, the cannonade began.

The bombardment of the outer earthworks continued for two hours. As the enemy began to return fire, the reverberating air was drenched with powder-laced acrid grey smoke. Soon, the twenty-four-pounders mounted on the city walls added a growling bass tone to the mix.

Andrey breathed deeply, then coughed in the tainted air. He thought he had become hardened to the roar of artillery, but the measure of this was something different. The grenadiers were not quite out of range of enemy guns. He must remain calm, appear confident, set an example. When, a few days ago he had returned to his regiment from his short spell of service on the staff, to his surprise he had found himself in temporary command of his former company. It seemed there had been little choice but to appoint him. Vengerov was still recovering from injuries sustained at Nur, Rosovsky had been retained by General Ugrumov, and casualties and disease had taken their toll among other officers in recent months.

He stood surveying the scene with Sergeant Sidorov among deserted homesteads and kitchen gardens. Months of Russian hesitation and delay had enabled the Poles to protect the vulnerable western edge of the city that was not flanked by the waters of the Vistula. The enemy army, assisted by eager citizens, had constructed a double range of intermittent fortified defences that stretched for several versts some distance outside the old town walls. The nearest earthworks were only dimly visible but they seemed substantial. Beyond them stood the Volya fortress, a closed redoubt with bastions, raised around a solid white rectangle, the Church of St Lawrence.

His men spoke in low voices. They seemed to be holding up well but, like him, must be tired and hungry. They had marched silently in full parade dress through the moonless night along narrow lanes, halting for some time at Chrzanów, two versts from the first line of fortifications. Before dawn they had been ordered to leave their packs behind and move to their current position.

Now they stood in battle order towards the rear of Count Pahlen's division of infantry, cavalry and artillery.

Andrey pulled out his glass, peered at the defences and turned to Sergeant Sidorov. 'The sides seem steep… no glacises… Do you think the men will manage to scale them?' While still in camp the company had made wooden siege ladders, which they had been ordered to bring with them, but now these seemed to have been forgotten or abandoned. Not for the first time, Andrey despaired of the casual approach of many of the troops when they thought they could get away with it.

The sergeant puffed out his cheeks. 'Well, if they're required to, sir, but I think the work will have been done by the time we're called on to assist…'

Before Andrey could enquire further about the fate of the ladders, a trumpet rang out. The guns fell silent. Sidorov ordered the troop to stand ready. Soon a group of volunteers from the guards, seeking death or glory, would make the first assault on the fort, supported by the first division of line infantry, led by Paskevich's second-in-command, Count Toll.

Colonel Chevakinsky, commanding the King of Prussia's regiment, gave the order to advance. A cannonball in flight from the direction of the city split the air overhead. Andrey judged that it would overshoot and that his men would be unscathed, but he glanced round all the same. A man shrieked. Some poor souls in the Emperor of Austria's regiment, drawn up to the rear, had been unlucky. As Andrey forced himself to march on steadily, the ground seemed to move beneath his feet. A series of ear-splitting explosions carried from the fort, accompanied by flashes and billows of smoke, and shortly followed by an eruption of high-flung debris.

'That's one of their ammo stores gone,' said Sidorov.

They were ordered to halt while the tumult of battle raged on around them. Word came that Russian troops had taken and overrun Volya's first defences. Some of the smaller structures, it seemed, had not even been manned. But the Poles within the fortress were putting up solid resistance. At eleven o'clock, however, the sound of heavy guns ceased, and the crackle of musket shot faded away. Andrey could see a Russian flag raised on the ramparts.

Sidorov spat tobacco onto the ground. 'That'll show them!' he said. 'They didn't think we'd go straight for the fort... boasted that if we attacked Volya, the fort would be our grave. Expected us to bear down on weaker spots...'

Cannon fire could still be heard in the distance. Andrey thought that perhaps the sergeant shouldn't speak too soon, but now came the order to move forward again. The grenadiers, preceded by two companies of carabiniers, were to occupy the fortress. As they passed the reduced earthworks of the outer fortifications, Andrey could see the church within the fort, a solid white cliff rising up. There were several holes in its roof and part of its tiered tower had been shot away.

Ahead, the carabiniers, bayonets raised, had almost reached the fort, when a shout and musket fire came from the direction of the city. The Poles were attempting a counter attack. The carabiniers knelt and opened fire on the enemy infantry, and then fell on their assailants with terrible ferocity, fighting hand to hand, the butts of their muskets swinging high into the air, cracking down to shatter their victims' heads and limbs. The Poles responded in kind, then wavered, but then came on again. The struggle continued for several minutes, but the enemy's reinforcements were deterred by renewed cannon fire from the ramparts of the fort. At last, the Poles fled in the direction of the city, leaving a scene of carnage behind them.

'Order the men to keep their eyes straight ahead,' Andrey told Sidorov as they approached the splintered gates. The remains of men and horses lay scattered around them and piled in the surrounding ditch. As they marched in, more corpses were being thrown from the walls.

Inside the fort, all was confusion. Troops wandered around; captured guns were being re-sited. A group of prisoners was huddled in a corner under guard. The bodies of Polish soldiers were being removed from the church, where a field hospital was being set up. As Andrey's company were directed to the graveyard nearby. he noticed that the guns had fallen silent. Negotiations must be taking place.

The men stood or sat at ease among the graves. Andrey's head was spinning. He was very hungry, but he had eaten his small ration of biscuit hours before. Sidorov and some of the other men had wisely shown more self-control and still had provisions, but many didn't. Yet again, Andrey despaired of the lack of organisation. Throughout the campaign, provisioning had been chaotic. He became more alarmed when he saw that men were distributing flasks of vodka.

'Don't worry, sir. They'll need a slug to wake them up, and I dare say some biscuit will follow.'

'Well, I hope so...' The stoicism of his men, and their capacity for drink, amazed him. He sank down onto a low square tomb. It must be late afternoon. If they remained here tonight it wouldn't be a comfortable billet. The slab now felt warm in the sun, but the nights were getting colder; they had neither blankets nor thick clothes.

Some parts of the high wall around the cemetery had collapsed under fire. From where he sat, he could see what had once been an orchard and vegetable plot that had been enclosed by the walls. Trees had been cut down for firewood, only stumps remained, and the beds had been trampled by military boots, but here and there a yellowing cabbage or skeletal fruit bush survived. Troops involved in the initial assault were leaving the fort. Wagons continued to bring in the wounded and remove the dead. Doctors and surgeons were arriving at the church in gigs, or riding on stocky cobs. Their sleeves already rolled up, one or two took precautionary swigs of spirit from leather flasks.

Andrey's stomach rumbled alarmingly. His head still felt light and he thought he was hallucinating when he saw a familiar figure approaching. It was Filipson, who nodded in recognition, and then stopped to speak for some time to an officer from the Siberian Grenadiers, who was making for the gates with his detachment. Their conversation concluded, Filipson greeted him warmly. 'Andrey Andreyevich! I'm glad to see you in one piece. I came to find my friend, Gagarin. He's with the Siberians... They were pretty active in the assault...'

'And is he alive?'

'Oh yes, very much so, although apparently some

shrapnel from a grenade sliced off the top of his helmet… But I've missed him. I'm told he's gone back to camp.'

As he spoke, Andrey noticed the arrival of a cart bringing biscuit from the field kitchens. 'Thank the Lord… some food. We've had nothing since yesterday.'

'Oh, I think we can do better than that.' With a flourish, Filipson pulled open the top of a sack that he was carrying. Andrey peered inside. It looked like a whole roast duck. His mouth started to water.

'Where did you get that?'

'Don't ask… but we've been standing in reserve all day at Czyste, just west of the road to the Jerusalem Gate, close to a farmstead. I expected to share it with Gagarin, but since he's chosen to depart…'

Taking along Borisov's replacement, a pale young ensign, Andrey and Filipson disappeared behind the walls of the church to a far corner of the cemetery. The resourceful Filipson had also managed to secure a bottle of wine and some gritty bread. Andrey tried not to think too deeply about the provenance of their dinner.

'The Siberians didn't take too many casualties, apparently,' Filipson said through a mouthful of duck. 'Although the fighting was tough. Our chaps killed General Savinsky, the commander of the fort. You know, the man whose leg we shot off at Borodino. He refused to concede, made a last stand in the church… he was bayonetted in front of the altar… took a lot of men with him.' Filipson wiped the back of his hand across his mouth. 'There were plenty of prisoners too, some officers and over a thousand men. They even caught Visotsky, the character from the cadet school who started the entire revolt.'

Andrey found it hard not to admire the Poles. Of course, they were fighting for their country's freedom, and many were volunteers, but their passion and bravery stood in marked contrast to the dogged resignation of his Russian troopers. His men never expressed any view about the purpose of their mission here, at least not in his hearing. In their way they could be as brave as the Poles, but they seemed more motivated by the avoidance of trouble than by patriotic enthusiasm.

Andrey chewed on his duck leg, his fingers becoming slick with grease. 'Do you think this ceasefire will hold?'

'I doubt it,' answered Filipson. 'Paskevich should have fought on. We were on the front foot. It seems General Toll argued that stopping to negotiate now would simply give the enemy the chance to regroup. But he was overruled, and so we'll have another night in the open.'

Andrey could see Sargeant Sidorov wandering among the gravestones. He was probably looking for him. He rose to his feet. The dubious duck lay heavy on his stomach. 'I must go, Filipson. I should be with the men.'

'Yes, and I must get back to Czyste. Well, if the truce doesn't hold, I dare say we'll both be in the thick of it tomorrow. Good luck to you.'

Andrey watched Filipson's broad form retreat. For a big man, he moved with surprising lightness of foot.

'Good news, sir!' Sidorov approached with a knowing smirk. 'It seems we're staying here until tomorrow and we need to select some of the lads for guard duty tonight!'

Andrey frowned. How would the men take the news? They wouldn't welcome this extra imposition. But in the event, the sergeant found willing volunteers without problem. Revived by their meagre rations, the men seemed to assume they were on the brink of victory and their spirits were high.

※

26th August 1831

At dawn, Andrey stood on the north-eastern bastion of the fort. The roofs of the settlement of Volya stretched towards the walls of Warsaw. He could trace the route of the main highway, which led between the low buildings to the city barrier. Many houses had been damaged, some completely destroyed, by the previous day's fighting. He looked through his glass at the distant city walls. Yesterday evening a crowd of townsfolk had gathered there to observe the besiegers, but now the walkways were empty. He thought he could make out the round maws of the heavy guns. They seemed to be unmanned.

He yawned and stretched, shivered and stamped his feet. It had been very cold last night, and no fires or lights had been permitted. The noise of sappers repairing parts of the fortress, combined with the constant rumble of wagons, had kept him awake. He needed a shave. As he wondered if it was safe to send for Morozov, there was movement below. On the track beneath the rampart, a detachment of the Chevalier Guard was trotting towards the city, their white uniforms and silver-grey breastplates gleaming in the morning light. He squinted down. Was Ivan Stenovsky riding with them? The commander-in-chief, Paskevich, followed, accompanied by the Emperor's brother, Grand Duke Michael, and Count Toll, the Chief of the General Staff. The group turned off to the left into the settlement. They must be meeting the Poles on neutral territory. Perhaps terms would be agreed. Several thousand soldiers now surrounded the city. Following the seizure of the Volya fort and several of the outer fortifications, the Russians had a clear advantage.

Andrey walked along the walls to review his men, who were keeping watch by the guns that now pointed towards the city. They seemed in good order, their green uniforms only a little grimy, their white crossbands as clean as could be expected, the stamped metal shako plates bright. He felt self-conscious and slightly awkward. Behind their rigid expressions perhaps they were laughing at him, at his youth and inexperience. He knew he should try to enjoy his new role, make the most of it. Once all this was over, his previous shortcomings might be remembered, and he could find himself once again a sub-lieutenant languishing in a distant garrison. On the other hand, if things went well, he might be able to return to the staff. Rosovsky had thought it possible and Filipson, ever optimistic, was sure of it. In time, that could mean a return to St Petersburg. First, however, he must survive the rest of the war.

He returned to the cemetery. His men were marched back from duty. Muskets were dismantled and cleaned, flints checked. Noon passed, then one o'clock. No further food was forthcoming, but fires for tea had been lit, and he had managed to shave. How long did they expect him and his men to survive on next to nothing? His shameful duck dinner had receded into the distant past. Stomach rumbling, he dozed in the sunlight.

A great roar shook him awake. He leapt to his feet and looked round for his sabre. His men grabbed their muskets. It seemed as though every piece of Russian ordinance had burst into life. Only Sidorov remained seated, whittling away at some wood with a small knife. 'That's just to encourage the Poles to make up their minds,' he said, not looking up.

'How do you know?'

'Well, I can't think of any other reason to fire. There's no sign of the enemy.'

The guns did indeed fall silent once more, but the men were now unsettled and within the hour a trumpet blew the call to arms. It seemed that the Polish Sejm was unable to accept Russian terms of surrender. Colonel Chevakinsky arrived at the fort, accompanied by several officers, including Kirill Rosovsky. He grasped Andrey's arm briefly as he passed and murmured, 'God be with you.' The Russian cannonade recommenced and the Poles were now returning fire.

At one-thirty, fighting restarted along the fortifications, but it was not until late afternoon that the King of Prussia's men were marched out to stand ready in the open fields to the right of the road to Warsaw. The Guards under Grand Duke Michael stood to the left, a detachment of light infantry, carabiniers, in advance. From where Andrey stood at the front of his company, it wasn't possible to make sense of much, but the presence of the guards implied that this would be the final push for the city.

His stomach was hollow and his heart was hammering. It was hot. His shirt stuck to his spine; his shako felt even heavier than usual. He patted his breast where he had concealed Nadezhda's glove as a talisman and briefly prayed for her and for himself. More settled, he checked his pistols, gripped the hilt of his half-sabre and shook his water canister. He hoped the men had obeyed instructions to fill their own. How would they perform? Would they obey his orders or mistrust his inexperience? Although sharp and responsive on the parade ground, they now faced something entirely different. Would those endless hours of drill help at all in the heat of battle? They had rarely fired real ammunition and many had little experience of confronting an enemy at close quarters.

The thunder of artillery rolled around the walls. The occasional bright blare of trumpets, shouts and the screams of men and horses came from the south. A fierce cavalry battle was raging in the fields before the Jerusalem Gate, but he could see nothing of it through the billowing smoke. The murk cleared briefly, and a company of hussars streaked past at a gallop towards the fight, their bright red jackets glowing, their grey horses like ghosts, surging forwards, forming and reforming among the clouds of fumes and dust.

As the King of Prussia's men continued to stand ready, Colonel Chevakinsky addressed them. He would shortly give the order to advance. The outer ring of fortifications having been overrun, Count Pahlen's infantry was now successfully storming the second line of the city's defences. The task of the grenadiers would be to take the last obstacle, the Volya city barrier. The streets of the intervening settlement were narrow so they could not advance as a body. If necessary, the Emperor of Austria's

Grenadiers would reinforce them from the rear. He wished them success; he had every confidence in them.

The men turned to the east for a moment of silent prayer and then shouted, 'Hurrah!' Chevakinsky led out the carabiniers, followed by the grenadiers, with Andrey's company to the fore. They marched in battle order along the main road to the edge of the settlement. The fortifications to left and right of the road had been cleared of the enemy and now flew Russian flags.

The windmills that circled the city were ablaze, huge torches against the darkening sky. As they approached the first house's they stepped round the corpses of a few carabiniers who had gone in some minutes earlier. It was clear that a direct march along the road through the settlement would be fraught with danger from snipers. A staff officer waved the grenadiers to the left.

'Keep together, lads!' Sidorov shouted as Andrey led his men into the narrow alleyways between the buildings. They flitted from house to house, clambering through kitchen gardens and over walls, trampling down hedges, coughing and spitting, breathing in fumes from smouldering roofs and fences. From time to time they kicked doors open, seeking the enemy. Packs of barking dogs darted past and the occasional chicken, witless with fear, flapped across their path, but the place seemed empty of people. At first they made good progress, although cannon shot whined overhead and, once, a ball fired from the city skipped and danced along the ground just a few yards away.

But now it turned out that they were not in fact alone. Struggling through smoke into the yard of an inn whose thatch was well alight, they found themselves facing a small troop of Polish infantry. It seemed they had been engaged for some time; their crossbands were blackened with powder, their faces were haggard. Some knelt and raised their muskets but their young officer, confronted by a solid body of freshly arrived grenadiers, ordered his men to fall back.

'They don't seem keen to fight,' said Sidorov. Andrey looked swiftly around. 'No, but they may not be alone…' As if to confirm his words, a shot rang out from a roof opposite the inn, felling a trooper.

'Take cover!'

But there was no follow up and, judging it to be relatively safe, Andrey led his men further to the left and then forward towards the city once more. Soon the way ahead was blocked by a long low barn, stretching across their path in both directions. Andrey could hear shots but could not judge from whence they came, and as the troop paused, a smouldering building collapsed to their right and burst into flames. There was now little choice but to move left again. At the corner of the barn, he halted to take stock. Across a piece of open ground, about seventy yards to the left, he could see the walls of a graveyard and a dark blue line – a hundred or so Polish soldiers, stood in two rows along its low wall. They were facing the other direction, firing repeated volleys across the graves, aiming to pick off Russian troops who were weaving between the tombs and monuments, making for Warsaw.

He hesitated. Should they mount an attack from the rear? They would take the enemy by surprise and would certainly kill a few of them, but they were clearly outnumbered. His orders were to take the Volya barrier, and he had already been forced some distance off the direct route to his goal. They must get past this damned barn, however. He peered cautiously round the edge. A handful of Polish pickets stood, muskets ready, covering the enemy's rear. They must be dealt with.

His guts felt liquid; blood was pulsing in his head. He took some deep breaths and forced himself to appear confident as he briefly conferred with Sidorov. He selected a platoon of men, then waited for the moment when the Polish musketeers in the front row were taking aim, and the rest were reloading. With one pistol primed, he led the men at speed along the exposed side of the barn. They swiftly overcame the first three pickets, but the fourth spotted them and shouted out; Andrey aimed his pistol, fired, and the man fell. He glanced towards the men strafing the cemetery. The picket's cry, it seemed, had gone unnoticed. The final picket attempted to fire his musket, but was rushed and brought down. The detachment reached the far corner of the barn unscathed, and quickly regrouped beside it, their muskets trained on the blue Polish line.

Now enjoying some cover, Sidorov waited for the right moment to order the remaining men to join their colleagues. It was too much to hope that this larger force would go undetected. Some of the Poles, surprised to find the enemy at their backs, turned away from the cemetery walls and opened fire. They shot erratically, too high. Andrey's men returned fire, taking several enemy soldiers down. A brace of grenadiers fell, but most were soon reunited with their comrades.

Andrey looked back. Would the Poles come after them? He prepared to order the men to form up and take aim in full view, to show that they would offer resistance. But it seemed that the Polish officers were reluctant to engage in an unlooked-for battle to their rear and, having released a few further shots, their forces, somewhat depleted, returned to the easier task of picking off Russians in the graveyard.

As Andrey led his men back into the relative safety of the settlement, the light was failing. It was almost dusk. He realised that his fear had changed to something close to rapture. This path led directly to the Volya barrier. He drew his sabre and urged his men on. Despite the shouts and gunfire ahead, they seemed keen to follow. From somewhere to the right, he could hear the rumble of the wheels of gun carriages heading towards the city.

Within a few minutes the grenadiers emerged from the last of the buildings onto the edge of a wide arc of open ground. Beneath the city walls, in the gathering gloom, a desperate struggle continued between its Polish defenders and Chevakinsky's avant-garde. As they paused for a moment, flames shot up from behind the walls, illuminating a vision from hell. An entangled body of men seethed back and forth, fighting with desperate intensity, musket pressed to musket. A sulphur-salted reek filled the air. Enemy shot poured down from above. Intermittently, a twenty-four-pounder nearby belched out thunderous waves of sound, muffling the cacophony of screams and yells.

At Andrey's signal, Sidorov bawled out the order to attack. The grenadiers needed little encouragement to join the fray. Andrey grasped his sabre and moved forward. His weapon was an improvement on the sword that it had recently replaced, but once again he longed for something more substantial.

Sidorov was at his side. 'Don't make yourself an easy target, sir.' He waved up at the walls. 'They'll be aiming at you officers – keep moving about. Stay close to the men, but not so close you get skewered.'

The advice was good, but difficult to follow. He advanced steadily on the walls, shouting encouragement, slashing to right and left with his sabre, increasingly elated as his men fought through. A Polish infantryman appeared ahead of him. A sensation of burning, like a sharp needle, dragged across his cheek. He expected a more lethal blow, but a grinning Russian carabinier, his shako askew, felled the Pole from behind with his rifle – but as quickly as he had come, he disappeared.

'You alright, sir?' Sidorov, flanked by two troopers, pulled Andrey away from the heart of the fight. He waved towards the barrier. 'I think they're flagging.' Andrey rubbed his hand across his face. It came away covered in blood. He wiped off what he could; it didn't seem too bad, didn't hurt. As he stood and caught his breath, he looked about him. The barrage from the walls seemed less intense; the defenders were wavering as they contemplated the presence of more green uniforms gathering at the edge of the settlement.

And then, like a vision, from the direction of the Jerusalem Gate a body of riderless horses appeared, in flight, it seemed, from the cavalry engagement. With empty stirrups flapping over disordered saddlecloths, the panicking chargers surged through the press of grappling men, scattering the living, and trampling the bodies of the fallen. A clear path to the walls opened up. A path despoiled by death, pooled with blood and excrement, strewn with discarded weaponry, but a path nonetheless.

Andrey broke away from Sidorov and, lifting his weapon, hurtled forward, sliding and splashing over what seemed like the floor of an abattoir. He looked back. His grenadiers were behind him. 'Come on, lads! Let's go and free Borisov!'

He waved them on and raced towards the barrier. A ball whined over his head but footsteps pounded at his back; his men were still with him! He paused to shout, 'Hurrah!' and raised his sabre. He heard a cry of triumph behind him; he jerked his head to look round. A heavy weight crashed into him. His legs seemed to disappear; he was flying through the air. He could taste blood. The dark earth rose to greet him, something cracked, then the world turned black and fell silent.

CHAPTER TWENTY-THREE

September 1831 – St Petersburg

Vasily stood at the Moscow barrier. His head ached. He took off his new hat and mopped his brow. It was late afternoon and flies, revived by recent rain, swarmed through the humid air. The police were inspecting goods moving in and out of the city. The long queue of wagons stretched back towards Tsarskoye Selo. Sporadic noisy arguments erupted as frustrated merchants haggled and argued. The practice of fumigating everything had been abandoned, but long-distance carriers were still obliged to transfer goods to local men at the edge of town.

'These sacks are damp!' a merchant complained. Vasily was not surprised. In the third week of August, thunder and heavy rain had dissipated the heat that had lingered over the city for weeks. This coincided with a couple of high tides and had caused unseasonable early flooding.

Whether it was the cooler weather or the effect of the floodwater, which had sluiced out the sewers and drains of the disease-struck city, the number of cases of cholera had at last started to fall. But the danger was not yet over, and people could not relax their guard. He noticed the queue of private citizens who were waiting outside the guardhouse for their papers to be examined. More than usual were returning to Petersburg. He asked the ensign on duty to send a patrol out to look for those who, unwilling to accept isolation, regularly attempted to find ways round the cordon.

A few soldiers marched off. Vasily yawned. He was hungry; it was time for his dinner. He called Smirnov and sent for his carriage. As he waited, he noticed a heavy wagon rumbling along the road from the city. Drawn by three horses, it was driven by a man who seemed to be going to a masquerade. He wore a hat with a feather, like an English cavalier, and a bright red velvet suit. Behind him sat several men and women, equally eccentrically dressed. One man flourished a bottle, and two were singing loudly.

'They're from the theatre,' muttered the ensign.

'Where are they going?'

'To Count Bolotin's country house, probably. He'll be throwing an evening entertainment...'

'But have they got papers?'

'Of sorts, I expect.' The soldier looked uncomfortable.

'Well, let's see.' Vasily walked up to the driver. 'I assume you have authority to leave the city?'

The driver smirked and pulled out a paper. It was perforated with pinpricks and stank of vinegar. It purported to be a permit from the Governor General to give the representatives permission to attend etc. It was obviously false.

'This won't do. I'll have to ask you to return to the city at once. You can't pass by here with this.'

A woman in the wagon turned and looked down at him. With surprise he realised that it was the dancer, Lyuba Lebedeva. She was wearing an extravagant white hat and a good deal of gauze, but little else. 'Oh, sir!' she said with a coy giggle, her eyes gleaming through her lashes. 'Let us through... please!'

'Yes please, sir!' chorused the other women. An aura of vanilla and patchouli oil hung in the still air.

'Where's the lieutenant? He always lets us pass,' a man said. The ensign shuffled, flushing with embarrassment.

'This is nonsense!' cried Lebedeva. 'Give the man something!'

'I don't think...' One of the men, recognising Vasily, realised that a bribe was inappropriate.

'You'll be in trouble if you don't let us through!' a woman in pink said irritably. 'Count Bolotin is a friend of your minister, Zakrevsky.'

'Of his wife, more likely!' cackled the cavalier, thrusting his folded whip repeatedly into the air. 'Whoo-hoo!'

Vasily tried to ignore him. 'I'm sorry,' he said. 'You must turn back. Otherwise these officers will be obliged to take you into custody.'

'You can all come with us to the party if you like,' crooned the woman in pink.

Vasily turned towards a small knot of policemen. They were looking on with interest and now shuffled forward. The ensign, seeing how things were developing, called some men from the guardhouse. They tumbled out and stood pulling on their shakos and gawping at the artists.

Lebedeva rose and surveyed the scene. She turned towards Vasily, her face rigid. 'You'll hear more of this, you lily-livered scribbler!' she spat. She looked surprisingly ugly. 'You don't know who's expecting us at the Count's. You'll be in real trouble!'

'No doubt someone of great importance, Madame, but the quarantine rules were made for a purpose, and I must ask you to respect them. If your permit was in order, of course it would be different. But it isn't.' Vasily, his face burning, knew that he sounded like a petty bureaucrat in a vaudeville. It seemed the performers thought so too. They howled with laughter. The man with the bottle flung it to the side of the road, where it exploded into shards. 'Come on,' he said. 'We'll find another way...'

'I wouldn't advise that,' Vasily said. 'Indeed, if that's your intention I shall have to detain you now.' He heard the ensign behind him call his men to order.

The cavalier shrugged, shook his head and took up the reins, turning his horses back towards St Petersburg. The actors and dancers jeered and cursed. As the vehicle drew away, Lebedeva cried out, 'How's your ginger squeeze, Count Belkin? Still screwing her on the English Embankment, are you?'

'I doubt it,' screeched another woman. 'I expect she's dumped him... I would – I'm told he can't get it up.'

Vasily turned back to face the guardsmen. To their credit they had the grace to try to hide their amusement. They understood the situation pretty well. Ivan had told him how, every summer, carriages filled with young women from the theatre and theatre school regularly poured out of town, headed for entertainments at the dachas of grandees. At these gatherings, theatre employees, the supervisors at the theatre school, even some of the board of directors, promoted liaisons between rich men and the artists, and indeed enjoyed them themselves. Money and favours would change hands for an introduction to a popular beauty. Vasily frowned. God knew he was no prude, but this was no ordinary summer and he knew he had been right to turn the party back.

Thank God! Here was his carriage at last…

On the way to the centre of the city, he stared out of the carriage window, avoiding Smirnov's gaze. This part of town was no longer fashionable. Larger houses, once the homes of gentlemen, had become crowded tenements. Shabby inns, wooden dwellings and manufactories lined the road.

He pulled off his hat with a sigh and loosened his neckcloth. No-one could fault his response to today's incident, but the role of an officious civil servant didn't suit him. Since the end of the rioting in July, his time had been spent enforcing such regulations as remained, and he had been obliged to prosecute some of the cases against those arrested during the disturbances. He had done his best and he knew that his work, and indeed his honesty, was appreciated by some, but the mindless and arbitrary brutality of the police and the venality of many of his fellow public servants had appalled him; they took bribes from the wealthy while they preyed on the superstition and ignorance of the poor. The only person who might bring about change was the Emperor, but the very nature of the system over which the autocrat presided meant that his ministers rarely told their master the truth, and even if they did, one man could not remedy everything.

The carriage was approaching the Admiralty District. Lebedeva's shrill jibes still rang in his ears. The dancer seemed not only to know his identity, but also details of his private life. Why could he possibly be of any interest to her? And how far from the truth her comment had been! If only Irina *had* been prepared to bring his daughter to live with him, and accept the gossip and minor scandal that would mean. They could be living quietly but happily at Dubovnoye. The harvest there should be in by now. Domed stooks of hay and straw would be standing golden in the fields. Sophia might be playing among them, or in the orchard, now heavy with fruit. He would be taking up his sketching again, refining his plans for the estate, and involving himself in local matters. There might in time be other children, and perhaps they would travel abroad, leaving Russia and its stifling rules and oppression behind, at least for a while. He shook his head. Yes, if only she would come to him. He would willingly give up everything, all prospect of rank, wealth and advancement, to fulfil that distant dream of freedom.

CHAPTER TWENTY-FOUR

September 1831 – Bashkatovo Estate, the province of Oryol

The rowing boat lurched violently and an oar teetered on the gunwale before sliding back into the boat with a crash.

'Oh! I'm so sorry, Nadezhda Gavrilovna, navigation isn't really my forte.' The young man pulled out his kerchief and blew his nose violently. He stared at the recalcitrant oar with dull eyes as the boat drifted into the middle of the lake.

Had she not been in despair, the clumsy mishaps of Konstantin Maksimovich – the second son of her family's illustrious neighbour, Prince Kukarin – would have caused Nadezhda to laugh out loud. But as it was, she could find little to amuse her. The overweight youth – she regarded him as a youth even though he was only a year her junior – had recently emerged as her parents' preferred choice of suitor. On paper he had much to recommend him – good family, lands adjacent to their own – but dexterity with the oars was just one of many skills he seemed to lack.

He had flunked cadet school and his only interests were hunting and dogs. What was more, his vacant expression, florid face and perpetually greasy black hair repelled her.

After half an hour or so, during which Konstantin Maksimovich's rowing skills failed to improve, she suggested that it would soon be time for dinner. Escaping up the path from the lake, her skirts sodden, she made for her rooms. When her maid had taken away her ruined dress, she sat on her window seat in her damp chemise and surveyed the trees in the park. The leaves were starting to turn and the green sward of parkland was luminous in the late afternoon light. One day this would all be hers, but it now seemed she must pay a high price for it.

What could she do? She had begged her parents not to marry her to an old man, however wealthy, and in selecting Konstantin they believed they had complied with her wishes. The closeness of the Kukarins' land to their own should be advantageous to the economics of their estate, so it was also hard to argue against the match on this account. But it seemed her fate was to be very different from what she had optimistically imagined. Perhaps she had misjudged things in St Petersburg. Instead of dreaming up deceitful schemes with Yevgeny, and allowing herself to fall in love, she should have been more hard-headed and prepared to compromise. But what was done was done, she *had* fallen in love, that couldn't be altered, and if marriage to Andrey was truly impossible, perhaps she should obstinately refuse to marry anyone. Her sister Lisa, when her prospects of marrying Mikhail seemed remote, had contemplated withdrawing to the female monastery in Oryol. But her religious faith was less strong than Lisa's and a life cut off from the world seemed inconceivable. Besides, if she gave up her rights, on the death of her father, the Laptev estate would pass to a distant cousin with his own established family. Her mother and aunt would be able to stay here, of course, but probably on sufferance. There would be no home for Lisa and Mikhail, if they were ever permitted to return from exile.

As she stared through the window, a small group of serfs was making its way home to the village across the garden. She recognised some of them, and her eyes filled with tears. She was gradually earning their love and respect. They knew she cared about their welfare. Could she abandon them to an unknown owner?

Perhaps she must indeed marry Konstantin Maksimovich and never enjoy the fruits of true love, never lie in the arms of a man without a sense of duty – or worse, of repulsion. She had been foolish to blindly believe the myth of "the right man", which had been woven with careless skill by her mother and her nurse, and described at length in French novels. If that "right man" was indeed Andrey Andreyevich, where was he now, when she needed him? She knew that the Polish war had recently ended in victory and she had written to him, but she knew she couldn't expect a reply. Besides, he may not even be alive; casualties were known to have been high.

Submerged in her distress, she did not hear her former nanny padding into the room. 'Oh Miss Nadya! You mustn't take on so…' The woman embraced her as she sobbed. 'There, there, it's not so bad.'

Nadezhda jerked from her arms. 'Yes it is! It's simply terrible!' she said with more passion than she intended.

She knew that her maid had gossiped to Nanya about the lieutenant, but the woman had avoided discussing the matter directly, probably believing it to be pointless, if not inappropriate. Generally practical, Nanya would certainly see the merits of the Kukarin match.

It was therefore a surprise when she responded, 'Now you listen carefully to me, Nadushka. God helps those who help themselves.' Her nurse's eyes held a glint of cunning. Did her kindly minder have a solution for her after all? 'You must go down to the village to see the widow of Boris Abramovich. Ask her about that giant painting Boris made for the Kukarins four years ago.'

A painting? What had that to do with anything? She remembered the picture, a family portrait complete with hunting dogs, set in the Kukarins' park. The artist's son, Piotr, had been obliged to finish it when his father died suddenly, and now it hung in the marble hall of the Kukarins' vast mansion.

'Why, Nanya? How can that possibly help me?'

Nanya compressed her lips. 'I've said quite enough, Nadezhda Gavrilovna.' The woman shook her greying head, her expression mulish. Nothing further would be forthcoming. But surely Nanya would not be so cruel as to give her empty hope? The weather seemed set fair; she would go to the village to see Boris's widow tomorrow.

※

Nadezhda drove the gig down the track to the edge of the village. The day was sunny and fresh. Ploughing had commenced and the golden fields were scarred with brown furrows. She stopped outside the izba that housed the artist's widow. The servant who had accompanied her handed her down. Several peasants emerged from their homes to greet her with a smile and a bow, and then stood staring as she walked to the door. There was no sign of life. Perhaps the widow was up at the house attending her mother? As she turned back, she heard singing coming from an outhouse. She knew this had once been Boris's studio, but had thought it was now used for other purposes.

'Hello!' she called.

A youth of around Matvey's age emerged from the open doorway, brushes and a pallet in his hands. It was Piotr, the widow's son.

'Piotr! I didn't expect to find you here, I thought you were away at art school.'

'I'm trapped here by the cholera. I came home for Easter, and have been unable to return. But it's said the cordons will be removed shortly, so I'll soon be going back to Arzamas.'

'I haven't seen you around the village,' she said.

'No, I have been working hard. Would you like to see my latest work, miss?'

She entered the bright studio that Piotr's father had created alongside their home. It was packed with images. There were pictures of the estate, of brightly dressed peasants, of a mother nursing a child, outlined against flat expanses of field, the silver snake of water, or the great house in the distance. Piotr was clearly painting for his own pleasure; these images of village life did not have an obvious market.

Having admired the pictures, she asked, 'Is your mother at home?'

'She's up at the house, Miss Nadezhda, did you need to speak to her?'

'I think you may be able to help me. Do you remember the large group picture your father was working on at the time of his death?'

'The Kukarin portrait? I won't forget that in a hurry! It was a lot of work, and I was hardly in the mood to take it on. I had to varnish the whole thing twice, and then arrange to have it framed and hung.'

'They were pleased with it?'

'I don't really know, but it's generally considered to be one of my father's best works. And of course, it was his last.' The youth paused and looked down at his feet. Nadezhda adjusted her bonnet. 'Can you tell me any more about it?'

Piotr frowned. 'Well, I can tell you this, miss: despite all their wealth, the Kukarins never paid the final, and largest, installment. Yevgraf, the steward, asked several times for the money but then gave up. It was embarrassing. As you know, your father has little interest in art, and although he was told about the debt, he took no action. We didn't understand why but said nothing. In other ways your father has been generous to us since my father died, as you know. It didn't seem right to trouble him.'

'But you were out of pocket?'

'Of course, but you know, at the time of his death my father was working on a series of portraits for Prince Uspenky's fellow officers. Those paid very well, so we certainly didn't starve!'

Nadezhda frowned. How would this information help her to avoid marriage to the odious Konstantin? But then her mind cleared. 'Do you think that the Kukarins could be less prosperous than they pretend? That perhaps they didn't pay the account because they couldn't?'

Piotr shrugged. 'It's possible. Not paying an artist's bill would be an easy choice If you're needing to tighten your belt. But I'm not really privy to that sort of information. You'd be best to talk to Yevgraf. He knows everything that goes on. And he'll want to help you, Nadezhda Gavrilovna, I'm sure of that. You shouldn't waste time; go to see him now!'

※

'You'd better be right about this, Nadezhda! And what will I say to your mother?'

Her father's face was a picture of misery as he turned away to contemplate the icons that hung in the corner of his study. Nadezhda had sought him out immediately on her return from the estate office. He had sat visibly drooping while, with ill-concealed relish, she had explained how, far from benefiting them all, the sizeable dowry payable on any marriage into the Kukarin family was likely to disappear into a black hole of debt.

He shook his head. If true, her story had exploded his hopes for an advantageous match with young Konstantin Maksimovich.

After her conversation with Piotr, Nadezhda had gone directly to the estate office, a place fragrant with the smell of ink and the sweet pine of the wooden walls.

Yevgraf was hunched over his ledgers. He had welcomed her warmly and invited her to sit in her father's high-backed chair.

'It's good to see you, miss. Have you come to find out how the sales from the harvest are going?'

'No, not today, Yevgraf. But I do have a particular question for you. I was speaking to Boris's son, Piotr, this morning. He told me that we were never paid for the big picture that his father painted of the Kukarin family. He didn't know why, but said you may be able to help me…'

The steward threw her a knowing look, not unlike that thrown by Nanya a little earlier. He whistled quietly under his breath for a moment and sucked his teeth. 'Well, I don't know if I should tell you, but I don't think matters are that rosy at the Kukarins. Haven't been for some time…'

'Surely my father knows this?'

'Well, I've dropped a few hints, but it isn't really my place. And if I were to be mistaken…' She nodded; the steward would be reluctant to question the solvency of a local nobleman without reason. He might be accused by his master of gossiping at best, troublemaking at worst.

'But I thought the family was so wealthy…'

Yevgraf shrugged. 'It seems their troubles are quite recent. They started during those bad harvests we had in the late '20s. Some folk managed better at the time than others, you see. Your father did alright. He sought guidance from God, or so he said, and the Good Lord told him to borrow money if he must, and hold off selling until the market price rose to reflect the shortages. Kukarin was less clever, I understand. We thought it strange at the time that he were in the market so early, but then there were rumours that his oldest son had lost his shirt gambling in Moscow. The prince had to apply to the foundling home bank for new lines of credit, and later, when they refused him, he borrowed elsewhere on poor terms. For a while things seemed to improve, but then the cholera came, and we heard that during the uprising in Warsaw, his business interests in Poland collapsed.'

'How do you know all this, Yevgraf?'

'I keep my ears open. What do you think people talk about when they stand about at the market? It's said the Kukarins' steward is fearful for his job...'

'Things are as bad as that?'

'It would seem so. Between ourselves, miss, I was holding myself back from speaking, knowing that the prince would likely soon be offering us a useful parcel of land. That piece down by the river. I kept it from your father. Although he can be shrewd enough, he has been known to be too eager to pay up for what he wants – land in particular – and I thought to wait until Kukarin really needed to sell. Perhaps I'm too sly for my own good, but it didn't do any harm to wait until the prize dropped into our laps, so to speak. I was biding my time, waiting for the right moment to mention the matter.'

'Oh! Thank you, Yevgraf!' She wanted to kiss the crafty old man, who was smiling broadly, but knew she shouldn't. Her heart was singing as she slipped from the leather seat and stood up. Although she had said nothing to him of her parents' plans for her, she was sure that he was aware of them.

'And the best of luck, miss,' he said, winking at her as he picked up his pen and turned back to his numbers. 'I doubt we'll be seeing any wedding celebrations this year, at least,' she heard him say to no-one in particular as she emerged into the sunshine.

CHAPTER TWENTY-FIVE

September 1831 – Warsaw

Voices come to him, but Andrey cannot respond. If he opens his eyes, the light offers nothing but pain. Better to drift back into dreams vivid and confused: home in Estonia, chickens scratching in the dusty yard, the wire-haired dog that was his faithful childhood companion, and that fine stallion, a yearling he had worked with for a whole summer. The heavy-shouldered figure of his grandfather stands by the barn, then thankfully fades and is replaced by another vision: Minnie laughing, champagne in hand, the scent of musk, a slick of greasepaint on her cheeks. He aches with desire, but as he moves to embrace her, she too disintegrates and another woman appears, slender and in blue, her back turned towards him, indistinct, unreachable. Who is she? Is it Nadezhda? Or that whore he had trifled with on the march in Pskov? But now she too disappears and he is on the desolate strand on Vasilevsky Island, small bitter waves slapping the shoreline. A crowd of peasants watch on, their caps clutched in their hands, while a group of grenadier officers stand to one side, their faces turned away. He knows he must fight, but he has no weapon. Where is his second? The pistols? He cannot shoot without a pistol! His opponent takes aim. He is going to die... he cries out...

'Steady on, Andrey...'

'Someone find Burov...'

He struggles to sit up, blinking in the light, but the pain in his chest and head defeat him. As he slumps back, arms catch him and hold him upright. Someone groans... or are they his groans? A bitter draught is forced between his lips. He falls away; the dreams return.

※

Much later, he woke again. His head felt clearer. The white-painted vault above him fractured and swam, but then took on firmer shape. Voices echoed outside in the street, a gun behind its limber rumbled on the cobbles, a faint trace of smoke curdled the air. Where was he? He had clearly been hurt, but this didn't seem to be a hospital. Had the Poles won? Was he a prisoner? He tried to sit up but the pain was harsh and he flopped back, stars bursting in showers behind his eyelids.

'Oh! You're awake, sir. That's good! We thought we might have lost you.' Morozov's kindly face was hovering above him. His servant was flushed, a faint smile on his lips. Not a prisoner then... His heart lifted.

'Where am I? How long have I been here?'

'We're in Warsaw, sir. In barracks.'

'So we took the city?'

'Yes, a few days ago. The Polish army has gone. Some of our men have gone after it, but the captain is here and a few others. Lieutenant Filipson arranged to bring you here before he went off to Modlin. The lieutenant said you'd not be safe in a hospital, that you'd certainly die. He seems to have his own doctor, a Doctor Burov – a friend of his, it seems, and some sort of magician…'

Andrey exhaled with some discomfort. Was there nothing that Filipson couldn't fix? But he must be grateful to him and to his doctor. He struggled to think back. He remembered the call to arms, then turning to the east for prayers before they marched behind the standards with drums and bugles, but the rest was a blank.

Morozov was waving a flask. 'The doctor says you're to drink more of this and then get more rest. I'll tell Captain Rosovsky that you're back among us, so to speak.'

Andrey struggled to sit up but Morozov gently pushed him back. 'No, sir, you're to move slowly. The doctor says your ribs have been smashed and your collarbone cracked, but that you were lucky and will be up and about in a few weeks if you rest quiet for now. He sorted out your face too…'

'I can smell smoke…'

'Some of the houses that were fired within the walls of the city are still smouldering. Many remain standing though. It's said that the Emperor doesn't want more damage than necessary. But I mustn't tire you, sir. I'll get hot water and sort you out. I suppose you'll have to try to sit up for a few minutes.'

Morozov, gentle as a nanny, dealt with his immediate needs. As he shaved him, he realised that his orderly was skirting a row of stitches. When he moved, the pain in his back and side were crushing. He tried again to remember what had happened. Some details of the storming of the city were coming back to him, but much remained unclear.

As Morozov helped him to lie down again, he heard footsteps on the stone flags of the passage outside the door. Doctor Burov stood on the threshold. 'Good, you've got him moving, Morozov. Well done. Now I want him to take another draught. Sleep is the thing… and tomorrow, perhaps some food.'

※

Captain Rosovsky wasted little time in coming to see him the following day. 'Well! How's the hero of Volya?' he asked, flipping up the tail of his jacket as he sat down on the stool by the bed. 'Feeling better?'

'I'm not sure how I felt before…'

'At least you're awake now. We were worried about you.'

'I can't remember much.'

'No, I don't expect you can. Our men took the Volya barrier. Do you remember that?'

Andrey shook his head. He struggled to sit up, but the room was spinning.

'Perhaps you were out of it by then,' Rosovsky was saying. 'I don't know. I was busy directing troops through the settlement. Anyway, I'm told it was you who led the charge, who seized the opportunity to go in. Sidorov made short work of the man that brought you down.'

'Did we lose many?'

'A few, but a lot more were wounded, including the colonel. He took a blow to the head, and one of his legs is broken. The fighting was tough for a time. But then the Poles suddenly seemed to give up and we took the walls. Of course, it was dark; we were fighting by the light of the burning houses. I think it was when the Sejm realised that buildings inside the ramparts were on fire that they stopped arguing among themselves, lost heart and capitulated. The Polish army are making for Modlin. They are hoping to regroup, although personally I think the war's pretty much over.

'What about Borisov? Any news of him?'

'He's fine. He was being held at the castle. We released him with a couple of hundred others. He's mortified of course, feels he should have escaped, but the Poles treated him fairly, I gather. No doubt he'll come to see you – if Burov lets him in, of course.' Relieved, Andrey sank back onto his pillow. 'Anyway, I'd better leave you to rest, you don't look too good. But you were lucky; it could have been a lot worse.'

As he rose, Rosovsky hesitated as if he wanted to say more, but then just added; 'I'll drop in again. We've a few things to discuss, but that can wait a while.'

<hr>

The doctor finally allowed Andrey to dress and get up three weeks later. He insisted that he wear a sling, and warned that he could not report for duty for several weeks. Morozov had kept him from a mirror, and now, when he saw his face, he realised why. The doctor had done his best, but down the left side of his face, a purpling scar ran from his temple to his chin. Burov had told him that it would fade in time, would be hardly noticeable, but the sight unsettled him. He looked like a stranger.

Not wishing to dwell on it, he sought out Rosovsky. It was clear they were remaining in Warsaw for some time. Perhaps he would find him something to do.

Rosovsky was confronted by a pile of what looked like receipts and a huge ledger. 'I can't make head or tail of these, Andrey. They're claims for payment from various sutlers and merchants, but I've no idea if they are valid. The organisation of provisioning was a disgrace, as I'm sure you remember, and these bills are the result.' He frowned, shoved them aside and rose from his desk. He walked to the door, looked up and down the passage outside, and then closed it. The he sat down and swung back in his chair. 'Have you decided what to do next?

Andrey said nothing for a moment. For months he had shied away from thinking about anything but the present. The next few days had felt uncertain enough. It had seemed pointless to speculate about the lawsuit, or indeed about Nadezhda. He shook his head.

'Not really, sir.'

'You don't need to stick to formalities with me, Andrey. Not here anyway. You're catching me up fast in any event. I'm sure you'll be confirmed as first lieutenant; you may even be promoted to captain. And that's the thing really. You made a very good impression both during the fighting, and while you were on the staff. I think you should think about putting in for a transfer.'

'I hadn't really intended to leave the regiment at present, Kirill.' It felt strange to use the captain's given name. He hurried on. 'I know that along with the Emperor of Austria's men, the Emperor has re-designated us a guards regiment. I'm not sure of the reason for that, but surely it will mean we'll spend more time in the capital – and in any event, Novgorod isn't so far distant. Besides, I like and respect the colonel.'

'Yes, but there are things you don't know. When you hear them, you may change your mind. For a start, sadly Chevakinsky is no longer in command, and there's little hope of our returning to Petersburg for some time, guards regiment or not.' Rosovsky sighed and picked up a pencil from his desk, weaving it between his fingers as he spoke. 'There's no easy way to tell you this…' His face was sombre. He took a deep breath. 'At the beginning of August we heard that there had been a series of uprisings in the military settlements around Novgorod. The trouble started just to the south in Staraya Rossiya, but soon spread to the settlements along the Volkhov River, including eventually our own regiment's.'

Andrey was shocked but not surprised. He remembered the rule book, the harsh punishments, the terrified faces of the cantonists.

'The whole idea always seemed ill-conceived to me,' Rosovsky continued. 'But cholera proved to be the final straw. The settlers got it into their heads that the remedies they were being given were not cures but poison. They were also convinced that the surrounding trees and fields had been contaminated by Polish spies. It didn't help that the authorities were secretive and started to dig graves before anyone actually died. In any event, despite the clergy working hard to calm the situation, in mid-July the men rose in a body, seized most of the officers, and tortured and murdered them.'

'Murdered them!' Andrey's voice rose in alarm. Then more quietly he said, 'Tortured them?' He recalled the carefree young officers with whom he had lodged and felt slightly sick. 'What about the married men? Their families?'

'The families were unhurt, although the wives were abused – not physically, but nonetheless... The rebels, after the so-called "executions" went on to pillage the officers' homes, burn the library and loot the kitchens.'

'But some officers escaped?'

'Yes, some saw the writing on the wall and fled to Novgorod; others were badly injured and spared. But I'm afraid the majority died, including the major in charge.'

'But most of them didn't see trouble coming?'

'No, it seems that on the eve of the disturbances, many were at an evening reception; others were quietly working at home on their affairs. When rioting broke out, they didn't realise in time that harsh words wouldn't do and that force was needed. Apparently it all happened very quickly; it was over in a couple of days. By the time Count Orlov arrived from St Petersburg, some sort of order had been restored by troops from active units nearby.'

Rosovsky fell silent for a moment, and then continued, 'The Emperor himself followed shortly afterwards. The settlers, of course, flung themselves to the earth and begged for mercy, but Nicholas was implacable. He insisted that the instigators must be given up before any idea of forgiveness was considered. A good number of offenders were rounded up. An investigation is continuing, but little mercy will be shown to those found guilty, I fear.'

Andrey, relieved that he had been spared, could imagine all too vividly the punishments that would be meted out in the name of the Emperor. Perhaps they could be justified. The cold-blooded murder of innocent men couldn't be tolerated. But Rosovsky was right that the system itself was really to blame.

'But the thing is this,' Rosovsky continued. 'It's now inevitable that plans for the regiment will change. God knows where the King of Prussia's men will go... it could be anywhere. I'm not sure what this new "guards" status means. But it will be some time before anyone returns to Petersburg. Like me, you need to be close to the capital. My family is there and you have business that you need to see to.'

Andrey felt weary and looked at his feet. That was of course true. The idea of retreating to some distant province for a while was strangely appealing, but of course it wouldn't do.

'Staff work is dull at times,' Rosovsky said, 'and sometimes goes unrecognised, but under the circumstances I believe it may suit you. You've proved yourself a brave, resourceful soldier, but now you'll need more than drill and guard duty to occupy you. It's my intention to try to return to my former regiment, to the Lifeguard Grenadiers. Just now, you're the hero of the hour, Andrey. If I were you, I'd seize the moment to seek a change too. I'll be setting off back to Petersburg once a peace is signed, and I suggest you consider coming with me.'

Andrey's heart lifted, warmed by the captain's praise. Clearly his performance during the war had been generally recognised and his worth acknowledged. Indeed, it seemed that his exploits at Nur and at the Volya barrier had made him something of a hero. Perhaps, at last, his fortunes were taking a turn for the better. He found himself wishing that his grandfather was alive to witness his success.

PART THREE

RESOLUTIONS

⊗

*'The Emperor of Russia is the source of all the
honours, all the riches of the state, all the titles
of nobility; the actual landed proprietors are, in
reality, only life tenants. There are only two classes
in Russia: the servants of the Tsar and the servants
of the gentry.'*

Speransky

CHAPTER TWENTY-SIX

November 1831

Winter approached and the number of cases of cholera in St Petersburg fell steeply. Travel restrictions were eased, society re-emerged, and life gradually returned to normal. Vasily resumed his work in the passport office. He had received some recognition for his efforts in public health in the form of another medal and elevation to the rank of Collegiate Assessor. The atmosphere in the Ministry was febrile however, and it seemed that there was to be no general celebration. The handling of the epidemic by the minister, Zakrevsky, had been widely blamed for the riots that had briefly shaken the city. The general had felt obliged to retire to his estates. As yet he had not been replaced.

One bleak November day, Vasily was quietly reading a news sheet at his desk when his idling was disturbed by the shadow of a clerk hovering at his door. 'You've a visitor, sir.'

'What kind of visitor? I've no appointments today.'

'No sir, but he says he is an aide to Full State Councillor Mordvinov. He says he has urgent business with you.'

'You'd better show him in.' Filled with curiosity mixed with disquiet, Vasily rose to meet his visitor. What could this mean? Following the recent death of his predecessor from cholera, Mordvinov had been appointed Director of the Third Section of the Imperial Chancery and was now Count Benkendorf's right-hand man. The Section's remit was to prevent and detect political crimes.

The small man's brisk footsteps rapped on the wooden floor. The eyes in his narrow face surveyed Vasily intently before he made his short bow. Vasily's stomach tightened. Was he here to question him? Had his past, which he had thought deeply buried, somehow been discovered? But after a moment of scrutiny, the officer allowed himself a thin smile, introduced himself as Collegiate Assessor Bagrov, and took the proffered seat.

Vasily cleared his throat. 'How can I help you, sir?'

'Some time ago I understand that you were offered a position with us, Count Belkin, which at the time you refused. Now that this troublesome year has passed, I have been sent by our new director to discover if you might have changed your mind?'

Vasily took a deep breath, uncertain how to respond. His whole being was repelled by the work he was being offered. Reporting directly to the Emperor, the power of the Third Section was extensive. Its intrusive and pervasive tentacles had wound their way into his work in the provinces, and he had encountered its agents again when handling criminal cases related to the epidemic.

'The thing is this, Belkin,' Bagrov continued. 'Following the recent unpleasantness in Poland, our work to purify the conscience of the nation, to root out dissent, is understandably expanding.' Vasily nodded and attempted to speak, but Bagrov raised his hand. 'No, hear me out, sir. You are just the sort of officer that we need. Your family has a history of service in the administration. You yourself have a reputation for honesty; you have been noticed performing with diligence here in the capital during these last difficult months. And, of course, you received high praise from your superiors in Oryol. You are also relatively young and have the energy to throw yourself into the work. I can promise you, if you continue as you have started, promotion will be rapid.' He gave a self-satisfied smirk and added, 'As I have discovered myself.' He unconsciously picked a bit of fluff from the knee of his trousers and rolled it in his fingers before dropping it to the floor.

Not for the first time, Vasily cursed his former colleagues in Oryol: Chudov, his charming but unreliable senior officer at the Ministry, and Strogov, the wise captain of gendarmes. Their commendations, generously intended, were largely undeserved. But now he must prevaricate.

'I am not at all sure I can accept at present, Bagrov. Once some family business in completed here I had hoped to return to Moscow to be nearer my estate,' he said.

'But that would be excellent! Officers are particularly needed in Moscow. Away from the influence of the court, people there think they can say and write what they wish. Here in the capital the cholera, however unfortunate its consequences, has worked very beneficially on public opinion. People have turned to religion and stopped thinking about politics, and of course they have seen at first-hand how their Sovereign loves them, and how concerned he is about their welfare.'

Vasily did not know how to respond. It seemed that Bagrov and his fellow officers were largely indifferent to recent suffering and thought the epidemic a price worth paying for an increase in reverence for the Emperor. But he must curb his rising distaste and deal with this carefully. The work of the Third Section was close to the Emperor's heart. An outright refusal might reflect badly, not just on himself but on his uncle and the prince.

'Look, Bagrov, forgive me, but I can't give you an answer now. You may well be aware of the Bogolyubov succession. The case has serious implications for my family, and now we are free to travel once more, I must devote myself to resolving the matter. I'm not sure how long that will take…'

Bagrov nodded. 'Yes, I am indeed aware of it, and I suspected that might be your immediate answer. I should tell you that the Emperor, who takes a great interest in such matters, is also watching the situation. I suggest, Count, that you bear that in mind.' Bagrov paused for a moment, fixed Vasily with a meaningful stare, and then, starting to rise, bestowed on him another delicate smile, apparently unconcerned at receiving no definite answer.

'I'll give you a response as soon as… err…' Vasily leapt to his feet and returned Bagrov's bow. He felt troubled and ashamed. He should have been honest and refused the man outright, but to offend either him or his all-powerful master felt unwise. Perhaps this was just a simple job offer, but it may also be some test of his loyalty.

'Yes, I am sure you will let me know in due course, Count.' On reaching the threshold, Bagrov turned. 'The offer remains open,' he said. 'I am sure you know it is in your interest to consider it carefully.'

Vasily sat down and breathed deeply. Once he had regained his composure, he called for Smirnov. 'I think the time has come to continue with my investigations into the prince's business,' he said. 'I'll be travelling south, to the Tver region. Please produce travel papers for me. I'll stamp them myself.'

※

Vasily waited for the frost to crisp the muddy roads. Then he set off with Yakov and Matvey to visit Count Angelov's sister at her home in the ancient town of Torzhok. Once he had completed his business he aimed to drive on to his estate, Dubovnoye, for Christmas and, on the return journey, to spend some time in Moscow, where the winter social season would be in progress.

The journey south coincided with the arrival of snow. On the second day of their journey, they switched to a sleigh and the pace of travel quickened. In Torzhok they put up in the Pozharsky Inn, close to the coach stop on the square. The Tversta River was starting to glaze with ice. A row of large houses, faced with white plasterwork, stood on the bank below the monastery. At this time of year Angelov's sister would certainly be found at home in one of these.

When Vasily, accompanied by Matvey, sent in his card, it turned out that the Count was also in residence.

Angelov hurried down to the spacious entrance hall. 'Good to meet you once again, Vasily Nikolayevich. I'm pleased to see you well!' His pink head glowed as he bowed.

'Yes, I too, sir. This is my ward, Matvey, who is helping me with my work at present. But, tell me, when did you return from Poland? Were you with the Grand Duke when he died?'

'No, once it was clear that war was inevitable, I headed home as quickly as I could; my soldiering days are long past. It wasn't an easy journey. I imagine it was the same for you.'

'Yes, sir.'

'And have you been in Petersburg throughout the epidemic? That must have been taxing.'

'It was my duty, sir, but there, as here, the problems have eased and I'm able to pursue the matter that I mentioned to you when we met in Lubartow. You said that your sister may have information about Astrella, Countess Bogolyubov, when she came here after the marriage in Petersburg in 1805.'

'She will willingly tell you what she knows, I'm sure of that. I suggest that you both stay and dine with us.'

❧

'Yes, Vasily Nikolayevich,' Countess Angelova was saying. 'Yes, I do remember Astrella Andreyevna quite clearly, although it was long ago.' Vasily and Matvey were sitting in the Angelovs' drawing room as the afternoon light faded over the river. 'The Bogolyubov estate is close to our own modest manor and we were regular visitors there,' the countess continued. 'Much to our surprise towards the end of the year, Astrella arrived, well attended by servants, but of course without Stepan Dmitryevich, who had re-joined his regiment. She brought a note from him, asking me to receive her kindly, and it was a pleasure to oblige. Stepan was charming, you know, always the life and soul of the party. We had no idea at all that he had financial problems – or at least, I had not.' She looked severely at her brother, who responded with a weak smile.

Vasily drew out the small portrait of Astrella. 'May I ask you, madam, is this the woman you remember?'

The countess sent for a magnifying glass and examined the picture for a few moments. 'My brother was correct, Vasily Nikolayevich. This is not the woman I knew as Countess Bogolyubov. The hair is quite a different shade, and the face quite other. I have to say our Astrella, if I can call her that, was not at all like this. Much more substantial.'

'Can you tell us more?' Vasily asked.

'Ah, she was a pretty thing! I would guess not very old. Younger than twenty, I would say. She had charming manners, spoke excellent French but also spoke Russian quite well. At home, of course, I suppose she spoke German. He accent was hard to place.'

'Well, she was supposed to come from Estonia…'

'That might account for it.'

'Tell me, did she speak about her home? Her parents?'

'Oh yes, indeed. I gathered that her family, while ancient, was no longer wealthy. She spoke a good deal of the farm and its problems.'

Vasily frowned. That was interesting. The woman may well not have been Astrella, but it seemed she did know the von Klein Sternberg estate. 'And that knowledge seemed to be based on experience?' he asked.

'Oh, I think so. I would say that she was well acquainted with the place.'

'Did she speak at all about her wedding, or weddings, because of course there was a Lutheran ceremony prior to the one in Petersburg.'

'No, I don't remember her talking about that. I can't say she concerned herself much with religion. She wasn't an assiduous church-goer. As far as I remember, we only saw her at special festivals. And, of course, after the news of Stepan's death, just after Christmas, it was discovered that a child was on the way…'

'A child?' Could that be von Klein? Surely not…

Matvey, who was taking notes, glanced up at Vasily, his eyebrows raised.

'Yes, a little girl; a sweet, tiny thing she was, but sadly we didn't enjoy seeing her for long.'

A girl! Well, it clearly couldn't be von Klein. And this Astrella, it seemed, was not his mother. But who was she, and what had happened to her and the child? 'You say you didn't enjoy her company for long, Countess?'

'No. When the child was about six months old, I suppose, the true financial situation at the Bogolyubov Estate finally came to light. Representatives of the court visited, followed by creditors, and within days Astrella had vanished, taking a quantity of jewellery with her. We assumed she had gone home to her parents in Estonia. Goodness, it was almost twenty-five years ago!'

'She can't have gone unaccompanied.

'No-one went missing permanently from the house, but someone may have gone with her. It was during the winter, and I was probably here in town.'

Angelov called for some wine. 'If I were you, Belkin,' he said, 'I'd go up to the village and ask around. Someone may remember something.'

'Didn't you know about the child, sir?' Matvey asked Angelov, putting down his pen. Vasily looked at Matvey. He was certainly becoming very self-assured, but then he had never been afraid to say his piece.

'I may have done, but I never thought much to it. Don't forget, I was away in the army during those years. By the time I got home the estate house was empty and, if not forgotten, Stepan Bogolyubov wasn't at the forefront of our minds.'

'Is it far to Kluchovo, to the Bogolyubov Estate?

'Only about nine versts from here. The estate was sold to try to defray some of the debts, of course, and the great house has now been pulled down. Great pity. There are many fine houses around here, and it was one of the best. But I have to say, Belkin, this is an odd situation. Two women, two children… There's no chance the girl might come forward to claim her share of the spoils?'

'She would only have a claim if the second marriage proves to be valid, which I'm inclined to doubt. If she is still alive and out in society, she cannot have failed to hear gossip about von Klein's claim, however. Perhaps both the mother and child died long ago.'

'If that's the case will still find it hard to dispute Andrey von Klein's rights to the legacy. As you know, it's my belief that it wasn't Astrella von Klein who married Stepan Bogolyubov in St Petersburg, but that was a quarter of a century ago and I'm not sure my recollection would satisfy the court. From what my sister has said, it seems that the woman who turned up here in 1805 was not Astrella von Klein either, and it is probable that she was the same woman who went through the marriage service. But once again you're relying on supposition and memories. Unless more can be discovered about the woman, I'm not sure that what you have at present would prevail against an attested entry in the register that has already been accepted as genuine. I would be happy to give evidence, to come to your aid, Belkin, but I'd say an assessor might not be persuaded to look again; they may even think your story a fabrication.'

'Surely not!' said the countess.

'When a lot is at stake, such schemes are not unheard of, particularly where the other party lacks power and influence,' said Angelov. They fell silent, and then Angelov said, 'You'll forgive me for asking, Belkin, but this business must be of great concern to you. I mean, it's generally known that if no heir can be established your family stands to benefit. It's said that the prince has hopes of naming you...'

'Yes, that's true, although over the past year I've had little time to dwell on it. And if I'm honest, I have mixed feelings. Of course, wealth and status is an attractive prospect, but in Russia it doesn't always come with freedom. Were the prince to gain permission of the Emperor to name me his heir, it would come at a price. And in truth, I have no burning wish to continue in government service or spend my life at court.'

Angelov nodded, evidently puzzled. 'But you're continuing to pursue the matter nonetheless?'

'Yes, of course, I must. It's of great importance to the prince, and also to my uncle. If they are obliged to admit the German's claim, our family expectations will certainly be reduced. We should get to the truth if we can.'

As they were leaving after dinner, Angelov said, 'Keep me in touch with developments, Vasily Nikolayevich. I would very much like to know how this all turns out, and of course I shall come to court to say my piece if needs be.'

'That's good of you, sir.'

'Good luck at Kluchovo. If you need to overnight out there, you should call on my steward; he'll find a bed for you. The local inn is nasty, to say the least.'

※

The following day, Yakov drove Vasily and Matvey out of town in a hooded kibitka. Stepan Bogolyubov's former estate lay on land skirted to the west and south by the Tversta. They travelled for around half an hour on smooth snowy tracks, sometimes through dense forest, sometimes through open farmland. Once or twice they saw a fine stone estate house or glimpsed a village; here and there an icicle-hung bridge crossed a frozen stream.

Vasily hoped to find the local priest. He might be able to think of someone who might remember 'our Astrella'. He might, indeed, remember her himself. The church that had once served the estate was no longer in use, and the present one was some distance from the settlement. It sat on the riverbank on a cushion of snow, a lonely structure with a fine stone bell tower, surrounded by the skeletal black branches of trees.

They found the priest inside, a gaunt man with a long beard and hair, both almost white. He held a small knife in one hand and a bowl in the other, and was engaged in removing wax from the candle racks that stood in front of the few icons propped before the unadorned screen. He set his tools aside as he raised his hand in blessing. Vasily and Matvey bowed their heads. A strong smell of incense mingled with a damp odour from the walls. Vasily pulled his fur-lined cloak closer about him.

'Welcome, gentlemen, to the Church of St Simeon. Are your needs spiritual or temporal?'

'Temporal, Holy Father, I regret,' said Vasily, who introduced himself and Matvey before embarking on his story.

'Yes, I remember the woman,' the priest said. 'I should say the countess, I suppose, but she wasn't here long. She rarely came to church and I was not often invited to the house. I did christen the child, however. I think we named her Elizaveta, but I would need to check that in the records, if I can find them.'

'So you have no idea where she went when she left here?'

'No, I'm sorry.'

'Is there anyone who might know. A former house serf? A bailiff or steward?'

The priest frowned, apparently sorting through his parishioners in his mind. 'Of course, you know that the house has been demolished. The estate is managed by a new steward on behalf of the current owner. The old nanny might have been able to help you, but she died a couple of years back. The house serfs have all gone. Working elsewhere, I suppose. And the field serfs, of course, aren't likely to know anything. If there had been any news of her, I think I would have heard it.'

Vasily was disappointed but not surprised. But now it seemed that the priest had remembered someone. 'There's a chance that Praskovya, the wife of the wheelwright, may have some recollection. She lived and worked at the house years ago, but I am not sure what she did there. If you can get past her husband, she may be able to answer your questions. She lives down in the village.'

※

The priest's warning about Praskovya's husband proved to be justified. While a brace of dogs barked with savage intent from a nearby compound, the well-muscled craftsman stood in front of his substantial wooden house and refused to allow Vasily and Matvey over the threshold. His wife, he said, was not at home. 'If your business is official then come with the proper papers,' he said, frowning. 'You're agents from the new owner, I suppose. I thought we'd seen the back of them. My wife's a free woman; she has nothing to do with the old house, or the family, anymore.'

Vasily now regretted not wearing his uniform. He and Matvey might well resemble an agent and his clerk. He was surprised to learn that the woman, Praskovya, was free – not a serf, as the priest had seemed to imply. And why was this man so anxious to obstruct them? 'We don't want to harm your wife, just want to find out if she remembers…'

'There have already been too many questions,' the wheelwright interrupted. 'And you, or others like you, have heard all the answers before. There's nothing here from the old house. Nothing at all.'

'We're not from the current owner, sir. I'm here on personal, family business, but I'm an officer from the Interior Ministry.' As soon as he spoke, Vasily realised that the revelation had probably been a mistake. The wheelwright scowled.

'And I'm Ivan the Terrible,' he said. 'Look, the family and house serfs have all gone, went years ago. Now, unless you want your vehicle mended, and it looks well enough to me, clear off or I'll let the dogs loose.' As he moved to shut the door, a shadow moved within the house. They heard a voice. 'Wait, Savva, I'll answer the gentleman's questions. Let him in.'

The wheelwright glowered. 'Well, if you feel you must…'

He held the door open with reluctance. The house was warm and very clean. Bright fabric hung at the windows and covered the table. High quality icons glowed in the holy corner. The samovar and pewter plates on the dresser gleamed and a bright carpet hung on the far wall. There was even a small fortepiano in the corner. Obviously, the wheelwright's trade was a lucrative one, and Praskovya a scrupulous housekeeper who was not without accomplishments.

The woman herself now stood in the centre of the room. She curtsied to Vasily, and offered a seat at the table. 'I am sorry about my husband's behaviour, your honour,' she said. 'He is over protective of me, and our home. No doubt you know the reason for that…'

'No I am not acquainted with your circumstances, Madame.'

'I see.'

Silence followed as Praskovya served tea. She was a slight woman in her forties. She wore a dark shawl over her blue high-waisted sarafan and a scarf covered the hair above her pleasant round face. The fabric of her garments was of good quality. Her voice was modulated, cultured. She was not at all what he had expected to find here. Had she been dressed differently she could have passed as gentry.

'So how can I help you, sir?'

'I understand from the priest at St Simeon's that you worked at the Kluchovo Mansion in the past.'

'Yes sir, that's the case. My mother was a servant there, and I followed in her footsteps, as is usual.'

'I am seeking information about the marriage of Stepan Bogolyubov in 1805. I am working on behalf of the head of the family, Prince Bogolyubov, a former officer of the Ministry I represent.'

'That was a very long time ago. I can hardly remember back that far…' The woman's face had flushed pink.

'But you remember the count?'

'Oh, one could hardly forget him, sir. Such a generous and handsome man, if rather fond of having his own way.'

Vasily wondered how the woman remembered him so well. She must have been just an infant when he joined the army, although presumably he had come back to the house from time to time.

'And do you remember when the Countess Astrella arrived here?'

'Yes, I do. We were much of an age and I was appointed her maid by my late mother, who was the housekeeper then. Astrella Andreyevna was good to me, very good. When the news came of the count's death, she was grief-stricken, and then of course she had the baby. But she looked after me. When she realised that the estate must be sold, she arranged for my husband, who was my admirer at the time, to pay for my freedom. He is a free man, you see, even though he runs his business here on the estate.'

'And that caused some trouble?'

'Yes, sir. The new owners weren't impressed by her actions. I wasn't the only serf who she freed for a small sum. She thought that the whole system was wrong. She said that where she came from there were no serfs. The creditors tried to force me, and others, to return but it was all done correctly through the agent and they failed. They also said that when she left, she took property from the family, money and jewels, that she wasn't entitled to.'

'And did she?'

'I don't know, sir, but I would not have blamed her if she had. She was left penniless; the count was heavily in debt. She had come to the marriage with no dowry that she might have claimed back. The count had made no provision for her. In fact, he hardly had time to do that, under the circumstances – the war and so on.'

'So she left the estate when she understood the difficulty of her position.'

'Yes, sir. We left within weeks. I went with her to Moscow with the child. We took the count's carriage to

Torzhok, and then the diligence. She must have had some money, I suppose, because at the start she put us up at the Hotel du Nord, which can't have been cheap. Then she started to look for work, as a housekeeper or governess. I thought it was strange that as a member of the nobility she knew no-one in Moscow, had no-one to help her, but it seemed that was the case. She called herself Madame von Klein Sternberg, using her old papers, I suppose.'

Vasily realised that the recitation, though hesitantly delivered, was well practised. He wondered who had coached her. The countess herself, perhaps, seeking to cover her tracks?

'It soon became clear that the child was a problem,' Praskovya continued. 'No-one wanted to take on a woman with a child and no references, so she tried to find a foster family for her. We looked about but couldn't find a place fit for the poor little soul. In the end she realised that she might have to take her to the Foundling Home. Her money was running out, she said, and I must return to Kluchovo. I sent to Savva and he came to Moscow to fetch me. We offered to take the child, but she said that the arrangement would be temporary until she could sort herself out, get a regular income, find a suitable childminder.'

'Did she take the child to the orphanage?'

'I'm not entirely sure, Sir, but I believe she may have had no choice.'

'And roughly when was this?'

'I left Moscow in the early spring of 1807. I was home just after Easter. Astrella Andreyevna had found work as a housekeeper for an older couple in the Bely-Gorod, and was intending to start work within days. She was in terrible distress at the prospect of abandoning her daughter, said she would try once again to find a decent foster home for her, said she hoped that in time her new employer might consent to take in the child. When we parted my heart was breaking for her. She didn't deserve her fate. She gave me a gold ring, said it should be my dowry. I married shortly afterwards.'

'Why didn't she go home to Estonia?'

'I understood there had been problems between her father and the count. She said she would return if there was no other choice, but that her father was unlikely to forgive her or take her in, and she would rather work in Moscow than Reval or Narva.'

Vasily thought that didn't ring true. Surely, had the woman been Astrella von Klein, her family would not turn their back on her and her child. But of course, she almost certainly wasn't. 'And you never heard from her again?'

'No, sir. Not a word. Some people came to the house trying to find her, but after a while they gave up. She vanished completely.'

'And the ring she gave you?'

'Oh, I sold that long ago. The money was welcome at the time.'

Vasily finally pulled out the miniature of Astrella and showed it to the woman. Praskovya barely glanced at it as she said, 'Oh yes, sir, I think that's likely her... if you say so... but it was many years ago and my eyes aren't what they were. I couldn't swear to it.'

She was clearly unwilling or unable to identify the woman, but much of her story rang true. He now had more to work with. He would be visiting Moscow shortly and could look at the housing register for the period in question, and make enquiries at the foundling home. He might soon have enough hard evidence to refute von Klein Sternberg's claim.

CHAPTER TWENTY-SEVEN

January 1832 – Moscow

It was the height of the winter season and the Great Hall of the Noble Assembly was crowded. A charity concert for families of the victims of cholera was in progress. Vasily sat with Matvey and an acquaintance from his school days, whom he had discovered at the English Club in Tverskaya on his first evening in the city.

He had come to Moscow directly from Dubovnoye, and had taken rooms at the Hotel Angleterre. It was nine years since he had spent time in the old capital at this busy time of year, but he had not been short of invitations. He was surprised that many people not only remembered who he was, but also recalled his father, the whereabouts of his family home that had been destroyed in the fire of 1812, and a good many other details, some of which were new to him.

As the music played, his mind drifted back to the estate. When the time had come to leave, his grandmother had been loath to let him go. She was becoming frail, and he had tried to encourage her to consider moving to St

Petersburg, where she could see more of her family and be properly cared for, but she continued to insist on remaining in the draughty old manor house with only her few servants and the former steward for company.

He had spent time in the estate office, pouring over numbers with the present steward. All had been under control. None of the serfs had fallen victim to cholera and, to his surprise, the controversial cattle were almost all alive and safely herded into the barn for the winter. The family had been offered a parcel of fertile land adjacent to their own. A small village was included. While he deplored serfdom, to buy it was a good way to expand his estate, and the peasants would be better off owned by his family than by their negligent current owner.

He had left the old manor house with reluctance, promising to return in the summer, and he would do what he could to keep his word. Surely by then he would have gone as far as he could with this von Klein business.

The concert was ending. As the musicians took their bows, he scanned the audience. Was there anyone here who might join them for supper?

And then he saw her. Irina Pavlovna was sitting a few rows away. As he watched, his former mistress rose from her seat and pulled her wrap about her. She was as beautiful as ever, but unusually overdressed. His heartbeat quickened. What was she doing here in Moscow? He had thought she was in the country. Her cousin Georgiy Kalinin, and his wife were with her.

Vasily hesitated. They knew him and did not entirely approve of him. But there was no help for that; he really must speak to her. He pushed his way through the crowd towards the back of the hall. By the time he reached the entrance, a flunkey was helping her into her cloak. As he approached, she looked up. 'Oh! Vasya!' she said. Her face flushed pink as she extended her hand.

'Good evening, Belkin.' Georgiy Kalinin looked down his nose in distaste, then turned away to assist his wife. Irina didn't smile, but seemed embarrassed, at a loss.

'I didn't expect to see you in Moscow,' he said at last.

'I'm staying with Georgiy over the winter. I decided not to remain in the country. Margarethe is away and it's lonely there.'

'Is Sophia here?'

'Yes, of course.'

'I should very much like to see her.'

'I expect you would, Vasily, but I don't know. You've not shown much interest in either of us over the past year or so. I've heard from Alexander Petrovich more regularly than you.'

'That's not very fair. The last few months have been difficult... you must realise that.'

Irina didn't respond. Of course, it had been a long time since they'd met. He hadn't written as often as he should and had been unable to visit. But he had some excuse: Poland, the cholera and its aftermath, and now the prince's investigation. Besides, she rarely wrote to him, and it had been her choices that had driven him away. With a stab of regret, he realised that a wall of resentment had developed between them.

She surveyed his new uniform and the two medals he was now obliged to wear. For a moment he thought she was going to remark on them, but she still said nothing. She was not making things easy, but he must see his daughter if he could. Surely she wouldn't prevent it?

'May I call on you tomorrow?' he persisted. 'I really would like to see Sonya.'

After a moment's further hesitation, she replied, 'The day after tomorrow would be more convenient. Don't come before eleven o'clock. We don't receive before then.' Dismissed, Vasily bowed, and she turned away, taking her cousin's arm. Having found his coat, he walked with heavy steps towards the doors. Out on Hunters' Row, fine needles of snow were falling. Crowds of people wandered about; laughing, greeting one another, seeking their servants, their sledges. He finally found Matvey and his friend waiting to take him for supper.

He climbed wearily into the sledge, catching Matvey's eye. The boy knew all was not well. 'Shall we eat in our rooms? I need some warming champagne,' Vasily said, attempting to laugh. The snow began to fall more thickly, further chilling his heart.

※

The next day they started their investigations. Aiming to search the police records of Moscow residents, Vasily called at the Ministry. He presented a letter from Alexander Petrovich to a senior officer. He had stayed at the home of the man in the past and was cheered by the friendly welcome he received. He sighed; things had come to a sorry pass when an encounter at the Interior Ministry improved his mood.

'I'm surprised these records weren't destroyed during the war,' Matvey observed as they clattered down the dusty steps into the archive.

'The Military Governor evacuated the government departments before Napoleon arrived, which started a general panic incidentally,' said Vasily. 'Although some records were lost in the fire, most were saved.'

They spent the morning perusing the bundles of paper and ledgers, including censuses and housing registers for 1807. They were looking for a Madame von Klein Sternberg in homes in Bely-Gorod, but drew a blank. They did not complete the task before dinner time and as they made their way to a restaurant, Matvey said he would return the next day to continue.

Vasily was grateful for his offer; the work had been dusty and frustrating. As he watched Matvey fall on his soup, he reflected that it had been a good idea to bring the boy with him. Although he continued to mourn the loss of Maltby, he had taken to the task of in hand with diligence and enthusiasm. Of course, he had a keen and enquiring mind, but he had been surprised at his acute perception and constructive suggestions.

Matvey was now polishing his bowl with a hunk of bread. He looked up and grinned, as he made a slightly off-colour remark in French about one of the serving women. As Vasily tried not to laugh, he realised that he was growing into a presentable young man; his pale olive skin had improved, his curly black hair shone in the candlelight. They must start to think about his future.

The Kalinins' Moscow house presented an austere facade of respectability to the world. It was a new residence close to the line of the old city walls, built after the fire almost twenty years before. As Vasily was admitted and relieved of his coat, hat and cane, he felt a flurry of nerves. Would Irina greet him more warmly than she had at the concert?

There was no sign of a child in the drawing room; there was no sign of anyone at all. He had been asked to wait, so he sat on a sofa, plush with bright cushions, and picked up a copy of the *Moscow Telegraph* from a mahogany side table. Time passed. Still no-one came. The words he was reading became blurred, his nerves more intrusive. It was ridiculous to be anxious, but he had not seen Irina for almost three years. Of course that was far too long. Their child would now be five years old.

At last he heard the sound of raised voices, of feet approaching, then halting, on the wooden floor of the hallway. Irina was trying to persuade their daughter to enter the room. He heard another voice, probably a nanny, murmuring encouragement in the background. The child shrieked. More shrieks followed and then faded away.

Should he excuse himself and leave?

Irina entered the drawing room. Her face was scarlet, her hair disordered and her eyes were bright with tears of frustration. Her shawl had slipped down her back. From old habit he swiftly moved to rearrange it around her shoulders, looking into her face, pulling her gently towards him. For a moment he thought she would come into his arms, but she drew back and offered her hand.

'It seems Sonya's unwilling to meet her father,' he said as he rose from his bow.

'No, no… well, yes… She's not used to strangers. I'm sorry, Vasily.'

'It's no more than I deserve, I suppose.'

'Don't say that.' She hesitated. 'It was unfair to complain the other night. I know that cholera has made travel difficult, and I heard from Pavel that you have been in Poland and were detained there.'

'Yes, he did me a great service helping me to get away.'

'He said nothing of that.'

'No.'

Silence fell between them. An air-splitting shriek was heard somewhere upstairs.

'Should I leave, Irina? I don't want to…'

'Oh no. Don't go. Sonya will calm down. Take a seat, I'll call for tea. I was so surprised to see you the other night. I had thought you busy elsewhere. I had hoped you might come to see us in the summer…'

'Yes, that was my intention.' He waited as she rang a bell and sent for tea. Today she wore the sort of dress that he was accustomed to: loose, light in colour, old-fashioned. She was little changed. Her red-brown hair was styled slightly differently, but curls still tumbled onto her pale brow and around her cheeks; the fine etched lines around her eyes were perhaps more pronounced, perhaps she was thinner. But as ever her beauty, her very presence, moved him. He had hoped that time might have altered his feelings towards her, but it had not, and now he must ask the inevitable question about her husband and receive the inevitable answer.

'And the baron?'

'Very much alive.' Vasily nodded his head. Of course he was. 'Pavel has recently seen him in Vienna. He's in Austria now, you know.'

'Yes, your brother was intending to travel to the west when we parted at Riga.'

'Margarethe has joined him, but I hope she'll return to Russia soon and then I suppose we shall return to Bryansk... back to the forests.' She looked down at her hands then, seeming to shiver, pulled her shawl about her.

He pitied her. Her life was not easy. He could go about as he wanted, fill his time with work, make new friends, take a mistress. She had fewer choices. Moreover, here in Moscow her ambiguous marital state would exclude her from much of society.

'And I gather you've found someone to comfort you,' she was saying. It was a statement, not a question. Her green-grey eyes held his. What might have been a smile played on her lips. She must mean Anna. As he had feared, her brother must have told her. Pavel had surely suspected something when they had been in Poland. Well, there was no need to lie.

'Yes, but that's over now. It could only ever have been a passing thing.'

'The general returned from the wars, I suppose?'

'Yes.'

'Really Vasya, you should be looking for a wife, not dallying with a married woman. Now your career's going so well, and you have the prospect of this legacy from

Dmitry Vladimirovich, surely that must be the right thing to do. You've been decorated twice and I understand from Alexander Petrovich that both the Tsar and the minister have spoken well of you. Girls must be falling over themselves to marry you…'

'If they have, I haven't noticed them. I don't want to marry; at least, not yet. And you should know, Irène, that rumours of the prospect of a more distinguished title, of great wealth, are premature. There's at least one man who may have a claim. There may even be others who might aspire to be the prince's heir. Then permission must be sought, of course…'

'But your uncle said that the Tsar…'

Vasily felt weary and not a little irritated. He didn't want to have to justify his intentions. Within moments of meeting again, it seemed that he and Irina had effortlessly fallen into a familiar pattern. She would tell him what was good for him, and he would be obliged to acknowledge the extent of her sacrifice in selflessly renouncing him and try to live up to it. It was a cycle he must break once and for all.

He stood up. 'I'm sorry, Irina. I was wrong to come. Nothing has changed, has it? Our differences remain the same. But I did want to see the child.'

'And so you shall.' Her voice rose. Was there a hint of despair?

'No, I must go. I repeat, nothing has changed. But if you want to know the truth, over the past months, I've risen effortlessly up the ranks doing a job I never wanted and in general dislike. I now may achieve power and status from a well-meaning benefactor, with the assent of an autocrat, whose service I find it hard to stomach. And you, the only woman I love, the mother of my child, are telling me to go away and marry someone else.'

'I didn't mean…' Irina, rising too, lifted her hand, and twisted and untwisted a curl.

'No. It just won't do, Irina. I have to take control of my life. When I've sorted out this interminable business of Dmitry's, I'm going abroad for a year or so, if I can get a passport, and then I shall go to Dubovnoye and grow old, content to live on the estate. If you wanted to come to me there, you'd both be very welcome. If not…'

She started to speak again, but then appeared to change her mind. She turned away from him, walked to the window and stood for a few moments, looking out. Her back was rigid, but then her head fell forward and her shoulders trembled. Was she weeping? This was unbearable. Why had he spoken so harshly? He stepped forwards and, standing behind her, wrapped her in his arms. She slackened a little. He could smell her citrus scent, a faint hint of soap. His head swam. He bent to kiss the back of her neck. Her hair was soft on his cheek. He clasped her shoulders and turned her to face him. He kissed her lips and tasted the salt of her tears. As he embraced her fully, he said, 'Surely the life you're living now can't satisfy you, Irène. Come back to Petersburg, to your apartment there. Margarethe will join you. It can be as it was before. We were both happy then, weren't we? And when this business of the prince's is over, we'll go away.'

She clung to him closely for a moment but then pulled back. He sighed; had he misread her?

'Give me some time to think about it, Vasya. You're right, my life *is* empty. Only Sonya brings me joy; she is in a way a part of you. Whatever happens, I shall never regret that we made her together.'

'Let's go and see if she's awake,' he said, now desperate to cheer her.

But Sophia was deeply asleep in her little bed, her hand clutching a wooden doll, her hair splayed, a dark halo on her lace pillow. She stirred a little but didn't wake.

'She seems like an angel now, of course…' said Irina.

Vasily looked at his daughter. Was this really the infant he had left behind? She did indeed resemble an angel, albeit rather a dark one. He would like to wake her, but perhaps he should leave well alone. Peace seemed, for the time being at least, to be reigning on all fronts, and perhaps he had reason to hope that he would see more of both her and her mother in the months to come.

※

The vast compound that encompassed the Moscow Foundling Home spread along the bank of the river. Of the several thousand children registered here, many lived beneath the three cupolas of the large white building.

Vasily and Matvey were directed to the newly built administrative offices at the rear, where they were to be met by an official. They climbed the steps and walked under a portico, supported by heavy columns. Inside all was light, clean and quiet. Vasily recalled that in addition to being an orphanage, this was also a bank, and indeed there was no sign of any children.

On the wall of the hallway was a picture of the home's former patron, Maria Feodorovna, the late mother of the Emperor, flanked by portraits of her sons. On the wall opposite hung a picture of an elderly man with surprised eyebrows and receding hair. He wore the uniform of a state councillor, embellished with the Imperial Order of St Ann. Without prompting, the officer remarked, 'That's General Ivan Tutolmin. He was the director of the Home who saved us from the fire in 1812. He fought the flames alongside his staff, and asked Napoleon himself for help to defend the children from looters. Without him there may have been no records to consult today.' He led them into his office. 'Now, how can I help you, gentlemen? I assume you are looking for one of our charges?'

'Yes, a child, or her mother.'

'The mother may be difficult. Most don't give their names; many we don't even see. They generally don't identify themselves unless they want to keep in contact with their children. And as for children, we rarely have their real names, as you will appreciate. The only question we ask, if we get the chance, is whether they have been christened.'

'We'll have to see. It's possible that the mother believed the arrangement to be temporary.'

Matvey gave Astrella's name, and the dates between which the child might have been brought to the home.

'That's some time ago, well before the fire. I'll have the relevant ledgers brought up to the board room. The job of sifting the records is difficult enough without the spiders.'

They sat at the large trustees' table and sorted through the ledgers and files. The papers made grim reading. Each child listed was represented as a number, sometimes with a note of their age. Those who had died were struck through or their names marked with a cross. There were far too many of these – perhaps more than half.

After some minutes Matvey gave a low moan. Vasily watched him walk to the window and stare out over the street. His face was white. 'This is terrible, sir, the number of deaths. I had thought that I had a difficult start in life, but this...'

Vasily should have realised that the records might disturb Matvey. He was, after all, an orphan too. 'Do you want to leave this job to me?'

The clerk looked up. 'Those are old records, sir. From over twenty years back. Things are better now; we generally have fewer deaths. You say that the child you are looking for was several months old when she arrived. If she was well cared for before we took her, her chances of survival are greater. It's the abandoned newborns that often cannot be saved, and they form the greatest part of our intake. Some are virtually dead when we receive them, but they still must be registered.'

'Surely any mother would seek to find an alternative to this?'

'Not necessarily. Many have no choice. But in fact, until recently, bringing a child here was seen by some as a risk worth taking. The rules have been tightened by the Emperor now, but in the past any child who survived and showed some promise may well have been among the five hundred or so who live here permanently. They are treated well, regarded as free citizens even if they are known to be born serfs, and all are taught a trade. Some even go to the university.'

'Can a mother stay in touch with her child?'

'Yes, of course, if they wish. Each mother is given a token so that they can identify them in the future. Sometimes they claim them back. The children can generally be traced until they are in their teens, sometimes beyond.'

'But not the reverse? A child cannot seek his or her mother?'

'No, hardly, sir. Some of our children come from surprisingly good homes. I'm afraid it wouldn't be appreciated if they were to turn up out of the blue claiming kinship.'

'No, I suppose not.'

For an hour or so they continued their dismal task without success. Tea was brought. Vasily began to doubt they would find anything. But soon Matvey gave a cry. 'It's here, sir! Look! The mother's name... it must be her.' Matvey was pointing to the very bottom of a page. 'Here, look! Goossens. Leonora Goossens. That's who the woman was. She must have eloped with the count! No wonder the old baron wanted no more to do with him!'

For a moment Vasily didn't understand, but then he remembered. The Flemish steward employed by the von Klein Sternberg family had indeed been called Goossens. Presumably the woman who married Stepan was a member of his family, perhaps his daughter. If she had fled from the farm with him, she would have retained her former identity papers, her passport. But most important for their purposes, as a foreigner, she should now be easier to find.

He recalled that Praskovya had said that 'Astrella' had claimed there were no serfs where she came from. However, the serfs in Estonia had only been freed after the war, long after 1806. He had thought the remark rather odd. But it would have been true if she did in fact come not from Estonia, but from Flanders.

The record yielded no more than a name and a date. Mother, Leonora Goossens; child, female; date of birth, June 1806. There was no signature. The father, as in almost every other entry, was recorded as unknown. There was nothing to indicate that the child had died. She would be twenty-four or twenty-five years old now, much the same age as Andrey Andreyevich. Stepan Bogolyubov had certainly been a busy man during those months before Austerlitz.

'Do you have more information about this child?'

'Since she seems to have survived, there may be something. I'll send down and see.'

The papers when they arrived were few, but they did record that the child had been registered as Elizaveta Goossens, and that initially sums of money had been sent for her benefit. There were three receipts between 1808 and 1812, and another in 1816. There was also a formal written agreement. Vasily perused it eagerly. In seemed that in 1818, when the child was twelve, she was transferred to the care of the Imperial Theatres and enrolled at the Theatre School in St Petersburg. There were no further entries in the file.

'So she must be an actress!'

'Perhaps, or she might have fallen by the wayside, not made the grade. It will be worth asking further questions when we return home, although under the circumstances it's possible that Dmitry Vladimirovich will want to let sleeping dogs lie. In any event, I think we have enough evidence now to prove that the woman who married Stepan Bogolyubov in 1805 wasn't Andrey Andreyevich's mother. Apart from anything else, she can't have been carrying two babies at once! There's no suggestion of twins. Baron von Klein Sternberg's suit has run its course, I think.'

Vasily turned to the officer. 'Do you send many children to the theatre school?'

'Fewer now than we did. Children, especially girls, went quite frequently in the past. I could try to see who else went that year, but you'd really be better to ask in St Petersburg. There should be a record there.'

Vasily thanked the officer for his help while Matvey took a copy of the registration ledger and noted the contents of the other documents. As they walked back to Tverskaya through the Kitay-Gorod, Vasily remembered with regret that somewhere in these busy trading streets, his family's warehouse had stood before the fire of 1812.

Vasily lingered in Moscow longer than he had intended. He and Matvey had completed their research within forty-eight hours of their visit to the foundling home and should have set out on the journey back to the capital immediately, but it hadn't been so easy. On the day that they felt that nothing further could be discovered about Leonora Goossens and her daughter, he had heard from Irina. To his disappointment, her note didn't make her intentions clear. She would like to come to St Petersburg, indeed now longed to be with him. But her cousin had raised the usual doubts in her mind about her lost sons, and about Vasily's, and indeed her own family's reputation. Her brother, Pavel, was now in Vienna and may have fresh news about the baron. She would like to consult him before committing to return to the English Embankment. In the meantime, she hoped that before he left for the capital, Vasily would come to visit her and Sonya again.

Vasily accepted that this was the best he could hope for. At least his proposal had not been entirely rejected. Before leaving Moscow, he called on Irina and his child several times, and finally found it difficult to tear himself away.

CHAPTER TWENTY-EIGHT

February 1832 – St Petersburg

'You certainly took your time, Vasily! We had expected you back before now.' Alexander Petrovich paced Dmitry's drawing room carpet while the prince sat by the fire, fondling the ears of his terriers. His uncle was clearly impatient to hear what he had discovered in Moscow.

'I was a little delayed, sir,' said Vasily. 'When I reached the city I discovered that Irina Pavlovna and Sophia were in town for the season. I spent some time seeing my daughter.' He observed Alexander's reaction. At first his uncle seemed to be cheered by the news. Vasily knew that he was fond of Irina; she had, after all, averted a family disaster six years ago.

But then Alexander frowned. 'Have you rekindled your affair?'

'Sasha, really! That's the boy's business,' the prince said.

'It's your business too if you want the Tsar to look kindly on Vasily. He needs to settle down, find a wife, have some legitimate children. It won't do for him to carry on openly with a married woman. The Emperor will think him no better than von Klein.'

Vasily wished that his uncle wouldn't discuss him as if he wasn't there.

'If the Emperor only chose his courtiers from faithful husbands, and indeed model wives, he would have trouble filling the court,' said the prince. 'And we can hardly take the moral high ground…'

'As it happens, sir, Irène has not decided whether or not to return to St Petersburg. I live in hope, but it's not certain,' Vasily said.

'That's all very well,' Alexander began. Then he reflected for a moment and sat down. 'I can't say I really blame you. She's a fine woman. You'll find a proper wife eventually, I suppose. But I don't know what your mother and Katya will say.' He sucked in his cheeks, and added, 'Just try not to have any more children. It's awkward being illegitimate, even in a loving family.'

'Let me tell you what Matvey and I discovered on our travels.' Vasily was keen to move onto safer ground. 'I think you'll be pleased with our progress.'

He related all that he had learned in Torzhok and in Moscow. As he spoke his uncle visibly brightened. 'But you don't know where the Goossens woman is?'

'No sir, but we now have strong evidence that the woman who married Stepan Bogolyubov was not Andrey Andreyevich's mother. It seems that his claim must therefore fail.'

'Well, that's good news, very good,' said the prince. 'But I have to say, I am curious to know more of the woman – and the child.'

'Once we had her name and knew she was a foreigner, we inspected the Moscow police records. Matvey soon found her; he is far more diligent and sharp-eyed than I. She became housekeeper to an elderly nobleman and subsequently married him.'

'She seems to be keen on getting married!'

'Yes, and this time there's no reason to believe the marriage to be anything but legal. She married in her own name. But in 1812 the couple left the city in the great exodus, and no-one knows where they went. We can't find any family connection, and there is no record of their return. No-one claimed any compensation for loss of property, as far as we can see.'

'So the trail goes cold.'

'In Moscow yes, but Matvey will check the records here to see if Goossens ever lived in Petersburg. We can also try to trace the child. We know that she came here to the theatre school in Petersburg aged around twelve. There should be records at the Imperial Theatre, which is, of course, overseen by our Ministry. It's my aim to go there in the next day or so to see what I can discover.'

'I suppose these inquiries are necessary?' said Alexander. 'We probably now have enough to see off von Klein.'

'Well, the child, Elizaveta, has no claim since the marriage between her parents was invalid for at least two reasons. Nonetheless she might prove an embarrassment. It might be as well to know who else might be interested in the case, but on the other hand it may be better to let things rest.'

'You may be right,' Alexander said.

'But if she is alive, still in Petersburg, and is aware of her past, she may already have taken notice of von Klein's suit,' Dmitry said. 'Sadly it has been something of a cause célèbre.'

'if you want me to stop investigating now, I can, sir.'

Vasily hoped that he might have done enough, but Dmitry said, 'No, if you don't mind I should like you to follow the matter through if you can. The woman in Torzhok lied about the picture so clearly isn't reliable; Angelov is getting on in years and his memory might be questioned. I confess I am curious to learn more. Who knows, I might like to help a pretty actress.'

Vasily thought this improbable, given the prince's age and tastes. However, it was the first time that he had heard Dmitry suggest that any of his newly found relations might be of interest to him. He was not surprised. The prince was usually generous and his conscience had clearly been pricked.

'Perhaps we should contact von Klein's agent?' Alexander said. 'Tell Rodionov we can overturn the court's recognition of the marriage.'

The prince shook his head. 'Do we really want to involve the man's agent, go back to court, risk raising more interest in this rather unsavoury story? I understand that the Emperor has got wind of the affair and has expressed some sympathy for von Klein, who he believes to be my heir, of course. It would be preferable to persuade the baron to withdraw quietly. We might approach him directly. Tell him the story, demonstrate that his case is hopeless and the circumstances scandalous. He'll probably retreat without making a fuss. I would like to draw a line under the whole sorry business, frankly, and once he learns the truth, I suspect he will too.'

'I'll meet him informally if you like,' said Vasily. 'Rosovsky and he have both returned to St Petersburg on leave from Poland. They've both been promoted. He's Captain von Klein Sternberg now it seems, and surprisingly, something of a hero.'

'Really?' said Alexander. 'That's probably what has attracted the attention of the Emperor. He likes to encourage young soldiers of promise, and he has a strong preference for Baltic Germans.'

Vasily turned to Dmitry. 'In the circumstances, and given the Emperor's interest, I wonder if you should help the man in some way, sir. I know his character is suspect, that he's been unreliable in the past, but I feel that he should receive something. His parents were after all legitimately married in the eyes of his own faith, and even though he's been deprived of his Russian birthright, he is one of your only surviving relations.'

'Yes, you're right, Vasya. Agree to meet him. I'll consider what I might offer him…'

※

Leaving the palace a couple of days later, Vasily encountered their neighbour, Luka Kuprin, approaching a shining new carriage. The man generally dressed as a merchant, and flanked by two liveried footmen, he looked incongruous in his round hat and fur coat. He spotted Vasily and touched his hat.

'Good morning, Count Belkin! Weather cold enough

for you? Do you want a ride anywhere? I wouldn't walk in these temperatures.'

'No thank you, Kuprin. The sun's out, and I'm not going far. And how is Madame Kuprina?' On his return from Moscow, Vasily had learned that following the death of his wife, the merchant had wasted no time in marrying his tenant, Madame Hélène.

'Excellent! Excellent! But she is a little out of sorts at the moment. A letter has upset her. I haven't pried, but suppose it must be from a dissatisfied customer. I think she frets that the manager isn't entirely on top of things, but it won't do for my wife to work.'

'Yes, no doubt it is hard to let go when one has built up a thriving business.'

'That's true, but as a nobleman's wife...' Having achieved the status of nobility, Kuprin was keen to remind people of the fact.

'Please remember me to Madame Hélène,' Vasily said. 'I suppose people still call her that?'

'Yes, indeed they do. Old habits die hard. I would prefer her to be known as Madame Kuprina now, of course. Well, farewell, Belkin!' He climbed into his carriage. His new wife obviously suited him. His bearded face, once marked by sombre calculation, now wore a genial smile. His customary stoop seemed to have vanished. Vasily stood on the pavement and watched as one of his lackeys, extravagantly clad in black with gold lace, slammed the door and the matched greys set off.

Although the sun was bright, there was a sharp breeze. Kuprin had been right about the cold. Vasily pulled up his muffler and stepped out briskly as he crossed the frozen

Moika River. Within a quarter of an hour, he had reached the snow-covered square confronting the columned facade of the Bolshoy Kamenny Theatre.

On making himself known, he was taken to the office of Raphael Zotov, the secretary to the director, Prince Gagarin. Zotov was a chubby middle-aged man with an incipient double chin. A poet, translator and dramatist in his own right, he had worked at the theatre for many years; there was little he didn't know about its innermost workings. They had met once before, during the unofficial inquiry into the actors' attempted excursion to Tsarskoye Selo during the epidemic last summer. When Vasily explained his business today, Zotov, clearly curious, raised an eyebrow.

'Is this a personal mission, Belkin? Or are you here in an official capacity?'

'Only indirectly, Zotov.' Vasily was deliberately vague. He didn't want to draw more attention than necessary to the von Klein affair.

Zotov shrugged. 'Well, I'm sure we'll have a record of the intake into the theatre school in 1818, and that will no doubt include some children from the foundling homes. We are seeing fewer from Moscow here now that the new theatre there is complete, and this Emperor is in any event less enthusiastic about training up orphans.'

'Where does the intake for the school come from now?'

'We still sometimes buy troops of artists, or individuals from large estates, but that can be pricey as they have to be freed, and as I say, a few still come from the orphanages. There are some from the professional and merchant classes, and increasingly we are seeing the children of the performers themselves entering the school. It's a trend we encourage. They generally have the most talent – inbred, I suppose. They come with different expectations, have more stable backgrounds, and the girls are less inclined to run after young bucks, hoping to be set up with a carriage and apartment on graduation. Unsurprisingly, they tend to be the ones who end up respectably married.'

Zotov rose, walked into the corridor and gave a shout. A young man appeared and the secretary sent him to find the relevant ledger. 'Would you like to look around backstage while we wait?'

They spent a full half an hour wandering the vast spaces behind the stage, admiring the scenery flats, watching a grotto and lake appearing under the oily brush of one of the scene painters. 'The whole building was refurbished quite recently and is now much better equipped,' Zotov remarked as they emerged from the wings onto the stage. He carried a lantern; even in the daytime, the backstage area was dark.

'I was here when poor Minnie met her theatrical end,' Vasily said.

'Yes, that was a great pity. I'll never understand quite how it happened, but the girl did take risks.' They both contemplated the edge of the stage, now lapped by the lower fringe of the curtain.

'Where is she now?'

'She's living in a room in Kolomna. She received some compensation from us, and will get a small pension for life, but it won't stretch very far.'

'Is Count Malyshev no longer with her?'

'What do you think?'

'I suppose not.'

'No. She was only ever going to be a passing fancy; it was unfortunate that it ended before she could extract some real value from the relationship. But all is not lost, I understand. A former lover of hers, a cavalryman, has been helping her to find some private pupils. She's now Madame Minette, apparently.'

Vasily realised he was talking about Ivan Stenovsky. Vanya still seemed to carry a torch for the girl. 'And her rival?' he enquired.

'Oh, Lebedeva's still with us, and has never danced better in my view. The two women present a good example of what I was saying, Belkin. Minnie came from the foundling home here in the capital. She had a poor attitude, lived carelessly, on the edge – literally, if you like – and disaster followed. Lebedeva, on the other hand, is quite different. She is the child of performers, understands the demands of a theatrical career, knows how to play her cards, if you know what I mean. There has never been a whiff of scandal, and I think that soon you'll hear that virtue has been rewarded. There will be news of an excellent marriage. This may be her last production.' Zotov preened himself. Did he, as had been suggested, personally benefit from promoting these liaisons?

'May I ask who the lucky man is?'

'Let's just say he's very well connected. But wouldn't you like to meet her? She's to dance tonight, and I expect she is already here… she's always well prepared.'

Vasily hesitated. His encounter with the dancer during the epidemic had been uncomfortable. She had laughed at him, insulted him. But it would be interesting to see the lovely Lyuba Lebedeva in her natural surroundings.

As they entered her dressing room he was overpowered by the aura of hot house flowers. Beneath the mirrors and on the floor, boxes containing gifts, tied with bright ribbons, and elegant drums of confectionary were piled high. As he contemplated the collection, something stirred in Vasily's memory, but he wasn't sure why. The dancer herself was sitting on a buttoned divan; she did not rise to greet them.

Zotov waved his hands at the pile of tributes. 'Most of this goes to charity. Unwanted gifts are sold for the benefit of the poor.'

'I always take some of the flowers home,' said the dancer as she extended her hand to Vasily. She looked at him closely. 'You're Count Belkin, the officer who spoilt our trip to the country, aren't you?'

'I am indeed, madame.'

'You were probably right to stop us, I suppose. Thank goodness all that cholera nonsense is behind us! But why are you visiting Rafael Mikhailovich? Has someone else done something wrong?'

'I'm not a policeman.'

'But you work for the Interior Ministry, I think.'

'The count is seeking some information for an enquiry that he is progressing.'

'Is this about the Bogolyubov legacy? I understand your patron the prince is refusing to acknowledge the aspiring German.' Vasily felt a twist of concern. Von Klein's claim did indeed seem to be common knowledge.

But there was no need to fuel further speculation. 'I'm afraid I can't discuss Ministry matters, Madame.'

Lyuba looked away, her lips compressed, unaccustomed to being refused. She looked older than she did on the stage. She was generously made, indeed, surprisingly solid. Her skin was very pale, her features almost too regular. She did not attract him; there was something formidable about her. She looked up and held his gaze. Her eyes were as blue and cold as a hole in the ice on the Neva. The scent of flowers was making his head spin a little. He murmured some pleasantries and backed towards the door.

Zotov seemed amused at his discomfiture. When they were out of earshot, he said, 'Not one for the artists, Count Belkin? Or is she just not to your taste?' The secretary gave him a sideways glance. For a brief moment Vasily thought that the man might offer an alternative.

When they returned to Zotov's office, the ledger from the theatre school lay open on the desk. 'Well, let's see. 1818.' Zotov found the appropriate page, took a ruler and ran it down the list. 'There are only five orphan entrants listed here, two boys, three girls. Just two from Moscow, a girl and a boy. There are no surnames of course. The girl was called Maria, but that doesn't signify. Most girls from the homes are named after their patroness, the dowager empress, or another member of the imperial family. We invariably change their names. We can't have an entire class called Ekaterina, Maria, or more recently, Alexandra!'

'Are those from Moscow still with you?'

'It seems not. One, the female, proved inadequate and was let go within a few weeks, according to the record.

And I know that the other, the male, died in the epidemic last year. He was an actor. Quite a good one. Sad story.'

'What would have happened to the girl you let go?'

'She would have been sent as an apprentice to the palace probably, to the kitchens or laundry. The Empress, the dowager empress at that time, took a personal interest in them all.'

'And is there any way of tracing her?'

'I doubt it, Belkin. We're speaking of some time ago now and her name will have been changed, as I said. You would have to make enquiries at the palace.'

'Are you sure there were only two children? The foundling home assured me there were three sent that year.'

'There's no record here, but that's not surprising. The lists are often inaccurate, and sometimes children go astray. Last year one child destined for the school took work at a post house en route, and others have simply disappeared.' Zotov seemed unconcerned at this casual loss of young people 'No, I'm sorry. I don't think we can help you further.' The secretary slapped the ledger closed, raising a cloud of dust.

Vasily sneezed. His nose itched and his eyes watered. There seemed to be nothing further to ask. 'Thank you, Zotov. My patron the prince would like to make a contribution to the theatre benevolent fund.'

'That's very kind, Count Belkin. If your family ever need last-minute tickets for the show – indeed, if I can be of any service to you – just let me know!'

Zotov saw him to the door, and then, with a smile and a theatrical bow, disappeared into the labyrinthine passages.

CHAPTER TWENTY-NINE

St Petersburg

Once the Poles had been chased over the Prussian border, Andrey's regiment was dispatched to winter quarters in Lithuania, from where it would keep watch over the re-subjugated territories.

Although late into the fray, the King of Prussia's men had been judged to have acquitted themselves well. All who had participated in the final attack on Warsaw received an inscribed silver medal, twenty-five soldiers from the lower ranks were awarded the Cross of St George, and two hundred or so were given the Polish order of Military Virtue. Acting First Lieutenant Andrey von Klein Sternberg was promoted to staff captain, and for his outstanding bravery in the storming of the Volya barrier, was awarded the prestigious Order of St Vladimir (4th class). Captain Rosovsky was promoted to major.

As planned, the two men sought and received leave of absence and travelled together to St Petersburg. Rosovsky was hoping to take advantage of the buoyant mood in the capital to be reinstated with his old regiment, the Lifeguards. Andrey had taken Rosovsky's advice, and was seeking a permanent position with the General Staff. He knew that if these hopes came to nothing, a return to the regiment was probably his best option. While the prince still lived, there seemed to be no way to escape the stalemate with regard to his legal suit.

Days after settling into their former billet, both men were invited to an imperial reception at the Anichkov Palace. On arrival, Rosovsky had been swiftly distracted by former acquaintance, so Andrey stood alone at the edge of the brightly painted hall, toying with a glass of champagne. He surveyed the crowd of newly promoted and decorated officers. The array of bright epaulettes and awards was dazzling, and the noise overwhelming. As he wondered how to penetrate this turbulent press, an imperial aide approached.

'Captain von Klein Sternberg?'

'Yes?'

'The Emperor has asked to meet you, sir.'

'Meet me?' He could not hide his surprise. Had his war exploits really been enough to justify this honour? He was led through a succession of bright rooms, his heart beating like an insistent drum.

'Ah, von Klein Sternberg,' the Emperor greeted him. 'Well done, Captain! You played a key part in the relief of Warsaw. Are you fully recovered from your wounds?' As Nicholas continued, it became obvious that he was not solely interested in congratulating him on his resourcefulness on the Nur and his bravery at Volya; he was also curious about the Bogolyubov lawsuit.

'I'm told that the court has confirmed your legitimacy, Captain,' Nicholas said. 'So what has the prince done to acknowledge your rights?'

'To date, sir, the prince has been unwilling to accept the judgement of the court.'

The Emperor's blue-grey eyes hardened, his face flushed, and he stared at his feet for some moments. 'That won't do at all,' he said. 'Since his retirement, we have seen little of Dmitry Vladimirovich at our court. He has shown no interest in serving again in the senate. It's time he started to pull his weight! And you, Count, should think about using your rightful title.'

'I feel I cannot do that while the prince refuses to acknowledge me, sir.'

'I suppose it is your choice, Captain, but it seems a pity. I shall take the matter up with the prince. The court has pronounced, and your claim cannot simply be brushed away...'

'No, sir. Thank you, sir.' Andrey waited for Nicholas to speak again, but to his relief, the Emperor of all the Russias was interrupted by an aide, and drawn away to other business. Andrey watched his imposing figure move away surrounded by courtiers, his imperial cords and awards tossing and flashing alarmingly. A crowd of men who had witnessed the exchange were staring at him and making comments to their neighbours. Trembling slightly, he took a deep breath. Now was no time for diffidence. He scanned the room with steady eyes and, nodding to an imaginary acquaintance in the adjacent saloon, paced away with measured steps.

When, a little later, he was driven back from the palace,

the implications of his exchange with the Tsar revolved in his head. His thoughts turned to Nadezhda. On his return to St Petersburg, he had found a letter from her. He knew she had left the city over a year ago and had contrived to send this from the country. He wondered who could have helped her. As he unsealed the letter, his heart quickening, he hoped that whoever it was had been discreet.

Bashkatovo, Oryol Province
December 1831

Andrey Andreyevich,

I understand that the campaign against the rebellious Poles is now successfully concluded, and pray that at some stage you will be returning to the capital. I am writing this in the earnest hope that you will receive it. We have heard in recent days from Princess Polunin that your name has appeared prominently in the list of awards and promotions. This news has gladdened my heart.

As I hope you discovered from the note I wrote before Easter, I have been on our estates in Oryol for some time. The fiction of my romantic attachment to Prince Uspensky ran its course some time ago when he resigned his commission and announced his intention to marry another. After a short period, when my 'disappointment' was deemed to have run its course, an alternative prospect was found, but fortunately this did not work out as my parents had hoped.

My mother, despairing of securing a local match, is hoping that my father will sanction a return to St Petersburg, I am praying that this will happen shortly now the cordon sanitaire has been removed, but she may wish to wait for better weather, and we shall come in the spring.

I hope that this letter reaches you and that you are in good health. I would give a good deal to hear news of you. I live on in the firm hope that we will soon meet once more. God bless you.
I remain,
Your Nadya

Andrey rubbed his finger along the scar on his face, as his raised eyebrows dropped to their customary position. As ever when thinking of Nadezhda Gavrilovna, he was torn between intense fascination and an uneasy sense of impropriety. He appreciated her direct approach, and of course, there was no denying her desirability. But she might also be considered unreflecting and altogether too forward, nothing like the sort of wife he had occasionally imagined.

He had set the letter aside. It was probably of no consequence in any event. The prospect of actually marrying any girl in the short term seemed remote, and by the time his ambitions were fulfilled, Nadezhda could be someone else's wife. It was pointless to offer for the girl now. He was now a captain, of course, but his financial position, while better than it had been, remained precarious. He would never be accepted.

But now, returning from the palace, his hopes were raised. If the prince bowed to pressure from the Emperor and recognised his claim, surely he might then write to the girl's father? There was a chance that as Count Bogolyubov, now a captain and a man with prospects, he would not be refused.

CHAPTER THIRTY

On his return from the theatre, as requested by the prince and Alexander Petrovich, Vasily sent a message to Captain von Klein Sternberg. He suggested they meet after dinner the following evening, in a private room at the English Inn on Galernaya Street.

It was a cold still night. The fat wedge of a half-moon shone above the almost empty streets. Vasily, well wrapped-up, decided to walk the short distance to the inn. He wondered how the baron would receive the bad news he must bring. During the duel on Vasilevsky Island, the man had possibly not been shown to best advantage, but he had clearly fought bravely in the recent campaign and achieved some distinction. Rosovsky had certainly warmed towards him. He might once have been the reprobate that Ivan had suggested, but if so, it seemed he had changed. Vasily sighed. Andrey Andreyevich might not have a legal right to anything, but he was after all Dmitry's flesh and blood, and had been cheated of his rights by his father's folly and negligence. Now his hopes would be completely dashed, but at least he could soften the blow. The prince had authorised him to offer the man quite a generous sum in compensation, more than enough to pay off most people's debts.

He took the route through Senate Square towards the bridge, turning under the arch leading into Galernaya Street. There had been snow showers that afternoon, and the pavements, powdered white, creaked beneath his boots as he approached the inn. He heard a slight hissing and turned round. A covered sledge was sliding along the street behind him, and seemed likely to run him down. Had the driver not seen him? As he gave a shout, the vehicle came to a halt. A large man climbed out and walked towards him.

'Excuse me, sir, do you want to pass?' Vasily said. 'I hadn't realised you were there.'

The man didn't answer, but took him by the arm. 'You're to come along with us, sir.'

Vasily was about to decline the invitation, when a figure emerged from a doorway and seized his other arm. What was this about? Were they going to rob him? Or had his past finally caught up with him?

'Let me go!' he exclaimed. 'You're welcome to my purse…'

He struggled to free himself. He must shout for help, but would the watchman back in the square hear him? He took a breath of freezing air, but his cry was cut short as a heavy fist swung into his face.

※

He seemed to be moving through space, bathing in soft white mist. The half-moon was drifting through a vault pricked with stars. He moved his head and felt snow touch his neck, and now the ground, solid and cold beneath him. He had lost his hat and cloak and his legs would not move. Where was he? There were lights in the distance. He could see the needle spire of the Admiralty across a glimmering blue-white plain. He was lying out on the frozen river, on the ice. He wouldn't survive here for long! Gripped by terror, he started to shiver uncontrollably. He must try to move, but his head was spinning. He tried once more, but once sitting upright, he couldn't control his numb hands to loosen the rope that tied his ankles. He beat his arms across his rapidly cooling body. He must stay awake, not lose consciousness. He shook himself and slapped and pounded his sides. But exhaustion and then creeping lassitude overwhelmed him and gradually and inexorably his eyes lost focus. All went dark and he sank into a cold, lonely place, from whence he knew he would not return.

***

When the note came from Count Belkin suggesting that they meet, Andrey considered refusing. His agent had warned him to be wary of direct contact with 'the other party'. But he knew that Rodionov wanted to retain control, and continue to collect his fees. It was time to meet his rival for the prince's money face to face. Perhaps they could reach some understanding.

He had decided to wear civilian clothes so left the barracks, where wearing uniform was mandatory, in a peaked cap, his tail coat concealed by a fur-lined cloak. The duty sentry would not be fooled by this camouflage, so he paid the expected toll. He took a droshky to the edge of Senate Square. Flickering oil lights threw shadows over the freshly fallen snow between the columns of the buildings, and contorted the outline of the monumental statue of the rearing horseman. The paving glistened brightly under his feet. He felt hopeful. Perhaps now, at last, his fortune might change.

As he approached the entrance to Galernaya Street he heard a warning shout and the jingle of harness. He was forced to step aside as a hooded sleigh veered past him and drove on at a hectic pace towards the river. Hard-pressed to keep his footing, he cursed the driver. Then, as he collected himself, he was almost toppled by a youth racing towards him.

'Careful! Watch where you're going!'

The boy, who was wearing a heavy fur coat and hat, was waving a stick crowned with a metal knob in the air. Shouting incoherently, he grabbed hold of Andrey's arms.

'Calm down, son. Tell me slowly.'

'They've got my master... taken him away... kidnapped him.'

'Who have?'

'The men there in the kibitka. I was walking a little way behind him, keeping an eye out. They were following him, but I didn't realise... We've got to go after them. They'll take him out onto the ice and rob him... leave him to die. We must go after them.'

The watchman posted on the corner had left the comfort of his hut and brazier. 'This is the third time this winter.' He shook his head. 'I'll raise the alarm.' As he spoke, a covered sledge, bells ringing, lanterns swinging, slid across the square towards them.

The youth turned to Andrey. 'Can we stop that carriage, sir? Ask them to help us?' Andrey considered for a moment. The lad seemed sincere and was, as far as he could tell, respectable. It seemed his master was indeed in trouble. His business with Belkin would have to wait.

Together they walked out into the path of the sledge. It came to a halt. A middle-aged couple sat inside, huddled in rugs and furs. The man stuck his head out from under the hood. 'Get out of the way, damn you! We're already late!'

'We need to borrow your vehicle, sir,' cried the youth. 'It's an emergency, a matter of life and death.'

'Well, you can't… we're in a hurry.' The woman said something from within, and the man's head drew back.

The watchman stepped forward. 'I'm commandeering this sledge and your driver. A crime has been committed and there's a need to pursue the criminals.'

'But it's freezing cold.'

'A man is out on the ice. He needs help,' Andrey said.

'You must get out, sir,' the youth insisted, a note of desperation in his voice. 'You can take refuge at the Polunin Palace. Tell them that Matvey sent you, and they'll arrange to take you wherever you want.'

'Oh, very well.' The Polunin name seemed to reassure.

'I'll conduct you to the palace on foot, your honour,' the watchman said. 'It's no more than five minutes' walk. Or you can stand by my fire while I look for a droshky.' Assisted by Matvey, the couple, now muttering words of concern, climbed out, wrapping their furs around them.

Andrey scrambled under the hood. Matvey pulled down his fur hat and urged on the startled driver. Moving as fast as the snow-covered paving of the square would allow, they approached the ramp that led onto the ice of the Neva. The sledge bucked and swayed over the rough surface. Andrey hoped that it could take the strain. He had heard stories of thieves abducting their victims and abandoning them on the ice, but he had not really believed them, thinking them one of the many fantastic myths that swirled around the salons of the capital, but the fresh tracks of the robbers' kibitka were clearly visible.

'Can you see them?'

'No, not yet.'

'Who is your master, Matvey?' He perhaps should have asked before embarking on this adventure.

'It's Vasily Nikolayevich, Count Belkin, sir. He was on his way to a meeting…'

Andrey almost laughed; this was an interesting development! Belkin had of course been on his way to meet him. Well, that was not of much consequence now. The man must be saved if possible. The lights of the city winked and faded as they moved out onto the empty expanses of the river that led towards the gulf.

'Look, there! They're coming back!' The kibitka was scudding towards them over the ice, heading back towards the city. 'Do you think my master's still with them?'

'I doubt it. I expect they've robbed and abandoned him. Pull aside. They may not see us.'

This proved a forlorn hope. As their sledge arced away, the approaching kibitka, drawn by a sure-footed shaggy pony, pulled up about twenty yards distant. Two men emerged, their bulky forms clear in the moonlight. One seemed to be groping for a weapon. Andrey wished he was better prepared. He clamped his cap firmly onto his head, threw aside his cloak, and climbed out of the sledge. Gasping in the grip of the icy air, he turned to the driver. 'Give me your whip.'

The whiplash sang out above the heads of the approaching men. They stopped in their tracks. Andrey cracked the whip once more, aiming lower, and the lash just kissed the boots of the man in front, who, surprised, staggered a little, almost fell. Andrey then advanced and, swinging out once again, curled the leather around the man's arm, and then wrenched back. The man pitched with a cry onto the ice. A pistol fell from his hand and skidded across the surface. With a further spin Andrey removed his companion's round hat. The man stood spellbound.

Matvey had jumped down from the box and, having watched this display with amazement, was now running across the ice towards the kibitka. The metal knob on his stick flashed in the moonlight. He bent to pick up the pistol.

'Be careful!' Andrey shouted. 'We just need to see them off... we don't have time for a bundle.'

Slithering on the slick surface, Matvey peered into the sleigh. 'He's not here.' He scuttled back towards Andrey, who relieved him of the gun.

The man on the ground shouted something to his hatless companion. Clearly not up for a fight, he lurched to his feet, and the two men retreated to their sleigh, which was soon careering away towards the city. If their purpose had been to delay their victim's rescue, they had succeeded.

'Will we ever find him out here, sir?' Matvey's voice quavered.

'I don't know.' Andrey threw on his cloak. They would probably find him, but in what state? Their driver was sitting on the box, his face rigid with fear. Matvey took the reins from his heavily gloved hands and Andrey threw him the whip. 'Just follow the tracks. Get a move on.'

It was hard to guess which tracks to follow, but in time they found Belkin. He seemed to be asleep, peacefully curled on the ice, his legs bound. The driver sat staring as if paralysed. 'For God's sake, help us!' Andrey shouted. The man came to life, and together they tipped Belkin into the sledge. Andrey looked at him. Was he dead? He must assume not. He had been very heavy. His coat had disappeared and his clothes seemed to have been doused with water. He felt around in the carriage. There were a couple of woollen rugs, but that was all.

'Can you drive?'

'Yes sir.' The coachman had recovered his composure.

Andrey turned to Matvey. 'We must take this off.' They struggled to ease off Belkin's jacket, which was already stiffening with frost. His body seemed to be warm, and it was clear he was still breathing. Matvey stripped off his fur coat and, creeping close, held him in his arms. Andrey wrapped them both in the fur and then covered them with his cloak, pulling a woollen blanket around his own shoulders.

'Alright... drive on.'

There was no sign of the robbers as they swung back towards the lights of Senate Square. Andrey could hear Matvey talking to Belkin. He was rubbing his fingers, his face and ears, and breathing on them gently, but Belkin didn't stir.

Once up the ramp, Andrey shouted that the driver should ignore all restrictions and drive directly to the front of the Polunin Palace, where there were plenty of hands available to lift Belkin out of the carriage and up the front steps. Above the murmur of agitated voices, someone was giving instructions.

Reluctant to confront the entire extended family, Andrey did not emerge from the sledge at once. He caught Matvey by the arm as he was extricating himself from Belkin's embrace, and said quietly, 'Tell them to put your master in a bath of cool water. Not hot – the shock, the pain, might kill him. And look out for frostbite.'

He retrieved his cloak, threw it around his shoulders, and slipped out of the sledge. Straightening his cap, he disappeared into the night.

※

They came to question him the next morning.

Having returned to the barracks, exhausted and chilled to the bone, Andrey had slipped past the sentry, who had been occupied collecting tribute from a group of drunken troopers. On achieving his rooms, he found that Morozov had thoughtfully fed the stove and put out a glass and a flask of red wine. He pulled off his clothes and put on his robe. He then slumped into his chair, and drank deeply, trying to make sense of what had happened. Belkin, it seemed, had been the victim of a robbery when on his way to their meeting. The count had been fortunate that his lad had been looking out for him. Tomorrow he must make contact with the family to check that he had survived, and to see if he could be of any assistance in identifying the perpetrators.

He finished his wine, fell into bed, and slept soundly.

He was woken by Morozov shaking him. 'The major wants to see you.'

'I'm on leave, Morozov...'

'I know, sir. But he says it's important.'

The guard room was full of people. Rosovsky, flanked by two military gendarmes, stood with a tall man in a civil service uniform who Andrey guessed was Belkin's uncle. In addition, Ivan Stenovsky, wearing his dark jacket with its red flashes, stood glowering in the corner. As Andrey arrived, he rewarded him with a self-satisfied smirk. His former rival seemed leaner than before the war, and had even less hair.

One of the gendarmes turned to him. 'We are here to question you, Captain, in connection with an incident yesterday evening in the Admiralty District.' He was momentarily shocked, but then understood. They thought him in some way responsible for Belkin's abduction. He was of course innocent of any wrongdoing, but it would be gratifying to give Stenovsky the chance to make a fool of himself.

'Do you know anything about this, Captain?' Rosovsky asked, evidently astonished.

'Well, I can't say I'm entirely ignorant of it, sir.'

Stenovsky leapt towards him, his hand on his sabre hilt. 'There you are, you see, Alexander Petrovich! I told you!' His spittle flew in Andrey's face. 'You knew that Count Belkin was on his way to the inn, and decided to do away with him! You think he is standing in the way of your vile ambitions…'

Andrey fought off a prickle of irritation. Stenovsky's antipathy towards him seemed to know no bounds. Surely he realised that it would be nonsensical for him to hire assassins to murder Belkin? Perhaps the man was still deranged by jealousy? Well, he must resist the urge to knock him to the floor.

'I'll neither explain myself to you, Stenovsky, nor allow myself to be taken in charge. I shall answer my superior officer's questions, if he has any for me, and that's all.'

'Rosovsky knows nothing about the matter,' Stenovsky retorted. 'You're plainly involved in some way. You crept out of the barracks in disguise…'

Belkin's uncle raised his hand. 'We don't know that, Ivan Alexandrovich. We're simply here to seek the truth. I'm not sure there is any need for an arrest. Let's hope we can quickly rule out any involvement on the part of Captain von Klein Sternberg.'

Andrey turned to him. 'If you want to get to the truth without delay, might I suggest that you summon the young servant who brought Count Belkin home last night?'

'Who? Matvey?'

'Yes. In his absence, I shall answer no further questions.'

Stenovsky snorted. He was about to speak again, but Alexander put a hand on his arm. The cavalryman's pink face deepened to purple and he turned away with a shrug. The deputation was escorted outside while Matvey was sent for.

'What is all this?' asked Rosovsky. 'You're not involved, I suppose?'

'Well, I am, but not in the way they imagine. They seem to regard me as some sort of pariah. All I want is what's rightfully mine, but obviously I'm not prepared to murder to achieve it.'

In time, informed that Matvey had arrived, Stenovsky, the gendarmes and Alexander Petrovich trooped back. As the boy entered, he looked about him with interest. He was an attractive lad. Andrey remembered his slightly Eastern features, but clearly he was no-one's servant. He was wearing a black frock coat, his cravat elegantly tied, his boots shiny. As Matvey saw him he smiled. 'Oh hello, sir! Why did you disappear off last night? I looked about for you but you had gone, and before we were able to thank you…'

'You know this man, Matvey?' asked Alexander.

'Oh yes, sir. He was the one that I told you about. The man who held those brigands off with a whip! It was quite something! You should have seen it, sir!'

'Yes, so you've said.'

Andrey turned to Matvey. 'And how is your… err… your master? Recovered, I hope.'

'Matvey is Vasily Nikolayevich's ward, Baron von Klein Sternberg,' Alexander said.

Matvey laughed. 'Oh! You're the pretender! Who'd have thought it!' Ivan Alexandrovich told the prince that you were a profligate wastrel!' He looked with renewed interest at Andrey. Then, remembering his question, he added, 'I think he'll live, but of course, he's not very comfortable. He yelled a great deal as he thawed out.'

'His fingers, toes?'

'Doctor Webster is concerned about one of his fingers, sir, but we'll have to wait and see, and of course…' Matvey was clearly happy to chatter on for some time. Stenovsky, snorting again, made as if to intervene, but Belkin's uncle, keen to bring the matter to a close, coughed and turned to him. 'Could you wait outside for a moment, Ivan Alexandrovich?'

Stenovsky swivelled on his heel and strutted from the room. Alexander, his face flushed, turned to Andrey.

'I have to apologise to you. Captain Stenovsky was much too quick to leap to conclusions. It seems that the attack on my nephew was, as I suspected, indeed a simple robbery, and that we are much indebted to you for your help.' He looked down at his boots. 'The truth is that everything to do with this business of the legacy has driven us all to a state close to lunacy. Vasily Nikolayevich was hoping to try to bring the matter to a sensible resolution.' He hesitated for a moment as if wanting to say more, but then thought better of it. 'He's not fit to speak to you now,' he continued. 'I hope he will not take too long to recover. May I send to you to rearrange your meeting? In the meantime, no doubt the regular police will be in touch about last night…'

Andrey gave a short bow of assent. An apology from Stenovsky seemed appropriate, but he doubted he would receive one. The man's continuing grudge had clearly led to this farce.

As the youth Matvey followed Alexander from the room, he turned and gave Andrey a sly wink. 'Now I know who you are sir, I'll put in a good word with… well, you know… send the other party news of you…'

What on earth was the young man talking about? But there was no time to seek clarification. He had gone.

Andrey sat down and then, remembering himself, stood again.

Rosovsky laughed. 'No, sit down, Andrey. It's not every day one's accused of murder.'

'It's almost enough to send me back to the regiment…'

'Come on! You can't give up now. You've got the prince on the run I think, especially after this. I'll tell you what. I have some paperwork to catch up with, but then we'll go somewhere for dinner.'

It was only much later, when he returned to his rooms, that Andrey understood Matvey's obscure remark. He must of course know Nadezhda, and was now intending to convey news to her about him. The thought lifted his heart.

CHAPTER THIRTY-ONE

March 1832 – St Petersburg

'Well, it obviously wasn't von Klein!' said Vasily. 'How can anyone have thought that it was in his interest to do away with me now? And how can Alexander Petrovich have embarrassed us all by going to the barracks and questioning him in the way he did?' He was more or less recovered from his ordeal on the ice, but his face was bruised, and one finger and his ears were still sore.

'It was Ivan Alexandrovich's idea,' said Matvey. 'When he heard that von Klein had failed to appear for your meeting at the inn, he suggested to your uncle that von Klein himself could have arranged to get rid of you. He knew you were going to meet him, after all, and it would have been a perfect opportunity. I don't think Alexander Petrovich thought it very likely, but he felt he should clear the matter up quickly.'

Vasily sighed. He had been careful to avoid discussing the progress of the case with Ivan, and so his volatile friend had jumped to unlikely conclusions. 'I don't think Ivan will ever forgive the German for appropriating Minnie. It makes him quite irrational.'

'But if it wasn't von Klein, who was it?' said Yakov, who, having recovered from the initial shock of almost losing his master, was now as keen as Matvey to unravel the mystery. 'It wasn't a robbery. Your purse was untouched; nothing was taken. There must have been some other motive.'

'It's probably best if the world believes it was a robbery,' said Vasily. 'Otherwise all sorts of questions will be raised. But you're right, Yakov. Someone wanted to frighten me or worse. I made a few enemies enforcing regulations during the epidemic, but more likely it has something to do with our research into the past.' He paused to consider for a moment. 'I must say, it's tempting to just let matters rest now, ask no further questions, and try to reach an accommodation with von Klein as we intended.'

Matvey shook his head. 'But we must continue to investigate, sir. You can't just ignore an attempt on your life. Whoever it was is bound to try again.'

Vasily shrugged off a stir of apprehension. Sadly, Matvey was right. 'In any event, I'm not looking forward to breaking the news to von Klein,' he said. 'Perhaps, in the light of recent events, the prince will see fit to offer him something more in compensation. I'll postpone my meeting with him for now, write to him, thank him for his invaluable, indeed vital, help and say that at present I am still indisposed.'

'And in the meantime, I need to make a start on the housing records here in St Petersburg,' said Matvey. 'The child came here in 1818, we know that. It's not impossible that the mother followed.'

'Fine, do that Matvey... but do be careful. And don't mention any of this to anyone, is that clear? Everything must remain confidential for now.'

The youth looked at him with reproach. 'Oh, yes sir. Absolutely,' he said, gravely. 'Mr Maltby taught me the importance of "absolute discretion" in such matters.'

※

A few days later Vasily once again found himself at the theatre. The Great Fast was approaching. Next week the house would go dark. Tonight, Lyuba Lebedeva was to give her farewell performance. With some difficulty, the prince had managed to secure a box for the occasion and even Alexander, not a great enthusiast for the theatre, had insisted on coming.

Vasily surveyed the scene, his eyes watering a little in the bluish haze. The orchestra was screeching, twangling. The spectacle would soon begin. The National Anthem played; the Emperor was arriving. As the curtain rose, the lights from the stage brightened the dim auditorium. Medals, ribbons and stars glowed; jewels flashed. The usual buzz of chatter arose as society recognised its acquaintance.

'Look! There's the captain!' said Matvey, as the first notes of the overture floated from the pit. Vasily scanned the ring of boxes. Major Rosovsky was seated nearby with his wife and sister. Captain von Klein Sternberg was with them. Both men glinted with awards from the recent campaign. An officer entered the box and shook both men's hands, presumably offering congratulation. Von Klein was laughing, his hair bright against the shadows behind him.

Katya raised her glasses to scrutinise him. 'He's actually very handsome…'

'Is he?' Vasily sat back, not wishing to be observed. 'Last time I saw him he didn't look so good, but of course, he was in fear of his life.'

'Well, he looks quite well now,' she said.

'He's not just handsome. He's damn courageous!' Matvey said. He was clearly much impressed by the captain.

'Matvey, no vulgar language, please.' Vasily spoke more sharply than he intended, beginning to feel outshone by all this adulation directed towards von Klein. He felt a twist of conscience. He couldn't delay his meeting with him much longer. Changing the subject, he asked Katya, 'Do you know why Lebedeva is retiring? Her career seemed to be going from strength to strength…'

'Oh, she's to marry Count Bolotin. Didn't you know? The count's mother is very distressed and his sisters are mortified, but he's so wealthy he can ignore the opprobrium of society, and probably that of the Emperor too. She won't appear on the stage again, in any event.'

The overture got underway and the spectacle began. The short programme was designed to include Lebedeva's most acclaimed numbers. Despite a vague feeling of distaste, which he found hard to throw off even here, Vasily had to admit that she looked quite stunning. At the end of her performance, a torrent of flowers poured onto the stage. A tribute of exotic blooms, a gift from Count Bolotin, was presented by a flurry of attendants. The Emperor rose to his feet and clapped with vigour. The audience followed his lead.

'Will she dance again?' asked Matvey.

'I expect she will,' Katya responded.

And, indeed, Lebedeva did dance one last piece: an exercise in grace and slow control that was greeted by the audience with a silence so profound that when the music ceased, it took some time for applause to recommence.

※

After the performance, Yakov was sent to find the prince's carriage and Vasily, having escorted his sister and his mother to their home on the English Embankment, returned home with his uncle and the prince. He knew that Matvey had today finished his investigations into the past of Leonora Goossens, and he was keen to hear what he had discovered.

They sat opposite one another in his study. Matvey was clearly still entranced by the spectacle at the theatre, and it took some time to bring him back to his task.

'Well, Motya? What do you have to tell me?'

Matvey pulled out his notes. As he spoke, Vasily rubbed the back of his neck. Could what he was hearing be true? Had he in fact known Leonora Goossens for some years? Was the woman he sought really the milliner who had sold goods to his mother, sister, Irina and almost every other woman of his acquaintance? It seemed barely credible.

But on reflection, perhaps it was not so surprising. There were few respectable, independent foreign woman of the right age in the city. If he had thought about it, he might have guessed. It was very plausible that Madame Hélène, flamboyant, slightly exotic, still alluring, might have been guilty of some youthful indiscretion, and might also, as Matvey had discovered, have outlived two husbands before her recent marriage to Kuprin, both widowers, each wealthier than the last. But would she, as Matvey seemed to suggest, have murdered each of their wives in turn? More importantly, would she have hired assassins to do away with him, thinking that he was on her trail? Could Madame Hélène really have done that?

Perhaps. The consequences of exposure would be disastrous; it might ruin both her business and her new marriage. He must try to find out.

❧

When, the following morning, he walked across the bright-hued carpet of her small drawing room, he knew at once that she had been expecting his call. As she extended her hand, her eyes were watchful. Rising from his bow, he noticed a hint of grey in her high-piled curls.

There was no attempt at denial. 'So you have found me out, Vasily Nikolayevich.' Her hands were twisting her kerchief into a tight coil. 'I thought it would be only a matter of time. It is hard for anyone, especially a foreigner, to hide their tracks in this land of bureaucrats, passports and registers.'

'You knew that I was looking for you?'

'Yes. As soon as I learnt about Baron von Klein Sternberg's claim, I was disturbed, but I thought that Prince Bogolyubov would accept him as his heir and that would close the matter. It surprised me when the prince decided to resist his suit. Of course, then I realised that the mistakes of my past might be revealed, although I believed that I would be hard to trace. But just recently, I heard that you had visited Praskovya in Kluchovo. I have paid her good money over the years to keep me informed, but not enough, it seems, to buy her silence.'

Of course, that would explain the opulence of the wheelwright's home. 'A visit from a government official is usually intimidating, Madame,' he said. 'And she could not deny the existence of a Countess Bogolyubov on the estate. Others also knew of your presence. But she didn't disclose your whereabouts to me. I had to work that out for myself. So you admit that it was you who married Stepan Dmitryevich in September 1805?'

'Yes, and I have regretted it ever after.'

'He had abandoned his wife, Astrella?'

Madame Hélène sat down. 'Yes. He married her under duress. He had carelessly compromised her when she was staying for the season with an aunt in Reval. He was waiting to march with his regiment to fight the French. Von Klein Sternberg, her father, was a very determined man, you might say a force of nature. He threatened Stepan with terrible retribution, reported him to his commanding officer, wrote to his father. Ultimately, he was unable to resist the demand that he marry his daughter. He stayed at the farm for some weeks after the wedding and the rows and arguments were terrible. It was impossible for Astrella.'

'Why didn't he just leave? He could have returned to the army.'

'He tried at least twice, but was prevented. The old man knew he was on extended leave. Stepan turned to me for some sanity and comfort. Finally we planned his escape together, and as the time approached he asked me to go with him. I was young, just seventeen, and love for him completely overwhelmed me. He had great charm, but more than that. Not many men can be said to possess pure physical beauty, but he was unusually striking. Few women could resist him. But of course, he was wild… wild and careless, and I later realised not very clever.' She dropped her head, cupped her chin in one hand and stared at the floor.

'You lived on the farm at the time?'

'Yes, my father had been steward there, but he and my mother decided to return home to the low countries. I remained behind and became Astrella's companion. We sewed and read together, played music, that sort of thing. My parents thought her influence would be good for me. But we didn't rub along very well. I was three years or so younger than her. She looked down on me; she was very proud. Towards the end, I suppose she was also jealous. As soon as Stepan arrived he made no secret of his admiration for me.'

'Was Stepan aware that his marriage in Estonia was – how should I put it? – incomplete.'

She looked up. 'Yes. he said that while legal, their marriage should be followed by an Orthodox ceremony, or at the very least, a solemn commitment to bring up any children as Orthodox, to be accepted in Russia. No such commitment had been made, and he wouldn't go through another ceremony. He didn't love Astrella and couldn't abide her family. He said he could extract himself from the relationship once the war was over. He never considered the fact that he had fathered a child whose future would be compromised. I was young and ignorant. He persuaded me that our own Orthodox marriage was the only valid one. I embraced the faith and all seemed as it should. But of course, irrespective of the fact that his marriage to Astrella was valid in law, stealing her papers, pretending to be her was impersonation, and that made our union void from the start. If Stepan had not died heavily in debt within a couple of months, I realise now that even though the old baron would have found it demeaning, he would have pursued us, investigated the case, appealed to Stepan's family, even to the Tsar. But of course, Stepan didn't live and they thought there was nothing but debts to shoulder. And not long after, Astrella herself died.'

'Had they appealed to the Tsar, Andrey might have inherited the Russian title, Orthodox marriage or no,' said Vasily. 'The situation was more fluid then.' But, he reflected, it was much more difficult now. Unlike his older brother, Alexander, the present Tsar, had declared himself unwilling to remedy issues that were better left to the auspices of the church.

'How did you find me?' Madame Hélène asked.

'We worked out who you were from the records at the foundling home. You used your real name.'

'Yes. You must think very ill of me for abandoning my daughter, but I had no choice. I was in deep trouble. I was guilty of impersonation, was being pursued by creditors, was penniless. I had to disappear, start again, stop being Astrella von Klein Sternberg and, having kept my old papers, risk reverting to the name of Goossens. I could not confess to a fatherless child. I needed to work.'

And do you know where your daughter is now?

'No.'

'We know you made contact with the foundling home several times…'

'I have lost touch with her.'

'But you know that she came here to St Petersburg, to the theatre school.'

'I was told that she did and I made enquiries, but I have been unable to find her…'

It seemed that Madame Hélène had, like him, hit a dead end. 'I can see that you may not be proud of your past, Madame Kuprina, but I have to wonder why you went to such lengths to try to silence me when you knew I was on your trail.'

'Silence you?' Her look of surprise seemed genuine.

'A week or so ago an attempt was made on my life. It has been passed off as an attempted robbery, but I can assure you it was not. It happened, I suspect, shortly after you received the letter from Praskovya telling you that I was investigating your past and might well reveal your fraudulent marriage. Perhaps this might not be enough to incite you to murder, but it's something of a coincidence that you have married three men, all of whom had wives that died shortly after you became acquainted with them.'

Matvey had insisted that this was significant, and such a discovery might afford another compelling reason to want to kill him. But Madame Hélène's hand had flown to her throat and she was shaking her head. 'People do die,' she said firmly. 'The first two women in question were elderly, and I assure you, they died of natural causes. Luka's wife, who was of course younger, died of the cholera. You yourself know that. I admit that their deaths were convenient, but I was not responsible.'

'The symptoms of cholera are indistinguishable from some forms of poisoning.'

Madame Hélène shook her head again and fell silent. She stared at her hands, as if weighing up the meaning of his words. Now she spoke almost in a whisper. 'You are right, Count Belkin. It was I who tried to silence you. I did not think I could bear the public shame of exposure as a fraud, and I did not want my husband, Luka, to learn the truth about me. But, as far as murdering my husbands' wives is concerned… that cannot be proved and I must deny it.'

'Are you prepared to make a statement to the police?'

Madame Hélène silently nodded, and again looked down.

Vasily felt uneasy; her denial of murdering her predecessors rang true. She did not seem to him like a killer. Surely Kuprin, conservative as he was, might forgive his wife her youthful indiscretion. His love for her was plain. And even if he did cast her off, surely separation would be a better fate than the long walk to prison in Siberia, the inevitable sentence for a criminal guilty of making an attempt on the life of a government officer?

'Tell me, Madame Hélène, who hired the assassins that tried to shoot me? I'm sure you did not seek them out yourself?'

'I asked a business acquaintance. A man we pay to protect our property from criminal activity.'

'May I know his name?'

'I would rather not say, for obvious reasons.'

'Well, I'll let that pass of now, but how did you know that I would be out on Vasilevsky Island that evening?'

'I… err… had you followed…'

Of course he had not been on the island, and although he had indeed been followed that night, no-one had tried to shoot him. The woman was inventing this. But why? Why would she want to blame herself for a terrible crime that she hadn't committed?

'Will you call the police?' Madame Hélène's face was pale.

He stroked the carved golden head of a winged sphinx that adorned the arm of a nearby chair. He couldn't involve the law now. He needed to know who had really tried to kill him, and must play for time. 'I would prefer to spare your reputation and the discomfort of an extended period in prison awaiting trial. I shall need to question you further in due course. But in my capacity as an officer of the Ministry of the Interior, I must require you not to leave the city while further enquiries are made.' The ease with which he was able to convince with nonsensical bureaucratic pomposity impressed even himself.

Madame Hélène looked up. 'I suppose Luka Ilyich must be told?'

'What you choose to tell your husband is up to you, madame, but, I repeat, you must not leave town.'

'I have no plans to do so. I have no passport at present in any event.'

Madame Hélène rose and turned from him; she seemed stooped, diminished. A girl hovered in the doorway, seeking to usher him out, but he stood for a moment and collected his thoughts. The woman had lied to him –presumably to protect someone she cared for more than she cared for her own life and reputation, someone who would be fatally damaged by his investigation. Of course, it was obvious! It must be the daughter! The daughter who Madame Hélène claimed to have lost must still be alive, and she was lying to protect her.

CHAPTER THIRTY-TWO

On his return from his interview with Madame Hélène, Vasily sent a note to Zotov at the theatre requesting another meeting. He knew that his earlier investigations had been too cursory. He had allowed himself to be diverted, confused by the heady distraction of Lebedeva's dressing room. He had accepted without question Zotov's story that there was no trace of a second girl child from the Moscow foundling home. This time, he wrote, he would like to personally examine the theatre school records for 1818 and beyond, and if necessary, ask further questions. Within a few hours he received a reply from Zotov's office. The theatre was now closed until Easter, the Director's secretary was away for a few days, but his assistant would be available to meet him if he arrived at three after noon the next day.

Yakov accompanied him, bearing Matvey's bronze-headed stick. Weak sunshine, promising warmer days, lit the stiff square facades of the buildings that edged Theatre Square. The usual imperial lackeys were absent, and they were greeted at the door to the administration offices by a stocky guard.

'We are here to see Zotov's assistant.'

The man checked a list, then pointed at Yakov. 'You can't bring him in here.'

'He's my man.'

'He aren't on the list. We can only allow in them on the list when the house is closed.'

Vasily looked at Yakov and shrugged. 'Give me an hour.' He knew that after that time Yakov would come looking for him, permitted or not. His servant took up a position by the door. The guard stared, but said nothing.

The last time Vasily had been here, the building had been busy. Now it was empty and completely silent, apart from the faint notes of a piano echoing through the shadows of the long stone corridors. He was shown to Zotov's office. A glossy young man sat at the desk. Like Zotov, he was rather overweight. His large teeth flashed as he smiled. He mumbled his name indistinctly and Vasily didn't catch it.

'How can we help you further, Count Belkin? If you have detailed questions then Secretary Zotov would be able to assist you better than I, I am afraid.' His teeth flashed again.

'I asked to see the admission records for the theatre school once more. Not just those for 1818, but for subsequent years.'

'Oh, did you? There's been no-one here to extract them. I'm afraid it might take a little time. I'll have to go myself…'

'That's alright. I can wait.'

'I'll tell you what. Why don't I take you along to the auditorium. Some of the students who have not left for the break are on the stage with Madame Lebedeva, taking advantage of the fact that there are no rehearsals at present.'

'So she's teaching here?'

'Oh, she always takes an interest in the pupils at the school, particularly the girls. I expect she will continue to do so when she marries.' Zotov's assistant took him to the loggia behind the second tier. There was scaffolding in place on the far side of the auditorium; some men with lanterns were touching up the gilding on the front of the boxes. 'I'm sorry I can't put you closer to the stage, but as you can see, restoration is in progress. 'I'll come and fetch you shortly.' The man lit a couple of lamps as he left.

Vasily looked down. He saw the piano that he had heard earlier. A group of six or seven young dancers were being coached by Lebedeva. She was dressed in a scarlet gown, which shimmered as she demonstrated the effect that she wanted her students to achieve.

He sat content for about twenty minutes, intrigued by what he was seeing. But then the piano fell silent and the class came to an end. A few other onlookers in one or two boxes had already departed. He waited for a few minutes. What had happened to Zotov's assistant? Surely it couldn't take this long to collect some ledgers. He should go to find him. He walked to the back of the box and twisted the doorhandle, but the door did not move. He rattled it. It was more robust than he expected and seemed to be locked. There must be some mistake.

He shouted out, but his voice disappeared unanswered into the empty passages. As he shouted again, his guts clenched with anxiety. He had been a fool; he was trapped here. He looked about. The theatre was quite dark. The workmen had gone, leaving only one lantern down in the pit, but the oil lamps in the box gave out a warm glow. He must try to escape, but how?

He looked down onto the parterre. It was a long drop, too far to jump, and to attempt to climb would be hazardous. His breath quickened. He must stay calm. Perhaps the next box wasn't locked. He could probably clamber round the two gilded columns that supported the arch. He took off his jacket, threw it into the adjacent box and, with some effort, edged his way round the twisted piers. He looked down; a mistake, his head swam. He pulled himself into the box and groped past the seats towards the door. Damn! It too was locked. Could he break it down? There was no time for that; footsteps were approaching along the stone flags in the corridor. Someone paused outside the box that he had just left. He heard the door crash open, followed by a grunt of disappointment. He must keep moving. Perhaps he could reach the scaffolding. As he climbed around the next set of pillars and entered a third box, footsteps sounded once again. Could he get much further? Still not entirely fit, he wasn't sure he would be quick or strong enough.

He could hear the lock of the adjacent box turning. The door squeaked open and then slammed shut. Perhaps his pursuer would give up now? In any event, he must try to take him by surprise. He pressed against the wall to the right of the door. A key rasped in the lock… any moment now…

The door beside him flew open, almost flattening him, and the guard who had admitted him to the building plunged into the box. He was gripping a club. Thrusting aside the chairs, he lurched towards the front of the loggia, apparently seeking to scan the auditorium. Vasily, behind him, delivered a kick of some force into the small of his back. The man staggered and, unbalanced, slumped over the plush banking. It now proved easy to move forward, grasp the back of his tunic and tip him head first into the gloom of the pit. A cry filled the darkness, then a crash reverberated from below.

'God forgive me!' Vasily muttered. But there was no time for reflection or remorse; he must get out. He emerged into the semi-circular passage behind the boxes. Someone else was approaching at a run. He drew back, but the steps slapped past the door without stopping. He heard shouts from the parterre below. The body of the guard had already been found. Careful not to hurry, he walked back along the corridors to the office. It was empty. The ledger he had requested was not there and there was no sign of the man with the teeth.

When he left the building, to his surprise the customary doorman in livery had reappeared. Yakov was where he had left him. 'I was just about to come in to find you, sir,' he said. 'But the guard looked again at the appointment book and it seemed that you were not in fact due to see the assistant manager until four. There had been some sort of mix-up, and apparently there's been an accident; a workman has fallen from some scaffolding...' He noticed that Vasily was sweating and breathing heavily. 'Are you alright, sir?'

'No, I'm not alright. Let's get away from here, Yakov.'

As they crossed the bridge over the Moika river, Vasily's body started to shake. His legs threatened to give way and, swaying alarmingly, he clasped the railings. Yakov supported him and looked around for a droshky.

'We must get you home, sir, and then I think we'd better call Doctor Webster.'

CHAPTER THIRTY-THREE

Webster's potion was powerful. Vasily slept solidly until the following afternoon, and when he awoke his first thought was of Irina. He had sensed her perfume in his dreams. Had she been here? It wasn't likely. He felt an ache of desolation. Perhaps once again her scruples had held her back, Perhaps, indeed, she would never come.

As Yakov opened the curtains, Vasily blinked against the light and sighed. He had obviously fallen into a trap in the theatre and been lucky to escape with his life. Perhaps he could protect himself from further trouble by instigating a formal inquiry into the incident, but that would attract unwanted attention. He suspected that in any event, no trace would be found of the man who had purported to be Zotov's assistant, and the death of his assailant would be passed off as an accident.

Matvey's head appeared round the door. 'Oh, you're awake, sir! You need to spruce yourself up; you have a visitor.'

But there was no time to wash. Irina was standing in the doorway. She had indeed visited him while he slept and now quickly moved to embrace him. The persistent tension lodged within his breast slowly eased. How he had missed her! How empty, how incomplete his life had seemed without her. He looked into her eyes, touched her soft skin. He knew he had needed her, had longed for her, but he had not realised how much.

She stroked his cheek. 'It's as well I've come… you need someone to keep you out of trouble, it seems.' Her words triggered a vision of the icy river, distant lights, the one-eyed moon. As he closed his eyes, involuntary tears spilled out. Her arms cradled him as the storm took its course.

He broke away at last, wiped his face and cleared his throat. 'It was good of you to visit me here,' he said.

'I have resolved not to hide away as much as I did. We don't need to flaunt our relationship, but…'

This was something new. In the past she had rarely come to his home. What could have altered things? He was about to ask when she said, 'So, Matvey tells me that the man you've been trying to discredit is something of a hero after all.'

'Yes. I suppose that's so. I've come to the conclusion that the prince should be generous and compromise, perhaps even accept the man's claim. And that's not an entirely selfless decision. I've been made fully aware that were Nicholas to agree to the prince's wishes and name me his heir, I'd have to make compromises.'

Irina fell silent for a moment, clearly weighing his words. 'But despite that, you've persisted with your enquiries?'

'There's someone who wants to kill me. I must try to discover who it is. I need to finish the business if I can.'

Irina frowned. 'Oh, my dear, do be careful. Promise me that you won't go out unattended again.'

'I think I can do that.'

She smiled faintly, shivered and took his hand.

'How is Sophia?' he asked.

'She loves it in the city. She spends hours looking out of the window at the river. She says she is waiting for the ice to melt. And she would like to see her papa.'

'I'll come to you very soon. I'm still a bit battered and bruised…'

'I think I can put up with that. And you know… I really want to… I mean… it's been so long.'

'I shall come tomorrow, the following day at the latest, but don't expect me to go home again. I know you don't want me wandering the city streets at night.'

He wondered if his shaving set and spare clothes were still in her dresser.

❧

That night he slept like a baby, and he was only woken by the arrival of Matvey, who started to creep from the room when he sat up. 'No, come in, Motya. I need to chew things over with you.'

Matvey opened the shutters and leant against the window sill. He listened in silence as Vasily described his eventful visit to the theatre. 'There's obviously something there someone doesn't want me to find, and it must be connected with the missing child, but I'm certain that that someone isn't Madame Hélène. I'm not sure what to do next.'

'You could start by talking to Minnie,' said Matvey.

'Minnie? What has she got to do with anything? She's no longer at the theatre, and anyway, I didn't know you were acquainted with her.' Vasily frowned. What had Matvey been up to now? Since when had he started making the acquaintance of retired dancers of doubtful reputation?

'She's been taken on by Princess Polunina as a dancing teacher for your nephew and some of his friends. I've met her at the palace.'

'Has she? I'd no idea.' But then he remembered that Zotov had told him that an old admirer, probably Ivan, had found the dancer work. 'I'm surprised that Katya agreed.'

'The princess did have her doubts, but I think she's done it as a favour to Captain Stenovsky. It's early days, but the children have taken to Minnie.'

'Oh, I see.'

'I know she's too young to have been at the theatre school in 1818,' Matvey continued. 'But she may be able to tell you something of use. It's another possible avenue of inquiry.' He paused to enjoy the ring of his words. 'I can arrange a meeting if you like.'

'Zotov told me that Minnie entered the school in 1824 at the age of eleven,' Vasily said. 'That would have been around nine years ago, several years after the arrival of Madame Hélène's daughter, who we know left Moscow in 1818. Elizaveta would have been seventeen, almost ready to leave and make her stage debut. I really wish that I had been able to look at those records again.'

Vasily thought he might try to rise. When he sat up, however, his head span and he lay back on his pillows once again.

'Shall I send for some tea, sir?' While Matvey went in search of a servant, Vasily revisited the facts of the case. He was not sure that Minnie would be able to help, but perhaps Matvey was right: he should at least make the effort to learn what, if anything, she could remember about the older girls at the theatre school. But then another, better, idea occurred to him, something he should have considered before. Madame Hélène's daughter would be about twenty-five or twenty-six now. That must be roughly the same age as Lyuba Lebedeva. Lebedeva had probably lived at home with her family, perhaps attending the school on a daily basis – or perhaps she had trained elsewhere, but she would still have known students who were of the same age as she. It would do no harm to try to find out, but he didn't find the idea of meeting the woman again very appealing. Nonetheless, he felt he should make one last effort to reveal the truth.

※

When Vasily had told her of his intention to question Lebedeva, Irina had insisted that he go accompanied by a more convincing bodyguard than either Yakov or Matvey. Three days later, therefore, after dinner, he went to her apartment near Theatre Square escorted by Ivan Stenovsky. The captain was still somewhat chastened by his foolish attempt to suggest that Andrey Andreyevich was a murderer, but he had helped Vasily to secure the meeting, and brought with him a cornet from his company and another well-built guardsman.

'I'm not much looking forward to this. I'm not sure that Madame Lebedeva is particularly fond of me,' Vasily commented as their carriage made its short journey through the city streets to the dancer's canal-side home. The evening was gloomy. A veil of thin moisture misted the glass of the carriage windows and the coach lights wavered in the dusk, flickering on carved stone heads and marble columns, throwing long shadows along the walls of the buildings.

'You go on up when we arrive,' said Ivan.' I'll wait for you in the hallway.' He indicated his fellow guardsmen. 'These two will stay in the coach but will be up there in a flash if I sound the alarm. I don't think there will be trouble. I know Lyuba quite well; she's a good, respectable girl. She was very carefully brought up by her adoptive parents. I'm pleased that she has found a future husband who is worthy of her.'

Vasily turned sharply towards him. 'Adoptive parents? I thought she was the Lebedevs' natural daughter?'

'Most people think she is, and indeed, she may be. I recall it was Minnie who told me that she had been adopted – but Minnie, understandably perhaps, is not fond of Lyuba and may just have been spreading tittle-tattle.'

'It would be easy enough to find out the truth,' Vasily said. He shifted in his seat uneasily. If Lyuba was not what she was generally thought to be, then what indeed was she? Surely she couldn't be... and if she was...

He felt a sharp beat of concern. Was he walking into another trap? He looked at Ivan and recalled those moments at school when he had relied on his burly presence for protection. The captain was sitting, impassive, wrapped in his cloak, a picture of confident solidity. He couldn't lose face by backing out of the meeting now.

'Stay here, close to the entrance,' Ivan instructed the coachman as they drew up at the building. 'Lebedeva's apartment is on the first floor.'

The entrance hall was brightly lit. The doorman emerged from his cubicle and asked them their business. 'My friend here has an appointment with Madame Lebedeva.' The doorman peered at Vasily with interest, then snorted derisively. 'It's quiet up there tonight,' he said. 'I'm not sure she's even at home.'

Vasily climbed up into the darkness, the soles of his boots clacking on the stone steps. As he reached the half landing, he paused. He could make out a sliver of light spilling from Lebedeva's apartment; one of the double doors seemed to be ajar. From somewhere above, he heard a noise. His heart throbbed, and he groped for his pistol. Damn it! He hadn't thought to prime it. Rooted to the spot, he listened as footsteps descended. A scrape of steel came from below; Ivan must have drawn his sword. The man on the stairs was almost upon him, and Vasily stepped back, seeking deeper shadow. A tall figure, wearing a forage cap, momentarily stood in the shaft of light. Vasily looked up, bracing himself for a shot or the impact of a fist.

'Good evening, sir.' The man touched his cap as he passed, and continued down the stairs. A moment later, Vasily heard him greet Ivan with the same words. Breathing more easily, Vasily grasped the banister as he mounted the final steps, then pushed against the door to the apartment.

There seemed to be no-one here. Surely there must at least be a few servants, a maid? The vestibule was lit, but the rooms leading from it were in darkness. He turned to the right, through double doors into what seemed to be a drawing room. In the far corner a red-shaded lamp glowed and a candelabra with two candles lit stood on a pianoforte. In the hearth, the embers of a fire flickered. Close to the lamp, in a high-backed armchair, he could make out a seated figure.

He coughed. 'Excuse me.'

There was no response. Whoever it was didn't stir. He could smell the heavy vanilla-sweet stench of hot house lilies as, almost tripping over a stool, he moved forward, his steps deadened by the thick carpet.

'Madame Lebedeva?'

Outside in the street he could hear passers-by hooting and laughing, disturbing the peace of the Fast, but here, in the room, all was silent. He approached the chair with slow steps, then skirted a small table. The dancer was sitting, her head lolling to one side, her fair curls tumbled over her brow. Her long lashes brushed her cheeks; she seemed to be sleeping.

'Madame?' he said more loudly. She didn't stir. He reached out to touch her. The white skin of her arm was soft and warm. An empty glass stood on the table. Surely she couldn't be drunk? He picked the glass up and sniffed it. Despite the cloying aroma of lilies, he could detect a faint spiritous bitterness. It was no drink he recognised.

He was briefly perplexed, but as the truth dawned he jerked away. He hurtled out into the hallway. 'Vanya! Quickly, come up… I think she's taken poison.'

Ivan took the steps two at a time. He ran heavily across the carpet and stood for some moments contemplating Lyuba's body. He lifted up the lamp. Her cheeks were flushed pink, but she did not seem to be breathing. 'I'll call for a doctor, but I'd say it's too late.'

'We should also call the police.'

'I wouldn't do that. I'll send the doorman to alert the watchman on the corner. We should leave here now, Vasily. The whole theatrical world will be here within the hour. It would be better that you were not here.'

CHAPTER THIRTY-FOUR

The news had travelled fast. As they drove away from Lebedeva's apartment, they had seen the hunched figure of Zotov accompanied by two other men, walking rapidly along the canal towards the apartment from the direction of the theatre. Now they sat in silence in the divan room at the Bogolyubov Palace, fortified by a shot of vodka.

Once Vasily was able to order his thoughts, everything started to fall into place. 'Of course, the first attempt on my life was just after I visited the theatre,' he said. 'I was seeking Eleanor Goossen's child, and asking about the intake from the foundling home in 1818. Presumably Lebedeva wanted to stop me from making further enquiries, knowing I would eventually learn about her origins. It was particularly crucial for her now that she was hoping to marry Bolotin.'

'But why kill herself now?' said Ivan.

'I suppose she thought that I had worked out the truth and had realised that it was she who had tried to kill me. That would, of course, have meant the end of her hopes of becoming the Countess Bolotina; she would have gone to prison, ultimately to Siberia. She thought that I was going to confront her tonight, perhaps to have her arrested. But she was wrong. I was taken in by the picture of respectability and the happy family background that Zotov had painted, and, as you know, simply wanted to ask her some questions. It was only when you mentioned in the carriage that she may not be what she seemed that I began to have doubts, to see the light.'

Vasily called for more vodka. He felt a sense of relief, but also of guilt. If he had let the matter lie, Lyuba would still be alive, but of course he would still have been in danger. 'Do you think there'll be an enquiry?' he asked. 'I really don't want to bring further gossip and scandal on our family, or indeed compromise at least one other party.' He thought of Madame Hélène. He recalled the milliner's distress when Lyuba had been booed that night at the theatre, and the regular delivery of flowers and chocolates that she had sent to the theatre, clearly intended for her daughter. How distressed she would be at her death!

'No. Zotov will do his best to cover the thing up,' said Ivan. 'They will concoct some story to explain the death and hide the tracks of all involved. Bolotin will be upset; as I know from personal experience he will have paid handsomely for the initial introduction to Lebedeva.' Ivan sighed and looked away, his face dark. When he spoke again, he abruptly changed the subject. 'Have you heard from my brother, from Misha?'

Vasily blinked. Ivan rarely mentioned his brother Mikhail, the state criminal, a source of potential social embarrassment.

'No, but I had a letter from Lisa some weeks ago. There are hopes that he will be released from prison next year, and Nikita a couple of years later.'

Well, that's something I suppose, although they'll not be allowed home.'

'Not while the current emperor lives.'

Ivan sighed. Although he would never admit it, Vasily realised that he missed his older brothers. Despite all appearances, his old schoolfriend was a lonely man who didn't find life easy. Although he was in better physical shape after his year of campaigning, he was certainly more subdued. Moreover, since his return from Poland, he had seemed less obsessed with the seedy milieu of the theatrical world.

When Ivan took his leave, Vasily sat back in his chair. How much, if any, of the mythology surrounding Lyuba had been true? Had she been an innocent pawn in the hands of theatre management? Or had she been complicit? Reaching out for the flask of vodka, he remembered Minnie, her spectacular plunge from the stage. Perhaps Matvey had been right to suspect foul play, perhaps Lyuba – or Elizaveta – had destroyed Minnie's future. She, like himself, had been a threat to her ambition. What had driven Lyuba to these desperate acts? Had she been damaged by her time at the orphanage and the toxic culture of exploitation at the theatre? Or had she simply inherited her father's wild carelessness along with his beauty? He supposed he would never know.

He felt very tired. Lebedeva's suicide had changed things, of course. Further threats to his life seemed unlikely, and he no longer had to waste time chasing elusive orphans through dusty ledgers. But he must visit Madame Hélène without delay.

※

He found her the next day at the shop on Nevsky Prospect. She was alone in her upper sitting room, staring down at the bonnets and hats of shoppers as they passed by. One of the girls announced him. The milliner gave no sign that she had heard him enter. He hesitated on the threshold. 'Madame Kuprina?'

There was no reply. He walked across the room and awkwardly stood before her. He stooped and reached for her hand. For a moment it lay in his palm, the fingers limp, but then her grip tightened. She looked up; her eyes were empty. Not knowing how to start, he raised her hand to his lips and bowed. The formality seemed to bring her to herself.

'Oh! Count Belkin. How good of you to call on me, sir.'

'I knew I must come back, and now of course…' How should he continue?

She rose to her feet. As if he were making a social call, she said, 'And how is your mother? Your dear sister, the princess? Are they downstairs? Do they need my help? Luka Ilyich, as you know, doesn't like me to serve in the shop these days, but the countess and the princess, of course, are special customers. Let me see what I can do for them. She started towards the door.

He spoke as gently as he could. 'No, they're not here. It's you and I who have business to complete, as I hope you'll remember.'

She turned and stared at him. 'Of course, I'm sorry. Of course we do. I'm sorry,' she repeated. 'Won't you sit down, sir? Shall I have tea brought?' She seemed quite distracted. Did she understand why he was here? Did she recall their previous meeting, their conversation?

'She's dead, you know,' she said suddenly. 'And I never said goodbye to her…'

'Your daughter, Elizaveta?'

'Ah! You even know her name!'

'Yes.'

'Of course you do.' Vasily detected a hint of bitterness. 'Then you must hear the rest of the story, I suppose.'

'It would help to understand what happened and why,' Vasily said.

As Madame Hélène started to speak, unheeded tears slipped down her cheeks. 'I lied to you of course when I said that I had lost touch with my daughter. When Elizaveta came to Petersburg, I was informed by the foundling home as I had requested. By that time, I was living on the small country estate of my husband, Serov, who had recently died. For want of anywhere better to go, I decided to come to the city too. I hoped to re-establish contact with her. But when I visited the theatre school, I was told that it was better not to meet her; my daughter was to be adopted by the Lebedevs, the theatrical family. I was persuaded that this was for the best, that it would give her a better chance to succeed on the stage. When I tried to contact her some years later, when I had married again, she refused to see me. She sent me a letter saying she didn't want to be known as the by-blow of a vulgar milliner and a bankrupt. She regarded herself as the Lebedevs' daughter.'

'That must have hurt,' Vasily said. It was still hard to find much to like about Elizaveta/Lyuba.

'Yes, but I felt that by abandoning her I had sacrificed any right to her affection. But I didn't let go entirely; I watched her progress with pride. I always sent her some chocolates or flowers on her opening nights.'

'Did she ever respond?'

'No.' She paused and looked at him. 'But you do know that there was never a breath of scandal surrounding her,' she hurried on. 'I truly believe she remained uncorrupted, that she managed to rise above impropriety. It's not completely unknown.'

'No, I'm sure it's not...'

Madame Hélène continued in a monotone. 'When Praskovya wrote from Kluchovo that an official had come asking questions about me, I feared for Elizaveta. If they could find me, they might find her too. So I sent to her, to warn her to be careful. After some hesitation she met me, but she seemed uninterested in my warnings. It was a difficult meeting. A week or so after that, the attempt was made on your life. I suppose that you went to the theatre asking questions?'

'Yes. I'm afraid I did. But my enquiries were quite general.'

'But specific enough, it seems. By the time you started to ferret around, Count, there was of course a lot at stake. Count Bolotin had been hooked in. He would have paid a high price for Elizaveta's hand. Certain people would profit handsomely from the match. I would prefer to think that perhaps the attempt on your life was made without her knowledge.' She looked at him hopefully.

'I'm sorry, Madame, but I fear that's not likely. If she knew nothing, why destroy herself? Revelations about her true parentage were possibly not so important, Bolotin may have been prepared to overlook them; but exposure for attempted murder would have meant not just loss of reputation, but a long march to prison in the east.'

For a moment she fell silent, but then she said, 'But I suppose your enquiries were necessary?'

Vasily shifted uneasily. Of course, he already had enough evidence to overturn von Klein's claim. 'The prince suggested that he might like to help her,' he said weakly.

'Did he? The best way to help her would have been to let her be!' Madame Hélène looked up at him. Her face was blotched, ravaged, but her eyes had lost their vacancy and were filled with anger. Unable to hold her gaze, Vasily looked out of the window. On the pavement in the street below, a pie-seller, a heavy wooden tray round his neck, stood on the corner seeking custom. Nearby two policemen were moving in on a vagrant. Shoppers were scurrying across the road, dodging the carts and carriages or staring avidly into shop windows. All had their faults, he supposed, their secrets, their weaknesses. Better perhaps not to scrutinise anyone too closely, not to push too far.

'What will happen now, Count Belkin?' Madame Hélène was saying. 'Will my past be revealed? Will hers?'

'Not if I can help it. I don't see why anyone needs to learn the truth. It can be proved that the woman who married Stepan Bogolyubov in St Petersburg was not Astrella von Klein. That should be enough for the prince's purposes. Only my young ward, myself and of course

Praskovya know that woman was you. As for Lyuba… well, the people at the theatre have no reason to reveal her past.'

'She can no longer care. Although I hope that she will be remembered with kindness.'

'And Kuprin?' asked Vasily. 'Does he know?'

'I have said nothing to him yet, but he is aware that something is wrong and the truth will out. He knows my past was colourful. He is not an unforgiving man.' Madame Hélène seemed more composed. 'And has it all been worthwhile, Count?' she said. 'It seems the young German baron will lose the prize.'

'I am not sure, Madame. I really can't say. But as things stand, no outcome seems entirely satisfactory.'

As he left, he kissed Madame Hélène's hand once again. 'I'm glad you didn't try to kill me, madame,' he said.

'You're a good boy, Vasily,' she murmured, staring at the wall somewhere above his head. He hesitated before making for the door, but could find no further words. He hoped Kuprin would be kind to her.

CHAPTER THIRTY-FIVE

March 1832 – St Petersburg

The morning mist had dispersed and the air was fresh with the hope of spring. Andrey Andreyevich, having little to occupy him, decided to ride out to enjoy the weak sunshine. As his horse trotted towards the monastery at the end of Nevsky Prospekt, he hummed to himself.

He passed Rodionov's office and remembered that he needed money. The transfer to the staff would come at a cost. There would be new uniforms to buy, perhaps a new horse, but the stipend would be higher. He may need to ask Rodionov to organise a further loan, but it would be worth it. If he could secure some additional work teaching at the cadet school that would help.

He had heard nothing further from Vasily Nikolayevich, apart from a note saying that he was not yet recovered from his ordeal on the ice. But surely the issue of the legacy might soon be resolved. The support of the Emperor must mean something, and, after all, he had recently saved his rival's life.

He reined in his horse as a duck with a brood crossed the road. He wondered when he would see young Matvey again. The lad had visited him a couple of days after Lebedeva's farewell performance. He had shown great interest in the military establishment – but of course, not being on official business or in uniform, he had not been allowed in. They had repaired to Wolf's coffee house, where the youth's ramblings had entertained him.

'Does Count Belkin know you're here?' he had asked.

Matvey remained silent. Clearly he did not. 'He wouldn't mind, of course,' Matvey said at last. 'But I don't like to upset him at present.' He muttered something about frost and bruises, and took a bite out of his pie, scattering pastry over the table, gathering up the crumbs with his hand and tipping them down his throat.

'So, what business do you have with me, Matvey?'

'I have been asked to relay news to you, sir. From Oryol.'

'Oh yes?' Andrey's heart leapt.

'Yes! Nadezhda Gavrilova's coming back to town with both her parents! She wanted you to know.' Matvey was triumphant.

The directness of the message startled him, but he was pleased at the news. If all went as he hoped, he could at least ask Count Laptev for permission to call on his daughter.

'You could reply through me if you like,' Matvey said. 'But I don't know when she will leave. I suppose they mean to come when the weather improves, so it could be a week or so yet.'

'What's your interest in all this?'

Matvey smiled. 'Oh, don't worry, sir. We're just friends… and anyway, even if we were more than that, she's too old for me and I have things to do before I settle down.'

Andrey found the young man engaging. He was really not much more than a boy. He wondered where Belkin had found him. 'Well, I don't know about settling down.'

'You're surely not going to jilt her, Sir.'

Andrey was taken aback. 'There's no understanding between us, Matvey. There can hardly be…'

'If you let her down, I'll call you out!' Matvey glared at him, his black eyes glittering.

Andrey tried not to laugh.

'I shall, sir!'

Andrey, saying nothing, looked at Matvey steadily for a few moments. Having sized up his potential opponent, the lad was already having second thoughts. He must let him off the hook. 'Well, you can write and tell her this, Matvey. I shall ask her parents for their permission to get to know her better. I can promise no more than that though. And,' he added, 'When you do see her, you can tell her that she is in my thoughts.'

'Can I have another pie, Sir?'

Andrey called the waiter.

Now, as he rode towards the monastery gates, he decided to call on Rodionov before returning to his rooms. In addition to the arrangement of a loan, he would take possession of the box that had been found on his father's estate. Its contents might be needed to support his claim when he finally met Vasily Nikolayevich.

Rodionov seemed unwilling to relinquish control of the property, but when Andrey insisted, he agreed that the box should be found and sent to the barracks. When Andrey reached his rooms it had already arrived. It was not very large. He pulled out the key from his pocket and unlocked it. There was not much inside: just a copy of the certificate of marriage, a poignant brief eve of battle note, presumably penned by his father, a small pile of long-unpaid bills, and another small bundle that seemed to be copies or drafts of letters. There were also some tiny baby clothes.

He picked up the certificate and looked at it. This was it! Proof of his right to the princedom! He examined it carefully, all seemed as it should be. He turned it over. There was writing on the back; his mother's name, Astrella von Klein, with the date of the marriage repeated. The signature, for that was what it was, was flamboyant, written in thick strokes with an alien flourish. He felt a stir of disquiet. Could this be this his mother's writing? His hands fumbled as he opened the bundle of papers, all written in the same hand. Feeling slightly sick, he pulled out from his bureau an old book of household remedies, the only example of Astrella's writing that he owned. No, this was quite different, fine, neat, precise. How had Rodionov not noticed? Very likely he had never seen his mother's writing and it had not been in his interest to check.

He read the draft letters through. They were copies of those written to his father in the weeks after his parents' marriage from an estate near Torzhok. They were brief but tender, and clearly not written by his mother, but by some other woman who sometimes signed herself 'your loving wife, Lena.'

As he absorbed the significance of his discovery, the walls of his room seemed to close in on him and then slowly disintegrate. There had certainly been a marriage in St Petersburg in 1805, but his mother had not been the bride. He had been cheated by a mirage, a fantasy. There was to be no sudden transformation, he was what he had always been, an anomaly, an oddity, unable to claim what many might see as his due.

He groaned and slumped forwards, blinking away tears. He envisaged Stenovsky's sneering delight when the truth was revealed, and the Belkin family's complaisant disdain. He would become the source of gossip again; society would mock him as a fraud and adventurer. There was, of course, no hope now of winning Nadezhda. And then there was the Emperor... what would he think? His military successes, such as they were, would probably soon be forgotten, and any preferment would inevitably go to another.

Disappointment cut into his soul like a knife but he found he was not really surprised. The whole idea of the legacy had always seemed too good to be true. Through his pain, he could hear his grandfather's voice: *'There is no easy way to achieve honour and respect! The route to glory lies in hard work, integrity, self-sacrifice, and of course, self-control.'* That may be true, but nonetheless the destruction of his hopes seemed cruelly unjust.

He pulled himself erect and tried to breathe deeply. He must think things through, not give way to despair. He could of course attempt to conceal the truth, but that couldn't be countenanced. He would live in constant fear of exposure and besides, his whole character revolted at such deceit. But his mind was too clouded; further reflection must wait until tomorrow.

'Morozov!' he shouted.

'Sir?'

'Fetch me a flask of vodka. No... bring two.'

He found a glass and threw himself onto his bed, determined to drink himself into a state of oblivion.

CHAPTER THIRTY-SIX

A few days after he had learned Madame Hélène's full story, Vasily received another visit from Bagrov. This time Mordvinov's aide arrived unannounced at the Bogolyubov Palace. Vasily received him in his own rooms, hoping that the prince and his uncle were unaware of this unwelcome visitor.

Having made the long walk from the street, up the stone staircase and through the staterooms, the secret policeman seemed impressed. 'You've a comfortable billet here, Vasily Nikolayevich,' he said.

'Yes, that's true, sir.' Vasily, filled with guilty discomfort, waved the insubstantial figure to a chair. 'So how can I help you?'

Avoiding Vasily's eye, Bagrov said, 'The family business that you have been engaged with is almost finished.' The words fell somewhere between a question and a statement.

'Not entirely, sir.'

'But I suspect near enough. It was in November when we had our last conversation. Spring is now on its way.'

Vasily said nothing as he struggled to think. How much did Bagrov know of his recent adventures? He would be aware of the 'robbery' on the ice, but surely he didn't know of his visit to the theatre or his part in the death of Lyuba. But Bagrov, it seemed, was exercised by none of these.

'The offer of employment I made you then remains open,' he said. 'I urge you to consider it seriously.' He paused. 'If you have misgivings, there would be no need to join us formally. You could remain in your present post and still operate as our agent. Many men do that.'

Vasily nodded; he was sure this was true. At times it felt that every other person in the city was an informer, vying to find sensitive information to divulge to the police, true or false.

To his alarm, Bagrov seemed to interpret his nod as agreement and he warmed to his theme. 'You won't regret it,' he said with a sly smile. 'Even if the Bogolyubov case is decided in your family's favour, I have it on good authority that as things stand, your ambition to inherit from the prince is unlikely to succeed. But if you made a gesture of real commitment…'

'Not my ambition, Bagrov, but the prince's hope.'

Bagrov shrugged. 'Be that as it may.' He rose to his feet and walked to the window from where he could see the walled garden between the wings of the great house. 'Doesn't it grieve you that all this could be lost to you?' he said. 'Our department has a good deal of power to change things. Some part at least could be saved for your family if you agree to my offer. The Emperor is more likely to look more kindly on the prince's petition if…'

As Bagrov's thin voice continued, Vasily wondered if this could be true. Was he really speaking for the Emperor? Did the recruitment of a single government agent matter so much? Perhaps it did. But he must cut this conversation short.

'The matter of the legacy is not yet settled, as you are aware,' Vasily said. 'I'm sorry to disappoint you, sir, but I fear that I would not be a suitable candidate for your department. I have other hopes and aspirations, which do not include continuing in government service.'

Bagrov looked grave but, it seemed, took him at his word. After a few expressions of regret and hollow pleasantries, he bowed and made his way towards the door. Vasily exhaled in relief. He had probably extinguished any hopes that the prince might still have of naming him his heir, but he could nothing else.

⁂

'I really don't know the best way ahead.' Prince Bogolyubov shook his head as he sat down behind his fine wooden desk. His expression was sombre. 'I've been given to understand that the Emperor is keen to see the von Klein affair settled.'

'Well, sir,' said Vasily. 'You have three options: allow von Klein to continue to pursue his suit in the courts, with the attendant probability of public scandal when, as it must be, the truth is revealed; tell von Klein the truth, compromise, as we had agreed, and hope that will satisfy the Emperor; or withdraw your appeal, allow the court's judgement to stand, and, despite all, allow him to inherit.'

He was sitting in the prince's study after dinner with his uncle, Alexander. He was to meet von Klein shortly, but Dmitry Vladimirovich was having difficulty deciding what exactly should be said to the baron. 'You know Vasya, Sasha. I made a mistake. I should have just accepted the situation and made the best of it... but I hoped to secure your future; I planned to try to avoid the loss of this house... the other estate...'

Vasily tried to conceal his irritation. Of course that is what Dmitry Vladimirovich should have done. However much one wanted to deny one's heir their birthright, they were, after all, one's kin. Unless they had behaved in a manner that was completely outrageous, it was cruel and sometimes impossible to disinherit them. In this case, von Klein's claim was fatally flawed, but that had never needed to come to light. The quest that he had been forced to undertake over recent months and years had cost him his freedom once, and twice almost cost him his life. Now it seemed that the story he had revealed turned out to be inconvenient. How galling it all was!

'If only the Emperor had not become interested!' Dmitry continued. Vasily watched as his patron, pursing his lips, absently picked up a quill and scratched behind his ear. It was of course the anticipated intervention of the autocrat that primarily exercised the prince. Nicholas's predilection for seeking out and promoting promising young acolytes was well known. Von Klein, the 'Hero of Volya', the brave grenadier, battle-scarred and handsome, over six feet tall and of German extraction, perfectly matched the preferred imperial blueprint.

'I allowed myself to be persuaded that von Klein was

a chip off the old block,' the prince continued. 'A gambler and libertine like my cousin, his father, and my uncle, his grandfather, before him. But it turns out that apart from one – admittedly major – slip up, he's quite a decent man… and of course he saved your life, Vasya.'

'Yes, he did.'

'And from what you tell me, a good deal of unpleasantness could come out if we seek to publicly refute the claim now. I know that my cousin's behaviour was scandalous, and for my part, for obvious reasons, I have been keen to avoid connection with open impropriety. It is why I was so keen to cut off that particular branch. But it's clear I shouldn't have been so hasty.

Vasily knew that in denying any impropriety on his own part, the prince was being somewhat disingenuous. 'There might be some talk, sir,' he said. 'Indeed, there has been a good deal of talk already. But the woman in the case hasn't been exposed. The gossip will soon die down.'

'No, but what about the attempts on your life; the daughter's suicide?'

'We have explained away the first incident, and no-one but us, and some shady characters, know anything about the second. The theatre management has already put out some story to explain Lyuba's death, which – like all the best lies – is close to the truth. They have claimed that she was not all she seemed and had been afraid of exposure as a fraud by blackmailers unspecified, and so on. Although Zotov certainly guessed my interest in the lost child was something to do with the lawsuit, I never revealed any details. But even if people at the theatre knew the whole story, which they don't, it wouldn't be in their interest to reveal it. I suspect that poor Bolotin might ask some questions though.'

'So we could tell von Klein that we won't contest the case – that when I die, he can inherit?'

Alexander, who had been sitting in pensive silence, looked up. 'You could, Dima. There is a risk that the truth emerges, but it is certainly one way forward.'

'But you'll both lose your home here – the palace will go to von Klein, and I won't be able to do all I want to for you, Vasya.'

'I think Vasily will get over his disappointment,' Alexander said. 'You have, after all, been generous to him up until now, and continue to be so. Isn't that right?'

Vasily nodded.

'And, as for me, I shall hardly be left destitute. Katya and Polunin would be happy to accommodate me. The truth is this, Dima, although you are unwilling to accept it: it's not in the Emperor's interest that you should have any heir – a genuine one or one of your own choosing. He's short of money after the war, and if von Klein's suit fails, he will want to see the title extinguished, and claim your hereditable property for the Crown. It is after all his right. He is highly unlikely to graciously accede to a request to bequeath it to me, or my family. Although he values your past service, and mine, he has more than once commented on our unusual lifestyle, your refusal to marry, and recently, your absence from court.'

Dmitry grunted. After a while, he said, 'I suppose you had better tell my cousin's son that I shall withdraw all objections to his claim, Vasily. We will shortly be calling von Klein Sternberg, Count Bogolyubov.'

CHAPTER THIRTY-SEVEN

Vasily finally met Andrey Andreyevich at the Polunin Palace. When he entered the anteroom, the captain was pacing up and down like a caged lion. Vasily returned his short stiff bow, and as he surveyed him he realised that he was quite changed from the defeated and diminished man he had seen on Vasilevsky Island eighteen months before. He stood tall and broad in his flawless uniform, his face weathered, his eyes cold. The scar on his cheek gave his regular features a sinister cast.

Vasily cleared his throat. 'Won't you sit down, Baron?'

The room was bright in the harsh light of early spring. They sat awkwardly facing one another on hard high-backed chairs. Vasily shifted in discomfort; there was something uncompromising, almost threatening, in the man's silent immobility. 'Firstly, I must thank you for saving my life. I am sorry that I have been so slow in acknowledging my debt to you,' he said.

Von Klein shrugged. 'Any decent person would have come to your aid, Count Belkin. It was fortunate that I was on my way to meet you.'

'All the same…' It was obvious that von Klein was not going to make this meeting easy. He must get straight to the point. 'The thing is this, sir, Prince Bogolyubov, your father's cousin, has asked me to convey to you that he is prepared to let the court judgement stand, and recognise you as his legitimate heir.'

The captain said nothing. If he was pleased by the news, he certainly did not show it. Vasily leant forward. 'He would like to meet you as soon as possible; he knows that he should have done so before. There is a lot to be sorted out…' Von Klein remained silent, his head slightly to one side. His eyes, an astonishing shade of blue, were no longer cold, but held a curious gleam that seemed to see into his very heart. Where had he seen those eyes before? Of course – they were Lyuba's.

'Aren't you content?' he asked finally.

'I'm sorry, Count,' the captain said. 'I cannot agree to go along with the prince's plan. In fact, I must tell you that it's my immediate intention to withdraw my claim to his property and title.'

'Why? Surely…' Vasily, with a twinge of disquiet, suspected that he already knew the answer, but he was unprepared for the ferocity with which von Klein Sternberg now interrupted him. 'I think you know why, Belkin, and you shouldn't dissemble.' His features hardened as he spat out the words. 'It's inconceivable that your extensive investigations haven't revealed by now that my father's marriage at St Andrew's was flawed; that the bride was not my mother; that, after all, I have no claim on the prince. What I can't understand, since I suspect you may have had the evidence for some time, is why it took you so long to refute my suit... and why, suddenly, you are prepared to accept it now.'

Vasily cleared his throat. Of course, the man was right, and there was no excuse for further pretence. It was not the time, perhaps, to mention the interest of the Emperor in the matter. 'When and how did you find out?'

'I see no reason to tell you that, and if you have said everything you wish to, I think I should leave.'

Vasily groaned inwardly. This was truly embarrassing. 'Don't leave, sir. We must discuss this further... I am sure that the prince will want to help you. He knows that his first impressions of you were mistaken, and, despite the legal situation, will certainly acknowledge your kinship. He is likely to be generous.'

Von Klein rose to his feet, his face rigid with contempt. 'I want absolutely nothing more to do with you, sir, with your family, or indeed with the prince,' he said. 'I shall be returning to my regiment within the week and that will be the end of it.' Before Vasily could reply he had spun round and left the room. Vasily dropped his head into his hands. He felt a complete fool. But what to do now? He must speak to Kirill Rosovsky. Perhaps the major could help to engineer a solution.

※

'So how did it go? Is the handsome captain delighted by his change in fortune?' Irina rose from her sofa to greet him. As he embraced her, Vasily produced something between a laugh and a moan. Irina drew him to sit beside her. 'Not well then?'

He took her hand, leant back and closed his eyes. 'I think between us we've created an impossible situation.'

'Surely the baron wasn't too proud to discuss the matter?'

'He is proud, of course, but that wasn't it. In essence he'd already discovered the truth and he is, of course, too honest to agree to our plan.' Vasily sat up and continued, 'The captain, von Klein Sternberg that is, was already there when I arrived. He looked quite different from the man he once was. I suppose he's been through a lot since then.'

'I expect he has. But so have you.'

'Yes, and to little purpose it seems.'

The door flew open. 'Papa! Papa!' Sonya, having heard his voice, had hauled her nanny from the nursery into the drawing room. She climbed onto his lap and anointed him with a kiss. She then insisted on taking him to the window, where, standing on a chair, she embarked on her regular commentary of all that she could see on the river.

'Shall I take her away, ma'am?' asked the nanny.

'Will she play quietly here?'

'I doubts it, ma'am. I was just going to take her out.'

When the nurse had removed the child, he said, 'I can't get used to being called "papa".'

'Does it trouble you?'

'No, of course not, but I still find it surprising.' He sat down, happy to talk about his daughter, reluctant to return to the subject of von Klein Sternberg. But Irina prompted him and after some hesitation, Vasily described his uncomfortable encounter with the captain.

'Oh dear! But how did he find out the truth? How long had he known?'

'I have no idea. I did ask, but he declined to tell me. I think he can only have made the discovery recently. When I met Rosovsky a few days ago, he told me that von Klein was very hopeful that his cause would succeed. I felt mortified, Irène. I asked him if he wouldn't at least meet Dmitry, that regardless of the legal situation he would be sure to help him, indeed was likely to be very generous. But he wanted nothing of it…'

'But that's not very sensible, Vasya. He should at least hear what Dmitry Vladimirovich has to say.'

'He is obviously disappointed and now understandably feels insulted by being asked to connive in what amounts to a fraud. I'm not surprised; in the unlikely event of the truth emerging, it would be difficult for all concerned, but for him most of all. No solution was perfect of course, but now I feel ashamed to have gone along with the one we chose. It was foolish.'

'So what's to be done?

'I'm not at all sure. The captain disappearing to Narva with nothing but his pride and his debts concerns me, and will upset Dmitry, and Matvey of course, and perhaps Nadezhda.'

'Is she in love with him?'

'I fear she might be. Matvey's hinted at it, but she barely knows him.'

'She's very young.'

'Less young than she was when they first met, and it would explain her behaviour. Why didn't Dmitry simply accept the man at the start? The claim seemed genuine enough. But now, unless von Klein unbends a little and agrees he has a moral, if not legal, right to some financial help, I don't see a happy outcome. And then there's the Emperor… he'll wonder what's going on, and will probably have to be told the truth.'

'He might prove to be part of a solution. After all, he makes the rules. He might be prevailed upon to remake them. He obviously favours von Klein.'

'Yes, but he's conservative when it comes to questions of family.'

'Von Klein isn't illegitimate. His parents were married.'

'But, for this purpose, not in the appropriate manner.'

'Estonia is part of the Empire. Surely the problem might be circumvented. After all, as I say, his parents were legally married in a Christian church, and had someone – his grandfather, for example – thought about it earlier they might have petitioned the previous tsar.

'Perhaps, although at that time it would have seemed unwise, given that there was nothing to inherit but obligations. But as you say, the situation is unusual. If the Emperor is so minded, he might find a way through. I'll suggest it to Dmitry. I doubt if he will relish making the approach. We need to stop von Klein leaving the city. I'll speak to Rosovsky today, see if he can persuade him or even order him to stay. I suppose I should be pleased that he's been seen off; it was, after all, my aim. But I was wrong about him, Irène. He seems to be a decent enough man, and will make a far better loyal servant of the state than I ever could.'

'Well, he still may…'

'Perhaps, if he can swallow his pride.'

Vasily fell silent and Irina moved towards him. Enjoying the close comfort of her softness, he kissed her neck and then her lips. Later he rose and walked to the window and traced his finger on the clouded glass. 'I admit, when all this started I was briefly attracted by the idea of wealth and status,' he said. 'But I've known for some time that the price I would have to pay for it would be too high. I hope my lack of ambition doesn't disappoint you.' He felt uneasy, remembering the lucrative position that he had again recently refused.

Irina shook her head. 'I think I can safely say, my love, that I won't blame you for turning your back on the rewards of high office. I know how you feel about serving the Emperor.'

They were interrupted by the return of Sonya and her nurse. To Vasily's relief, the matter of the prince's legacy was set aside.

※

On leaving the Polunin Palace, Andrey turned west and walked along the English Embankment as far as the shipyards. His discussion with Belkin had enraged him, and anger felt better than nagging disappointment. What was the prince thinking of? How dare he and the Belkin family suggest that he collude in fraud? What sort of person did they think he was? What sort of people were they? He wondered how quickly he could conclude his business and return to the reassurance and certainty of army routine in the purer air of the countryside. The weather was getting warmer; he should try to leave before the thaw took hold.

He continued to walk the streets for some time. As he passed the Polunin Palace once again, he looked up at the windows. When would Nadezhda arrive? Perhaps she was already here. But there was no question now of paying a speculative call, of approaching her father, Count Laptev. He would write to her before he left the city, assure her of his eternal regard and explain that there was no way he could now pursue his suit. His pace slowed and he turned towards the river and, idling for a moment, he contemplated the now-melting surface. Of course, they may not in the end have suited one another, but it would have been good to have had the chance to find out.

Later, returning to his rooms, he called Morozov and told him that they would be leaving within the next three days. That would give him time to see Rodionov and withdraw his application for transfer to the staff. He must also relinquish the option on the fine horse that he had seen a day or so ago. That was a pity.

The next morning he slept late, and then started to sort through his papers and prepare for his journey. A little later, Morozov knocked and told him that the major wanted to see him.

'I thought you were on leave, Kirill,' he said as he walked into Rosovsky's office.

'I am, but there still seem to be things to attend to. Look, Andrey, have you got a few minutes? I want to talk to you. Sit down.' Rosovsky didn't meet his gaze.

Andrey was immediately suspicious and slightly irritated. What did Rosovsky know? Fond as he was of the major, he really didn't want him to know everything about his affairs. 'You've been talking to Belkin, haven't you?' Rosovsky flushed and shuffled the papers on his desk. 'Don't bother trying to persuade me to stay, to fall in with his dirty subterfuge. The thing is finished once and for all. I'm going back to the regiment. I can't afford to do anything else.'

'Hold on. I know that you're disappointed, but don't be too hasty. Vasily Nikolayevich hopes that you will agree to meet him again. He feels very uncomfortable. He says at the very least you deserve to hear his point of view and learn something of what he has discovered about what happened in 1805.'

'I don't see why. I've survived perfectly well without knowing all these years.'

'Have you really? I'm not sure that's true. But in any event, think for a moment. Do you really want to live the rest of your life like so many other impoverished officers, hoping for a war to come along to push you further up the ranks? You'll marry, if at all, still a captain, at about forty-five, because you've been sending any pittance you've saved back to your desperate family in Wesenburgh. You're a decent man, Andrey, and a first-class soldier. You owe it to yourself to try to reach some accommodation with the prince. You owe it to me too. I've done all I can to support you. And there's someone else you've forgotten.'

'Who?'

'The Emperor, of course. You know that he's taken an interest in your case. He can't just be fobbed off.'

'Oh, he'll soon forget about it.'

'I wouldn't be too sure about that. Once Nicholas decides a man is worth backing, he tends to see it through. His capacity for meddling in small personal matters is notorious. Look, Andrey, I can't order you to stay, although I'd like to, but I earnestly request you not to leave in a hurry.'

Andrey did not reply. He had thought that once the Emperor knew the truth he would inevitably withdraw his support, but perhaps he couldn't assume that.

'Please, Andrey,' Rosovsky continued. 'You're feeling angry and hurt, but don't let your pride stand in the way of accepting help from people who have developed some regard for you. You must try to make the best of things.' Without waiting for a reply the major rose to his feet. 'I suppose this isn't the best time to tell you, but I, at least, have had some good news. Thanks to General Ugrumov's intervention, I'm permitted to return to the Lifeguard Grenadiers here in Petersburg. I need to look at a couple of horses, get measured up for some boots… Come with me.'

Andrey hesitated. Did he really want to watch Rosovsky preparing for his new life? But despite his own problems he was pleased for his friend, and after all, preparing to leave, sorting out his possessions in his gloomy rooms, wasn't an enticing prospect.

'And then we'll go and get some dinner somewhere,' Rosovsky was saying.

It felt awkward to continue to resist, and in truth he didn't want to. He was soon walking out, past the guardhouse and into the city.

※

'You wanted to meet again, Count Belkin, and as you see, I am here.' Von Klein was regarding him, his eyes glinting with suspicion, while his tall frame seemed to dominate the room. Vasily had already invited him to sit down. Since he couldn't ask him again, it seemed they must stand and confront one another across his desk. When Rosovsky had told him that Andrey Andreyevich had reluctantly agreed to talk to him, he had decided to meet at the Ministry, where their encounter should be unobserved and undisturbed. But even here on his own territory, he felt at a disadvantage.

'I wanted to apologise to you,' he said. 'I know that the prince's decision to accept your claim was flawed, actually worse than flawed, and we all would have come to realise that in time.'

Andrey said nothing.

'In any event,' he hurried on, 'I trust that you've decided not to leave the city. As I said when we last met, Dmitry Vladimirovich is determined to help you. And you ought to know the full truth about your father, even though it isn't a very edifying tale.'

'No, I don't expect it is.'

'Look, please sit down, Captain,' Vasily said. 'My story won't be a short one.'

The tall grenadier inclined his head. The lining of his jacket flashed red as he flicked out its tails. Vasily watched him stretch out his legs and cross his arms. The chair creaked. As he spoke, Vasily realised that he was revealing more detail than was strictly necessary, but painting a full picture might lead to a better understanding between them.

Having listened in silence and with concentration, Andrey Andreyevich did not react until Vasily started to talk about the child, abandoned in the foundling home. 'Is she still alive?' he asked.

'No, I'm afraid not.'

The captain frowned and looked down. Vasily called for some tea and continued. When he explained how Stepan Dmitriyevich's bride had been discovered, he said, 'I hope you will forgive me if I don't reveal the woman's identity. She is still alive and is known in society. No useful purpose would be served in exposing her.'

Von Klein shrugged. He had shown little emotion when told about the abandonment of his mother and the perfidy of his father, but, when he heard the identity of his late half-sister, he rubbed his forehead.

'What a pity,' he said quietly. 'I have always longed to have brothers and sisters, although I must admit that the woman in question does not seem to have been very admirable.'

Vasily nodded. Perhaps it would be wise not to reveal his suspicions that in addition to her attempts on his own life, it had been Andrey's half sibling who may have caused the downfall of his former mistress, Minnie. Once again, he wondered if he should have pursued the case to its end, but under the circumstances there was no way that Andrey and his half-sister could have been happily reunited. The death of the dancer being the end of the story, Vasily fell silent.

'That's very interesting, Count,' Andrey said. 'But I see no reason why I should now stay here in St Petersburg. Your patron, the prince, can write to me if he has any proposal for my consideration.'

'We really hope you will stay, Captain. It is no secret

that, like Rosovsky, you were hoping to transfer to a new regiment here.'

'That was true, but it seems impossible now.'

Vasily felt he must keep trying. 'I don't think that's so. I had intended to put to you the offer of compensation that we had prepared the night we failed to meet at the English Tavern. But Dmitry Vladimirovich doesn't want to make you some impersonal financial offer through a third party. He wants to meet you himself, would like to recognise the ties of blood between you.'

Andrey's brows rose. 'It seems a little late. I suppose this hitherto unfelt desire to meet me has occurred to him since the intervention of the Emperor?'

'I can't deny that's partly so, but he had already begun to recognise you to be a better man than you seemed, and he was much affected when he realised that you had saved my life. You must know that for years he believed your side of the Bogolyubov family to be degenerate and unworthy of attention, and when he first heard of your… err… recent activities from Stenovsky, his long-held prejudices seemed confirmed.'

'I see.' The hint of a smile touched von Klein's lips. 'So, if I agree, how do you see this rapprochement being brought about?'

'Well, of course you can meet Dmitry Vladimirovich privately at any time you wish. But we thought it would be very advantageous to both sides if you were seen to be accepted by him in a public setting, so that the talk of irreconcilable differences between you – and there has been a good deal of talk – might be refuted. You could for example attend one of my sister's open morning calls; the prince often attends... where you could be seen to meet on good terms and then withdraw for a private conversation.'

Von Klein did not seem much taken by the idea. 'A private meeting surely would be better...'

'The thing is this, Baron von Klein Sternberg, in the light of all that has happened, I would very much like you to become accepted by my family and put all the bad blood and suspicion behind us. I confess that I too misjudged you and of course, I owe my life to you.' He paused and then continued, 'I also know you might have other, more personal reasons to seek some sort of reconciliation.'

Would von Klein take the bait, or would he have to spell it out? If Matvey was right the man might be quick enough see this not just as a route to a settlement, but a way to progress any hopes he had regarding Nadya. The captain at first looked puzzled, but now light seemed to be dawning. He uncrossed his arms, reflected for a moment, and leant forward. 'Very well, Count Belkin. I shall do as you ask. I suppose I have little more to lose than I have already, and something, at least, to gain. Rosovsky has made that plain enough.'

'Good! I'm very pleased, Captain. I know that the major has your best interests at heart. I suppose it's too early to say that you and I will grow to trust one another, become friends, but with goodwill on both sides I do not see why not.'

As they walked together towards the stairs, Andrey asked, 'Do you intend to stay in Petersburg when this affair is over, Count?'

'No, probably not. Although bred for it, I'm not cut out for the life of a state bureaucrat.'

'I find that hard to believe… your attention to detail… perseverance…'

'But I don't really like the work. There are more fulfilling ways to spend one's time.'

They reached the hallway. The long case clock chimed noon. 'My sister's next reception is on Thursday, the day after tomorrow. Can I rely on you to be there?'

'Well, yes, I suppose so.' As the captain took his leave, he favoured Vasily with a tentative smile that transformed his flawed features. Perhaps Nadya's enthusiasm for the man was understandable. In fact, on closer acquaintance, the soldier didn't seem unpleasant, just proud and rather reserved, and he had, after all, recently suffered a major disappointment. But now he must pen a message to Katya, to warn her of the invitation issued in her name. She would be surprised of course, but he knew she could be trusted to smooth Andrey's path. He gave the note to a clerk, who later confirmed that the message had been delivered.

'I handed it to Prince Polunin myself,' he said.

CHAPTER THIRTY-EIGHT

After long days on the road, the bright comfort and warmth of the Polunin Palace was a blessing. Nadezhda had excused herself from Katya's reception in the adjacent saloon and curled up with a book in the small drawing room.

Downstairs, she could hear a lively tune played over and over, overlayed by the thump of a cane keeping time. Young Prince Nikolay and his friends must be taking their dancing lesson with Madame Minnie. Her parents were in the saloon with Katya, and soon their voices were joined by that of Ivan Stenovsky. She wriggled down behind the sofa's high back; she really didn't want to be bored by him!

More guests arrived. The buzz of their chatter and the clink of fine china increased. But now all had fallen silent. What could be happening? She rose and walked to the door. The great room was more crowded than she had realised and all eyes seemed focussed on some object of interest on the far side. She stood on tiptoe and peered through the cluster of heads. Oh blessed mother of God! It was him!

Andrey Andreyevich stood between the distant

double doors on the threshold of the saloon, a row of plaster cherubs cavorting on the lintel above his head. His epaulettes gleamed on his parade uniform, his medals shone on his breast. He seemed somewhat altered – something odd had happened to his face – but nonetheless, he was an impressive sight. Apparently unaware of the interest he had aroused, he sought out his hostess, his shoes ringing out on the wooden floor.

Katya, clearly surprised, automatically proffered her hand. Pink washed her cheeks. 'Baron von Klein Sternberg,' she said, her voice a tremulous warble.

'Princess Polunina. Your brother Count Belkin suggested I call this morning. I expected him to be here, but I do not see him.'

'Uh, he must have been delayed. But... err... how good to see you.'

'I am delighted to be here.'

When it was clear that this surprising guest was, after all, going to be received rather than ejected, a group by the window turned away and resumed their conversation. Soon the room resounded with voices once more, but from time to time a pair of lorgnettes, accompanied by an expression of curiosity, flashed towards the tall grenadier. Her mother was staring at the baron with horrified fascination, and beside her, Ivan Stenovsky's face was rigid with supressed fury.

Nadezhda took a step back, her hand at her throat. She retreated into the small drawing room and almost fell over Matvey. He had been escorting Sonya and her nurse to the dancing class and had now come to see what was going on upstairs.

'He's here, Motya!' she hissed.

'Who? Vasily Nikolayevich? He was intending to come...'

'No, not him, the captain, Andrey Andreyevich!'

Matvey peered into the saloon. 'He's talking to old Count Sverdlov,' he said. 'He's unscathed so far, but you must find a way to talk to him.'

'Do you think so?' There was nothing she wanted more, but as she stepped forward she could see that Stenovsky's surly face was watchful, and her mother's anxious eyes were scanning the room like two carriage lamps. She stepped back again.

'Of course! He must be seen to stake his claim. Leave it to me.' Before she could prevent it, Matvey had straightened his cravat and entered the saloon. Bowing to right and left, he walked towards Andrey, who was still talking to the elderly count. 'I'm sorry to trouble you, sir,' he said. 'There's someone who urgently needs to speak to you.'

Andrey excused himself and stepped briskly into the small drawing room. He stopped dead on the threshold. 'Nadezhda Gavrilovna... I had not thought to find you here...'

'No, we have only just arrived...' His blue gaze seemed to dazzle her for some seconds, before he bowed, kissed her hand and did not release it! But the sweet moment was swiftly interrupted. The buzz of conversation next door subsided.

'What are you doing in there, Nadya?' Her mother's shrill voice wailed.

Nadezhda sighed. How very irritating this was! Why

couldn't they be left alone, if only for few minutes. She felt Andrey squeeze her hand gently. His voice was calm. 'I think, my love, that you should make a fighting retreat.' Her heart lifted. His love! He had called her his love! But she couldn't dwell on that now. The advice was sound. She let his hand drop, stepped forward and faced the crowd with what she hoped was an appropriately haughty expression.

'What's going on? I thought that damned German had learned his lesson!' Stenovsky barked out, rapidly approaching from the flank. Prince Polunin moved to restrain him. 'Ivan Alexandrovich, Ivan Alexandrovich, you must let this go now, admit defeat… let things take their course.'

As if deaf to this eruption, Nadezhda walked through the saloon towards the far doors. Her heart beat against her ribs like a drum, but her step was firm and her head high. Anyone who did not know her well would have thought that the soldier's approach had been an unsought intrusion.

※

Vasily knew he was late; not just late but disastrously so. Delayed at the Department by a summons from the minister, he had then failed to find transport. As a result he had arrived at the Polunin Palace half an hour after the appointed hour. Now it seemed, due to an oversight on the part of Prince Polunin, that his carefully worded note to Katya explaining his invitation to von Klein had failed to reach his sister's hands.

Aware that his face must be purple, he entered the saloon breathing heavily, just as Nadezhda was making her exit. What was she doing here? Surely the Laptev family had not been expected until later in the week? And where was Andrey Andreyevich? His intention had been to meet the captain in the lobby, make a discreet appearance together, effect some quiet introductions, and then hold their private meeting with Dmitry Vladimirovich. But it seemed the captain had felt obliged to make an entrance on his own.

'Good day, Captain von Klein Sternberg,' he said, approaching him. 'I am sorry this didn't quite work out as I had intended. I had hoped…'

'Don't worry, Count. No-one has yet tried to eject me, although I fear that Captain Stenovsky still bears me a grudge, and I didn't expect to meet Nadezhda Gavrilovna or her parents here.'

'No, I thought they were still on the road from Moscow.'

'It was a pleasure to meet her once again.' If Andrey Andreyevich was embarrassed, he did not show it. In fact, the situation seemed to amuse him. To his relief, Vasily heard Prince Bogolyubov and his uncle being announced. Once the necessary introductions were made, they could all escape.

The initial encounter between the prince and the baron went as well as could be expected. As Vasily had hoped, a good crowd witnessed their first conversation and those expecting any acrimony were disappointed. Whatever accommodation was now actually reached between Dmitry and von Klein could be safely concluded away from prying eyes.

As soon as was polite, Vasily, the prince, Alexander Petrovich and von Klein Sternberg withdrew to a nearby anteroom. As he left, Vasily attempted to calm Ivan Stenovsky's fury, reminding him that Mademoiselle Minnie would now be concluding her class downstairs. He guessed that Ivan would not miss the opportunity to greet the former dancer.

So, at last, Vasily sat round a table with the people most interested in the prince's legacy.

Dmitry Vladimirovich's proposal was a simple one. He would pay Andrey's debts, which were not excessive, and would support him in securing his transfer to the staff. He would provide him with an annual allowance for his life, which even without his stipend from the army, would enable him to live, if not in luxury, in reasonable comfort and send funds to his family in Estonia. Until the prince's death, the captain could avail himself of accommodation at the Bogolyubov Palace and would be welcome to dine there. He had, he said, discussed these arrangements with his friends, the Counts Belkin, and they were in perfect agreement.

Von Klein looked away, swallowed, and rubbed his scarred cheek. For a moment Vasily thought that he might refuse, but Rosovsky had prepared the ground well. 'That's extremely generous of you, sir,' he said at last.

'Not really, my boy, it's a small part of what you might have expected had things turned out differently. But are you content?'

'Yes, yes, of course. More than content... I...' His voice was hoarse.

Dmitry Vladimirovich raised his hand. 'There is no need for thanks. You are, after all, my family and I was wrong to blindly believe the stories about you. With that in mind there is one other thing to mention. As you are aware, when I die, on account of having no legal heir, my heritable property, my lands in the provinces, such as they are, and the palace will revert to the Crown. And of course the title will lapse. The loss does not mean there will be nothing left, but a fair proportion could well vanish into the imperial coffers.' The prince paused, pursed his lips and blew his nose. 'I still hope for some flexibility from Nicholas; I know he has taken an interest in your case. When he learns the facts surrounding your birth, he may or may not decide to make some further concessions. I really don't know, but I shall go to see him.'

'Thank you Sir.' Andrey shook his head slightly as if in disbelief.

Their business complete, they walked down the steps of the palace to the lower hall. The prince turned to Andrey and said, 'If you are not engaged this evening, Andrey Andreyevich, I hope you will take your first dinner with us. You will be coming with Irène, I think, Vasily?'

'Yes, sir.'

'Good, and afterwards we can discuss further details, and you can tell me more of your plans for the future.'

Later at dinner, they drank champagne. Vasily felt at one with the world; at last perhaps the future was settled. The prince's round head was bobbing with pleasure and even Alexander looked cheerful. Von Klein appeared to be at ease. Irina seemed much taken with the captain, but how long she would sustain her interest in details of topography and military strategy he was not sure.

As dessert was being served, a lackey trotted into the dining room bearing a fat vellum missive for the prince.

The company fell silent.

Dmitry Vladimirovich eyed the letter with dismay, immediately recognising the elaborate seal. 'It's from the palace, from the Emperor,' he said. 'I fear I have been pre-empted.'

※

Andrey's own summons to the palace followed a few days later. Unlike Prince Bogolyubov, he was not ushered into the imperial presence, but was obliged to answer a list of questions put to him by a court functionary clad in old-fashioned breeches and a scramble of gold braid. The Emperor's decision would be made known to him within a few weeks.

He decided not to call at the Polunin Palace again until his position was settled. Through Matvey, he had sent a message to Nadezhda asking her to have patience. He took possession of the rooms that had been prepared for him at the Bogolyubov Palace, but did not move into them.

Rodionov sent him a large bill for his services, which he set to one side, and then he waited. In the event he did not have to wait long. Within the week, the Emperor Nicholas requested his presence at the Imperial Palace at the early hour of seven in the morning. Rosovsky advised him that Morozov must brush his uniform until not a speck of dust was visible, and that anything that could not be brushed should be polished. His orderly must then accompany him to the gates to remove anything that might have attached to his person enroute. He had added that Andrey must be honest. Nicholas was adept at drawing people out and was quick to detect falsehood. And he should call him 'sir', nothing more elevated. Nicholas liked to think that they were all soldiers together.

Andrey's stomach tightened as he progressed along the seemingly endless enfilade. Each chamber was more extravagant than the next, each decorated wooden floor more sinuous, the crown of each column more thickly frosted with white and gold. But when he reached the Emperor's rooms, he found them austere and chill. Nicholas, in an unadorned field uniform, was writing at his desk in a room that resembled both a study and military headquarters.

Andrey stood rigid, unmoving as he was announced. After a few seconds Nicholas looked up. The lips beneath his small moustache were smiling but his eyes were pebble cold as they scrutinised his shoes, his trousers, his jacket. 'You may stand at ease, Captain,' he said, apparently satisfied. He picked up what seemed to be a report from his desk and frowned at it. 'Von Klein Sternberg,' he said. 'I know one or two good officers of that name. Tell me, are you related to the General, Baron Karl von Klein Sternberg?'

'Not very closely, sir. He is a distant cousin, and of course not of my generation.'

'No, no, of course.' Nicholas looked again at the report. 'I recall that your performance in Poland was creditable, very creditable. And now I see that you have put in for a transfer to join the General Staff.'

'Yes sir, I would prefer to be based here in the capital, and enjoyed the short time that I spent on the staff in Poland.'

'And you feel you can afford to live here?'

'Prince Bogolyubov's support will help, sir.'

'I see. Tell me, what help have you received from him, Captain?' Andrey felt Nicholas's eyes scrutinising him as he outlined the details of the prince's settlement. 'Why do you think he decided to reach such an accommodation with you now?' the Emperor asked.

'I can't really say, sir. It's true that he was resistant when I first sought to be recognised as his heir. He thought me unsuitable to inherit. However, by the time my claim proved to be invalid, he had come to think better of me and now, I think, believes that fate had dealt with me unfairly.'

The Emperor's eyes drifted away. 'You might say he could have been more generous under the circumstances?'

'I don't think so, sir. After all, he's not obliged to grant me anything, and there are others to whom he is closer, who care for him and rely on his generosity. And of course, if he has no legal heir, he will have less wealth to distribute.'

'Yes, of course that is true. A good portion of his property will revert to the state, as is proper.' Nicholas cleared his throat and looked at him directly once more. 'But tell me, Captain, how did you find out that your claim would not hold? All looked very promising at the start, I think, and the court accepted it.'

'I realised that my case was hopeless when I was able to examine a copy of the marriage certificate and some other papers. They were not in my mother's hand.' His response was perhaps limited, but it was the truth and he saw no reason to mention Vasily Nikolayevich's investigations.

'You might have concealed that fact.'

'It did not seem honest to do so, sir.'

Nicholas nodded, and fell silent for a good minute before he spoke again. 'Dmitry Vladimirovich has earnestly asked me to look favourably on your right to inherit his estates and title. I must confess your position is quite unusual, but not unknown. As I expect you are aware, my brother Alexander, in his time, occasionally exercised his discretion to remedy problems of this type. However, when I came to the throne I decided to no longer consider such cases, realising that investigating questions of birth and legitimacy was complex, time-consuming and best governed by the precepts of the Church. But, I repeat, your position is unusual. You are clearly regarded as legitimate within the Lutheran faith, and your rights and title, through your grandfather, appear valid.

'For that reason, I did ask for the matter to be examined. But I am afraid that, as I feared, the Patriarch is adamant that under the terms of the original grant of nobility, you have no right to inherit property or title in Russia. That being the case, all heritable lands, which of course originally emanated by gift of the Tsar, must return to the state on Prince Bogolyubov's death. Dmitry Vladimirovich really should have made some effort to produce issue of his own, or taken more timely notice of the fortunes of his extended family. Had he done so, all this uncertainty might have been avoided.'

Andrey had expected no other outcome. He waited to be dismissed, but Nicholas did not seem to have finished. The Emperor rose to his feet. His smile was somewhat unnerving. Speaking again, he seemed to adopt the ingratiating tone of a father rewarding a child. 'However, Captain,' he said, 'I am not unaware of your real merit as a soldier, and would hope to see you continue in the service of Russia for many years.' He stopped, clearly expecting some comment.

'Yes, sir. I plan to pursue my career in the Russian army, and hope to do my best...' Andrey felt all eloquence desert him.

Nicholas contemplated the deep blue and pink morning sky through the window. From somewhere nearby a military band was playing – encouragement, perhaps, for the imperial family to rise.

'Everyone must serve,' Nicholas said, his eyes fixed on the heavens. 'I regard the goal all of human life to be nothing more than service. Recent events have shown us all the importance of loyalty, of dedication. I want to encourage these virtues in all men here in Russia, but in soldiers in particular. I have always held the military in the highest esteem.' The Tsar's eyes seemed to be moist. He returned to his desk and picked up another document. 'Your promotion to captain is recent, I think.'

'Yes, sir.'

'And now you want to transfer to the staff?'

'Yes, sir.'

Nicholas frowned and looked him up and down. 'I don't think that would be appropriate.'

What did this mean? Was it the Emperor's will that he return to the King of Prussia's grenadiers? Leave the capital?

'You don't want to join the staff!' the Emperor said. 'Dull work, too much headwork, maps, manoeuvres and the like. No, I see you in the Chevalier Guards, or the Life Horse guards. You like horses, I believe.'

'Yes, of course, sir, but I have never really thought that...'

'Too costly, I suppose?'

'Well, yes, certainly, and my family hadn't the connections...'

'Good, well that's settled. I shall speak to my brother, Mikhail. Consider it done! I'm sure Prince Bogolyubov will agree that you will make a fine cavalry officer. And, in time, perhaps you may be able to serve on my own staff here at the palace, acquire some gold knots...'

'Thank you, sir.' A post at the palace! This was all too much to absorb.

'As regards the Bogolyubov affair, given the unusual nature of your current position, I shall consider awarding you a hereditary Russian title in due course, probably that of count, like your father. But it will be dependent on continued loyal service, and must be a new creation. The Bogolyubov title will die with the prince.' The Emperor gave a faint smile of satisfaction. The thought of extinguishing a princedom clearly pleased him.

Andrey felt his heart lift; this he had not expected. 'In my own name, sir?'

'Yes, I do not think you really want to assume your father's name under the circumstances. That whole affair would be better forgotten, I think. Besides, I hope you are proud of your grandfather's family.

'Yes, sir, of course.'

'It will please me to bestow the title when in time you decide to marry. It must be a proper marriage in a proper church, of course. Normally the grant of a title would come with some land, but in this case, I propose to delay that privilege until the death of the prince. Provided you fulfil your service obligations diligently, when his property reverts to the Crown, I shall return around two or three hundred souls to pass on to your own heirs.'

Land too, and although only a small proportion of the prince's worth, a reasonable amount, but the grant would be delayed. Andrey felt enveloped in a web of contingencies, conditions and obligations. He could not join the staff, as he had hoped, must probably change his religion, would be bound to state service for many years, have little autonomy. But how much freedom would he have if he refused? And besides, he could hardly spurn the Emperor's munificence.

'Thank you, sir. You are most generous.'

'Well, that will be all, Captain.' The autocrat's mind had turned to his next duty. His smile had vanished.

Andrey walked briskly across Palace Square, trying to untangle the implications of the Emperor's will. It seemed that his status in society would now be as far as possible regularised. He could look forward to a comfortable, if not luxurious, life and enjoy many things unattainable in the past. He could send funds to his family, perhaps marry well, perhaps aspire to approach Nadezhda. And of course, it had been his childhood dream to serve as a cavalry officer. But his good fortune came with a price: he must become part of a system of duty, obligation and dependence; inhabit a gilded cage, from which he may never escape.

CHAPTER THIRTY-NINE

April 1832 – St Petersburg

The surface of the Neva had begun to craze and crack. Soon it would splinter and shards of ice would drift out towards the gulf. Walking from the Ministry to the English Embankment, Vasily could sense some warmth in the sun, feel the beginning of spring. His sister Katya had sent to him that morning, asking him to call on his way home, wherever home was these days. Content with his small family, he was spending much of his time with Irina.

His sister was in her small drawing room. There was no sign of Prince Polunin, or of Nadezhda's parents, who seemed to have taken up permanent residence at the palace.

'Thank you for coming, Vasya,' she said. 'How's life at the Ministry?'

'Oh, as dull as ever. It was good to have an excuse to get away. I don't know how our uncle has tolerated working there all these years.'

'You don't think you'll be there much longer? Alexander will be disappointed. He is sure you will be promoted again if you stay. You really should consider it.'

'No. Now this business of the legacy seems to be resolved I'll be leaving for Dubovnoye soon. Working here was never supposed to be a permanent arrangement, although I think he hoped it would become so.'

'Will Baroness von Steiner stay here in Petersburg when you leave?'

Vasily knew that his relationship with Irina both intrigued and troubled his sister. 'No.'

'No?'

'No.'

Katya waited, but when he said nothing further, she shrugged and continued, 'Nadezhda's father has had a letter from Captain von Klein Sternberg. He seeks permission to call on her.'

'I expect he does.'

'You don't seem surprised.'

'Well, no. Are you?'

'Somewhat... I thought she had been persuaded to forget him.'

'Why should you think that?'

'It seems I was wrong, but how can we discourage the baron without causing offence?'

'Do we want to discourage him?'

'Oh, I think so. His position is much improved of course, but he can't be said to be rich, he's a German, and a serious question mark remains over his background. She could do very much better.'

'I don't think she could.'

'Really? You've certainly changed your tune, Vasya.'

'I suppose I have. But you know he's proved himself

an honest man, he's actually far more amusing than he seems, and now he has caught Nicholas's eye, his prospects seem good. I'd be happy to see them married if she wishes it, but Andrey Andreyevich may not step up once he gets to know her better.'

'What do you mean "not step up"? She's a wonderful catch.'

'Perhaps she is, but she's still immature and flighty.'

'Oh really, Vasya. You could say that Andrey Andreyevich is proud and rather dull.'

'Well, there you are. Neither may take to the other, but they should have the opportunity to try, don't you think?'

'I'm not sure Count Laptev will see it like that. The countess certainly has higher hopes for her daughter. After all, there seems little prospect that Lisa and Mikhail will ever return from Siberia. Nadya is their only hope of securing a respectable connection.'

'All the more reason for her to marry a solid and reliable servant of the state.'

'I think you'll have to persuade her father of his value…'

'I've persuaded him of more difficult things in the past. I'll go up to see him.'

Katya fell silent for a moment. 'So, will the baroness be going to her estates in Bryansk when you leave?'

He hesitated. Why couldn't his sister contain her curiosity and leave the question alone? He wasn't going to enlighten her. She and the prince were reluctant to receive Irina, and he wasn't prepared to give her ammunition for gossip. 'Leave it, Katya. Is Gavril Ivanovich at home?'

Katya pouted and turned away. 'Yes, both Laptevs are upstairs in their rooms.'

'I'll go up now. Tell me, has Ivan continued to slander von Klein?'

'No, he seems more interested in ogling Mademoiselle Minnie. It's a pity he can't settle down with someone respectable.'

'I somehow think that's not very likely,' Vasily said. 'I believe he'll leave Petersburg shortly, return to the Caucasus. Parade ground soldiering doesn't suit him, and he's obviously not interested in marriage at present.'

He excused himself and went to look for Nadezhda's father.

❧

Vasily left the palace an hour or so later. His conversation with Laptev had been inconclusive, but the Count had listened to the arguments in favour of Andrey Andreyevich, and said he would pray on the matter. This was promising. When Gavril Ivanovich made difficult decisions, he liked the Almighty to bear the responsibility.

He walked along the English Embankment towards Irina's apartment. The sun was low in the west and shone in his eyes, so that he did not immediately recognise the approaching figure of a man, his shadow preceding him. 'Good evening, Vasily Nikolayevich.'

'Kalinin! I didn't think to see you back in Russia.' Why was it that Pavel Pavlovich always materialised when he was least expected?

'I have just arrived and was coming to seek you out, Vasily. I have important news.'

'News?'

'Yes, you had better come up. You seem to regard my home as your own in any event.'

The colonel's baggage was piled in the hallway. There was no sign of Irina, or indeed of Kalinin's mistress, Margarethe. Kalinin indicated that they should go into his study. He shut the door, put two glasses on the table and, taking a flask of vodka from the bookshelf, poured two shots. 'Sit down, and then drink that.' He reached for his glass.

'Is Margarethe here?'

'No, we've parted.' Kalinin's expression did not encourage further questions.

'Oh, I'm sorry.'

The colonel shrugged. He drained his glass and watched in silence as Vasily drained his. He poured a second, downed it swiftly and once again waited for Vasily to follow. He then cleared his throat. 'I have some news for you, Vasily. The baron is dead.'

Vasily's head spun as the vodka hit home. Which baron? Obviously not the one who had absorbed his attention in recent months. Kalinin must be talking about Irina's husband, the Austrian, who had for years refused to divorce or release her.

'That means...' Vasily started, his head spinning more insistently.

'It means, Vasily Nikolayevich, that you are now free to marry my sister. And marry her you will. Your affair has gone on long enough. I shall visit your uncle tomorrow to discuss the settlement and then it's off to church with you. I assume you have no objections?'

'No, none at all, of course. But how did he die?'

'It seems it was the cholera. The symptoms certainly implied that.'

'Does Irina know?'

'Of course she does, and you'll find her impatiently waiting for you now in the drawing room with my niece. But she asked me to break the news to you, and I wanted to make my feelings on the matter plain.'

Vasily frowned. He didn't need Kalinin to remind him of his duty. He had wanted to marry Irina since the day they had met almost seven years ago.

Kalinin leant forward, refilled his own glass once more and then stoppered the flask. His hand was shaking. 'Well, off you go.' Kalinin turned away, gave a profound sigh, and gazed out at the splintering surface of the icy river.

Vasily wanted say something encouraging, but he couldn't find appropriate words. When he stepped into the drawing room, his head still whirling, Sonya ran to greet him. A few moments later the nanny came to sweep the child away. Irina stood, her face flushed, gazing at the carpet.

'Well, Vasya?' She wouldn't meet his eye. Surely she didn't doubt him? Unable to speak, he took her in his arms and stroked her soft curls. At last, she raised her face to look at him and he kissed her lips. The sense of relief when she responded was almost painful. He knew she would now be entirely his. There would no longer be any need for secrecy, for discretion, no need to tolerate the intolerance of others. He felt tears on his cheeks and his heart filled with gratitude at this unexpected change in fortune.

'Now, finally, we shall marry,' he said. It was not a question and did not need an answer. He drew her down and held her as she settled close to him. Despite his joy, he was faintly troubled. Von Steiner's death was remarkably convenient. Hadn't Kalinin said that he had died of cholera? The symptoms of cholera were very like that of poison, as he himself had remarked to Madame Hélène. He recalled how Kalinin had taken leave of him at Riga and disappeared to Austria on the pretext of family business. Was murder that business? Kalinin had noticed his growing attachment to Anna. Had he thought that she might replace his sister in his affections? And had Irina already known of the death of her husband? Since she had come from Moscow, she had been uncharacteristically careless of gossip. He felt slightly sick. No, surely that couldn't be. His recent adventures had deranged him. He imagined murder and conspiracy everywhere. But he must put the question.

'Did you know... Irène... did you suspect that your husband was dead?'

'I had some reason to hope,' she said. 'But no, I didn't know for sure until Pavel confirmed the news.'

Her answer resolved nothing. He was about to try another approach, but she silenced his next question with a kiss. As they settled into a deeper embrace, it occurred to him that sometimes it was better to let matters lie. After all, many things in life, good and bad, happen by chance.

Andrey Andreyevich was to call on her today! Nadezhda paced the small drawing room, unable to settle to her stitching or her book. They had only met briefly since her return and now she found it hard to visualise him. Was he really as she had imagined him? If only she could meet with him alone. She glanced at Katya, who had settled on a carved chair at the edge of the room, her eyes on her handwork, but her ears clearly ready to absorb every word.

He was very punctual. The clock struck three as he was announced. The captain was wearing his new horse guards' uniform, an assemblage that seemed to eclipse the plush glitter of the room. She rose as he entered. He bowed, clicking his heels, and then regarded her steadily. How very formal he was! He was certainly still handsome but he was different from the kind, fresh-faced young man who had danced with her at the palace more than two years before. The fading scar on his cheek had altered him: he looked older, harsher, his hair seemed duller and, perhaps, thinner.

'Please don't stand on ceremony with me, sir.' Aware that she sounded like her mother, she waved him to a chair. Unable to meet his eye, blood rushed to her cheeks. A terrible silence ensued. Then she heard him clear his throat twice. He seemed as nervous as she! But he had asked to call, surely he must now find something to say to her? Finally they both spoke at once, then fell silent again. Katya, a faint smile on her lips, set aside her work. She ordered tea and dominated all further conversation until, finally, Andrey Andreyevich bowed and left.

Tears filled Nadezhda's eyes. 'Oh Katya! This is impossible. I don't know him at all. How can I marry a man I don't know?'

Katya frowned. 'Well, firstly you don't have to commit yourself to anything at present, and secondly I wouldn't worry too much about getting to know him. I barely knew Polunin at all when we agreed to marry.' Nadezhda nodded, unconvinced. The Polunins' marriage of convenience had worked out well enough, but of course that couldn't be guaranteed. Perhaps the doubts of her parents were valid after all? Was it really in her interest to encourage him? She did have other options, probably.

'How would you feel if you never saw Captain von Klein Sternberg again?' Katya asked. 'I can ask Vasya to tell him it was all a mistake. He'll do it gently. He's good at that sort of thing…'

How *did* she feel? Had it been the man himself that she loved, thought she still loved, that had led her to pursue him? Or was it some mirage of perfection that had fed her dreams all this time? How to know? She must meet him again, if only to find out.

'No, I must see him again. I can't leave it like this.'

Katya sighed and shook her head. 'I'll see what can be arranged.'

※

On a bright morning, a week or so later, Andrey found himself pacing back and forth at the entrance to the Summer Garden. He stopped occasionally to contemplate the sinuous metal snakes on the heads of Medusa that adorned the railings. His new uniform still felt strange, but he knew that it suited him well, and he had enjoyed his first days with the horse guards.

Princess Polunina had sent to him suggesting that he joined Countess Laptev, Nadezhda and herself for a walk, and perhaps a visit to the tea house. The invitation had both pleased and unnerved him. When he had seen Nadezhda once again her beauty had, as always, moved him. More than that, he had persuaded himself that her determination to deflect other suitors was evidence of true affection. But how to make that clear to her, particularly under the eagle eyes of her chaperone? He must take the initiative, but how?

A carriage drawn by four fine greys was rolling up. Recognising the Polunin crest, he straightened his shoulders and took a deep breath. A lackey leapt from the rear, opened the door and pulled down the steps with a clunk. Katya led the way, holding the edge of her wide-brimmed hat. Nadezhda's mother followed and then Nadezhda herself, her gown silver-blue under a dark mantle. Her expression was unreadable. Andrey approached and bowed, blinking at the array of bright billowing skirts and sleeves.

'Ah, Baron!' Katya said. 'How good of you to agree to accompany us on our walk. I think we will be lucky; we may be spared from the rain.'

He forbore from glancing up at the cloudless sky, and agreed. The princess took his arm and, followed by a maid, the group processed along the main alley towards the Neva. After a few minutes, Katya shivered and turned to look back. 'Goodness Antonina! It's colder than I realised!

I should very much like some coffee! Wouldn't you? But don't let us spoil your walk, Andrey Andreyevich, Nadya. The maid will accompany you... we'll see you in, say, half an hour or so.'

Finding himself abandoned, he turned to Nadezhda. She stood gazing down at the path, her face flushed with embarrassment. Her cousin's ploy had not been very subtle. He took her arm, drawing her as close as her wide skirts would allow, and they walked on together between the white marble statues that stood, as if holding their breath, beneath the early-budding branches of the trees.

They sat on a bench beneath a marble nymph who gazed down from her plinth, her inquisitive head to one side. He told Nadezhda something of his past, his mistakes, his more recent triumphs. He didn't omit his affair with Minnie and its disastrous consequences. He told her about his meeting with the Emperor, and Nicholas's conditional promise to grant him his father's title on marriage, but in his own name.

She nodded. 'I knew that the Tsar had shown you favour,' she said. 'That you can expect his support, and that Prince Bogolyubov has recognised some obligation towards you. It seems that has been sufficient to persuade my father to allow you to call. I knew nothing further.'

'No, up to now I've told no-one of what precisely the Emperor said to me. I think he is sincere and, if all goes well, will honour his commitment... who knows. But I want you to know, Nadezhda Gavrilovna, that my feelings for you have little to do with the Tsar and his promises. I have often relived that afternoon I first saw you, and our meeting in the church. Those memories and your letter sustained me during the war, and when I was wounded you came to me in my dreams.' He paused. Now he must come to the point. 'But you must have no illusions. Preferment comes at a price, and nothing is certain. I shall be expected to serve diligently for years, and whoever becomes my wife will have to understand that.' He paused for a moment, uncertain how to continue. 'You shouldn't... can't...'

He felt blood rush to his cheeks. Need he express his doubts now? Did it really matter that she had sometimes surprised, even shocked him, in the past? Of course, that had been part of her attraction. He knew he couldn't love a simpering doll.

'We'll get to know one another better,' she said. Her tone was firm. 'There's no need to hurry. I'm not like my sainted sister, who travelled six thousand versts to marry a man she had known for less than three months. I can wait. But my heart tells me that we can make one another happy, can find a way to face the world together, create a good partnership.'

She turned towards him and took his hand, then quickly released it. He looked away and swallowed, overcome by a wave of tenderness and gratitude accompanied by a sharp ache of desire. Reaching inside his jacket, he pulled out the glove that he had kept since their meeting at the cathedral. It was crumpled and stained. He smoothed it out on his knee.

'You still have it!' As she stretched out to touch the glove, he covered her hand with his.

'Of course,' he said. 'And I'm sure it preserved me...'

She smiled up into his face, her eyes bright. The restraint, which had seemed to hang like a fine mist between them, had dissipated. He glanced around and, reassured that they were unobserved, leant forwards and kissed her lips.

CHAPTER FORTY

May 1832 – St Petersburg

'I'm sorry uncle, I can't stay here much longer.' The disappointment on Alexander's face was difficult to bear, but Vasily was determined. He must leave the capital. His betrothal meant his financial circumstances had improved. After his imminent wedding, he wanted to take Irina home to Dubovnoye, and this winter perhaps go abroad to see Italy at last. But he must try to soften the blow. 'It won't be forever, but there is a great deal I want to do on the estate. The house must be renovated before it finally falls down. We have to fully incorporate the new land we've bought and perhaps buy some more, and look into improving our farming methods further.'

'Good luck with that!' Alexander said.

'I know that the peasants will resist anything new, but if I live there among them for a while, I think I can achieve something. Generally, change never gets bedded in and the manager hasn't the patience to try.' He decided not to mention Italy.

Alexander looked down at his desk. 'I can't really argue

with your reasoning.' he said. 'If Irina can be content with life in the country, then it's a good plan. But Dmitry and I will miss you.'

'Irina claims she'll be happy, and in any event we'll probably go to Moscow for the season. And you know, Dmitry has Andrey Andreyevich to talk to now.'

'Yes, and despite everything they seem to rub along surprisingly well. But it's not the same – at least, he says it's not. He's always loved you, Vasya.'

'He's been more than generous, and I really appreciate it, but…'

Alexander shook his head. 'He understands, but he had set his heart on his plans for you. And I too, of course, am sorry that it all came to nothing.'

Vasily could not bring himself to tell the truth, that the failure of Dmitry's ambitions had in the end come as a relief. Years ago, he had vowed to oppose the autocratic system. His experience in Poland and the time he had spent combatting cholera on the government's behalf had done nothing to alter his views. Since its defeat in the war, Poland was now subject to extreme oppression. Many Polish leaders had been exiled and Russia's grip on power had been savagely reinforced. The nature of the regime here in St Petersburg would remain unchanged, and he had no wish to become a permanent cog in its inexorable grinding wheel.

Alexander nodded his head, as if he could read his thoughts. 'You'll take Matvey with you, I suppose.'

'For a while, but Matvey has plans. When Thomas died, the boy wrote to Golovkin. You remember the journalist who runs the school in Oryol? Golovkin suggested that he go back to study with him to prepare for the university. It's a good idea. Motya is fond of his old teacher, and is concerned to fulfil Maltby's wish that he make something of himself.'

'I always said he should go back to school, but you've resisted the idea in the past.'

'I think the time has come now, but he knows he will always have a home with us.'

'He's happy about your marriage?'

'I think so. Irina's certainly fond of him and Sonya idolises him. But although it may have contributed to his decision, he's clever enough to know he must learn to stand on his own feet.'

The hollow sound of the gong sounded for dinner. Alexander rose. 'Well, Vasya. I'll be sad to see you go. But I do understand. And I'm content that you finally have the life and the woman you wanted.'

❧

June 1832 – Dubovnoye Estate, Moscow Region

It was early evening. Out in the park, the shadows of ancient trees had begun to lengthen. Woodpigeons crooned their doubled tones over the reviving grass. Within the cool depths of the house, Sonya chirruped as she was put to bed. On the terrace, sparrows dipped for crumbs around the samovar while Vasily's grandmother snored gently in her rocking chair, the lace of her kerchief trailing from her lap onto the planked floor.

Irina set down her book and, speaking quietly so as not to wake the old woman said to Vasily, 'Matvey had a letter from Nadezhda today. It seems Andrey Andreyevich's courtship is progressing. She went with Katya to see him exercising his new horses at the manège. That certainly seemed to impress her! She's talking of taking to the saddle herself.'

'I'm not sure that Andrey would approve of that.' Vasily wondered how the newly minted cavalry officer would react to Nadezhda's enthusiasms.

'Oh, I don't know… not in Petersburg perhaps, but I suppose that they'll spend some time in the country.'

'Not very much. His duties will keep him in the capital a good deal of the time, and in the summer, he'll be obliged to go on manoeuvres at Krasnoye Selo, or run around the Emperor and his family. I really don't envy him. Getting away from town, having the freedom to live our lives as we want, has changed everything for the better, for me at least.'

He leaned back in his chair and yawned. It was true that from the moment he had left St Petersburg his spirit had seemed to lighten. Now he had started to build what he hoped could be his new life. With Matvey's help, he had ordered books for the library, Dmitry had written to say that he was looking out some pictures to send to them.

'I got out my sketch pad today…' he said.

'Did you?'

'Yes, I need to get my eye in if we're to go travelling in the winter'

'Ah!' Irina looked away.

'Ah, what?

'I've been waiting for the right time to tell you.'

'Tell me?'

'I think we're having another child. In fact, I know we are. Travelling might have to be postponed.'

Vasily leapt to his feet. 'That's marvellous! When?'

His grandmother, startled, looked up and, apparently reassured, nodded off once again.

Irina laughed. 'Some time after new year, before the spring comes.'

Trying to process the news, he stepped to the edge of the veranda and looked up at the house. 'We must get on with the building works, make this old place really weather-proof. We'll get some plans drawn up at once. I should like the child to be born here, but perhaps you'll want to go to Moscow?'

'No, I'm content to stay. It already feels like home. I'm not sure about the local doctor, but I have confidence in the wise woman Agafya; and it's right that your heir be born at Dubovnoye.'

'Yes, of course it's right.'

He looked out over the park. His heir! The notion seemed strange and a little disturbing. Although he had resolved that Sophia would always be cherished, his precious little daughter born out of wedlock had no automatic rights of inheritance and could not take his title. He now knew how difficult and complicated, even fatal, such matters could be. But now he allowed his excitement and happiness to grow. He must write to his uncle and mother at once, and summon an architect from Moscow. As he made his way to his study, Annika the deerhound, who had been asleep on the grass, started to bark. Shouts were coming from the stable yard.

'What now?' He walked down the steps onto the

gravel. The serf Grisha, seated on a shaggy pony, was leading his own horse towards the house. 'The cows are out again, sir! They need you to come...'

It seemed his plans must wait. He spoke some words of cheer to his grandmother, took leave of Irina, and ran upstairs, calling for Yakov. Then, with Annika in pursuit, he rode with Grisha down to the village. As they approached the first huts, they heard a cacophony of whistling, cries and groans. A large ginger heifer and her calf lumbered towards them, pursued by a group of stick-waving villagers. As the beasts veered away in the direction of their pen, Vasily surveyed the damage. More cattle stood in the kitchen gardens surrounded by flattened fencing, their hooves churning up a pitted confusion of earth as they grazed among the vegetables. The men eyed him knowingly as they drove the beasts off. He knew they blamed him for this mayhem, but in their hearts surely they accepted that, on the whole, the cow experiment had been a success? If only they would keep them fenced in!

The last of the cattle was secured, and peace descended. Having promised compensation to the owners of the gardens, Vasily mounted his horse and rode back towards the estate house. The rays of the setting sun burnished the silvered bark cupolas of the small church where, just a week ago, he and Irina had repeated their vows.

He reined in at the edge of the park. The scenes of chaos in the village faded away; his ordeals of the past two years now seemed like a bad dream. A sliver of moon hung in the transparent air, bats dipped and whirled above the river, a late blackbird sang. Beyond the cemetery and the swathe of smooth grass sweeping up to the manor, a dark rampart of trees stood, firm against the world. He smiled. There was nothing more precious than this: his home, his family. There was nothing that he prized more. He watched as lamps, newly lit, gleamed at each window in turn, until the old wooden house glowed, a safe haven of consolation, in the gathering dusk.

HISTORICAL NOTE

The specific family difficulties that form the basis of the plot of *Fortune's Price* are of course fictional, as are most of the characters involved. However, issues of legitimacy, heredity, nobility and religion were matters of great importance in nineteenth-century Russia, not least because of the sharp differences in life expectations experienced by those of different rank. Only the nobility were allowed to own land and serfs, and were exempt from taxation. The higher ranks of the civil service and army were, in most cases, open only to them. The laws of inheritance were also restrictive, landowners having little freedom to dispose of patrimonial land as they wished.

Rulings about such issues were generally the sphere of the courts, with the important proviso that the emperor, as the embodiment of the law, was able to override their decisions, and was often petitioned to do so. The period in which *Fortune's Price* is set saw an increasing reluctance on the part of Nicholas I to exercise this discretion in the area of family law, a fact which is reflected in the plot of the book.

I have tried to ensure that the background and events against which my characters play their parts are as historically accurate as possible.

Sources

The Emperor, Nicholas the First, plays a pivotal role in the plot. There are a number of works, more or less flattering, that, taken together, give a good idea of his character and physical appearance. Probably the most comprehensive of these is W. Bruce Lincoln's *Nicholas I, Emperor and Autocrat of All the Russians* (London, 1978). Nicholas's propensity for preferring Baltic Germans over the Russian nobility, and his quite unpredictable tendency to pick out individuals for particular exceptional favour, or indeed opprobrium, are well attested.

Descriptions of St Petersburg, other parts of Russia and the journey from St Petersburg to Warsaw are mainly based on contemporary images and the accounts of non-Russian travellers. Particularly important was the work of Augustus Bozzi Granville, a doctor, who travelled widely in Eastern Europe and Russia in the years shortly prior to the opening of the novel.

Aspects of Andrey's family background, as an Estonian of German extraction, is based loosely on that of the Decembrist, Baron Andrey Rosen (1800–1884), whose family circumstances were described in *The Rebel on the Bridge*, by Glynn R. Barratt (1975).

The character of Prince Yevgeny Uspensky was, as in the prequel to the current book, *Small Acts of Kindness*, based on the memoires of the writer and socialite Count

Mikhail Dmitryevich Buterlin (1807–1876), who once again managed to be in the right place at the right time.

The cholera epidemic that afflicted Russia, and indeed the rest of Europe, in the early 1830s is well described by Roderick E. McGrew's *Russia and the Cholera (1823–1832)* (1965). The description of the rioting in Sennaya Square in the summer of 1831 was vividly brought to life by an active participant, the ensign (later Major General) Ivan Romanovich van der Khoven (1812–1881).

There is a good deal of information in English on the Polish Uprising of 1830 online. Books in English include a broad military overview in *The Russian Army under Nicholas 1st (1825–1855)* by John Shelton Curtiss, and the political background is exhaustively described in *Polish Politics and the Revolution of 1830* by R.F. Leslie (1956).

General information about the Russian Army in the pre-revolutionary period can be found in *Soldiers of the Tsar. Army and Society in Russia 1462–1874* (1985). The principle source of the activities of Andrey's regiment was *The History of the St. Petersburg Grenadiers, King Frederick William the Third's Regiment (1726–1890)* (1892) by General F.F. Orlov. Other sources were Alexander Puzirevsky's *The Russian Polish War of 1831* (1890), and Karnovich's *Biography of Grand Duke Constantine* (1899). The story about Englishman George Fanshaw and the sad fate of his brother, Frederick, comes from the article 'Englishmen in Russian Service' in Colburn's *United Service Magazine and Naval and Military Journal Part 2* (1846).

Eyewitness accounts of the Polish campaign can be found in the memoirs of two young officers, Grigory

Ivanovich Filipson (1809-1882) (later General Filipson), who appears as a character in the novel, and Staff Officer, Nikolay Dmitryevich Neelov (1800-1850).

Information on the Russian theatre and its milieu can be found in Richard Stites's *Serfdom, Society and the Arts in Imperial Russia* (2005) and on actresses and dancers in particular in Wendy Rosslyn's article *'Petersburg Actresses on and off the Stage'* in ed. Cross, *St Petersburg 1703 to 1825.* (2003). Some background on the laws of inheritance and problems of legitimacy are provided in *The illegitimate children of the Russian Nobility in law and practice (1700 to 1860)* by Olga Glagoleva (Kritika, 2005), and I would like to thank Ms. Glagoleva for access to this article. The creation and operation of the Moscow Foundling Home is described in *Mothers of Misery, Child Abandonment in Russia,* by David Ransel (1988).

ACKNOWLEDGEMENTS

I have been astonished and gratified by the help and encouragement I have received from so many people following the publication of my first novel, *Small Acts of Kindness* in 2022. Without their enthusiasm and requests for "what comes next", *Fortune's Price* may not have been written.

Special mention must go to early readers, Julia Payne, Hilary Taylor, David Carse and Brian Moody. Also to Kate Harris at Harris and Harris Booksellers in Clare, and to Susie Keepin at Woodbridge Books for valuable advice on presentation and marketing. Others offering valuable support were Rachel Taylor at Sudbury Library and many members of The Arts Society, Stour Valley, including in particular John and Carole Ashton and Carol van de Sande. I must not forget my old schoolfriends from Wroxall Abbey, Angela Sage, Pippa Gray and Vicky Hamill and particular mention must go to all participants at the annual Russian Summer School in Cambridge, especially to Tanya Yurasova and Ellina Konovalova.

Thanks also to Justine Antill, Joy Baker, Hugh Belsey, Mark Bills, David Brummell, Christine Brouet Menzies, Elizabeth Cooper, Simon Edge, Barbara Emerson, Jessica Fleming, Andrei Gaidamaka, Christine Hodgson, Wendy Gibson, Arabella McKessar, Jackie Newbury, Fiona Pearson, Kate Rizzo, Joanna Spicer, Isabella Warren and Angela Winwood.

And also to the team at The Book Guild.

Last but not least, thanks to my family: my long-suffering husband, Nick, for his endless patience; and my sons Matthew and Thomas. Also to Danielle, my daughter-in-law; her mother, Linda Farmer; and her father, Ken Farmer, for his essential advice on military matters.

ABOUT THE AUTHOR

Jennifer Antill studied Russian Language, Literature and Politics at UCL School of Slavonic and East European Studies and has travelled extensively in the country. She gives talks on Russian cultural topics to a wide variety of organisations and writes a blog on her website. Her first book, *Small Acts of Kindness, a tale of the first Russian revolution*, was published in November 2022. In a former life she worked in the City of London as an investment analyst, and has also served as a local councillor. Jennifer is married to Nick, has two adult sons, Matthew and Thomas, and lives near Sudbury in Suffolk.

For more information go to: https://jenniferantill.com/